WE ARE ALL CREW

A NOVEL BY BILL LANDAUER

KAYLIE JONES BOOKS

This is a work of fiction. Names, characters, places, and incidents are a product of the author's imagination. Mostly. In one case, the author imagined that real celebrities who died actually survived to sing some of their old songs and say things they never actually said. Also, the author wishes he imagined the words of certain real politicians, but regrettably, their quotes are genuine and footnoted. Otherwise, any resemblance to real events or persons, living or dead, is entirely coincidental.

Published by Akashic Books
©2015 Bill Landauer

ISBN: 978-1-61775-356-5
eISBN: 978-1-61775-371-8
Library of Congress Control Number: 2013957097

Kaylie Jones Books
c/o Akashic Books
Twitter: @AkashicBooks
Facebook: AkashicBooks
info@akashicbooks.com
www.akashicbooks.com

For Kaylie Jones . . .
who told me I should write it . . .
who believed when no one else did . . .
and by whose laughter its success was gauged.
Also for my parents.

Any issue that seems to put plants and animals above humans is one that we cannot support.
—Dr. James Dobson

There are no passengers on Spaceship Earth. We are all crew.
—Marshall McLuhan

AUTHOR'S NOTE

Since Europeans first encountered this continent five hundred or so years ago, they have been looking for an expedient way to cross it without having to get out of their boats and soil their boots—and without risking the pesky ice flows that used to make sailing the Northwest Passage such fun.

In 1995, the author William Least Heat-Moon said he crossed the continent with a gasoline-powered boat and a canoe. He claimed to have traveled only two hundred of the thousands of miles overland, and that he could have made it by crossing only seventy-five miles of earth. Who knows what he could have accomplished if he'd been a cartologist or a navigator instead of a poet/writer?

The story that follows is a depiction one such attempt to cross the continent. However, readers looking to recreate the voyage of the boat described herein are likely to be disappointed. This is a work of fiction.

For example, don't bother to search for the Allwyn River. The Allwyn doesn't exist any more than Crofton, Kentucky; Lynnbrook, Ohio; or Blysse, Missouri, exist. They are inventions of the author, created to fit the story. Other locations, characters, and animals, however, are entirely factual.

The author begs forgiveness for these indulgences and little white lies, which were necessary to get to a larger truth.

PART ONE

Crazy-Ass Boat

Who holds back the electric car? . . . We do! We do!
—The Simpsons

the trees

The trees tried to murder the boys.

They'd tracked them for a day and a half. Through the ends of their branches and within the folds of their barks they'd sensed a dozen or so boys and a few adults cleaving the rush of the stream and blotting out the birdsongs with their talking. They spread the word downstream through their interconnecting webwork of root systems, sapling to sapling, Methuselah pine to oak.

Intruders among us.

They did nothing, not even when the boys stacked their limbs and lit them ablaze. The yearlings seethed. In their midst, boys audaciously danced and cackled before a pyre of the trees' dead kinsmen. Some of the boys decorated themselves with orbs, knickknacks, and baubles made of plastic, a material forged by fire that caused poisonous rain to fall upon the trees' heads.

If only we could move, the younger trees said. *We could scoop up the boys and impale them with our branches. We could beckon the boys deeper into our midst, into the places where we blot out the sun. Then it would be a different story.*

At midday, the trees got their chance. Two of the smaller boys broke from the herd. They climbed out of the river, scrambled over the rocks and through the soft vegetation at the water's edge, and plunged into the trees, deep into their darkest recesses.

Vengeance.

trees suck

In the real-time wilderness, trees want to kill you.

They're nothing like the trees in *Heckenluber*, this video game I played to train for this mission. In that game, trees are part of the background—big gray-and-jade blocks off of which the hero (I always select Klaus, the archer) bounces harmlessly. Back home in Philly, trees are either fingers trapped in circles of sidewalk or green stuff on hillsides you never think about.

But along the river, they're monsters. With claws. When we first abandoned our canoe, they scraped me and ripped the sleeve of my best black turtleneck. While Arthur scrambled ahead of me, I stopped and looked at the long, red scratch snaking down from my shoulder to my elbow. For a second I was back at the jungle gym behind my house, and I'd scraped my knee and wanted the Moms to spray on a little Bactine and tell me it was going to be all right. And that gave me bleary eyes and shaky hands until the scratch on my arm looked like this jagged mouth grinning at me, the way this kid from school, Burton Trotsky, grins at me when I'm being a little wuss boy.

Wimp, the mouth said.

In this interview I once saw, Fang, the lead singer of the Red Grizzlies, said he took all the fear and pain he'd ever experienced and shoved it deep down into this big reservoir in his belly. Then he used it in his music. I've been practicing Fang's method for a year now, and I've got to say, I'm getting some major tunes out of it. Once Trotsky and the other guys and I launch our own musical campaign in Trotsky's garage, they will rock hardcore.

The Grizzlies are why Arthur and I ran away. Just a few hours ago, we ditched Godspeed Summer Camp—a gaggle of dorky *Boys' Life* marshmallow cookers singing "Kumbaya," paddling down the Allwyn River in central Pennsylvania—for the Grizzlies' only North American stop on their worldwide tour: San Francisco, California. In ten days.

the french

The trees knew people had died here before.

A couple of hundred years earlier, three French trappers had camped along the riverbed. It was late fall and cold, so they chopped down one of the trees and built a fire. A cougar attacked them in the night: it ate one of the trappers, and another suffered a slash to his belly and a broken leg. He had tried to make it downstream but fell and bled to death on the rocks. The third trapper drowned. Their fire went out, and weeds grew up through its charred remains. A new tree grew where the tree that the trappers had chopped for their fire once stood. The rotting corpses were eaten by animals, and their bones turned to meal, a fragment of which became lodged in the shoe tread of the one called Winthrop.

Nobody knew about it except for the trees, and since they wanted to kill the boys, they would not tell.

arthur

Anyway, I shove Wimp Winthrop—my nickname for the wimpy part of myself—deep down inside my songwriting reservoir and focus on Arthur. Arthur is stumbling, his chewed Nike running shoes getting caught in the rocks. Arthur is a gangly, freckled kid with a big tower of curls and sunken eyes. Attached to his chest is a loudspeaker welded to a tan metal box. From its side, a wire runs behind his back and clips to his T-shirt. I've seen two of these mad big things—PA systems; the one he's wearing now has a waterproof plastic shell.

He hasn't said a word in more than an hour. He's walking slower. I'm sure he's crying. That worries me, so I lay this on him: "*When the lightning flashes and the thunder rolls, I will not yield. I will stand fast and resolute.*"

I've been jamming to that one on the mental iPhone, since the Jesus freaks back at Godspeed Summer Camp stole my real-time phone. When you listen to that cut off the Red Grizzlies' *Journeys* album, the sounds fill even the shadowy parts of your head you hadn't known were there before. I sing it out loud because I think it'll give Arthur a kick. Instead, it disappears into the trees.

These monster trees are everywhere. You can't see a house, a road, or any other sign of human life.

It's getting darker; the orange beach ball is dipping below the mountains. The woods look more horrorshow by the minute, but it's not just the darkness. Evil things are glowing: sometimes eyes, sometimes fireflies going off like tracer fire.

In that movie *Zombie Cannibals*, the teenaged co-ed zombie bait went in circles for days and couldn't find their car . . .

Wimp, says the voice. I shove my fear back down.

Arthur lists from side to side.

"Yeah," I say, practically yelling. "Going over these rocks is probably tough for the average dude, but my sensei back home told me I have the most catlike balance in my dojo. I could take ninjitsu if I really wanted to."

You took one karate class when you were six years old, wimp, the voice says, *and Moms had to carry you out bawling like a nancy boy because you got scared when they yelled.*

"You know who said that?" I repeat.

Arthur marches on.

"My sensei," I say, and now I'm mentally kicking my own ass for making shit up.

I stare at my Timberlands. I bought them because the blond, sky-eyed twenty-something wearing them in the online ad looked like the sort of guy for whom a girl would remove all her clothing. I wore them because they were ghetto *and* functional, but after walking through the river and then over the hard rocks and roots, brown thread is sprouting from the leather. Slime covers my Prada shorts. Hopefully our rescuers won't be ladies.

Arthur is freaking me out. I had my eye on the kid since the first day of camp, when a black BMW zipped into the Godspeed Summer Camp compound and he emerged from the rear. He'd squinted in the sunlight beneath the big welcoming banner they'd strung across the entrance with the motto *Conquering Nature* written across it in blue script. A man and a woman disembarked from the front. She was wearing a navy suit and lunged at the boy the minute his Nikes touched the gravel, dabbed his face with a silk handkerchief and made cooing noises. The man wore pastel Ralph Laurens and kept his ear glued to his cell phone and eyes glued to his Rolex until it was time to go, which I heard him say wasn't soon enough.

We'd been there about an hour when the jockstraps started in on him. One kid stopped Arthur and grabbed the horn of his PA system between his bear claws. It was the guy who'd already established himself as the camp leader and probably the only one who'd get laid. He had this iron-colored 'do that just seemed to lay effortlessly in the coolest Abercrombie way, and wore off-the-rack clothes like he didn't even need to try. I hated him. I buy designer black-on-black stuff because it makes me look badass, but this kid didn't even need to try to have a *style* because he had a *body* underneath his Old Navys. I'm a skinny runt. Style is the refuge of a runt.

"Darth Vader," the kid said, hanging onto Arthur's bullhorn like it was a trophy they give to popular kids. The group of sheep he'd already pulled in with his cool tractor beam thought that was a howler.

Behind the canoe where I was hiding, I stifled a laugh. I hated myself for it. Two minutes earlier, the same guys had labeled me Eddie Munster and made fun of me for the way I talk. Totes. Like the word bling isn't the bomb, yo. My Oxford Edition American Street Lingo dictionary lists "bling" as the No. 2 most-used slang word on the streets, next to "the bomb." And Eddie Munster? Real freaking original, guys. Like I haven't heard that one before. I mean, hello? The average height of a fourteen-year-old is five feet and I'm four foot eleven.

The big kid swung Arthur around by his bullhorn. Arthur's arms and legs flailed. His eyes filled with tears, and his mouth trembled. Counselors shooed the big boys away.

Arthur sat down on a bench and trembled for a while. Then he wiped his eyes, jammed his hand into his pocket, and pulled out a pocketknife and a piece of wood. He started whittling.

By then, I'd already decided I needed a partner to escape from camp, a conspirator to help me ditch the canoe once the flotilla started down the Allwyn the next day, a lookout, a bag carrier, and a friend.

This kid needed lessons in how to be cool.

This kid needed me more than I needed him.

"That's quite a piece of artwork you've got there," I said, sitting next to him.

Arthur stiffened. He peered at me out of the corner of his eye and stuck his teeth out in what I took for a smile.

Click. "THANK YOU."

"From the looks of things, I'd say that's a dinosaur?"

Click. Whistle. "AN ALLOSAURAUS, ACTUALLY."

"What's that?"

Click. "BIPEDAL CARNIVOROUS THEROPOD FROM THE LATE JURASSIC PERIOD. VIRTUALLY DISAPPEARED WHEN THE (*whistle*) TYRANNOSAUR APPEARED IN THE CRETACEOUS PERIOD."

"Interesting."

We sat there quietly for a minute. Arthur looked at his whittling and sliced off a thick band of wood around what might have been a leg.

"Interesting," I repeated. "Listen, does that thing have a volume control?"

Click. "IT'S ON LOW NOW, I'M AFRAID."

"Why, may I ask, do you have to use that?"

Click. "IT IS A BIRTH DEFECT THAT HAS PARTIALLY PARALYZED MY VOCAL CHORDS. I CAN SPEAK, BUT ONLY SOFTLY."

"Interesting."

Arthur stuck his teeth out again. "IT MAKES POLITE CONVERSATION SOMEWHAT, WELL ... *bzzz crrck bzzz* ... PROBLEMATIC."

"Well, if it's any consolation, I can hear you just fine with it."

Click. "THANK YOU."

We slipped back into silence once again.

"Are you, by chance, a fan of The Greatest Band on Earth?" I blurted.

Click. "I LOVE THE GRIZZLIES!" He was wicked excited. I could tell I had him. Arthur was probably in my grade, but he looked like a gangly version of a little kid. Dinky blue eyes darted at the breeze. Washes of freckles speckled his cheeks and forearms. Not even *my* friends would have sat with him at lunch.

"Did you catch any of their shows this season?"

Click. "THEY'RE ALL OVERSEAS, I'M AFRAID. EXCEPT THAT ONE SHOW IN SAN FRAN."

"I was so tempted to cross the pond."

For two days the counselors taught us how to row and steer, how to make flotation devices out of our pants should we capsize. The other seven boys hit on the four chicks. Arthur and I schemed.

He was a member of my caste. At the end of the previous school year, we'd studied India's caste system, and if I'm realistic I'm most likely a *harijan,* one of the untouchables who live outside the city walls. Within the *harijan,* however, there are hierarchies. I am the Kung Fu Master, the A No. 1 King of the *harijan* at Primrose School, and Arthur is definitely a bottom-runger. He has no style. His gravestone of hair is more like an epidermis problem than a style. He wears a dorky skintight T-shirt tucked into jorts. Moving up within one's caste isn't impossible, and I'm sure with the right moves, the right coaching, and Fang's never-fail method of pain and fear stockpiling, Arthur can be totally cool. I need a friend, and I want my friend to be at least a little cool—but certainly not cooler than me.

The only real strike against him in my book is his height. Truth be told, people, he's probably a foot taller than me. I assured myself it would serve a purpose and hoped that whatever ladies we encountered would understand who was the teacher and who was the student.

He agreed to my plan without hesitation. I think he would have just as soon taken on the evil Sith in *Star Wars* than stick around the jockstraps in that camp for a whole week of torment on a backwoods Pennsylvania creek bed.

But now that we're alone, walking along the river without an adult in sight, he's wigging. I'm honestly not far from it either, even with Fang's methodology.

If only we could get clear of these monster trees. Why would anybody ever want to save the forest? There's this handful of Birkenstock-wearing glue sniffers back at school—the kinds of people my father, His Eminence, refers to as *tree huggers* or, when he's really mad, *spotted owl fuckers*—who used to hand out fliers and give book reports about saving tree-covered places like this from logging companies. Why? Plow the monsters under and pave it all, I say. At least that way I'd be able to see a house or a road or a way to California.

the car

The young ones stopped to rest at a pile of charred metal that sat at the edge of the river. Had they thought about it, they would have realized it had been a car.

The car had belonged to a man who had once lived in a house about three miles away. The man did not like the car because it had cost him more money than he could afford to keep it filled with gasoline, but he could not afford a new car. So one day he drove the car through the woods. He ran over a family of rabbits, killing most of them, and knocked over saplings until he reached the Allwyn. He set the car on fire and watched it burn. Then he went back to his house, called his insurance company, and reported the car stolen. The insurance company bought him a replacement that used less gasoline. By then, however, the price of gasoline had risen so high that his employer could no longer afford to pay him and the man could no longer afford to live in his house. He never told anyone about the car, and nobody ever found out about it—except for the rabbits, the trees, and the river, and they were not telling.

arthur climbs a tree

Click. "THE BATTERIES ON THIS THING ARE ONLY GOOD FOR TWENTY-FOUR HOURS," Arthur says through his speaker system. "I NEED TO RECHARGE. I HOPE WE FIND SOMETHING SOON."

His Eminence would call Arthur a weak choice. I disagree. He's a Grizzlies fan. He has a great sense of humor—I can tell because he laughs at all my jokes. He'll make up for what he lacks in the confidence department once he starts his own pain and fear reservoir. I'm certain I can turn Arthur into a badass friend.

We're looking at these trees all wrong. We need to get up on top of them, way up there, and then we'll be able to check out the scene for miles.

People climb trees all the time—in old movies, dads built kids little playrooms up in the treetops in the backyards. (Not my father. The most His Eminence ever did for me was commission his IT staff to assemble a security camera in my room.) But how do they climb them? Out here in the sticks, there are probably millions of feral monkey-kids who can scale a tree in seconds, but I'm wicked stumped. I try, but most of the branches I can reach are so freaking brittle they break off in my palms. This one big branch hangs low enough for me to reach, but the most I can do is strain against it until it scrapes my forearms and I tumble back, flushed and sweaty.

I coax Arthur into giving it a go. He loops a long arm over the same branch, lassoing it. Then he plants a Nike on the trunk and walks up it, throws a leg across the limb, and swings himself around it until he's riding it like a horse. He works his way up the tree, stretching out his long, skinny frame until it looks like it might snap, then grabbing a limb, wrestling up to his chin, and pulling himself up.

I order him along. "That's it. No, that branch is too skinny, Arthur. Cool. Now . . ."

Soon I lose him in the white Xs of limbs. The tree shivers. I can hear his bullhorn scraping the branches.

I give him a few minutes and then ask what he sees. I'm hoping the PA system will announce that he's spotted Route 81 or whatever highway I limoed in on, or at least that he sees a hint of macadam a couple clicks away that we can walk toward.

the old oak
The old oak had seen when the French trappers had been killed along

the river, had watched the houses being built three miles from the trees and the man who burned his car. When the tree had been a sapling, it, too, would have clawed at boys the way the other trees clawed at them, but now it was too old and had grown too large and no longer shivered when breezes swept past it like the wild younger trees. Its branches were too large and too high to be of much use for clawing.

Now it groaned and shook as an animal grabbed its branches and scraped against it. *What's happening to me?* it wondered.

It was the first time a mammal of this size had ever dared come this close. Fish and birds and lizards made sense to it, but mammals perplexed the wise old tree. It did not understand why they feared death, why they clung to life the way the oak clung to the soil.

But the tree understood the message: boys were enemies.

So when the boy reached a branch that was too small to support his weight, the tree allowed that branch to snap.

arthur takes a tumble

I hear a cracking sound. The tree sways, and the air is still for a second. Then something thuds against the growth on the opposite side.

It's Arthur. I guess he landed on his right Nike because when he tries to stand, his leg buckles, and he lies on his back clutching his ankle. All that extra height and tree-climbing ability can't help him stand upright any more. His face looks funny, but he must not have his PA system turned on because I can't hear him. I guess he's crying, even though it's getting hard to see him now.

After he strips off the Nike and sock, his ankle swells up like a throw pillow. He rolls around and holds onto it for maybe five minutes, his face all contorted. Then he lies flat, and his little blue eyes look up into the branches like he just smoked a blunt.

I ask him if he thinks he can climb up there again, but that seems to annoy him. I coax him to try standing, but when he tries out his swollen ankle, his face screws up and he falls over and rolls around.

I sit and try to remember what they taught us in health class. Mr. Volmer said you're supposed to apply pressure to a wound. That makes sense; maybe the goo blistering Arthur's ankle might go back where it came from if I squeeze it like a tube of toothpaste.

But squeezing it only makes his eyes widen and his face tighten into a scream that can't be heard, and he thrashes around and shoves me until I quit. His ankle looks bigger now.

Volmer also taught us about tourniquets, which involve tying bandages really tightly around the wound. So I sling his discarded sock around his ankle, but when he sees what I'm doing he pushes me away.

I ask if he remembers passing any plants or berries that could be used as an herbal remedy. He clicks on his PA system and says, *Click.* "PLEASE, WINTHROP, DON'T HELP. JUST LET ME LIE HERE A MINUTE, OKAY?"

Well, that chafes me. I'm just trying to help. After all, Arthur wouldn't even *be* here if it wasn't for me. He'd still be fending off the abuse of the jocks at camp. But the kid is probably in pain and forgetting who his real friends are.

So I sit next to him.

"Okay," I say. "I think I'm safe in saying that this blows big time. But chill. It's 2,711.26 miles to San Francisco. If we hitch, and with a little bit of luck, we can make it in two or three days. I know this sounds FUBAR, Arthur, but we'll be perfectly safe. You rest that ankle, and we'll be on our way. The highways of the United States are well-equipped for safety. There are police call boxes at nearly every mile marker. There are rest areas and sources of food. As long as we remain vigilant, we needn't worry about traveling with someone unscrupulous. You see, Arthur, it's not so risky. Granted, there are risks, but remember what Fang said: *It's a bold adventure you're going on.*"

Arthur still has the mute button pressed. I continue: "We need to get clear of these woods. We'll pass a road by tomorrow and hitch our way out to the main highway. This is Pennsylvania, for crying out loud, not the Serengeti. It's their only American stop on the tour. It'll all be worth it, Arthur, you'll see."

Arthur continues with the silent treatment. It occurs to me that I haven't seen a TV set in three days. No phone, no Netflix, no HBO Go.

"It's Tuesday, Arthur. Did you know that?"

Click. "SNIPER DUDE X!"

"That's right! *Sniper Dude X!*" It's my favorite show. It's about this badass who's a surfer by day and a government assassin by night who actually offs baddies with the blade of his board. "They're starting the whole series over again from the first one, when he gets the samurai board from Tibet. You know, maybe you should turn that thing off, Arthur. I don't want to alarm you, but who knows who or what is out in these woods at this hour."

I peer at the stars through the trees. A bank of clouds has crept into view, so only half the sky looks back at me. "I love that show. God, I'd miss that show terribly if anything ever happened. Wouldn't you? Of course, we'd also miss *Sargent Storm . . .*"

I tire of doing all the talking, so I stretch out on the rocks and go over all the episodes of *Sniper Dude X* I've memorized until I fall asleep.

I have this screwed-up dream I only sort of remember when I wake up. Arthur and I were in my chemistry classroom. Steel bars covered the door. The cool kid from camp was in there with us, mussing my hair and swinging Arthur around by his bullhorn. Outside this guard kept walking past and looking in at us. I couldn't see his face, but whenever he yelled in through the bars, the voice sounded an awful lot like His Eminence's.

There was this TV set on a heavy metal cart in the front of the room. Most of the kids in the classroom with us just stared at it and didn't move. Suddenly Arthur jumped up and ran at the TV set and tried to push it out of the way. The cool kid was yelling at him, and outside the guard was fumbling with the door. I helped Arthur push the cart out of the way, and underneath it, bored into the floor, was a deep pit. Arthur jumped into it. I followed him. The walls were rushing past my head as the ground below was getting closer and closer and closer . . .

I don't know how long I'm out, but it's pitch-black and raining when I wake up. Arthur is snoring. I listen to the forest noises and the pattering of the rain on the boughs overhead. The moss, the tree bark, the leaves, the animals, and the junk people leave behind combine to form a powerful odor that feels like somebody is poking my sinuses with a dirty stick. Then the rain really opens up and turns into a roar overhead, and lightning pops. The breeze blowing off the river makes me shake like a mofo.

I think about my mother. Not my father. The second I allow His Eminence to materialize as an image in the old temporal lobe is when I come down with another case of Wimp Winthrop real quick. When His Eminence says anything, it's like somebody ripping off my Halloween mask and spoiling the whole show.

But the Moms . . . well, frankly what bothers me is the fact that I can't quite picture her. I mean, I see her every day. She's always nagging, pestering, and slobbering all over me like I'm three years old or something, and yet I can't quite remember the exact color of her hair, the precise shade of her eyes, or the strict layout of her face.

What I can remember, for some reason is her forearms: the squashy, pale, hairless part of them that the sun doesn't reach, with red pucker marks smack in the middle of this part—two rectangular reddish boxes, one on each drumstick, like she's been leaning on them and her weight left a welt behind. I mostly noticed them when she tucked me into bed at night, which she just a year ago gave up on insisting.

Thoughts like this make the woods seem extra cold and dark, so I shake them off. After all, this whole thing is going to slap her pretty hard. *Good*, I tell myself. They blindsided me with this summer camp trip. They gave it to me as a birthday present during a party where they'd refused to invite my friends—His Eminence saddled my clique with the name "Paste Eaters" because we all looked like righteous psychos: pale white and always wearing black—and instead invited only His Eminence's clan: bronze men in various stages of gray flanked by women in various stages of plastic surgery regimens.

Godspeed Summer Camp, the flier said. *Come and share His Life and His Word with Us.* They told me it was a canoe trip with a bunch of other kids down the Allwyn River for ten days. His Eminence, they explained, had worked very hard to secure me a place in the camp, which is run by some of his government cronies.

I was expecting concert tickets.

The Red Grizzlies were coming that same week. *Music Freak* magazine had just given them a cover story about how their show in Germany sent shockwaves echoing down the Rhine, and all of Europe was in an uproar for this "must-see-do-not-miss-under-penalty-of-lameness show." *Do not miss!* I'd explained to them my need to go to the show, that I'd missed them when they played at the Spectrum the year before, that my grades were up at school, and that they'd promised—especially if I stopped asking them repeatedly. Burton Trotsky's folks had gotten him tickets, after all, and his dad was only a minor undersecretary for the Defense Department—not even one of the Primrose School's most elite.

But this camp, the Moms explained, was for my own good. They didn't need another summer of their first and only mooning about desolately inside the compound watching George Lucas movies on the plasma screen.

Trotsky had chided me mercilessly. So I told him he'd see me there. Front row center. "Count on it," I'd said.

I look at Arthur's ankle in the dark. I was hoping the swelling might have gone down a little and that he'd be able to try the tree again. But it's more swollen than ever.

What if he broke something? I definitely can't fix that. Maybe the ankle is even getting worse just lying here. In sports, when somebody breaks something, they stop everything and send out the doctors, strap on a cast, and haul the player off in an ambulance. Maybe Arthur needs a doctor right away. Maybe if I wait until morning, he'll never walk again.

Then I'd *really* get it.

It'll be all over the news: *Mortimer Brubaker's son ran away, crippled an already disabled boy, and left him for dead in the woods.* His Eminence has a whole staff of interns whose only job it is to scour the headlines, surf the Web, and watch TV to find any mention of his name in the media. When it's good news, he's on top of the world, marching through the house humming "Battle Hymn of the Republic," chatting with the help or instructing them on some sort of housekeeping business in his authoritarian, leader-of-men voice. But when the media gives him a black eye, he sulks, insists upon my joining one Young Republicans organization or another, or worse yet, tries talking to me.

And this time, when his personal e-mail floods with incoming bad news that can't wait, the bad news will include *my* name, his son's name, listed as the culprit . . .

I peer into the blue-black crisscrossing lines of branches and weeds. Maybe I can find a house somewhere with a phone, call an ambulance anonymously, tell them roughly where Arthur is, and then run away into the night before anybody knows my identity. But I'm only like 75 percent sure I'll be able to find Arthur again or be able to tell an ambulance crew how to locate him, so I'll probably have to wait with him. Then they'll summon our parents, and I'll have to answer to His Eminence anyway.

I wander back in what I thought was the direction we'd come from. I don't get far before I'm wishing I'd waited until morning.

Walking through a black, rain-soaked woods blows. It's not just a football field with trees sticking up; it's hills, boulders, rocks, roots, and broken tree limbs. It's old radial tires full of water, rusted metal, old boxes, and sheets of cardboard. Branches loaded with briars rip you open, and you slip and tear the hell out of your elbows and knees.

I stumble around for about an hour before I realize I've twisted and turned around so much I no longer know where I am. I thought I'd eventually reach the river and the canoe because I figured Arthur and I had walked in a straight line, but maybe we've been going in circles. I don't know where the river is, and I don't know how to get back to Arthur.

I sit on a rock, soaked and bleeding and scared worse than anything. I made things worse. Trotsky'll tease me. *Yeah, front row center,* he'll say. *You couldn't even make it out of the woods.* We'll spend a night in the rain and then find help in the daylight.

But what if we don't?

Mortimer Brubaker today mourns the loss of his son, who was eaten by wolves after getting lost in the woods during a camping expedition in central PA . . .

The whole thing, I realize, is my fault. If not for me, Arthur and I would be back at camp, and maybe the Moms would have been right: it would have been for my own, stupid good.

The retaining walls of my pain and fear reservoir fail. The rain sounds like footsteps everywhere: cracks and moans and pops all over the place, and each one makes me bug out worse.

the mountain lion

Trees weren't the only things following the boy.

Hunger had driven the mountain lion from the hills. It was summer, and she had been surviving on mice, which were easy prey.

But she wanted to kill the boy for revenge. She had lost mates and companions to starvation, homelessness, and bullets. She had long wanted to kill one of the creatures responsible, one of the hairless dogs that walk like birds. And now, here was a young one, sitting alone and defenseless.

She waited in the dark, tail swishing back and forth. She waited to see if the boy would stay or move on.

Now she was sure. He'd been sitting on the rock not moving for a long time.

She lifted her haunches and prepared for what she'd been made for: the great rush forward at blinding speeds, every muscle in perfect harmony, every tooth and claw synchronized perfectly to knock her prey over and sever his spinal cord.

Then she saw the light.

Out away from the boy, a man was walking—and glowing. Light meant men. Men meant weapons.

She held her ground.

the blue light

Ahead of me, swaying slowly back and forth, is this pale light. It's dim, but it's moving right to left, pausing, and then left to right.

I go toward it, careful not to lose it when a stump or a ridge throws me to the ground. As I get closer, it becomes a bluish flicker, which is mad spooky—maybe it's a ghost, or worse. In *Zombie Cannibals*, the decaying orbit of the satellite that caused the dead to rise from the grave produced this blue light that glowed out of the graves right before the zombies poked their heads up. So I try stealth: I hide behind trees. I crawl on hand and knee. Now I can see this dude pacing with the blue light, and I hear a voice muttering through the rain.

The light snaps off, but I can still barely make out the dude. His long hair is silver and white. It pokes straight up like an afro and then cascades down the back.

It isn't hair—it's a headdress.

An Indian headdress.

He turns toward me, arms at his sides, legs spread slightly. His lips form a hard, stoic line. His eyes glow in the dark.

I stare into them.

They stare back at me.

CHAPTER TWO

we hitch

My video game training says the situation calls for a little left trigger, with the A and X buttons tapped twice in unison.

I ninjitsu out of the trees, helicoptering, no feeling but drizzle and wind until his jawbone turns to crumbling Cheetos beneath the toe of my Timberlands.

Then: X, Y, X, Y, twice in succession. Fist punches bloody the midsection, sending baddy back into the brush.

Select button.

Arsenal menu.

Chainsaw.

The Activision sound card blasts a killer bee storm as I lower it and Cuisinart baddy into monster tree food.

He is an Indian—blinged up like one, anyhow. He wears a leather headband with white and silver feathers that crest down his back. He has finger-painted a circle with lines poking out of it on his chest the way a kid would draw the sun. Old school yellow leather pants with fringe cover his bottom half, and he wears what looks like His Eminence's bedroom slippers. His tats are badass, people. Swoops and swirls swish around his arms rockstarlike.

When he doesn't make a move to John Wayne Gacey me, I tell him about Arthur's ankle, and he follows me into the woods. Afterward, while we hoof it around the brush looking for Arthur, I figure I'm stupid asking him for help. Maybe trusting some crazy guy fronting squaw isn't my Mensa moment, but I'm too scared of the trees and the rain and the creeping things to care.

TV and movie Indians superman it through fields and forests, flashing through trees and tall grass like stampeding wolves, but remain ghost quiet while the cowboys they sneak up on make a racket around their campfires.

Not this guy. He's a dork, stubbing his toes on the same roots where I stub mine, slipping and making a racket even though he doesn't talk.

The two of us dick around in the brush for a while, crashing into rocks and trees and sliding like goons. I yell, "Arthur!" the whole time and begin to get the worryshakes that I seriously lost the kid for good. But after a half hour, I hear a low, "Winthrop," blip out from somewhere. We follow his voice and there he is, lying where I left him, little blue eyes gaping over what I harpooned in the way of help.

Crazy Indian Guy keeps mute, and before Arthur has time to flinch, he stoops and swings him over a tatted shoulder like a sack of dog food, and we make for the exit, or whatever destination Crazy Indian Guy has in mind.

Tapping the escape key is crossing my mind, people, truth be told. Arthur has his help. I've been lucky to find anybody, and now Arthur has his ambulance ride without me having to nursemaid him and give up the San Fran show. But it's not like I'm leaving Arthur with a nuclear family in a house with a white picket fence, am I? What if he's a serial killer? I can't just leave him here to get Dahmered by Crazy Horse. So I keep on behind them, barking my shins on the slippery stuff and praying to the gods of civilization to show me a road.

a change of orders

The world had changed.

Moments before, vengeance had been so sure. The two young ones had been alone. One had already been felled by the old oak. That a man had arrived meant little; one man was of almost no consequence to trees that had stood by the river long before any two-footed beast.

It began as a shivering through the interconnecting webwork of root systems, where earlier the message had been of intruders and hostility, which the trees felt the way trees feel all things, as heat and bluster.

This was a message of stillness.

Pull back your branches. Let this one pass.

It puzzled some of the yearlings, who wondered what blood tasted like. But even they followed the example of the older trees, who knew better than to ask.

i meet the *tamzene*

A gurgling noise starts in. The woods thin, the monster trees stop scraping, and we find the river. It has fattened in the rain. On it is a boat so bizarre it makes all the tunes on my mental iPhone skip.

I guess it's a boat. His Eminence considers himself a beast on yachting—when he isn't parlaying business, he's going off about his own hundred footer anchored off the Schuykill, which is how I know all about anything that floats. But this thing is like nothing I've ever seen floating in Annapolis harbor.

It's about fifteen feet tall and rests on what I know is a pontoon. Above it are several other pontoons of different shapes and sizes. The pontoons all connect on a dial that looks like the bullet spindle on a six shooter. On top of the dial is the wooden hull of a boat right out of a history book. Plank upon plank wrap around the pointed bow and the wide stern. Portholes are cut into the planks, and grooved gunwales spread across the top of the hull.

A large cabin rises near the center of the deck. It looks modern, made of fiberglass, with sheer plastic for the windows. To the rear of the cabin, a mushroom-shaped smokestack painted a rusty red points skyward.

Beneath the forecastle, a figurine stares ahead—the wooden form of an old man with a toothy grin and a '70s-style three-piece suit. I recognize it from school: it's a statue of former president Jimmy Carter.

Near the bow, the name of the boat is spelled in blue letters: the *Tamzene.*

We wade through the water and climb up a rope ladder to the

deck. The Indian lays Arthur down, signals us to wait, and then goes around the cabin.

From this height, the monster trees don't seem so big. The Allwyn River sweeps past and disappears behind an outcropping of rocks and bushes. In the cabin, I can make out the silhouettes of a steering wheel and radio equipment.

Static hisses. A voice chatters on a radio in the cabin: "*How to prepare . . . Fill your gas tank regularly.*"[1]

I kneel next to Arthur. He's wigging out like a mofo. If we'd been on *Sniper Dude X* or a movie or the *Psycho Car Thievery* video game, I could lay a wicked line on him, like, "I won't let them hurt you, man," or, "I'll avenge you." Instead, I say, "You don't think this guy is going eat us, do you?" which makes him shiver even more.

The Indian guy reemerges, but not alone. A bald guy follows him. He has a circle of hair with muttonchops that drift down both cheeks like dog legs. A paw of red hair pokes out from the neck of the brownish undershirt he wears tucked into plaid boxer shorts. He stares at us for a minute or two, his big bushy unibrow making a V between his eyes.

Finally, he says, "Who are they?"

Nobody says anything.

"You." He nods at Arthur. "Who are you? What's going on?"

Arthur is still shaking.

Bald guy looks him over. "Your ankle," he says. "What happened? Who are you?" He gets down on one knee and observes Arthur's bad ankle. Arthur just lies there like a sack.

Well I, of course, am schitzing hardcore, people. The brain bungee jumps past rock songs, movie lines, game graphics, and comes to a thud on His Eminence. When reporters fire questions at him about fossil fuel emissions and air pollutants, he lasers them with a smile, and the even tone in his voice knocks them back like a weapon. *Publicspeak*, I call it. A masterclass shit talker, that's what he is, the Moms always says. We Brubakers could talk our way out of a lethal injection if we were already bound to the chair.

"He can't speak, sir," I say, trying on His Eminence's publicspeak. I'm rebuilding the reservoir leeves. "He's got disabled vocal chords. That's why he's wearing that stereo on his chest, if you understand what I'm saying. To make himself heard. Audibly heard." I offer him a smile so big it hurts my cheek muscles.

The bald head pivots toward me. I shrink back a little.

"Who are you?"

"Well, his name is Arthur. And I'm Winthrop. Winthrop Snake. And thank heavens you two came along here. We were separated from our camp—Godspeed Summer Camp? Like, Christians, you know? My friend Arthur here busted his ankle up pretty bad and your, I guess, friend there was, um, magnificent enough to help us out."

The bald guy frowns at me and tells Arthur to wiggle his toes. "Nothing is broken," he says. "Looks as though you've sprained it."

He pushes himself up, a big meat slab of a guy: middle ballooning out and hairy arms that look like they could do some damage if they wanted to. In a video game: X, Y, X, Y, a scissor kick to the solar plexus, and a Japanese throwing star to the forehead would off his ass.

"Well," I say, still fronting publicspeak and holding down Wimp Winthrop, "thank our Lord and Savior-guy Jesus Christ for this holiest of holies. Our friends at the Christian camp will be so happy."

A vertical wrinkle flickers above the unibrow V on bald dude's head. He turns to the Indian. "What can we do?" he asks.

The Indian just stares back at him like he didn't say anything. He looks at Arthur, then back at me, and then Arthur again, smacking his lips. My mental plasma screen boils with some mad freak show. I'm alone in the woods, and His Eminence and the Moms are probably still clueless as to my exact GPS coordinates. Weak little girly arms, pale fragile skin that monster trees can make mincemeat—I'm probably the kind of thing this guy eats for breakfast.

"Okay," he says finally. "Okay, I guess we can't just leave them here. Mr. Snake." He looks at me. "A few miles downriver from here, we'll reach the outskirts of a town called Snow Shoe. There's bound to be a phone there somewhere, even in this day and age. Kang here"—he points at the Indian—"will carry you to a pay phone or something. I'd like to do more for you, but we just . . . we just can't. In the meantime, you and your friend here are to sit very quietly and still, and above all, *do not touch anything*. And after we've dropped you off, I want you to forget you ever saw us. We were never here." He leans in horror-movie close. He smells like pipe tobacco. "Is that clear?"

CHAPTER THREE

i take a boat ride

Monster tree arms grope at the boat for miles. From the boat's deck, and with morning lighting things up, they look less badass—more tree than monster. Still, I'm glad we ditched them because they're everywhere, and we might never have found our way out.

The *Tamzene* chugs along, making whirring noises as it moves. The Indian—Kang—and the bald guy fooled around with some instruments and stuff that dreamed up the purr. Smoke pours out of the big mushroom-shaped smokestack, and metal arms in the rear pump like boxers throwing jabs. I haven't gotten a good look at anything. In keeping with the bald guy's instructions, Arthur and I stay where we are, behind the cabin on the deck, and try not to notice anything.

The bald guy seems cheesed at Kang for bringing us aboard. He doesn't say a thing to us after he says to pretend he doesn't exist, and he barely speaks to the Indian. He grumps around fiddling with levers and knobs, walking past us with that unibrow still in V formation. He's dark and depressed. I don't mean he looks like he's going to cry, but he sure doesn't look like he'll laugh. When he's not messing with the controls, he stands at the side of the boat and looks into the trees or fiddles with his key chain. He has this big key chain—a silver cross about as big as the palm of his hand. He keeps it in the pocket of the khaki pants he'd pulled on after the *Tamzene* started out this morning. It must have cost a chunk of change; he's always polishing it with his thumb, staring at his reflection on its surface, and rubbing fingerprints off on his shirt.

Kang, of course, says even less. Every once in a while he flashes past us, following whatever the bald guy says, which is stuff like: "Check the burner level." "Make sure the O2 is stable." "Synchronize the timing." He doesn't look like a laugher or a weeper either, but he doesn't seem as dark as baldy—he seems more robotic. His mouth is a straight line, and his eyes remain focused on their work. His tats rule, though, people. Swirls and symbols circle his biceps.

As for yourstruly, now that I know they aren't pervs, I feel a lot better. We're on our way. And Arthur's ankle isn't broken. We'll get him to a doctor, and since the two guys escorting us want us to forget they exist, I don't have to worry about them calling His Eminence.

But I've got to admit, I'm curious: who are these guys? What is this boat, and why the hell don't they want us outing them?

"Do you think they're drug dealers?" I whisper to Arthur.

He's lying on his back next to me, forearm pressed to the bridge of his nose to shield his eyes from the sun, which has baked the sky yellow. The PA system on his chest is so big it could strangle him. Without moving his forearm, he shrugs.

"I'll bet that's what they are," I whisper. "I'll bet this boat-thing is loaded to the gills with ganja. Maybe before we get off at that town, we ought to think about buying some off them. It's better than trying to find it on the road, after all. Whaddaya say? You down?"

I'm trying to sound cool again. Truth be told, I've never smoked the stuff. Wimp Winthrop wouldn't allow it. A short kid is horrified by anything even rumored to stunt your growth. Once a spurt raises me some, I've always figured I'll hit the pipe. Most of the non-lame kids from my class have smoked homegrown out of soda cans. Some of the cooler kids even have brass pipes, or so they say. Trotsky told me he scores his weed from this Puerto Rican guy who lives by an underpass on Broad Street.

But, of course, I want Arthur to think I'm cool.

He lifts his forearm. Red veins crisscross his small blue eyes.

"What?" I whisper. "You're not down? How else do you think we're going to get it? My right Timberland is stuffed full of Benjamins

I've liberated from His Eminence. I thought we might use them to get a hotel and score us a stash for the trip."

Arthur covers his eyes again.

"What, are you lame or something?" I hiss. "This is a golden opportunity here, Arthur. You smoke, don't you?"

He just lies there.

"Oh come on," I say. "How do your friends let you get away with that?"

He looks at me again. "I don't have friends," he mouths, his face tense.

Well, that shuts me up. In that one sentence I know his life story: in the morning he always sits in an empty bus seat instead of with another dude, his face to the window, pretending not to notice how even the little kids use him—his look, disability, and punchline features—to climb their ladders. In the cafeteria at lunch, even Paste Eaters can jump levels by pelting him with rubber bands, spit wads, and food. Gym class is a dungeon of horror, him the lone prisoner to tens of other guards. School chews him all day, every day, spits him out at night, and starts over again before the first bell.

But can you blame them? The too-tight shirt. The jorts. The guy has never smoked a doob. No status. He's obviously not an athlete, despite his height; he's obviously not a hipster; he's obviously not a badass. He isn't even Paste Eater.

You have to listen to people, watch them—what they wear, do what's cool. We say what they say on TV and in the movies. I mean, the other guys laugh at how I talk sometimes, but you keep trying and working at it until you get the right combo. You get a cold smackdown if you don't at least feign badassness and say you've smoked weed. That's how you get friends.

So when Arthur says he has none, I get it. I've been there.

We let the river talk splishsplash with the *Tamzene*. Not a house nor a street shows itself no matter how hard I crane my neck. But you were here, people, and you left your trash behind: your plastic Mountain

Dew bottles and cigarette boxes pepper the edges of the river where the water stalls and smells like dead fish.

This one time in history class, we studied a population density map of the US where clusters of people were represented by lights. The northeast corner, where we are, was like a firework in freeze-frame; almost all of it was lit up. Who knew it'd be nothing but river static and bird cackles for miles in Pennsylvania? I want those soda bottles *filled* and sitting on a *shelf* in a *store* next to a *hotel* where I can take a *shower*.

My junk reeks—smells like Campbell's chicken noodle soup, if you can imagine. My skin is slippery with my own filth, and my 'do is all matted and gross.

I will stand fast and resolute, Fang sings. I try to shove this nastiness below, but again I'm thinking about my house and the hum His Eminence's plasma screen makes a split second before coming to life. In a few hours, *Little Gnomes* will be on the Cartoon Channel, followed by the early morning repeat of *Attack Bears*. Ordinarily I'd be sitting in the Barca lounger, Prada jean–encased legs propped in front of me, a cool glass of Pepsi bubbling on the end table.

the trout

The trout heard the boat coming and darted to the bottom of the river.

He looked up, waiting for the V to pass. He hated boats; they left trails of black water in their wakes. Black water made it hard to breathe. He supposed the boat was another device of the two-legged creatures, and he long ago learned not to truck with their kind.

He was a strong fish; he had learned to swim to the bottom when a V cut the water above. Some of the older trout had simply given up. The river had changed, they said. It was too shallow. The food was gone. The water had soured and could no longer be breathed.

The time of the trout, they said, was gone.

But this trout believed the other talk. There were those who said the time of the two-legged beasts was at hand, that the world above was as bleak a wasteland as the world below. So he swam deep, fought for air, and waited.

The V passed overhead. The trout swam on. Its gills detected the clearness of the water—whatever had passed seemed not to sour it.

Strange, the fish thought.

After some time, a new sound sent him below again. As he watched, three more Vs skimmed white across the surface, following the first one. Soon he found himself drowning in the black water from their wakes.

i think of his eminence

"My dad's going to kill me," I hear myself say at last—and there it is, people, the thought I've been dreading because with it comes all the other thoughts that tag along with His Eminence.

I am a disappointment. A scrawny runt. I'm not the kid he wants. By the time he was my age, His Eminence was a jock. Five foot five, I've read on his football roster. I've seen the pictures: the old football uniform, hair that didn't need product, and a killer smile, even at fourteen. I've often searched for his face in the mirror, but His Eminence is a DNA cul-de-sac. The freakishly slender nose? Not too good on my melon head. The girlish arch to the eyebrows? Not too cute when you've got little girl arms to match.

One time, back when he was a kid, he and some college buddies ripped off a dean's car and drove all the way to California and back. His Eminence already had publicspeak working for him in those days, and it took some fancy maneuvering, but he got out of it without a blemish to his good name.

He'd hoped I'd be like him, but Wimp Winthrop had too big a grip on me. I could already see the disappointment in his eyes when I pleaded with him not to make me go to camp. I stood in his office beneath the Bitchin' Poster—my favorite thing he owned. I'd admired it for as long as I could remember: a black metal frame with the snarling, profiled face of a cougar in the center, its fangs exposed beneath bloodshot eyes. The letter C cupped the cougar's head from the left side of its face. The cougar appeared to be spitting at a large letter S on the right side of the frame. Circling it are the words, *Duty to God*,

Country, and Species. I don't know what the C and the S stand for; His Eminence never bothered to explain.

"You're going," he said. "End of story." *You're pale. You're girly. All you do is sit inside. How could you be my son?*

I've never openly defied him before, though I'm sure being a Paste Eater probably cheeses him off. This one might mean military school, but you never know. I'd be lying, people, if I said I don't sort of hope that maybe he'll pick me up when this is all said and done and that disapproving look of his might actually go away because the little runt might not be such a wimp after all.

The Allwyn pisses along, and so do we on its grimy, stinking water. It twists, squawks, and chatters over the rocks the bald guy steers us around. It sighs when it gets wider and deeper.

The sun is nearly straight overhead when the Allwyn finally stretches out its banks on both sides and dumps into a big lake. The bald sad sack sticks to the cabin, leaning on the steering wheel and staring out the mosquito gut–speckled windshield. Kang joins him. Up until the Allwyn took this breather, he'd stood in the bow watching for rocks.

It's summer, all right, hot as a mofo and not even noon, although there's a mountain range of storm clouds leaning on the trees. Gnats, mosquitoes, and dragonflies have been buzzing all day, but here, where the water has slowed, their swarms violate all the holes in your head and hum in your ears.

And that's what I first think the other boats are: a buzzing dragonfly or a horsefly or a gnat humming in my ears. But when I see Kang's face go sour as he stands and walks out of the cabin, I hear their engines.

Three identical white yachts are humming along behind us. His Eminence would drool over them. Their white paint reflects the sun, the rails are spit polished, and their drivers are probably nice and cool and showered behind the tinted windows that seal the cabins.

All three run parallel to one another, lazily droning along. Actually, no—they seem to be coming up on our asses, plowing white water trails, though they are still probably a football field away. I'm not sure exactly where they came from—the part of the river we'd been in before the Allwyn turned to lake was too narrow for a yacht. The town the bald guy mentioned must be nearby, which means civilization. Upscale civilization, from the looks of these boats. I can already feel the warm hotel shower, water washing off the river slime, and me all clean and mapping out the quickest route to California.

"Check it out, Arthur," I say.

But when I turn back to the deck, Kang is clearly the one to watch. He still isn't laughing or crying, but the sun he painted on his chest bends at right angles atop his tense muscles. His moccasins are planted parallel the deck center, and his eyebrows are caving the rest of his face in. He shoots the white boats a stare that would make me want to change course if I was one of them.

"Put them below," Baldy says. I jump. He's stepped in behind me so that he and Kang have me sandwiched. The wrinkles around his eyes and mouth gather before he turns and goes back to the cabin. When he looks over his shoulder, his face has gone red as a Coke can.

"Now, Kang, goddamn it!" he yells—spraying it, not saying it.

Evidently Arthur and I are the stuff Baldy wants below—the Indian stoops and puts Arthur over his shoulder, then grabs me by the wrist. He takes us to the opposite side of the cabin, where a retractable stairway leads down to blackness. Baldy puts on a head of steam—I can tell because the the trees are now whirring past.

Kang marches us down the steps and leaves us there, retracting the stairway and closing the hatch without turning on the light.

It's hot and close. The ammonia smell of cleaning solution wafts through the room. Beneath my Timberlands is a hard metal floor, and I guess beneath that is the pontoon dial I saw before coming aboard. Up above, Baldy is hauling ass—I can feel the water chopping against the hull.

I'm mad scared. It was only two years ago that I threw out the Power Rangers nightlight the Moms had plugged in next to my dresser because it was too pussy, but the dark still isn't my bitch. Every noise emitted from the two men scraping around overhead makes me strain more desperately into the darkness, but it's black as a coffin. I am going to bawl for sure.

Then the explosions start.

I have this majorly cool DVD called *Hell's Boat,* which is about this submarine during World War II. The Germans dump barrels full of explosives into the sea, which go off all over the place—wicked close to the submarine. You see it shimmy and shake, and the crew members just get thrown ass over ears. On surround sound in the living room it practically shakes the whole house down, the Moms always says.

Whatever's exploding around the *Tamzene* is like that, only louder— like somebody going up to the parapet that overlooks the courtyard at the Primrose School and shoving shelves full of hardcovers from the library over the edge. Giant fists punch the water next to the boat. I hear the bald guy and Kang running around yelling.

This is it, I'm going to die, I can't help thinking.

Every time it booms, I lose my balance, smack my head, and see those white fountains that flow behind your eyelids when you hit your head in the dark.

I see all kinds of things in the dark. I see the foyer in my house. I'm a kid. I look through the arms of potted plants and pretend they're a jungle. I can stand up straight and still hide. The Moms chases me on her hands and knees. She pretends she's a hippo. I slip and fall, but it doesn't hurt, and the Moms leaps on me like an animal attacking. Instead of ripping my flesh, she attacks me with kisses, and our giggles echo through the marble hall.

Then, through all the banging and shouting and crashing water, I hear a voice.

It is a short distance behind us, electronic and piped through a public address system: "*Crew of the* Tamzene. *Crew of the* Tamzene. *Cut your engines, drop anchor, and prepare to be boarded. If you do not comply we will fire. Repeat: cut your engines . . .*"

The cops!

A Paste Eater's rep as being anti-society *requires* me to loathe five-oh. And of course the cops would *definitely* call our parents and totally rub out our trip to California. *Senator Mortimer Brubaker's son was arrested with a pair of drug dealers in central PA*, the cable channels would tease.

Well, I'd be lying, people . . . and I hate myself for saying this . . . but I'm sort of relieved. The cops are going to off a couple of drug dealers. Lying down here in the dark with a bunch of people I don't know and explosions going off, I felt pretty damn warm toward cops. Fuck California, and fuck the Grizzlies. We're saved. In a few minutes we'll probably be at police headquarters. "We got lost, and Arthur hurt his leg, and these guys offered us a ride," I'll say. His Eminence will send somebody to pick me up. Then he'll glower at me for a while, but I'll still be back in Philly in time for *Sniper Dude X*. I might get to see a real-time shoot-out once Baldy and Indian realize it's pointless to try outrunning the cops' cool boats.

But the *Tamzene* doesn't slow down. As a matter of fact, it churns even faster. And the electronic voice from the cop yachts gives up pleading.

More explosions.

CHAPTER FOUR

the heavens

Twisting, supercooled shapes of vapor curled in absolute freedom until the word came to be.

The world was a thought from an unseen mind, and when it appeared, the undulating parabolas, parallelograms, and spirals stopped and took their necessary forms.

Warm air rose. Ice crystals collided with crackling blue light.

Then the rain began.

the *tamzene* gets hit by a storm

I've taken bullets at point-blank range before.

Once, on the streets of LA in broad daylight, some Chicano dude in flannel glocked me in the front of the skull. I've been riddled with machine-gun fire in a castle in Bavaria, whacked by lightsabers about a million times, and had some really big cats pummel my head with lead pipes over and over again. Not a big deal. In *Castle Wolfenstein*, that just means finding a couple of medical bags and running over them, and then you're all good again.

But there's nothing like that down here in the hold. We'll get offed, and that'll be that. One of the explosions will smash the hull, it'll fill with water, and Arthur and I will drown.

I want to tell him it's okay that he doesn't have style or friends or anything because he had the balls to ditch camp and try to get to California, which makes him all right in my book. But the combined roar of the water and the engine is too loud. Since it's pitch-black and we've been thrown around so much, I don't know how Arthur's doing. I hear him breathing—wheezing, actually—every time the boat lurches.

Soon I hear another noise on top of the explosions and shouts. It starts softly—a faint tapping against the hull that you can barely hear over the engine—but soon gets louder. It hisses.

I also hear a new explosion. It's different from whatever the cops are shooting at our boat. This one is distant, a low rumble, as if another boat might be being fired upon in another river somewhere nearby. Then it gets louder, like dozens of rifles firing at once. These explosions are big, but they don't shake the boat. Still, the *Tamzene* begins to pitch and sway as if a giant is using it as a cat toy.

The stairway descends again, the bald man with it. Above him, sickly white flashes fall down the stairs.

"We need your help," he says. Now he's wearing a brimmed rain hat and a slicker.

On deck, the sky has turned the color of the Grizzlies' *Bruiser* album, a bloody purple. Lightning crackles. Sheets of rain soak me, and the wind nearly hurls me from the deck. The monster trees are gone. Somehow, we've wound up in the center of a lake. Big swells pick us up, then waves slap us back down.

The white yachts, the five-oh, are gone.

Inside the cabin, Kang, also sealed in a black slicker and rain hat, has turned on a light. He grips the wheel.

I can barely see water other than when spray shoots up over the boat. Occasionally, in the purple void over the gunwales, white bursts of spray break over the big rocks that whiz past.

The bald man throws me this thing that looks like two tentacles attached to a bicycle pump. He tries to shout over the wind, but I can't make out what he's saying.

He pulls me close and shouts in my ear. "It's a pump! We need to pump out this water or it'll swamp us!"

From the cabin the bald man produces a second pump and jams the end onto the deck beneath a half-inch of water. He pitches one of the hoses over the deck and lets it dangle against the gunwale. Then he pumps the pump, sucking water through the hose and overboard.

I try to do as he asks but can't get started. The boat is rudderless, pitching about on these big-ass swells, and I fall around the deck, running into soaked cardboard boxes full of equipment. Big rocks loom up out of the darkness, but the boat darts out of the way just in time.

The bald man runs around lashing boxes and other equipment to railings with rope. A fire extinguisher breaks free and smashes into the plastic window of the cabin, making a broken star.

Through the rain, electric lights appear on the side of the river. I realize the boat is passing a town—my first sign of civilization in days. But I'm still scared shitless, and soon the lights fade from view.

The storm goes on and on. Then, almost all at once, it stops, the river calms, and the thunder wanders away. The boat slides into a narrows, and trees wrap their arms around us.

"Well, that'll make you old," the bald man says. He tears off his rain cap. Sweat or rain has plastered his gray hair to his bald head. "That most certainly will make you old."

By now, I'm shivering in the aft corner. Every part of my body aches, and my wet shorts and turtleneck have chafed me like a bitch.

The bald guy takes a white towel from a cabinet beneath the steering wheel and throws it to me. Then he sheds his slicker, and from his hip pocket produces an enormous pipe, a hookah shaped like a seventeenth-century warship. From his breast pocket he pulls a canvas bag of tobacco. He loads the pipe with the tobacco and lights it with a Zippo by sucking and exhaling quick puffs of smoke, all the while eyeing me.

"Mr. Snake," he says after a while, "I believe we passed the town of Snow Shoe in the storm. And I'm sorry, but we can't turn around."

Because the cops would nail your drug dealer ass, I'm thinking, but I don't say anything.

He puffs his pipe some more. He's looking at me weird, which is worrisome because I've been in a bunch of His Eminence's PR photos—me and the Moms grinning like crazy while he wraps his arms around us like we're a real, honest-to-goodness nuke family. If he remembers me—well, who knows what he'll do? Ransom my ass, maybe?

But I guess he can't place me, because after a while, he says, "We'll look at the maps and find the next closest town. Meantime, why don't you go take care of your friend?"

Kang leads me back down to the hold, but this time he leaves the light on before he closes the hatch. Arthur is sprawled in the center, sweat beading all over him.

The dark room in which we're being held prisoner is a long storage area. The iron floors and ceiling are painted white, and long metal supports that look like ribs run up the sides. Between the ribs poke long pipes.

Half the room—the side where they tied us before—is empty. But on the other half, they've stacked flat white sacks clear to the ceiling. In the storm, one of the sacks fell and ripped open. Brownish moss spills from it. I sniff it.

"It's weed! I told you! I told you! These guys are drug runners!"

Ordinarily, people, I'd think that was wicked badass. But the sight of it scares me. You can *hear* about stuff like bong hits and hypos full of Whitey Herzog and think it's cool; when some bald post-grunger squeals about it in one of his jams, doobage and all of it sounds righteous psycho and mind-expanding. The danger seems wicked cool, and you're sure you wouldn't be one of those geeky DARE momma's boys if given half the chance—and if it didn't threaten any future growth spurts. I'm telling you, though, in reality it gives you the shakes. Because connected to it is all the stuff the Moms was trying to protect me from—the pale dudes with bluish lips and tracks all over their arms, guys killing one another with chainsaws like Pacino in that one movie where he's supposed to be Chicano. And suddenly I'm aware that about a million monster trees separate me from the Moms—with her pucker-marked arms that definitely won't tuck me in tonight—and I want to curl up and cry until they come and get me.

Which is what I do. When I wake up hours later Kang is shaking me. I don't know how long I was out, but the swelling's down in Arthur's ankle, and he's able to hobble around on both feet.

We go up the stairway again. It's night now; fireflies flit through the trees over the gunwales, and the stars look like a mad big city. Stars don't shine very bright in Philly, so you usually forget that they're there, but out here they're like blue daylight.

Baldy is listening to a little radio in the cabin. He's switched on the overhead light and is leaning back in a wooden swivel chair with his legs propped on the dash. He smiles at us when we walk into the cabin.

". . . authorities are continuing their search and rescue operations for both boys after their canoe and gear were located," the radio is saying. *"To repeat, the son of Pennsylvania Republican Senator Mortimer Brubaker has been reported missing. The fourteen-year-old had been attending a downriver Christian summer camp in central Pennsylvania. Winthrop Brubaker and another boy became separated from the rest of the camp . . ."*

Back home the Moms and His Eminence have probably loaded up into the Bentley, bound for Godspeed Summer Camp, the Moms with her usual hangdog expression and His Eminence trying out disappointed glares. They could be there in two hours, which would give them plenty of time to stew.

Baldy is still smiling at us. Me in particular.

"So you're Senator Brubaker's kid?" he asks.

we hatch a plan

Cat: out of bag. I stammer.

"I recognized you," the bald guy says. "You were in his campaign brochure. Kang, you picked up Mortimer Brubaker's kid. Do you believe that? The . . . the irony of that?"

Kang's eyes shoot razors at me, not exactly the way he looked at those white yachts, but close enough to make me feel a little like puking.

Baldy keeps smiling. "The head of the Committee on the Environment and Public Works," he says slowly. His grin doesn't look happy, but that might have been the Indian at his shoulder looking like he might eat me up.

"So you've heard of him?" I manage.

"Heard of him!" The bald guy bends at the waist, raps the table with a hairy fist, and lets out a series of bleats that rouse some cackles from the woods. "Heard of Senator Mortimer Brubaker! Who hasn't? You might say we're big fans of your father's work, Mr. Brubaker. Tremendous fans. He's a brilliant politician. Who else could successfully siphon a billion in funding from the National Science Foundation labs and put it—just where it belongs—in the Defense Department. And don't forget that your old man was, of course, the quintessential vote in the Senate—the big push, you might say, behind lowering carbon dioxide emission standards in the EPA Act . . ."

On and on he rambles about all kinds of stuff they admire about my dad. It relieves me that they like him so much, but the smile on his face and the amount of saliva he's working up in the corners of his mouth make my skin crawl.

". . . and of course when somebody offers him a cost-effective alternative fuel source—something that works, mind you, we're living proof here—when somebody calls him with that and thinks maybe he could put his money where his oh-so-eloquent mouth is and ante up some government funding, what does Senator Mortimer Brubaker do? Why, he courageously refuses to return a *phone call*. And just what are you *doing* out here in the woods, Mr. Brubaker?"

I try to put on some publicspeak again, but all I can do is stammer out the same junk I told him before: that we got lost from our camp and are trying to find our way back. The guy doesn't look like he really believes me, so instead I just spill it about how we ran away and are heading to California to see the Grizzlies show.

When I let him in on the state where the Grizzlies will play, Baldy does a double take. He puts his smile away and glances at Kang, whose eyebrows shrug. A thought seems to be filling Baldy's dome. His eyes slowly grow bigger, and he blinks like he's trying to hold them in. Then he lets out a breath and says, no, that wouldn't be right because we're just kids and it's dirty pool.

Kang keeps pointing at us. Finally, the bald guy rubs his chin and says, "Well, we can't just leave them in the woods, after all, can we?"

I don't need to tell you how freaky this is, people. Somehow he can make sense of the weird gestures this Indian guy makes, which don't look like sign language to me; it's like seeing this guy talk to himself.

Baldy looks at his shoes. Then he looks back at me with another smile, this one sort of tired around the eyes, but a lot more friendly.

"You're in luck," he says. "You might say this is a very fortuitous coincidence, our crossing paths, Mr. Brubaker. We, too, are on our way to California. Here's what we're proposing: you ride along with us for just a little while longer, and we'll drop you at the next town. In the meantime, we'll let you in on all the secrets of the *Tamzene*. You see, the success of our voyage here is definitely something your father would be very interested in."

There's a lot of ganja stacked in the hold, I'm thinking. Maybe His Eminence is on a DEA oversight committee.

"Why?" I ask.

"Because of its potential alternative fuel source capabilities. The *Tamzene*, Mr. Brubaker, is powered by hemp. We've attempted to solicit help from Congress before but haven't found the right channel for funding. But believe me, the *Tamzene* is an important invention, and being a part of its introduction to the world would be of great political importance to your father. Is it a deal?"

The whirring crickets sound like one of those flying cars from the *Jetsons*. Why don't I just jump at the chance? What choice do we have, after all, out here among the trees and junk without a clue where we are? But I can't shake the idea that the bald dude and the Indian aren't pot dealers. I mean, who knows? Maybe we're safer monster-treeing it alone. Maybe Kang and Baldy are making up a story just so we won't put up a fight when they take us somewhere and off us.

On TV, it's usually not hard to tell baddy from good guy. In *Sniper Dude X*, the EALs (Evil Assassin League) all wear black leather and have red eyes. But this is real time. The bald guy is just standing there with that tired-eye smile on his face, waiting for me to say something. He doesn't look like a drug dealer, who TV says are mostly swarthy-looking guys with lots of bling and greased-back hair. This guy wears khakis like an army dude but has wild hippie hair under the bald, tangled gray that meshes into his muttonchops. His dome is full of smart wrinkles: horizontal lines streak across his forehead, and crow's-feet sprout from the corners of his eyes.

"I don't know," I say after a minute.

"Okay," he says. "At least hear my sales pitch. Maybe that'll help you make up your minds."

He opens a cabinet beneath the dashboard, and there sits a small color TV—the old-fashioned kind that looks like a big gray eye—and what I recognize as a VCR.

This just got better. I ask him if he has a satellite dish, because I'm thinking we can still catch the late-night *Sniper Dude X* repeat.

But that doesn't seem like it's on the program. Kang fumbles through boxes while Baldy drags two lawn chairs up from the hold and two bottles from a small refrigerator in the cabin and hands them to us. The bottles are full of green liquid.

"Don't you have any Pepsi?" I ask.

He snorts. "Soft drinks? Never," he says. "This is an organic concoction of citrus juices and seaweed concentrate. Try it. You'll like it."

"It's green."

"Sixteen years ago Coca-Cola said it would use recycled plastics in its bottles, but it never did. They use it in New Zealand, Australia, and Europe, but not in the US."

"What about Pepsi?"

He smiles at me. "The human body stops making bone at age thirty. Soft drinks are found to have pH levels of 3.4 or higher. And they're habit forming. Addictive poisons. Corporations want you weak and dependent. Seaweed citrus juice is delicious and promotes robust health."

I haven't had a thing to drink in a day and don't realize how parched I am until the green stuff hits the back of my throat. It tastes like sugary grass. Arthur gulps his down in about two seconds and rips out a belch.

The bald guy hits the play button on the VCR. The screen flashes and the title appears: *The* Tamzene: *Manifest Destiny, Part II.*

The production quality isn't Peter Jackson. It starts off with smog-covered cities, people wearing surgical masks, and smokestacks. Some guy I swear is the same dude who narrated the *Importance of Hygiene* DVD they made us watch in the fourth grade starts spewing statistics, like three million people worldwide die each year from causes related to air pollution. And it says the highway system is worse because automobiles emit 90 percent of the carbon monoxide and produce at least half of the pollutants that create smog. The guy on the tape says the answer to all these problems is the *Tamzene* and Doctor Marion Seabrook, which, it turns out, is the bald guy's name. Then the video shows us how the boat works, how it runs on burning hemp and this other chemical for fuel. And it's not just a boat—underneath there's this rack thing with wheels on it, and the boat can actually drive over land on this hemp fuel for up to one hundred miles. "It has the cargo capacity of four large tractor trailers," the video says, and a fleet of these things would greatly lessen the dependence on the trucking industry and fossil fuels. Finally, it says that Doctor Seabrook is taking the boat on its maiden voyage on rivers across the continental US.

"The *Tamzene*," Seabrook says when the screen goes black, "is a prototype. After the success of her first voyage—once we've proven she's the sort of vessel that can change not only the environmental but economic landscape in this country—we're hopeful we can find investors and begin mass production. Of course, government subsidy and potential tax breaks for whoever the lucky bidder is would be advantageous to us, and this is where your father comes in."

"So his office never called you back?" I ask. After all, His Eminence has a whole staff of cronies—mostly college kids—who field calls from people with ideas for stuff like superpowered windmills. They usually jot down the ideas, study them, give them each a ranking, and post them on a cork board in the Dirksen Senate office building marked *Crackpot Ideas of the Week*.

"Of course," Seabrook says, "we made inquiries with several government offices and corporations. But without results, we're just a pipe dream." He smiles. "So, do we have a deal?"

"So what's up with five-oh?" I ask. "Why are the cops after you?"

He frowns. He looks at the trees. "That's not the police," he mutters.

"DEA, then."

"No," he says. "To be honest I don't know who they are."

"Well, the name on the boats was the Green Police . . ."

He looks back at me and gives me this I-really-don't-want-to-smile-but-I've-got-to-smile smile. "Let's just say we're not without enemies. Your dad, in Congress, he has his share of enemies, doesn't he? Well, it's the same out here." He looks back at the river.

Well, *enemies* I can understand. His Eminence often says tree huggers are a bigger threat to this country than any turban-clad wack

job. Personally, I don't agree with His Eminence—albeit most ordinary
people would pick a nice parking lot over a shitload of monster trees
any day, but how someone believing the reverse constitutes a threat
doesn't compute with me. And, since air pollution is foul, foul stuff, I
can't see how anybody would have a problem with somebody wanting
a solution. I tell Seabrook so.

He shrugs. "They've merely thrown us off course. We'll get back
en route to California, but it will take some doing."

"Why?"

"It's not that simple, is it? Here, have a look at this." From the long
drawer under the steering wheel he pulls a large piece of paper. He
turns it to face us, unfurling it, and it hangs over his knees. The map
is called *Rivers and Waterways of the US*. On it, the old US of A looks
like an animal—the head of the beast being Maine, Texas and Florida
its legs, and California its butt. Rivers spider across it, forming streaks
everywhere. They look like the beast's skeleton.

"There are over fifty-one thousand miles of streams in the
Mid-Atlantic Highlands alone! Then there are storm systems like this
one blowing us off course. We run out of hemp every six months and
have to get more, no simple task." He smiles that uncomfortable smile
again. "But it'll be worth it, Mr. Brubaker. Someone needs to develop
something to eliminate the fear, you see. Your dad could lead this ef-
fort, and we hope to give him the chance. It's not just clean air that's
at play here, Mr. Brubaker. It's economics. The *Tamzene*, if used to
its potential, might threaten the US oil industry. The US economy is
dependent upon oil; oil is its lifeblood. Take it away, and what happens? The economy and US industry sputter and die. Now what is an
industry? Sounds like a nebulous sort of thing—big faceless factories
and smokestacks and automobile assembly lines and all that. But an
industry is *really* made up of *people*. *People* work those jobs. *People*
need the economy. You take away the oil, take away the factories, and
these people can't support themselves. But somebody needs to show
the world there's a better way . . ."

He keeps rambling. He doesn't talk to us like we're kids, and he reminds me a hell of a lot of His Eminence. If His Eminence flipped his publicspeak to treehuggerdom, he'd be Seabrook. So it occurs to me that maybe this might be just what my trip needs: I'd get to see the show, and the my-son's-a-lame-o looks from His Eminence would go the way of grunge music because I actually helped the man find a gimmick to further his political career. Yay me.

"Okay," I tell him. "We'll hang with you guys for a while."

"Excellent," Seabrook says. "Two standing rules: I am captain of this vessel, so when I tell you to do something, Mr. Brubaker, you are to follow my orders."

Well, that sounds a little scary. My face must tell him that I think so, because he says, "Don't worry. You're our guests here. But I need to make sure you're safe."

"Okay," I say.

"And secondly, I do not allow the practice of religion aboard this vessel." Seabrook's face darkens. "I am well aware of your father's Evangelical leanings, Mr. Brubaker. And, like you said before, you came from a Christian camp. If you need to pray, I suggest you do so silently or wait until you're ashore."

I know full well that in the pocket of those khaki pants of his is a silver crucifix he can't stop playing with. But as to His Eminence's "leanings," we only go to church for photo ops, and religious discussion only comes in press conferences.

"So the deal is you're going to get a patent on this puppy and sell it for billions. Is that it?" I say.

He smiles, tired again. "Something like that."

"Well, why else would you invent this thing?" I feel like I'm interviewing him for the *Tonight Show*.

"Well, there's the fact that it really could help reduce emissions," he says.

"And you did all this by yourself?"

He doesn't answer. Arthur's chin is dropping and resting on the speaker of his PA system. You can hear him snoring. The Indian's eyes stay open, but he sits very still, and his breathing has grown deep.

Seabrook offers us sheets and blankets and says he plans to pilot the boat for several more hours, in case the white boats have regrouped and choose to search the area. He also gives Arthur a pad and pen. "So you can write messages instead of shouting through that thing at all hours," Seabrook says.

Arthur and I huddle next to one another. Kang disappears into the long shadows cast by the boat, while Seabrook takes the wheel and pilots the craft out of the shoal.

Leaning on an elbow, Arthur scribbles on his pad and shoves it at me. *I thought you said this guy was a drug runner?*

"Well," I whisper, "maybe he's not."

You're not really thinking of hitching with this guy to California, are you?

"He's heading in the right direction at the moment, at least," I whisper. "I say we go with him for as long as we can. At least until we see some civilization."

Arthur frowns. *But how do you know that they aren't drug dealers? Or that they won't try something desperate? Or what if we meet up with those people again?*

"Would you rather he leave us out here in the woods?"

Seabrook leans over the wheel and peers ahead, steering the boat between the trees into the night. Before I drift off, I watch his hand dart into his front pocket. Just for a second. Like he wants to make sure the crucifix is still there.

PART TWO

Bum Tribe

I was suddenly sensible of such sweet and beneficent society in Nature, in the very pattering of the drops, and in every sound and sight around my house, an infinite and unaccountable friendliness all at once like an atmosphere sustaining me, as made the fancied advantages of human neighborhood insignificant, and I have never thought of them since.

—Henry David Thoreau

the warning

Steel birds lined the valley floor in long rows.

The valley, which stretched for miles between twin green mountains, belonged to the steel birds, and the rumbling bears who rolled between them, and the men who lived in the box houses.

A fence of wire filed to sharpened points separated the valley from the mountains. Along the fence at intervals were large metal sheets with marks on them that looked like this:

Property United States Air Force
No Trespassing
Violators Will Be Fired Upon

The fence was not necessary. No other men lived in the green mountains that overlooked the steel birds' valley, and the birds, deer, mice, bears, and squirrels who lived in the trees stayed away. The steel birds belched fire and made a terrible racket when taking flight, the rolling bears farted blue fumes, and the men carried guns.

The mountains were peaceful. Some of the animals had heard tales of men with guns killing animals for sport, of the foulness spread by men on other mountains. Here, the wire fence seemed to keep the men away. The animals drank from clear water that trickled down the mountainside and ate from the unspoiled greenery. Generations were spawned and lived entire lifespans, and when they died new generations formed. Some of the young ones still flinched when the steel birds roared through the valley, but even that had lessened with each succeeding bloodline, as if knowledge of the steel birds had become hereditary.

Then came the warning.

It came on the heels of a storm that rolled through the valley, as if it was actually part of the thunder, lightning, and rain. It blew through the mountains, within seconds shredding the old ways forever.

Before the warning, each animal was its own keeper; every desire or fear was the animal's own. But the warning obliterated individuality. In an instant, thoughts of survival that had passed from generation to generation disappeared. A burst of whiteness swept across the animals' minds, wiping clean each synapse, instinct, and memory.

What replaced them was a heightened awareness, as if each brain was no longer an individual consciousness but a collective whole.

They rose from burrows. Figures some had never seen before—haggard beasts with long teeth and razor claws, puffing and drooling; bears that had grown fat in their tranquility; deer with racks of sharpened antlers; even scrambling gray mice and squirrels—gathered together on the forest floor. Pile upon pile of moaning, snarling, chattering animals teemed until both hillsides swarmed with life. Overhead, birds rose flapping from every tree until they blotted out the sky.

The thought coursing through their collective consciousness made them all turn in unison toward the base of the mountain, down into the valley, and past the wire fence to where the steel birds sat, waiting.

And then they marched.

we head downriver

Hard work isn't so bad. Back home, I did all I could to get out of the chores the Moms stuck me with. When she told me to straighten my room or tidy the bathroom, I told her my back hurt or I was so hungry I had the shakes or that I was so tired I felt like I was going to die.

But on the *Tamzene*, working's just cool. It gives my thoughts a rhythm. Everything about the *Tamzene* is rhythm: the *whoosh-whoosh* of the engine, the sloshing of the creek against the hull. Even the work schedule has this ebb and flow, so that the harder we work, the better my head works.

Seabrook didn't exactly *ask* us to start working when we woke this morning; he simply said matter-of-factly, "The hemp chamber is low and needs filling." Then he looked at us with eyebrows raised, and Kang appeared from nowhere, motioning for us to follow.

For two hours we've been hauling bags of hemp up the stairs from the hold to the metal dome in front of the smokestack in the aft portion of the boat. Kang stands on a small platform just above the metal dome, takes the bags from us, tears them open, and dumps the contents into the metal chamber. Then he pokes them with a stick, seeking out seeds that might hurt the equipment by exploding during the heating process, as Seabrook explained.

At first, the weight of the bags and the plodding up and down the stairs sucked big time. My arms ached, I sweated like a mofo, and my chest felt like it was going to explode. But soon, the mindless back-and-forth marching unhitches my brain and it's the best thing ever, like being half-asleep and half-awake. Trudge, trudge, boom. Turn. Trudge, trudge, boom. Turn. I compose two whole songs and come up with album cover designs and stage show concepts for my band's upcoming tours.

Arthur takes a break to "chat" with Kang. It looks like chatting, at any rate. The two silently point and wave, making shapes with their hands and noises by trumpeting their lips. Kang motions at the metal dome with the hemp in it, and at the water and the trees.

This one time when I pass Arthur on the steps, I make like I'm mute and mouth a couple of silent words. He frowns like he can't hear me. I move on and when we cross paths again, I mouth gibberish at him a second time. He stops and narrows his eyes and leans in close like he's trying to hear. So I sort of wiggle my hands, make bird shapes, point at stuff, and mouth things at him. Just goofing around, you know. Guys do that with their buddies, because nothing is off limits when it's just a joke.

When he gets that I'm just goofing, he looks at the ground and smiles and pushes past me. Oh man, it's about as low as I've ever felt. The kid is obviously used to it. He's conditioned because everybody else probably picks on him the same way. This one time at Primrose, one of the football players threw his cheeseburger at me in the cafeteria, and I dropped my tray with this mad loud crash and everybody laughed because I had mustard and ketchup and meat all over me and was standing above this mound of food and broken plates and spilled milk. And you can't cry because that just makes it worse. All you can do is smile and act like you're in on the joke. It's the saddest thing in the world.

I swear to myself then and there that I'll never make fun of Arthur ever again.

Seabrook stands rigidly behind the wheel and scans the banks of the river with his woolly caterpillar eyebrows at half-mast. He tells Kang we probably won't stop until we clear Pennsylvania, just in case the white boats are still out looking for us.

The weather stays hot and weighs down on us, and bugs that spawned in the night cloud the deck. They bite me like crazy until Seabrook hands Arthur and me each our own personal bottle of bug repellant from his private stash. It's a lotion, he says, but it smells like my shorts. "An invention," he reassures us.

After I rub on a coat of the stuff, the bugs form a wide path when I come near them. But the lotion reeks something chronic. I tell Seabrook so.

He laughs. "Yeah, smelly as hell. But it works, doesn't it?"

"Wicked," I say. "And you *invented* this goop?"

Well, I must have stuck my foot in my mouth, because he looks at his feet and mutters at me and then goes into the cabin. I'm about to ask him what he said when I bump into Kang, who is looking at him with that same lump-of-coal expression he always wears.

"What's his deal?" I ask, pointing at the Doctor, who is wiping the dashboard he cleaned just five minutes ago.

Kang makes some signs at Arthur. Arthur scribbles on his pad: *His wife invented the bug repellant. She was a scientist too. She died.*

What do you say in a moment like this? This one time, Joe Kennedy's old man passed on, and nobody talked to the guy for eons. Then a month afterward Hugo Frist tried telling him a joke, and Joe went home sick for the day. You never know with dead people, you know? Nobody talked to Hugo for a long time after that, the stupid dork.

I don't want to piss Seabrook off. He doesn't talk much. Mostly he just goes about his work real determined, or else he sits there like he's treading water in his own thoughts, staring at that crucifix key chain and stroking it. He's always nice when he talks to us, even though he uses big words. He calls me Mr. Brubaker, which makes me feel like a grown-up.

So I work harder than before and hope not to pop off something else that stupid. Seabrook, after all, has to be a genius to have built this messed up boat.

The *Tamzene* is insane, people. Seabrook assembled it from a hodgepodge of boat parts and secondhand machinery. The top portion looks like an eighteenth-century trawler. Lacquered planks form the prow, the name *Tamzene* stenciled near the bow. Seabrook explains that he took the wood from a retired British warship that used to serve as the gift shop for a museum/casino in Reno, Nevada, before it went out of business. "It was the perfect size to anchor the rest of the boat," he tells us.

Plastic and fiberglass sheets form the cabin, where there are two wheels for steering: one for the rudder, and another for the tires the boat uses to drive through streams too shallow to float on the pontoons.

Beneath the wheel is a CB radio. Seabrook says he used to use it to listen in on his pursuers—until they changed their frequency. Now the radio mostly spits static with only occasional snatches of talking.

The hemp cooker—a hulking mushroom dome of red metal with a hatch that hides the burning hemp in its belly—takes up most of the aft side. The fire chamber burns beneath the larger cap portion of the mushroom, which holds water. When the water boils, two large steel pistons attached to its sides pump in and out. These are connected by steel pipes to the *Tamzene*'s propulsion system, two small wheels directly beneath the stern.

"The idea, I'm afraid, came from the drug industry," Seabrook says. "A device called a bong, used for the smoking of marijuana, routes the smoke through water and makes it cleaner for the inhaler. I've just built a larger version for the burning of the hemp—just without the electric motor, so it's actually more energy efficient. The smoke gets piped from the cooker through the turbine with copper tubing."

"Yeah," I say, "it's like a huge bong."

Seabrook smiles. "Not exactly, like I said," he says. "It has no electric power source. So it's cleaner than a bong."

"Dude," I say, "a bong is just a chamber with water in it. You hook the pipe up to it and suck from the other end and it cleans the smoke. You don't need electricity."

"I'm quite sure about this," he says. "I've studied it quite closely, and a bong is an electric device."

Then he sulks, and I feel bad again. I mean, it isn't a big deal that he doesn't know anything about bongs. He's still about the smartest guy I ever met. I guess he doesn't like being wrong. His Eminence hates being wrong too. If he gets a fact out of whack and you call him out on it, it's like you've taken away his iPhone.

The radio hisses and crackles. A voice bubbles up through the white noise: "*. . . costly efforts to curb greenhouse gas emissions could devastate the American economy and would only nominally reduce global temperatures. Further, many scientists are not convinced that the planet is warming beyond normal cyclical patterns.*"[2]

Kang fixes the broken glass from the storm with duct tape and patches some of the places where the boards had come loose.

When we aren't hauling hemp or sweeping the dust that always seems to cover the deck, we watch the trees, bushes, and weeds drift past. Sometimes we go beneath the long cement legs of a bridge. Here

and there we see the burned-out wreckage of a car, and in one case a
pair of Nike sneakers with the laces tied together slung over the limb
of a tree.

People dump all kinds of shit into the river. It is a big flowing
garbage can. There are pipes everywhere, snaking down banks and
spewing brown gunk and green sludge that kills the fish. Dead fish
are all over the place, floating upside down or scattered through the
rocks, plastic six-pack holders, and rotting pizza boxes on the banks.
We don't see a soul for hours.

For lunch Seabrook serves TV dinners. I've never eaten one before. It's Salisbury steak and waterlogged tater tots. "Sorry about this,
guys," Seabrook says. "We brought food that could be frozen easily.
We must conserve."

Arthur doesn't wait for utensils—he picks up the brown, greasy
lump of meat with his fingers and finishes it in three bites. Kang does
the same, and both race to down their drinks. I sip my seaweed citrus
juice and wonder if I'll be able to keep everything down.

"I suppose it's not like we could get Domino's Pizza to deliver out
here," I say.

Seabrook pats my shoulder. "We'll get you pizza when we reach
the border."

"Why Ohio?"

Seabrook frowns. "I'll be confident that we put enough water between ourselves and our pursuers by then to rest."

Kang lets out a tremendous belch. Arthur smiles.

I lean toward Seabrook. "What, if you don't mind my asking, is his
story?" I nod toward Kang.

Seabrook tells us he first met Kang when he was setting off from
New Orleans. Kang responded to an ad Seabrook had placed in the
Times-Picayune for an "able-bodied seaman."

"Come to think of it, that ad never actually made the newspaper,
so I'm not certain how he responded," Seabrook says. Kang had been
the only applicant. They hit it off, probably because Kang can't talk,
which is always a great trait to have in your help. Seabrook didn't have

the money to pay him in anything other than food, so he made Kang his partner. And it all works out because the traveling helps Kang with his own quest.

"What quest?" I ask.

Just then, Kang takes the bowie knife out of the scabbard on his waist and sharpens it on a gray whetstone. Arthur watches like it's TV.

"Kang is a Milliconquit."

"A what?"

"A Milliconquit. A tribe of Native Americans that originated in New Orleans. A rather small, mostly unknown group that excelled in trade with other Native American tribes. Specifically, you see, the Milliconquit specialized in the production of a device for the protection of Native American feet."

"Shoes?"

"Kind of, yeah. The tribe Milliconquit mostly subsisted on trading these items with other tribes, and as a result their population circulated throughout what we call today the continental United States, sometimes taking up residence with various other tribes, taking wives, bearing children. To tribes like the Iroquois and the Apache, the resident Milliconquit was considered to be something of a holy man. And the footwear they produced was considered so important to the other Indians that wars were actually fought over these shoes."

"We've never discussed the Milliconquit in history class."

Seabrook shakes his head. "You've likely never heard of the Arawaks either—the Indians Columbus first encountered and later slaughtered. The Milliconquit, as a tribe, were wiped away by European genocide. They were so dispersed throughout the continent that they've been forgotten. In fact, I'd never heard of them myself until I met Kang. I personally believe that Kang here is the last of the Milliconquit."

"Really?"

"Yeah, but don't tell him that. You see, Kang is on a quest to find his lost tribe. He's traveling the country looking for remnants."

"Like Caine in *Kung Fu*!" I say. "Just walking the earth. Or that guy in *The Last of the Mohicans*!" I beam at Kang. "That's badass, man. Bad*ass*."

Then, I whisper to Seabrook: "Why does he glow at night?"

"Excuse me?"

"That first night, he was . . . never mind."

You can't tell which way you're going on a river because it's all twists and turns. One minute you're on what looks like a big lake with the sun burning a hole through your back, and then a minute later the sun is in front of you, the trees are clawing at you on either side, and it's hard to tell there's water under you at all. Sometimes there's a fork in the river and you don't know if it's the start of some new waterway or if the one you're on has split in two.

It gives me a headache, but Seabrook gets all ramped up by it. I mean, he has a GPS locator, but he gets giggles out of figuring things out on paper. He spots a landmark, unfurls his map, and scrawls in a little spiral notebook full of numbers he keeps in the cabin. Then runs back to the hemp cooker and twists a few knobs. That makes the cooker's *whoosh-whoosh* noise hiss and the big pistons move faster or slower.

We run into a three-pronged fork. There's a wide, tree-lined mouth on the right and a narrow trickle of water on the left—or we can head straight the way we're going, downriver and around a bend. Seabrook frowns and scrawls on his pad, then erases it, sticks his tongue in the corner of his mouth, and replaces it with more writing.

"Mr. Brubaker," he says, "get my pocket compass. It's there on the top shelf."

Arthur and I have been helping Kang with the anchor while Seabrook figures out where we're going. I go to the far end of the cabin and look at the tall set of shelves.

"Where?" I ask.

"Top shelf," Seabrook says again.

I look up at the shelves. They must be about six feet tall, so I should be able to reach, but I stand on tiptoe and can't get it.

"Mr. Brubaker?" Seabrook's back is to me, and he's chewing the top of his eraser over his equations.

It's embarrassing. Four foot eleven. Another half inch and I could get it. I strain. I grab the shelves. Maybe I could climb them, but they are these rickety metal things that would probably teeter over on top of me if I risked it.

Something bumps into my rear and I turn. It's an empty plastic crate that was sitting near the door. It clicks that I can stand on the crate to reach the compass.

I see Arthur standing next to Seabrook. I can tell he's glancing at me out of the corner of his eye.

I give the compass to Seabrook and stand next to Arthur.

If you're tall—or at least normal height—it probably doesn't mean much to you, but this was a cool move. Arthur could have just come over and grabbed the compass and handed it to Seabrook himself, which would have dissed me big time, even if he didn't mean to. More often than not, when my shrimp frame shames me, there's somebody—a Paste Eater or His Eminence or even the Moms—there to remind me what a little freakshow I am.

But Arthur bumped the crate at me nonchalantly and then pretended it didn't happen. He's a gangly kid, a good head and a half taller than yourstruly, but it's like he knows what it's like to be me.

I stand next to him and watch the water churn by. "So what are you going to do when you grow up, man?"

"*Law school*," he writes on his pad.

Well that doesn't compute. With some guys, you can just tell what they're going to be. Burton Trotsky, for instance—if our band doesn't save him from it—is going to be a lawyer. He doesn't have publicspeak like His Eminence, but the kid is a born schmoozer.

I'm sticking to my vow never to insult Arthur, so I don't mention the obvious—lawyers usually gab a little better than he does. "That's cool, man," I say.

Arthur shrugs. "*My dad went to Harvard, and he says I'm going there*."

"So did mine," I say. No big surprise. Everybody I know is Harvard grad spawn. And His Eminence never told me specifically I'm going there, but he often says "When you're at Harvard in a couple years" like it's a given.

"*Dad works for the NSA,*" Arthur writes. "*Hush hush stuff. Says I'm going to be a legacy there. That's why I was at Godspeed Summer Camp. First step.*"

"Well, what do you want to do?"

He shrugs again. "*I like dinosaurs. I've thought about archaeology or anthropology, but of course my dad won't have any of it.*"

"Wow, that sucks," I say. "You see, me and my boys are starting this band. We're wicked psycho. Doesn't matter what my folks say—come eighteen, I'm out the door."

We talk for a while longer until Seabrook yells, "Weigh anchor. We're going to starboard. We'll keep to the trees and hope they don't spot us."

Arthur is geeky, people, but I'm beginning to learn that he isn't such a bad dude.

He tells me his dad does all kinds of secret agent stuff for the NSA. Everything is super quiet where he works: people mumble in sound-proof rooms, phone conversations are whispered. They don't even talk around the watercoolers like they do in the offices you see on TV. Co-workers only nod at one another when they pass in the hallways. One time, Arthur says, he went with his dad to a government-mandated father-son day, and people shot him dirty looks because of the soft noises his sneakers made when he tiptoed on the carpet. Things are so soundless at work that, when Arthur's old man gets home, he needs a break from all the peace and quiet and relaxes with a little noise and tension. Every night, he turns up the TV set full blast, throws his briefcase down with a loud *kerplunk*, and hollers at his wife. And she shouts back, Arthur figures, because she knows how much he loves noise and tension, and she's grown to love it over the years too.

"What's for dinner tonight!" he shrieks.

"Pot roast!" she yells back.

"Again?! Can't you speak to the help, dear? Chef just made pot roast last week! Do I have to do everything around here?"

Up until Arthur could actually speak, he looked as if he'd be a world-class loudmouth too. His *goo-goos* were loud enough to make the French doors to his nursery wobble. During his christening, church members actually stuck cotton balls in their ears to try to get some relief from the piercing sounds of his crying.

It wasn't until he was old enough to actually speak that his parents noticed the volume coming down.

"Dinosaurs, Arthur?" his father would shout at him. "What good do you think you're possibly going to get out of playing with dinosaurs?"

"Why don't you play football, Arthur? How are you ever going to make friends if you don't play football?"

"Why do you sit inside and read constantly? Why don't you go outside and play, for God's sake?"

Arthur tried to answer, but it was like somebody was twisting his sound knob to the left. Arthur kept speaking more and more softly until he was barely whispering.

At first, Arthur's pediatrician said it was a mental thing. But his old man was convinced that wasn't the answer. So they took the kid to other doctors, who hooked him up to machines that X-rayed his throat and scanned his brain. They jabbed him with needles and looked at his blood under microscopes. Arthur went to fifty of these other doctors in all, and none of them could find a thing wrong with him—physically, that is.

Then one day Arthur's old man came home, kerplunked his brief-case down, and yelled about how he'd been right all along. One of the doctors who had just checked Arthur out had phoned and told him so. It wasn't psycho-something. It was a birth defect. There was bad stuff in Arthur's throat, this cloud of muscle that encircled his vocal chords. As Arthur got older, the muscle kept getting bigger and bigger and tighter and tighter around the vocal chords, which in turn kept getting weaker and weaker and littler and littler. It was incurable; surgery would have killed him. But the condition wouldn't—it just meant he wouldn't be able to talk above a whisper.

So the doctors outfitted him with the PA system that could pick up the tiny squeaks he made and blow them up into a voice that could be heard. That's when the kids at school started in on him.

The whole thing freaked his mom out; after that she wouldn't let him outdoors and slobbered all over him. She paraded him around the big social functions they hosted at their home in the DC suburbs so more people could cry over what a little freakshow he was.

His old man kept yelling. He yelled that Arthur needed to get his nose out of books and go outside. He yelled that he'd pulled some strings and had gotten him into Godspeed Summer Camp where he'd hang out with kids with normal voices.

Chapter Seven

we pass pittsburgh

When we hit shallow spots the *Tamzene* creeps over the rocks on its wheels, and that shakes the boat so badly that the boxes rattle against the floor and bottles and cans fall off tables. That doesn't happen all that often, though. When the river widens and deepens, except for the crazy rhythms of the engine, the *Tamzene* slides along silently. We don't pass anything at all for the rest of the day.

When the sun sets, Seabrook unfurls his map across the small table in the cabin, grips his chin, and announces that we should make Ohio by midday tomorrow.

That night, Kang cooks four steaks on the gas grill that's lashed to the side of the cabin and takes over the piloting duties. I stand with him for a while and watch him work the controls. On closer inspection, his tats are not 100 percent Indian. The Nike swoosh is in there. Somebody has stenciled some squares and lines around it to hide it, but it's the Nike swoosh all right.

The way he sort of fades into the deck at night freaks me out. And I still have no idea what that blue light was the night I spotted him. When I ask him, all he does is shrug and look back at whatever he's doing.

Seabrook takes a pack of playing cards from one of the containers and asks us to play pinochle. The only card game I know is video poker, and I haven't played in months since I lost $1,500 to a website that operates out of Kuala Lumpur, and His Eminence, after noting it on the credit card bill, took the Internet access out of my room. So Seabrook lights his hookah and teaches us how to play as Kang drives the boat through the trees, with only the occasional crackling noise and cricket pulsing above the hum of the engine.

We play until after midnight, and then unpack our bedding and lie down on the deck. I fall right to sleep.

I wake up in the dark. I was dreaming about the pink marks on the Moms's forearms. I don't know why I'd never thought of this before, but I know where they come from. Every night, the Moms leans on the brick wall that surrounds our house, which His Eminence refers to as the Compound. The Moms is out there every night, leaning on her forearms against that brick wall, staring out at the trees. I was dreaming that she was out there again, staring up at the same sky that I'd been looking at.

But that's not what I see when I wake up. The trees are gone. Glowing towers roped with what look like Christmas tree lights have grown up in their place. They spike for miles, everywhere I can see, and lift into the darkness, blotting out the stars. Between the towers I can make out narrow blacktop corridors lined with cement walkways. Headlights whisk past on the roads. Three lighted bridges stretch across the river.

The hissing radio burps in the cabin. A voice crackles: "*We need an energy bill that encourages consumption.*"[3]

I rub my eyes. It must be Pittsburgh. I haven't seen a city in days. I've never seen a city from the water before, and it feels like I'm watching a movie with the sound off—I can see the blinking lights, the cars driving past, even antlike people moving about on the walkways, but I hear only the gentle *whoosh-whoosh* of the *Tamzene*. Philadelphia has this loud-ass buzz. It's big and everywhere. This city doesn't seem real.

At first I consider waking Arthur. The two of us could slip into the water like secret agents and swim for shore, then maybe hitchhike like we originally planned. I prop myself up to get a better look at the city, but Seabrook, who is lying next to me on the deck, pulls me down by the shoulder.

"Mr. Brubaker," he whispers, "we have to be quiet now. They'll be expecting us to stop someplace like Pittsburgh. They may be watching us right now."

"Who the hell are these people following you?" I whisper back.

So he tells me what he knows, which isn't much. After they built the *Tamzene* near Seabrook's lab in New Orleans and started searching for investors, they got a visit from some dude who looked like a government goon. The guy offered to buy the *Tamzene* from Seabrook for a briefcase containing $5 million. Well, first off, Seabrook knew his invention could potentially fetch a boatload more in the Benjamin department, and secondly, something about this dude didn't seem big potatoes enough. So he turned the guy down. About a month before Arthur and I arrived at Godspeed Summer Camp, Seabrook set out from New Orleans. And that's when he first started seeing them.

"What?" I ask.

"Those boats," he says. Even in the dark, I can tell he's frowning. "The Green Police."

He first noticed them when rounding Florida—a couple of white boats cruising nonchalantly around the Key West harbor. Seabrook wouldn't even have noticed them if it wasn't for the names on their hull: *Green Police*. "I thought maybe they were kindred spirits. Perhaps that promotional video we'd made had found its way to the Web, and we were attracting sympathizers."

Then he started seeing white boats everywhere. Four were anchored at the port in Savannah, with dudes gawking at the *Tamzene* through binoculars. In Baltimore, one of the white boats came within a few yards of the ship. When Seabrook tried to hail the man on deck, he hoisted a camera with a telephoto lens and started snapping pictures.

By the time he'd sailed to New York, the white boats were following his wake. He tried to hail them on the radio, but they didn't respond. He managed to pick up their frequency on his own radio, and beneath their coded transmissions he thought he heard an order.

"Shoot to kill," someone had said.

Then, when he turned onto the Hudson, they started shouting at him through their PA systems. And then they fired at him. They used a big gun—or maybe more like a mortar—like they wanted to blow the boat out of the water. The blast hit very close beneath the pontoon and sent the boat reeling from side to side. Seabrook said he was lucky there wasn't any major damage, but it seemed to affect his radio because after that, all he picked up were snatches of conversations on one frequency.

Needless to say, Seabrook tried to avoid traveling by day. He hid the boat and altered his advertised route, turning into the small rivers of Pennsylvania to start his trip westward. He'd had run-ins with the Green Police twice since then, including the one on the Allwyn.

"So who are they?" I ask again.

Seabrook shakes his head. "Well, Mr. Brubaker, the environmental movement in this country is not without its enemies. I suggest you try and get some sleep and hope they don't find us again."

"Why didn't you call the cops on them?"

"I tried," he says. When the white boats first started shooting and the *Tamzene* got away, Seabrook stopped at a town and called the police. They told him to sit tight and wait for an officer to show up at the dock. But that's when he saw those damn white boats a second time and nearly got sunk hauling ass out of the harbor. I tell him it sounds like the five-oh really *were* in those boats tailing him, but he says he doesn't think so because he'd heard nothing on his police scanner about the boat. "And why would they want to stop us?" he asks.

"I don't get it," I say. "Why, if people are trying to kill you, don't you just stop? There are other ways to make a buck."

Seabrook doesn't say anything for a while. Finally he says, "Go to sleep," and rolls over on his side.

I lie down on my back. The air doesn't smell like city either; it smells like the river always has—like dead fish and chemicals. I watch the undersides of the bridges as we pass beneath them, and then the yellow glow of the city dims and the sky once again goes dark. *The band Carmine is from Pittsburgh*, I think. They have big stadiums there I could scout for venues for my arena rock shows. And TV! My chest starts to ache as I think about how recently, late at night, Cartoon Channel had been showing reruns of *Hot Force*—the shoot-'em-up cartoon with the chick in lingerie—one of my all-time favorites.

I glance at Arthur, who lies with his arm draped over the speaker of his powerless PA system, which he refuses to take off. Here, at least, we're headed in the right direction. I might have made a discovery that'll help His Eminence's political career. We're dry. We have food.

I close my eyes and try to go back to sleep. In the cabin, the radio hisses and buzzes. "*If we are saying that the loss of species in and of itself is inherently bad—I don't think we know enough about how the world works to say that.*"[4]

the river

The men and women who live in this part of the world have found a new way to be happy.

They discovered that, if they dig through the ground and find a certain rock, they can extract a form of fuel from the rock that other men and women will pay through the nose to get because they can burn it to heat their homes for less money.

But men and women are never neat, and so, when they extracted this fuel, it leeched into the soil and collected into the groundwater, which gathered in subterranean streams and spilled into the river.

The river changed. It knew that one day it would burn the same way another river further west, the one men and women called the Cuyahoga, had burned years before.

The river didn't hate. It didn't love. It didn't judge. It just flowed forever west.

However, when a boat capsized, or when someone fell into its depths and failed to surface . . . well . . . let's just say after this whole fracking business, as it was called, the river could live with that.

Which is why when the thought came that night to throw up its arms in the form of a great fog and allow itself to be sucked into the air around a thing as insignificant as a boat, one might understand how the notion gave the waterway pause.

The river flowed forever west without judgment, but it threw up its fog and allowed the boat to pass unseen through the night around the city.

the orange

I think I am still dreaming when I wake up the second time. The monster trees, the rocks, the dirt—everything is pinkish yellow. The river has changed. Purplish ectoplasm swirls all around us, and the foam breaking off the *Tamzene*'s hull is like cotton candy.

Behind us, the river and the trees and the banks make roughly a U shape out of the horizon. At the base of the U, a glowing blob is rising. On the surface of the water, it paints a neon orange strip, more orange than a neon sign on Broad Street. Then another. And another.

After a few minutes, a big blood orange that seems lit from the inside climbs up out of the river and sprays pink light over all of the hills and trees and sky. As it climbs higher, it paints more neon pink and orange streaks on the water, one after another after another, until there's a path of them in the water to our stern.

I try waking Arthur so he can see, but nothing doing. It's the coolest thing I've ever seen—and I've seen every *Star Wars* flick at least five times. But in those movies, it's different because you can see everything. Out here, the screen in my head can't hold it all. That almost makes me feel like giving up and not looking, but I can't help myself. I go to the cabin and explain how it feels to Kang, but he just nods and smiles.

giant head

Breakfast is cinnamon Pop-Tarts and black coffee. The night cooled the air, and fog surrounds the boat. Trees streak the fog, and we can barely make out the river in front of us. The city is long gone.

As we gather our bedding, Seabrook says, "We'll be in Ohio before you know it."

It's getting close to lunchtime when we cross the state line, and Seabrook slows down. I'm not sure what river we're on, but when we change states it spreads out, which in the fog is science-fiction scary.

Water stretches on all sides of us and disappears into fog banks. I guess Seabrook can tell what direction we're headed, but I sure can't.

I look over the side of the boat and watch the black water while the radio crackles in the cabin: "... *never been one case—documented case—of groundwater contamination in the history of the thousands and thousands of hydraulic fracturing.*"[5]

I see a face looking back at me.

Well, it freaks me out something fierce. The big face is a couple feet down. I can't make it out very well, but it's definitely grinning. I holler for Seabrook to stop the engine. He does, and we drift downriver a moment until he tosses the anchor in, then joins me.

"What is it?" he says, grumpy as hell.

I point at the face, and he frowns and peers deep into the river.

"Kang, give me the hook," he says.

Seabrook equipped the *Tamzene* with this long skinny pole with a hook on the end of it. He uses it to grab posts or trees when he's docking. When he plunges it into the water, the face disappears behind a brown haze. Seabrook shoves the pole around for a bit, hooks it, and pulls it to the surface.

It's a poster.

It's made of white plastic and was probably once in somebody's front yard on a metal hanger. On one side is the face, a smiling older guy with jowls and a ridged nose and bald head.

On the other side, blue letters read: *Keep Lynnbrook on the winning path. Reelect Councilman Bob Schwartz.*

Seabrook unhooks it and lets it slide back into the water. "People and their trash. Please don't ask me to stop again, Mr. Brubaker, unless it's something important."

"I just thought it was a real person down there," I say.

I guess he can tell the face really made me wiggy, because he softens a bit. "A real person would most likely float. The fog can play tricks on you. Just keep an eye out for rocks, and I'll worry about any dead bodies, okay?"

CHAPTER EIGHT

we see more faces

Arthur and I mop the deck and then sit down with Kang to learn how to tie knots, which is like trying to learn the Gettysburg Address from a guy who only speaks Arabic. He makes hand motions and tries to demonstrate knot tying by coiling bits of rope between his fingers; I find myself saying "What?" a lot. It's boring as hell, so I start drifting off again to thoughts of TV. I'm thinking of my favorite episode of *Hot Force* when I see another face.

The river has narrowed, and through the fog, trees are visible on the opposite bank. Between two pines, people, I swear I see a dude.

The dude is mostly in the shadow of a tree. His back is in silhouette, but his face is clearly in view: a pale white face with crazy hair and a beard. It glares at the boat for an instant and then disappears into the trees.

Kang continues to show us how to tie what Seabrook calls a sheep shank. Arthur, who has no trouble following Kang, ties the knot like he's tying his shoelaces.

I look over at Seabrook, who is driving the boat, puffing his crazy pipe, and whistling old people music. I assume, since no one reacts, that my eyes are fucked up. Probably the result of too many hours without exposure to television.

I'm settling back in to try to absorb more of Kang's instructions when I see two more faces among the trees on the riverbank. The people who own the faces dart back behind trees to hide when they see me looking.

"What the fuck?" I say. Kang looks at me like he doesn't know what I'm gabbing about.

I get up and lean against the cabin, looking into the woods for more of these people. Seabrook continues to whistle. Then he looks at me, smiles, and sings: "*Tin soldiers and Nixon coming. We're finally on our own.*"

"Huh?" I don't know what he was talking about, and don't much care, because right then two more of these fog freakos appear and then disappear back into the trees.

Seabrook whistles a few more bars. "Man, what they don't teach you anymore. Crosby, Stills, Nash, and Young's finest—"

I interrupt him and point at a trio of dudes who dart into the woods. All three are holding long, skinny poles. Seabrook turns to look at the trees the second they disappear.

He looks back at me, frowning.

"What did you see?"

"People. It looked like people."

Seabrook again glances into the forest and then back at me. He smiles. "Maybe you did. I can't say we're near any town at this point, but there could certainly be hikers in the woods here. After all, we aren't all that far from Lynnbrook."

A few minutes later, Seabrook pulls the *Tamzene* under the low-hanging branches of a tree so you can't see the boat from the river.

"Here we are, gentlemen," he says.

I look into the same monster trees we'd been getting our fill of for what seems like forever. "Where?" I say.

"End of the line," he says. "We're a short walk to the town of Lynnbrook, Ohio. Kang and I are heading there to pick up some supplies, but I believe I owe you a pizza. Afterward, we'll put you on a bus to wherever you'd like to go."

We're making it! I give Arthur's arm a squeeze. He grins at me. We've got a badass head start, people. Ohio and California aren't that far apart. I can't wait to see Burton Trotsky. *What did I tell you, punk?* I'll say. *Who did you think you were talking to?*

Before I can climb down the ladder, Seabrook stops me.

"I assume you're a man of your word," he says. He hoists his eyebrows.

"What?"

"You'll be telling your father about the success of this venture?"

"Of course," I say. "Why wouldn't I?"

I mean it too. The *Tamzene* is a freakshow, no doubt, but it really works. And once His Eminence scoops this little beauty up and shows his constituents what it can do without using a drop of gas, the next election is in the bag. And that means fewer campaign stops where yourstruly would have to put on a dorky suit.

"That's great," Seabrook says, smiling. "It's been a pleasure."

We climb down onto the pebbles and rusting cans at the edge of the river. Kang, leading the way, walks into the woods. I'm straining to catch a glimpse of the town through these big dancing monster trees. I see nothing, but I hear a hissing noise—an electric buzzing, maybe a few cars.

We're not more than a few yards in when a man jumps out and scares the living shit out of me.

He's bare chested and speckled all over with bits of straw, paper, and brown shit, and a long, matted, grayish-brown beard brushes his stomach. A wild look parts the place in the beard where his mouth should be and continues up into his eyes, which are crazy and rolling around.

A full minute seems to pass. A few birds squawk. The river gurgles.

"Wraaaaaiths," the man says. It's a horror show voice, a hiss from lungs coated in something thick and drippy.

As if that's not enough to wig us all out, he hefts a piece of wood with a sharp stone point and a few pigeon feathers tied to the end and threatens us with it.

Well, Kang is like double this guy's size, so I feel like he'll push him over and we'll get on with our day, no problem. But then another guy leaps up out of the brush, also with a spear.

The *Tamzene* is a short jog back behind us, and I'm all for turning around and finding another way to town. I'm not alone, I realize, because

Seabrook has also turned, but then a few more of these half-naked guys crawl out of the woods.

"Just take what you want," Seabrook says. He plunges a hand into his pocket, but one of the men jabs him in the throat with his spear.

And now it's too late to run for it because there are ten of them, waving spears and circling around us, mumbling about wraiths in this low, guttural drone. Fucks me up. It's like that *Ambling Corpses* show come to life.

A guy with a crooked anarchy symbol prison-tattooed on his arm steps out of the pack. The other guys go quiet. He has mangy blond hair that's turning into natural dreds from no washing. He's ripped, but not Abercrombie model ripped—muscles cling sharply to his bones. He circles around us, pushing his buddy's spear away from Seabrook's throat.

"The fuck you doing here?" he says.

"We're just trying to get to town," Seabrook says.

He leans in real close and sniffs Seabrook. Then he makes a face like he doesn't like the smell.

"This is private property," he says, never taking his eyes off the doctor.

"My apologies," Seabrook says. "We'll turn around and get out of your hair."

The blond guy shakes his head. "No, no, no, no, no," he says. "Too late for that."

He wanders around to each of us in turn and leans in wicked close to me. The smell! A hundred locker rooms and a hundred port-a-potties stirred into pudding send a shockwave through my fear-shriveled stomach.

"Look," Seabrook says, "we'll give you whatever you want."

"You ain't got nothing I want, wraith," the blond guy says. He smiles. I wish he wouldn't. He's gumming two broken pieces of cement I realize are his teeth.

"Fellas," he says, "let's take these boys to Bob."

we learn about the shells of the sweetworm

Burton Trotsky has this mad funny video called *Bumfights* where homeless guys whale on each other. The other Paste Eaters and I love that DVD. It's a howler—toothless winos and crackheads duking it out for cheap liquor. This one time, we thought about maybe making our own *Bumfights* on Trotsky's Canon XL, but chickened out when these two assholes from LA got busted for smacking homeless people around with baseball bats and said they were inspired by the same flick. People are so sensitive. Those videos are mad funny.

I've never seen a real-life homeless person up close. Every now and then, I see a couple from the window of the Bentley on the way to Primrose, but they're just part of the background, brown and green dudes I'm just happy to be separated from by a pane of glass.

These Ohio guys look like the guys from *Bumfights*: hair sprouting out all over, jagged shards for teeth, grime, and the white parts of their eyes all yellow. There are some differences, though. First of all, as far as I know, the *Bumfights* bums and Philly's homeless don't travel in packs. Second, the men on the river are dressed weird. Even for bums. They wear pants, but they knot the legs around their waists and let the waists of the pants cover their junk, so their asses are exposed. Dozens of pale, hairy balloons lead us through the woods. Third, there's the jewelry. Around each of their necks, looped through a piece of twine, are at least twenty crushed soda cans apiece—Pepsi, Sunkist, and Coke. I've seen bums picking up soda cans before, but never wearing them. And fourth, I've seen bums pushing shopping carts or cradling paper bags, but I've never seen them toting spears.

I've also never heard of a boat mugging before. It'd look freaky on CNN: "*Senator Mortimer Brubaker's son killed in a boat mugging in Ohio.*"

There's a hoard of them. One points a spear at Kang, whose eyes have gone crazy, and his muscles ropier than ever. The blond one has a spear on Seabrook, and another is threatening Arthur—who has gone all *Rain Man*—and me.

I'm thinking: *Select button. Arsenal. Gatling gun. A and B buttons tapped three times with the trigger on. I leap, hold down the trigger, and spin, and the Gatling gun mows all of them down in a cloud of vaporized blood.*

They're all dressed the same: soda can necklaces and jeans, or flannel shirts worn as belts to cover their privates. They march us at spear-point into the woods.

Arthur glances at the spears and trips over roots, skinning his knees. Kang looks wicked pissed, shifting his eyes from side to side and walking with muscles tensed. Seabrook stops and tries talking to them, but then they jab him with a spear and he keeps walking.

As for yourstruly, I can't seem to find my pain and fear reservoir, and all the songs on the mental iPhone are coming up File Not Found. Sometimes when you get really scared you don't think about the situation you're in—like, what is this ever-growing group of smelly homeless guys going to do with us in these woods?—and you focus on something else. Well, people, for me the twenty-twenties can't stop lasering these crushed soda can necklaces. There are black dudes, Chicanos, Asians, and white guys among them, and the only thing they all have in common is their nasty uncleanliness and that crazy-ass bling.

"Doctor Seabrook?" I whisper as we march along.

"What?"

"Why are they wearing soda cans around their necks?"

He looks at me like I have orcs crawling out of my nostrils. "That's what you want to know?" he whispers. "*Why are they wearing aluminum cans?*"

The blond freako must have heard. He gives me a nasty look. "What do you want to know?" he asks. He pushes through the others and stands in front of me.

"Chill, man," I say.

Kang turns and lowers his shoulders like he's going to rush the blonde, but one of the others points a spear at his throat.

The blonde holds the stone point of his spear a fraction of an inch from my nose.

"Not cool," I say, burying my face into Seabrook's stomach. "Not cool, man."

"You know what's good for you," he says, "you'll shut your yap about cans." With his free hand, he cradles the clunking, rust-colored caterpillar he has tied around his neck. "These are the shells of the sweetworm."

Some of shirtless guys snicker. Blond guy grins up at them, showing his little gray spade teeth. I don't get it. At any rate, I guess the blond dude feels he's adequately terrorized me, because he pulls away and lowers his spear.

We continue into the woods until we can't hear the river anymore. They keep us on a path of sorts. Ferns and briars scrape us as we walk, but we don't have to scramble over any stumps or fallen limbs, and the forest's thicker growth rises up on either side. Birds and bugs and other monsters scream.

There's also that other sound, the noise I heard whispering when we first got off the boat. It comes from a long way off—barely a hiss. I hardly notice it at first, but soon it's clear as an electric guitar chord and sounds just as familiar.

After a while the trees peter out, and we reach a big clearing that stretches about the length of a football field. In the center of the clearing, towering nearly as high as the trees, is a collection of charred logs, roped together in what once was a big bonfire. Next to it is a man in a cage. The cage is a dome of chicken wire with pointy ends that have been shoved into the ground. The man, a sickly looking guy with red hair, loops his fingers into the wire and stares at us as we enter the camp. He's a little better dressed than the bums who took us hostage. That is to say he wears his clothes normally, legs in pant legs and shirt buttoned over his chest.

Surrounding the bonfire are row upon row of cardboard boxes and packaging containers. On some of the flaps are brand names like Whirlpool and Kenmore. The boxes have been set on their sides and appointed like homes—rotting cushions, rags, and other junk spill from their mouths.

On the opposite side of the clearing, a large pile of these packing crates stands nearly as tall as the bonfire.

Between the rows of cardboard boxes, there must be a hundred of these homeless people. They're dressed the same as the guys who took us, although the women cover their boobs by knotting shirts around their chests. They dart in and out of boxes or stand talking to one another while others sit around sharpening their spears.

When we march into the clearing, the pack of derelicts and winos stops and stares at us.

we meet shwo-rez

The dudes with the spears march us into a central corridor between the boxes. The other bums step out of the way, staring at us like we're a freak show. The center of town is hot and close, and I might hurl from the smell of sweat pressing in from all sides.

Nobody says a word. A freckled woman with red hair that falls down to her waist clutches a naked baby to her boobs. A bony old man with hair sprouting from nearly every inch of skin chews on God knows what as he watches us, never once blinking. Filthy kids—some probably about my age—wrapped only in T-shirts or pants, who had moments before been playing some sort of game with what looked like the remnants of a baseball, stop and stare at me like I'm something sick.

No plasma screens. No iPhones. No iPads.

It's unreal.

It occurs to me, people, that maybe it isn't real. Maybe it's TV's version of real. Follow me here. Maybe it's reality TV—maybe like another *Bumfights*. And they can't talk to outsiders because that's part of the contract. Or maybe *they're* the contestants, and it's one of those shows where to win you have to dress in garbage, refuse to bathe, and eat grubs and worms.

"George!" hollers the man in the cage. "This is crazy, George!"

One of the hunter dudes hisses at the man. "Shut up, Clarence," he says. "This don't concern you."

"Come on, show some pride, now!" the man hollers again. "Ain't no need to do what he says. This is crazy, and you know it!"

"I said shut up and mind your own," the hunter says. The blond leader looks at him like he's pissed, and he quiets down.

As we pass through the cardboard box town, people drop what they're doing and follow us. Men drop their tools, women clutch their kids, and, never taking their eyes off us, fall behind us in a trance.

I still can't spot the cameras.

Our silent parade makes its way up the path toward the tall pile of boxes on the opposite end of the field. There's no noise but the yelping and tittering of the things in the woods, along with that hissing noise I still can't place.

By the time we arrive at the big pile, the entire town is following us. Someone has stacked the crates one on top of another and then fastened them together at the sides with sharpened twigs bent like staples. Together they make a big house with no windows. The sides are scratched or punctured. Rainwater has turned them white with mildew.

The blonde raps on the side of one of the crates.

From inside the box house, a man's voice says, "Who knocks?"

"Yellow-Hunter," the blonde says. "We come to see him."

A flap opens and a short man with a few wisps of gray hair sprouting from his temples steps out. A well-fed old bum—a round, hairy belly bulges over a flannel shirt, which he's tied over his waist to cover himself. The wrinkles on his forehead are pursed like he's pissed at first, but when he sees us, he gapes. He and the blond guy mumble to each other, and then he goes back into the box and closes the flap.

We wait. I look over at Arthur, who is rocking back and forth at the waist with his eyes fixed on the tips of those spears—unless there's a noise from the forest, and then he looks off in that direction. Kang grips his shoulder as if holding Arthur upright. Seabrook's head hasn't stopped moving since we arrived in the village; he cranes his neck to look at the town, then up at the mounds of packing crates. He doesn't look frightened—he didn't even look frightened when that storm almost sank his boat. He just looks mega pissed. As for yourstruly, I've stopped trying to stuff things down in the pain and fear reservoir. I still hear the same hissing noise—that soft buzzing way off in the distance. I know I've heard it before. It drowns out the crazy freaks around us, the sweat smells, the reality TV show set we are stuck on, and the pointy spears.

Then the flap opens and the gray-haired man appears.

He says: "You may enter the palace of Shwo-Rez."

WTF, right? But we have no time to think about it, because they make us duck inside this stinking mound of cardboard. There's enough room for Seabrook to stand up straight without hitting his head, but Kang has to stoop. The air is hotter and the BO thicker, and I can feel the food barreling upward as I stumble down the corridor. The gray-haired man shuts the flap, and all is dark except for shafts of light knifing in through the cardboard holes.

At the far end we walk back out, and we're standing in a court-yard. The containers loom over everyone's heads on all sides. There's enough room for about forty people in here.

In front of us is a heap of old pillows. They look like somebody's trash, which is fitting with the whole decor—some are mildewed and patched. Even the newer ones are torn and leaking silver wisps of stuffing.

Tall, pointed sticks are shoved around the edges of the pillows. Spitted upon these are beige spheres with long mops of yellow and brown hair hanging from them. I nearly go schitzo, but as we walk closer I breathe a little easier. They're the heads of department store mannequins.

Sitting on the pillows is a chubby guy with long white hair. His jowls dangle and around his neck are many necklaces—more than I can count—made of twine and crushed beer and soda cans.

He looks familiar.

The man is smoking a cigarette, but as we approach his jaw goes slack, and the cigarette falls from his lips onto the pants he tied around his waist. He jumps up to stamp it out.

In his lap, he caresses the sides of an old cigar box. El Rey del Mundos. I recognize the brand. His Eminence gets those things by the gross. It's supposed to be hush-hush because they're illegal here.

"Horrors!" he says when we walk in. "Horrors!"

Towering right there behind him, like a mirage, is the skyline of a small city on a mountain. It must be several miles off. Skyscrapers climb, radio towers blink, church steeples point—the hissing noise I'm hearing is civilization. I haven't heard it in days, since cruising past silent Pittsburgh didn't count.

"A city!" I say. "What city is that?"

"I don't know, Mr. Brubaker," Seabrook murmurs. "It's got to be Lynnbrook, Ohio."

We are pushed closer. I fall into place beside Arthur, who hasn't stopped being catatonic. Seabrook keeps craning his neck, his eyes bugging out. Kang's muscles look like skin-covered piles of rocks. I would think twice about messing with him if I were one of the bums with the spears.

Yellow-Hunter steps up and bows from the waist and says some gibberish like, "Great and mighty Shwo-Rez, we have brought you four captive wraiths." This might read just like *Lord of the Rings*, except Yellow-Hunter sounds like a longshoreman.

Now I'm really thinking this is a reality show. Has to be. Nobody talks like that.

Then the gray-haired guy steps in and tells Shwo-Rez that it's impossible because he and the "Shrub People" have proven that "wraiths" do not exist. He isn't much more convincing than Yellow-Hunter, which is why reality TV jumped the shark, people—regular folks off the street are lousy actors.

The Shwo-Rez guy says that wraiths must exist because here we stand, and he waves at us.

The gray one, whom Shwo-Rez calls Gray-Aide, keeps saying we aren't, because wraiths don't exist. And Shwo-Rez doesn't know what to think. They keep going on and on in circles until Shwo-Rez waves his arm and says they should chant until they figure out what's what.

All three of them close their eyes, hold each other's hands, and start singing, real somber-like:

*"Flintstones
Meet the Flintstones
They're the modern Stone Age fam-i-leee!"*

Dr. Seabrook is watching everything with a calm, serene expression, like the whole show couldn't be more normal. Even though these homeless guys are singing a TV show theme song, they're acting like it's a sacred thing, like a chant or one of those songs I hear the congregants sing during photo ops at church.

And Seabrook doesn't like religion. Not one bit.

So all at once Seabrook hollers, "Your majesty!"

And that's when things get weird.

things get weird

"Don't let it speak, your grace," Gray-Aide says. He stumbles over the pillows and draws near to Shwo-Rez's side. He whispers in Shwo-Rez's ear, but still loud enough for us to hear: "Who knows what could happen? They could hex you."

Shwo-Rez raises his hand and motions for Gray-Aide to move away from him. "We will allow it to speak."

Gray-Aide opens his mouth to argue, seems to think better of it, and hangs his head. He sits just below Shwo-Rez on a rotting couch cushion and stares streams of ice water at Seabrook.

In fact, all eyes are on the doctor, who clears his throat.

"Your majesty," he says, bowing from the waist, as the other Shrub Men did. "Most humbly, we the crew of the *Tamzene* bid you greetings." It's like he's reading from the same cheesy script as them. It impresses the hell out of me that he could just pull it out of his ass like this. After my band hits it big, I'll land a part or two in a movie, and I might be smart to listen to how this dude wings it. "My name is Doctor Seabrook. This is my partner, Kang, and our other crew members are but mere boys—Mr. Winthrop Brubaker and his associate, Arthur, uh . . ."

"Wraith gibberish, my liege!" Gray-Aide cries.

"Silence," Shwo-Rez says. "You have come from the evil mountains?"

"Sir?"

"The evil mountains," Shwo-Rez repeats. He points over his shoulder.

Above the tops of the boxes, the trees hold a milky morning sky. Thin clouds streak across it, and sparrows and pigeons swoop in the haze.

"Oh," says Seabrook. "Do you mean Lynnbrook, Ohio? No, your grace, we come from much farther away."

"Lynn-brook?" Shwo-Rez repeats, apparently mystified.

"Begging your majesty's indulgence," Seabrook says, bowing again, "what town is that on the horizon?"

"Town?" Shwo-Rez repeats, rubbing his chin.

"Yes, the city skyline there."

"Siii-teeee?"

Silence falls on the courtyard. Off in the distance I hear the honks of car horns and the tapping of music. Is it? It is! I can hear, "*When the lightning crashes and the thunder rolls . . .*" I need the Grizzlies now more than ever. If this is a reality TV show, these producers are cruel sons of bitches.

"Wraithery!" Gray-Aide exclaims after a moment, pointing a finger at Seabrook.

Maybe it's the frustration of being so close to an actual town. Maybe it's Seabrook's smile. Maybe it's the spears. But mostly, it's because His Eminence taught me to never, *ever*, under any circumstances— especially not among liberals or on national TV—tolerate shit.

I am officially done playing nice.

"All right," I say. "This is ridiculous."

Shwo-Rez smiles at me like a goon. "Yes, my child?" he says.

"Come on. Where are the cameras? You guys might be getting paid to act like this, but we're not."

"Mr. Brubaker," Seabrook whispers. "Perhaps it's best not to—"

"Oh, come off it, Doctor," I say. "Evil mountains, my ass. That's a city over there, *Shwo-Rez*. Civilization. Made by human beings."

"Blasphemy!" Gray-Aide says. "No wraith or man could ever build a mountain! Why, it would take more digging stones than we have in all of Eden."

I stoop and begin picking up throw pillows, searching for the hidden cameras and microphones. "And we're not ghosts, psycho. We're human beings. You have no idea, do you? You have no clue who you're messing with. I'm Winthrop Brubaker, freako."

"Yellow-Hunter! Remove them from this place!" Gray-Aide shouts. He trembles, and a patchy red blot—a hive—bubbles on his forehead.

Seabrook moves toward me like he wants me to shut up, but Yellow-Hunter points a spear at him.

"Gray-Aide!" Shwo-Rez loses his temper.

"Don't you people know reality TV has been done to death? Hour-long crime dramas are where it's at now. If you want this take to count, people, you're going to have to let us sign a release form or something. I know contracts. My old man is a congressman, for God's sake. I demand a trailer and a quick ride to town."

"The great debate among those in Eden has long been about wraiths, you see," Shwo-Rez says. "There are the wraith believers, like Yellow-Hunter, and the non-believers, such as Gray-Aide."

"What do you believe these wraiths to be, your majesty?" Seabrook asks.

"Spirits," Shwo-Rez says. "The dead."

"You're not fooling anybody! This is scripted! This is scripted! The least your douchey producers could do if they're going to write scripts is to give you a decent trailer. Seriously. They build you a cardboard shantytown? Why do you stand for that shit?"

Shwo-Rez laughs. "Is this a joke? How is it possible to *make* something that comes from earth? Shrub People build their homes from the bark of trees that we find on the ground."

"Fine. Fine. What about those clothes you're wearing?"

"The skins of animals."

"You are so full of shit!" I shout at the fat king of the bums.

"Enough, Mr. Brubaker . . ." Seabrook says.

"Right," I mutter. "Those *shells* around your neck are just gross squashed soda cans."

"Enough!" Shwo-Rez leaps to his feet. His goes all red, and saliva falls from his lips. "You go too far in your blasphemy, wraith. The sweetworm is a gift from heaven. It leaves its shell for us. Sometimes, when we find these beautiful shells, some of their nectar has been left behind within them, and this is a truly precious gift from above, and blessed is he who drinks from it. Now, I know you speak evil. To suggest a sweetworm is wraithery from the evil mountains is pure mischief. Remove them."

Quick as they came, my king-sized balls crawl back up into me. Boxes and everything start spinning.

When they jab him with a spear, Arthur jolts as if someone hooked jumper cables to his toes. He whirls, and the bullhorn of his PA system strikes one of the hunters in the belly, knocking him to the floor. He scrambles toward the flap in the cardboard boxes where we entered the courtyard, but Yellow-Hunter and another Shrub Man overtake him. They drag him back in by the shoulders.

Kang moves to help the kid, but a hunter jams a spear into the skin under his chin.

Shwo-Rez stands. "We must execute them," he says. "We must make haste, and hope that if others come they will be as easily slain."

I will stand fast and resolute . . . I will stand fast and resolute . . . I grab at the song, but the lyrics slip through my fingers. The world continues to spin.

Shwo-Rez stops glaring and looks at the sky. And now I recognize him. The face. The face from the poster in the river.

It's Councilman Bob Schwartz.

The Gray-Aide guy looks horror-struck. "But perhaps doing evil to evil will only bring more evil upon us," he says. "This must be thought on, your majesty."

Shwo-Rez waves at him dismissively. He picks up his box of illegal cigars and caresses its side as lovingly as Seabrook fingers his crucifix.

"Yellow-Hunter," he says. "Put them in the cage."

CHAPTER NINE

---

birds

It looked no different than any other smoke the town of Lynnbrook produced—a black, roiling pall that poured from the towers. Some felt a tingling under their wings; others sensed a change had happened within themselves.

By that spring, they knew. No bird was a mother. The eggs that were laid were weak. Mothers crushed babies in their nests before they could become pink things gasping for food. Instead of the cries of thousands of tiny voices, there was only the wind in the trees and the melting of the snow.

Some knew it was the smoke. Others thought it was another trick men had played on them on purpose.

Some, however, recognized that the stone yards where the men laid their dead had grown larger that season.

The smoke stopped altogether. Not just the poisoned smoke, but everything that had come from the towers stopped flowing. The silent trees became filled with another cry, one the birds hadn't heard before at such volume.

Some of the men moved into the trees and ate what they could find on the ground.

The birds watched them and sang.

i meet esmerelda

Yellow-Hunter forces us into the chicken wire dome next to the bonfire logs. The whole town surrounds us. They yell and poke us through the chicken wire with spears and sticks. Some call us wraiths. Then

Yellow-Hunter gets between our cage and the crowd and tells the crazies that the prisoners must be left unharmed, and that the great Shwo-Rez will let them all know by nightfall what he's decided.

Even after Yellow-Hunter calms them down, most of the crowd hangs around, gawking at us like we're the monkey cage at the Philly zoo.

Arthur crouches and rocks back and forth. He isn't bawling anymore but he looks plenty scared, so I sit next to him and say: "*When the lightning flashes and the thunder rolls* . . . you know . . ."

Frowning, he stands and goes to the other side of the cage.

I follow him. "So what do you think they're going to do to us?" I ask. "Our dads do have a lot of cash after all. Maybe they recognized me from TV . . ."

His frown gets darker, and he turns his back on me.

"So I was wrong about the reality TV thing. I can admit it," I say. "I mean, who would really think that actual homeless people would talk like that without a script? You have to admit, though, it'd make for a pretty good show—kidnapping people and throwing *Lord of the Rings* at them . . ."

While I'm talking, Arthur picks up a branch from the ground. In the dirt in front of him, he draws the words, GO AWAY. Then he takes out his pocketknife—the Shrub People must not have seen it—and starts whittling the branch.

What a pantload! I feel like reminding the kid that if it hadn't been for me, he'd still be back in Pennsylvania like a little loser.

So I just say, "What-*ev*-er, man," real cold and walk away from him.

Eventually the crowd peters down, and the crazies return to their cardboard boxes, leaving us alone. Kang and Doctor Seabrook examine the cage—a dome of chicken wire with long sharp ends the hunters have shoved into the ground. Kang could probably push the cage over no problem, but the hunters positioned us in the center of town. Every time we move a Shrub Person has his eye on us.

"Don't bother," Clarence says.

I forgot he was here. When they brought us into the camp he hollered at the homeless guys who captured us, but since then he's shut up. He's sitting Indian style in a corner of the cage. The chicken wire's shadow creates crosses over his skeleton-like body.

"They'll nail you with a spear if you try to escape." His voice is phlegmy. "I've been here two days, I have."

"Why didn't you yell for the police?" Seabrook asks.

He snorts. "Police. There's no such thing out here. Besides, you really think they'd put old Bob Schwartz away?"

"I knew it!" I shout.

"Ain't you all from Lynnbrook?" Clarence asks.

"No," Seabrook says.

"*They're not even from Lynnbrook!*" Clarence shouts. Nobody cares.

"The guy running the show here is Bob Schwartz," he continues. "Used to be on the city council. Took so many bribes he's still the richest man in the county. And this here is his land."

"Listen," Seabrook says. "Who are all these people, and what do they want from us?"

"It ain't them," Clarence says. "It's Schwartz. Most of these people don't care about you any more than I do. Schwartz runs the show, and all of them do anything Schwartz says. Except me, and that's why they put me in here."

"What does he tell them to do?" Seabrook asks.

"You got to act nuts. You got to put your duds on all funny and sing songs and parade around. You got to believe in ghosts. You got to say Schwartz is your king. And you got to change your name. All that for some free food and a cardboard box to keep the rain off your head."

"And if you don't?" Seabrook asks.

Clarence smiles. I think he might have one tooth, but it's way back in his head and I can barely see it. "They put you in here," he says. "I come here from Lynnbrook, I did. Cops are hassling you all the time in Lynnbrook. So people say all the time, *Go out to Bob Schwartz's land.*

There's free food and free junk. So I come on out here. But when I got here, I seen them all acting like this. I tried it out for a bit like the rest of them, but the whole thing is just so damn silly. I raised hell. Put on my clothes normal-like and stopped acting like a damn fool, and they shut me up in here!" He shakes his head and looks at his lap. "If we all just hung together, we could have it real nice out here, we could. But then I guess old Shwo-Rez would pout that we don't want to play no more and kick us off his land. Or worse."

"But what do they want with us?" Seabrook asks. "Why won't they let me get back to my ship?"

"They're pretending you're ghosts. They do that with all the outsiders."

"But what do they want with us?"

"You ain't pretending. They want you to."

Seabrook sighs. "Again, sir. If we don't pretend, what happens?"

Again, Clarence shows us the hollows where his teeth should be. "River's only a couple of miles that way," he says, pointing over our heads. "Runs clear into Lake Erie. One time an old buddy of mine, Bob Shanks, got hopped up something fierce and fell in right around these parts. Never did find no body. See, the county dredges that river so it's almost like a canal. No branches or nothing. Nothing for a body to get snagged on. A body'll float for a long time before it'll sink. And Lake Erie's over two hundred feet deep in some places, and so dark and polluted down there, nobody'd ever find a corpse. Not in a million years."

Arthur whittles. Seabrook fiddles with his crucifix key chain. Kang sits and stares. The bums lie in their boxes.

I stand, lean against the cage, and stare at the city on the mountain. I can just make out lights on the radio towers and in the office buildings over the tops of the trees.

From here, it looks like the forest could strangle the city if it wanted to. The monster trees could lasso the buildings with their branches and pull them down. It's up to the people in the cities to keep beating the forest back, keep hacking down the vines and bushes and limbs with machetes to preserve their Nintendo Wiis and plasma screen televisions.

Just as I'm starting to zone out, I notice this chick watching me.

She has reddish-blond hair—a little older than yourstruly, maybe, and a good head taller, though that isn't saying much. She wears a black T-shirt knotted over her breasts and a pair of ratty-looking blue jeans wrapped around her waist. Her navel gawks at me above the jeans, and her skin is brown all over. She's pulled her hair back from her face and clipped it with a clothespin. She leans against a refrigerator box a few yards from the cage with her arms crossed.

Girls are coming my way soon enough—that is, after Trotsky and I launch our band and the first disc drops, I know the chickies will be coming in droves. But for now . . . in school, the girls make it plain they want nothing to do with me. I've been on one official date—a prearranged movie His Eminence concocted for me with Millicent Fouquet, the six-foot-tall daughter of his chief of staff, Maximilian Fouquet. We looked like a freak show. After the security detail had secured the perimeter and dropped us off at the Cineplex where we'd agreed to watch an *X-Men* film together, Fouquet's lips snarled and she said she planned to meet her girlfriends to watch the latest Zac Efron chick flick, and that she didn't give a flying fuck what I did so long as I didn't sit within forty yards of her. So we watched movies separately, and I wrote this wicked sad power ballad, the best I've ever written.

I don't have an aversion to girls. Far from it. Hip-hop videos on YouTube have more than a few hotties—chicks with jiggly rumps and boobs like howitzers chewing gum and staring longingly through spiked eyelashes at the camera. Many is the night I sit alone in the parlor at the edge of the Barcalounger, afghan coiled in my lap, just waiting for one of those videos to flash on the screen and imagining what girl flesh might feel like.

I know, I know, people. Pathetic to be all of fourteen and to never have *done it*.

But the point is, you can see then why this chick noticing me temporarily makes me forget the deep shit we're bathing in. Here is a chick wearing very little clothing checking yourstruly out. And, damn it, I haven't showered or brushed my teeth in days. My body smells not much better than the average Shrub Person and, though I haven't seen a mirror recently, I'm positive my hair is inadvertently doing a greasy flip thing like that band A Flock of Seagulls I once saw on VH1's *I Love the '80s*.

The girl comes to my side of the cage and loops her fingers through the chicken wire. I back up a little. Her blond hair is mangy, her tan dirty, and her boyish hands callused and mutilated from biting her nails. Little black hairs peek out from beneath her pits, and her legs need a good shaving. The teeth are crooked, and one of her front ones is broken.

"Who are you?" she whispers.

I stand back so she won't catch a whiff of me. "Winthrop," I whisper back.

"Look, you'd better get out of here."

"I think so too," I say.

"That guy Shwo-Rez ain't exactly all there," she says. She has a dusky voice, hoarse and low. I'd put her at sixteen. "And he don't like outsiders." Her bad grammar sounds hot in a wrong-side-of-the-tracks way.

It is the most I've ever seen of a real-time hottie, and though she's more strategic than some of the other Shrub People (you can't see any bits or pieces), you can see practically everything. I think. I'm trying hard not to stare, like seeing a bearly nude chickie is just as run-of-the-mill as lobster night at the compound.

"So," I say, slipping into His Eminence's publicspeak, "you from around here?"

Seabrook and Kang come over, and Seabrook asks who she is. She says her name is Esmerelda Chicklis, and that she's lived with the Shrub People for about a month. Again, she says the Shwo-Rez guy is messed up in the head and that if we don't get out of here, who knows what he might do.

"What about your parents?" Seabrook asks.

"I can help you guys get out," Esmerelda continues, ignoring him. "On one condition."

"What do you want?" Seabrook asks.

"Take me with you," she says. "If we make it to your boat, take me to the next town or something and drop me off. Is it a deal?"

"She's crazy," Clarence says. "Y'all will never make it."

"How can you help?" Seabrook asks.

"Well, when it gets dark, Shwo Rez will walk through town. At that point they dance. They'll carry on so long that I can ease us on out of here unseen. I know the way."

I'm surprised that a homeless chick like Esmerelda—someone His Eminence would refer to as lazy and shiftless and a barnacle on the bottom of the ship that is the US economy—could be a bona fide hottie if she'd slather on a little makeup and shave her pits. In fact, I am running through movie scripts trying to find a line that won't sound made up, preferably dialogue from a movie she would not have seen. So I settle on a passage from this episode of *Sniper Dude X* from the seldom-viewed third season.

"Esmerelda," I say, cutting off Seabrook, "your days of fear are at an end."

Everybody—including the hottie—looks at me like I'm out of my mind. So I lower my head and continue to listen to Esmerelda and the Doctor parlay about the homeless weirdos.

The chickies are coming, people. After my band's first disc drops, they're coming. In droves.

CHAPTER TEN

arthur becomes dinosaur king

So, you're probably thinking I'm a bubble boy since I haven't taken a toke of Mary Jane (yet) and because the Shrub People are the first homeless I've seen up close. Not so. I may be young, but I've seen my share of action.

Check this out—two thousand tons of poured concrete. Think about that. That's what surrounds the Compound at Westchester. The wall is feet thick. Yards thick. Yards high. There's razor wire atop it and cameras at every door. Machine gunners—Ralph, Harold, Sven, Gunther, Michael, and Ray—watch from twin fifty-foot guard towers at the lone entrance to the compound. There's this kick-ass Jason Bourne–ified alarm system that's been known to freak out if a squirrel farts somewhere nearby.

I breach it all the time.

I'm telling you, His Eminence's head of security is a Nazi. Nothing ever goes in or out of the compound without him checking it out. And there's also the chambermaids and the butlers and the black suits with the shades and dangly earpieces on the prowl. But I bust this security down. I've got inside men—Gunther in particular—who help me out. Unbeknownst to anyone, I sneak entertainment past them that would, frankly, cheese off the Moms and His Eminence big time. Entertainment some of you might find immoral. And probably illegal.

Dirty movies.

You have to be seventeen to watch *Zombie Cannibals*, what with chicks showing their breasts and that scene where the zombie makes the girl eat her own belly button. I've also seen *Teenage Nuns II: Holy*

Water Sports and *The Boobsie Twins*. NC-17 movies, people.

Download them, you say? Please. The 'rents monitor my Internet history like it's a stock ticker.

Gunther gets my DVDs for me. That took some convincing. The first time I approached him, he waved me off and said he'd have to speak to my old man first. I told him to forget the whole thing and not to mention it to anybody. I thought I was sunk. So it was weird when the next day Gunther *came to me* and told me he reconsidered and would get me whatever I asked to see.

Anyway, since I'm able to break through the Compound's airtight security on a nearly weekly basis, it should be easy to push over the chicken wire dome the Shrub People have us caged in. Instead, we wait for dark to arrive, for Shwo-Rez to march through the town, and for the dancing to start, which is when Esmerelda says she'll set us free.

After not talking to me for a long while, a pretty big pile of wood chips covers the ground at Arthur's feet. He's whittled another dinosaur, this one out of anger at me, I guess—a wicked-looking four-legged beastie with a beak and big horns. By the time he finishes, a crowd of little Shrub People has eked out of the boxes and edged up close to the cage. Grade-schoolers, some gaining on me in the height department, but all still scarcely breaking the plane at Arthur's waist. Five of them—hair filthy, matted, and shoulder length; mud and grime streaking their little butt-naked bods; and hands and fingers smudged black.

"What is that?" says a shrub kid with scary-big moss-green eyes.

Arthur writes on the ground with a twig, *TRICERATOPS*.

The green-eyed kid is quiet a minute and then says, "It's cool, man."

Arthur smiles and nods.

"Do they have animals like that where you're from?" the kid asks.

Arthur will try writing out an explanation on the ground if I don't cut him off. "Yo, kid. It's a dinosaur."

The green eyes remain unblinking.

"You know, one of those lizards that went extinct ages ago. Come on, didn't you get that in first grade?"

"Don't have school," he chirps.

Lucky little bastard! A bonus to the Shrub People, forgoing that whole snoozefest. I guess it isn't all bad here, and I'm about to say so when Arthur hands him the dinosaur through the cage. Filthy little fingers take it and cradle it, and his lips fall slack. Then all these little monsters start running around, oohing and ahing over this wooden dinosaur. So Arthur reaches into his pocket and pulls out the allosaurus he whittled at Godspeed Summer Camp and passes it through the chicken wire.

Well, next thing you know there are Shrub Kids everywhere. "Come see the dinosaur man!" they yell at each other, or, to their moms and dads, "Please, Mommy, I want to go see the dinosaur man." They take turns holding the toys Arthur made and then they stare at Arthur like he's a rock star. Arthur writes things like CRETACEOUS PERIOD and HERBIVOROUS in response. He doesn't seem so shy, actually; he looks like he's having a good time there in the cage. I doubt the kid has ever gotten this much positive attention in his whole life. It seems to warm him, even when the adults come by—including a couple who don't have kids in tow.

"You sure know a lot about dinosaurs," says one of the men who is here by himself. "My little girl'd love to talk to you. When she was real little, I used to buy her stuffed dinosaurs by the truckload. She's probably about your age now. Ain't seen her myself in three years. They got her in a foster home somewheres. They didn't have this place back then, this town for homeless folks, so the state come and took her away. If I ever see her again, though, I'll tell her I met somebody her own age that knew everything there was to know about dinosaurs."

Arthur doesn't shy away. He stands and smiles and writes things on the ground.

These are the people from the boxes closest to the cage, understand. The big stack of boxes, the palace where we were taken—Shwo-Rez's palace—sits still. Nobody goes in or out, but we keep looking up that way, waiting.

The rest of the Shrub People don't seem so scary. They seem just like super poor people (which you'd think would be scary).

We don't notice at first when Gladys comes. All the other Shrub People run away.

"Y'all think we crazy," she hisses. Gladys is a black woman—a Shrub Person with this giant nest of hair that's full of little knots. She's naked to the waist, though you can't see anything because she's holding this little white bundle up in front of her. It's a baby.

"Y'all think we crazy," she says again. Behind her a handful of Shrub People peer out of the mouths of some of the boxes. Gladys has a thick face, but her body is all ashy and bony, with flesh hanging off it like an old dress two sizes too big.

"Y'all think we crazy."

I want to say, *Can you blame us*, but I'm scared.

"I don't know who ya'll is coming in here, but we ain't crazy," she says, rocking from side to side, I guess to soothe the little bundle she's carrying. "I'm doing what I need to do to take care of me and mine. We ain't all crazy. After Super Corp. go down, what you expect us to do? A body got to eat, you know?"

"You're just as bad as they are, Gladys!" Clarence says. He rushes over to the side of the cage next to me. "You don't have to pretend, damn it!"

"Fuck you, Clarence!" she yells. "You tryin' to spoil it all!" She looks back at me. "Ain't nothing on the streets of Lynnbrook for us. That unemployment check stop coming, and you can't pay the rent. Then what you expect us to do? Some of us turn to junk just to make our minds forget what's happening to our bodies. But some of us got little ones to take care of. What you expect a body to do? Find a job? Move where the work is? Well, how'm I gonna do that when there ain't no more job and nobody hire no old bag lady with no clothes and no family 'cept this little one? So we hear tell that the councilman gone crazy come out here and set up a place for us to go, and that there food and there place to keep out the cold."

"*You don't have to pretend, Gladys, goddamn it!*" Clarence yells. "If we all hung together, they'd never . . ."

She ignores him. "Sure, it ain't decent. Got to pretend all kind of things, like ain't no city over there and ain't no God, and got to put on clothes like crazy people 'cause that old councilman Shwo-Rez gone lost his mind. What you expect? When you need food you can't afford believing in beliefs no more. You just go on with what he say and get to live without nobody hassling you. So why you have to hassle us now? I'm glad y'all in there, and I'm glad what they going do to you, but I know there be more of you. I see you lookin' at me like I'm crazy, white boy. But I ain't crazy."

It occurs to me the whole time she's moving that the bundle—her baby—doesn't budge.

It just hangs there.

At dusk they light the bonfire with torches and old newspaper (I wonder what they call newspaper—palm leaves, maybe?) and the fire grows up and licks the tall logs.

Seabrook leans against the cage. He's been leaning against the cage most of the day. And he's been staring at his crucifix key chain, rubbing it with his thumb. That's Seabrook. He's all the time gloomy, quiet. Friendly when you talk to him, a blur of limbs when he has a chart or technical readouts, but sad and soundless the rest of the time.

"I hope this doesn't taint your opinion of the *Tamzene*, Mr. Brubaker," Seabrook says. "Once we get out of here, we'll drop you off at the next town and call your father."

But that seems unlikely as we sit here watching the fire burn. I want His Eminence to burst in with some guys with submachine guns to take out Shwo-Rez and these hunter guys. Not so much the other homeless people. I'm not sure why, exactly. They don't seem so crazy anymore—just in need of some serious grooming. His Eminence says the homeless are animals that you can't feed too much, or they get fat and spoiled. I'm not sure where he gets the farming imagery from, or when he might have tested his theory of feeding them too much. But if he saw the little Shrub Kids, maybe he'd understand that they're prisoners too.

Still, they stuck us in this cage, and some of them are acting like mental cases.

I ask Seabrook what he thinks might be wrong with them. He agrees with me that it isn't the homeless people's fault but Shwo-Rez's, and maybe a handful of others. From what he knows of Lynnbrook, a few years ago the town faced an air pollution disaster that killed off a lot of people, forcing the company responsible for the disaster to close down. The closing cost a lot of Lynnbrook residents their jobs.

"But how does that explain them acting like we're ghosts or something?" I ask.

Seabrook is sulking again. More than that—he has his crucifix in his right hand, and he's rubbing it so hard he's shaking with the other. Something has him pissed off.

"Well, it's like His Eminence says, I guess," I say. "They're all a bunch of wackos."

"Who?"

"Bums. Homeless. These people. Following everything that Shwo-Rez guy says just for some cardboard cribs."

Seabrook shifts his weight from his right foot to his left. He opens his mouth to speak and then closes it.

"Sometimes I forget who I'm talking to," he says eventually.

I realize I've stuck my foot in my mouth again, and I apologize. But he just gives me this uncomfortable smile and says it isn't his place and that maybe I should talk to His Eminence about it. About what, I'm not sure.

"Besides," he says, "what they're doing isn't so different from what your d—what some people in the government do every day."

"What's that?"

"It's good policy to pretend nature doesn't exist. In fact, in some offices it's a fireable offense to consider rocks and trees and animals and air as real things. And nobody bats an eye. So why is it such a surprise that a government official would do the reverse and pretend that buildings and litter and civilization don't exist?

"You can fill people's heads with all kinds of nonsense," he continues, and even though he is talking to me, it's like he's not anymore. He looks back at his crucifix key chain. "People will believe anything."

"SHWO-REEEEEEEEEZ!" shouts someone from the crowd. It's just starting to get dark, and Shrub People are filling the courtyard. And here's the Shrub King, moseying along out of his cardboard box palace down the main corridor toward the bonfire. Shwo-Rez is a pile of flesh that ripples when he walks. He smiles and nods at the collected Shrub People.

A yell goes up, then falls, then rises up again in a chant: "Shwo-Rez! Shwo-Rez!" Some of them start acting like Beatles fans in a black-and-white movie, screaming like they're ready to climb out of themselves just to touch the wrinkly fat guy with the soda cans around his neck. Others seem to think the whole thing is hilarious, smiling and nudging one another. And others just look like they want to go back to their boxes, but they're chanting anyway: "Shwo-Rez! Shwo-Rez!"

Shwo-Rez looks like His Eminence on a campaign photo op. A big smile slackens his neck. He waves and points to people in the crowd. He stops and kisses a few babies, musses the hair of a couple of youngsters.

"There he is," Clarence mutters. "The king fruit nut."

The gray-haired guy I recognize from the palace is following him; Bob Schwartz called him Gray-Aide. When his sweeping eyes land on us in the cage, he looks away.

"Friends of the great Eden!" Shwo-Rez shouts when he reaches the bonfire. The crowd falls silent. "Today is a monumental day in the history of our people. For we have proven that not only does evil exist—but that it walks among us."

A great roar erupts from the crowd. A couple of the hunters run to the cage and jab us with spears.

"Tonight," Shwo-Rez continues, "after our celebration, we will put these evil spirits to their death by lighting them ablaze on our sacred fire."

Well, that wigs us out something fierce. The crowd goes wild again, lifting their spears into the night and chanting, "Shwo-Rez! Shwo-Rez!"

"Your devotion is truly super," Shwo-Rez says, smiling. Then the crowd stops chanting his name and there's nothing, no noise but the crackling of the fire and the sound of bugs fizzing. Some of the Shrub People look at their feet and toe the ground.

The smile slips from Shwo-Rez's lips, and he looks off past the tops of the trees. He stares at the city in the distance. "Super," he mutters absently, as if he can't get past the word. "Super . . . super . . ." His body seems to melt, and he staggers backward. "Super . . ." The crowd flinches.

Gray-Aide leaps to his side and wraps his arm around Shwo-Rez's shoulder. "The great Shwo-Rez is overcome by your worship in the face of such evil!" Gray-Aide shouts. "And tonight, he will reward us all by ridding us of this scourge!"

The crowd goes nuts. Shwo-Rez blinks. Then the smile grows across his face again, and he lifts his arms above his head and howls at the sliver of moon on the horizon:

"I don't wanna grow up
I'm a Toys 'R' Us kid . . ."

And they dance.

It's like a crowd of people having seizures. One woman tucks her hands into her armpits, leans forward, and does a chicken dance, then does jumping jacks with her feet and head flopping. Another man falls onto his back and thrusts his arms and legs into the air, shakes them like he's doing the hokey pokey, sits back up, runs in a circle, then falls down and does it all again.

"There's a million toys in Toys 'R' Us
That I can play with!"

"Here we go," Esmerelda says. She's sneaked up on the side of the cage where I'm leaning. Her breath warms my ear, and I smell her sweat. Female sweat is sharper than male sweat—a little more acidic, maybe, more alluring than man sweat but not much better smelling. I can only see her silhouette in the dark, but I picture her in designer hip-huggers and a belly shirt with her navel pierced.

Then her shadow disappears and the cage inches upward.

Shwo-Rez sits on a rotting La-Z-Boy recliner next to the bonfire and watches the dancers, smiling, the giant glow of the fire and the shadows from the thrashing Shrub People flashing red on his face. He doesn't seem to notice us.

"Coming?" Seabrook says to Clarence.

"You're dead," Clarence hisses at us. "They'll kill you for sure. Better to stay here and take my chances than to take a spear in the ass, it is." He turns, goes to a corner of the cage, and sits X-ing his arms and legs and V-ing his eyebrows at us.

"Follow me," says a voice, but it's not Esmerelda.

It's the big guy with the gray hair. Gray-Aide.

"What do you think you're doing?" Seabrook hisses.

"Saving you," Gray-Aide says. He glances back at Shwo-Rez and the dancing figures and lowers himself to the ground. "Everybody get down and stay behind me if you want to make it out of here alive."

I trip and fall on my face. I'm about to stand up again when I notice the others crawling on their bellies until the shadows cover them.

We creep through the box city. The shadows undulate and ripple over us like moonlight on water.

When we're halfway there, the singing dies off. Ahead of me, the crawling figure of Gray-Aide freezes. His head turns, and he looks at us with satellite dish eyes.

I hold my breath. Will the hunter guys see that we're gone? The bonfire crackles. I squeeze my leg muscles and get ready to leap toward the tree line yards ahead of us through the corridor of musty-smelling cardboard.

Then someone yelps, and the bad singing continues. It's a song I think I recognize from a Honda commercial.

Eventually, we're back in the trees. After we've crawled far enough so that the bonfire and the dancing figures are safely out of view, Gray-Aide stands. He's cradling that box of Cuban cigars the big Shrub King had earlier.

"This is private property," he says. There's something shaky and uncertain in his voice. None of the "my liege" crap we'd heard before. He's slipped back into sanity. "You're trespassing."

"So call the police," Seabrook says.

He laughs. "Okay, okay," he says. "All we wanted was to be left alone. Bob and me."

"What about the Shrub People?" Seabrook asks.

"Ambience. It's really not so bad for them . . . Doctor Seabrook, was it? And it's not like we're not providing them a service. The homeless shelters got full in Lynnbrook after Super Corp. poisoned the entire area and was forced to close down. Here, at least they have food. They look after one another. They need Bob. Bob needs them."

"Who are you?" Seabrook snaps.

"We're not bad people, Doctor Seabrook. We're a licensed charity. Bob Schwartz is—was—a city councilman—"

The singing halts, again, and Gray-Aide's voice trails off. We all stand frozen for what seems like an entire double episode of *Sniper Dude X*.

After a moment, the singing starts again:

"We are Flintstone Kids. Ten million strong . . ."

"I was city administrator," Gray-Aide continues, more quietly this time. "That was . . . a year ago. Back then, Bob Schwartz was going to run for the state senate. Maybe even governor. You might not believe this, but that crazy son of a bitch might well one day have been president of the United States."

"What about Super Corp.?" Seabrook asks.

Gray-Aide snaps, "Super Corp. was the biggest development deal in Lynnbrook history. Thousands of jobs, all right? They single-handedly lowered the unemployment rate by two percentage points. Bob Schwartz made that happen. He greased the tracks. It's what great men do. He signed the papers. Didn't want to, but he did. You gotta let a little bad happen, so you, personally, can do a little good."

"Yes, and he killed two thousand people," Seabrook says.

Gray-Aide shrugs. "They never could prove a damn thing. I mean, people. Hell. They die all the time."

"But you couldn't convince Shwo-Rez of that. Could you?"

"No. Stupid son of a bitch. If he would have just stayed on the council a little longer we would have beaten that federal investigation. But after his wife and kid died of lung cancer the poor bastard lost his mind. I tendered his resignation myself. Then, when they let him out of the loony bin, that very same day, I followed him out here. This is his land, private property. He was going to build a new estate out here three years ago when the whole Super Corp. mess started, and I worked out a 501(c)(3) deal. We're providing a service."

"Some charity."

Gray-Aide shrugs again. "All you see is the crazy. He stripped off his suit and tie and started talking about the evil mountains and how tin cans are shells. Tied his pants around his waist and said it was the skin of some beast. What am I supposed to do? Look at the big picture. You have to do a little bad to do a lot of good, right? This place is good for him, you know? I mean, okay, with the threatening to burn people at the stake thing he's taking it a little too far, maybe . . ."

Esmerelda snorts.

"But, look, nobody's been hurt," Gray-Aide says. "No harm, no foul. Get the hell back on your boat and leave us alone."

A noise pops over the sounds of the Shrub People's chanting. It echoes into the forest, and after a pause, the Shrub People start to scream. When he hears the noise, Gray-Aide's smile droops and his eyes widen. Just then these huge floodlights go on and it looks like broad daylight.

More pops. *Pop, pop, pop.* I've heard this sound in practically every video game I own, so I know damn well what it is.

A machine gun.

Another burst of machine-gun fire. An electronic voice in the distance, piped through a PA system, says, "*Federal officers. Put your hands on your heads and lie on the ground.*"

Gray-Aide scrambles to the edge of the woods. He stands there a moment, kind of shimmying, his big bare ass pointed at us. Then he darts back to where we're standing.

His huge eyes dart from each one of us to the other. "That's the Green Police out there!" Gray-Aide says. "They wouldn't come here for Bob and me. Who are you people?"

Seabrook, who stands a good head taller than the Shrub Man, grabs him by the shoulders.

"*Federal officers,*" repeats the electronic voice.

"What do you know about the Green Police?" Seabrook asks.

"You don't *know?*"

"Who is that out there?"

Gray-Aide flashes this sick smile and goes limp. "They don't know," he says. His eyes glaze. "Dead men in their graves just waiting for the dirt to come down, and they don't know."

"Kang . . ." Seabrook growls.

Kang grabs the old man by the throat so tightly the loose flesh on his neck bulges between his fingers. The cigar box slips from Gray-Aide's hands and clatters to the forest floor, spilling bits of paper and flat, round things.

"The FBI?" Gray-Aide offers in a choked voice. "The CIA? The National Security Agency? Children, Seabrook. Just children with toy guns and plastic badges compared to these people . . . they don't play games."

Kang lets go of him and backs away. "You're telling me the Green Police," Seabrook says, "is . . . is what? The *government?*"

"*We're looking for Doctor Marion Seabrook and his crew,*" says the voice on the PA system. "*We have warrants for their arrest. Anyone who doesn't assist us will be arrested and charged with obstructing a federal investigation.*"

"Government?" Gray-Aide laughs. "They're over the government. Over and around it. They don't play games. If they want you, you're dead already. And anybody standing within five feet of you, probably."

Kang and Seabrook exchange looks.

Gray-Aide drops to his knees. He picks something up—one of the round objects that fell from the cigar box. He scrambles out of the woods, waving it over his head.

"They're here!" he screams. "We're on your side! They're right here!"

Men in black surround him. They raise their rifles and point them at Gray-Aide's head.

"We're with you!" he yells in the face of one of the men with the rifles, the one who has drawn closest to him. The man flips his gun over and slams it into Gray-Aide's stomach. The Shrub Man crumples inward and falls to his knees. A second blow from the butt of the rifle catches him in the back of the head. He drops to his stomach.

"Move," Seabrook spits under his breath. We start into the woods.

"Not that way," Esmerelda says. "Follow me." She leads us along the edge of the clearing.

On the way out I trip for, like, the millionth time on a stupid monster tree root. I look down at it and realize it's not a root or a rut, but Shwo Rez's cigar box. And all around it are bits of paper and crap. I pick something up, a circular thing that looks like a DVD. Whatever it is, it's fabric.

"Hurry," Seabrook says.

I stuff the circle into my pocket and start running.

On the opposite end of the clearing are several wicked-looking soldier guys dressed in black leather, black helmets, and visors that hide their eyes. They hug assault rifles. They point them at the crowd of Shrub People, who have stopped dancing and singing to lie on the ground, spread out like a carpet of pink flesh, hair, and rags. They whisper. Once in a while one of them screams. Above them the huge bonfire crackles.

The men in black wander through the boxes. Occasionally they find a hiding Shrub Person, whom they flush out and force to join the group lying before the fire.

"This way," Esmerelda hisses.

The Shrub People haven't cleared a path here, so the woods are thick. Briars tear at us, and we stumble over ruts and roots. The light from the bonfire is enough to see by, though. We start going around the clearing toward the river.

By this time, my turtleneck is a goner, people, a collection of rips and blood and pit stains and dirty streaks. I wish I didn't leave my Gucci backpack full of designer labels on the canoe when we'd ditched camp—especially with Esmerelda, the blond hottie, along for the ride.

We're almost past the clearing when Seabrook stoops behind a tree. The others keep moving, but I'm curious, so I stand next to him.

The clearing opens up in front of us. The big tongue of the bonfire pokes up a few yards away. The guys in black march through the supine forms of the Shrub People, occasionally pausing in front of one or two of the cowering figures to fire off a question.

A few feet from the edge of the woods, crouching behind a row of cardboard box homes, is Shwo-Rez. He's looking around the edge of the boxes at the Shrub People, his back to us. The row of cardboard homes beside him is wet, and I smell something that reminds me of long rides in the Bentley—a smell that always seems to waft in trace amounts through Philly. It's gasoline. I don't place it immediately because I haven't smelled it in days.

Shwo-Rez has soaked the boxes with it. There is a red metal canister next to him. When the officers burst into the clearing, Shwo-Rez must have run off to hide before he was noticed, and had this container hidden somewhere.

He is fumbling with a Zippo lighter.

He is going to go Waco on the place.

It wouldn't take much more than a spark. The whole place is as moistureless as the pages of the 1963 *X-Men* issue no. 1 I keep in a plastic sleeve in my bedroom. And in the fire would be the boxes, the leaves and branches and grass, the men in black, their guns, and the Shrub People.

The homeless woman carrying the dead baby pops into my head. Will she try to save the thing she carries, even though it's not moving? Will the kids with Arthur's dinosaurs hold on to Arthur's gifts to protect them from the fire? Will Clarence run? The man who once bought his little girl dinosaurs—will his little girl ever find out what happened? Would she visit him one day?

And then I'm thinking about people that aren't even there: faces of people rushing past the Bentley window on the morning commute to school, the ones His Eminence calls "a bunch of wackos."

My stomach hurts.

Then I realize Seabrook is no longer kneeling next to me. He's inching toward the Shrub King, who's flicking his lighter next to the cardboard box beside him.

Seabrook grabs Shwo-Rez by the arm. Shwo-Rez bellows. Seabrook pulls him over like a sack of pale flab. They struggle for the lighter, Seabrook astride Schwartz. The doctor raises his arm and brings his fist down hard onto Shwo-Rez's jaw. Shwo-Rez drops the lighter on impact, and its flame snuffs out in the grass.

Seabrook hits him again.

A guard comes running through the boxes. "You there!" he shouts. "Put your hands on your head and come out of there!"

Seabrook lands a final blow on Shwo-Rez's jaw, and the Shrub King stops moving. Then Seabrook scrambles back toward the tree line, where I'm waving at him like crazy.

"Halt!" The man with the gun shouts. He fires a single shot.

The bullet catches Seabrook in the back.

It sounds like someone pounding a melon with a rubber mallet.

A red mist fills the air as the impact of the shot throws him to the ground.

The man with the gun lowers his shoulders and charges toward Seabrook, who pushes himself to his feet and stumbles into the woods next to me. Wind whistles in and out of his mouth.

"Come on," he moans between breaths. "We've got to move."

But he doesn't move.

He leans against me.

I think he might have passed out.

I can't drag him.

The guard is coming.

the metal crate

The guard chasing Seabrook stops. He turns and walks in the other direction. Some of the other guys in black push their way through the boxes, rolling this big metal crate on wheels. It's taller than all of them, and the top part is made of mesh. They wheel it up to the edge of the woods where the doctor is lying against me.

Then they back away.

I can't see where they went. All I see is the big metal crate.

I shake Seabrook, but he doesn't budge. His breath is really whistling now, like he's got asthma or something. I elbow him and slap his cheeks.

There's a loud hissing sound and a pop, and fire leaps up out of the crate.

Some of the sparks hit the gas-covered boxes, which explode, blowing rags of flame across the box city.

Then these little black things begin to boil out of the crate. Living things. They make chattering noises and swarm up like a big plume of giant bugs.

They swarm at us.

I scream at the doctor to get up. He must have seen the creatures too, because next thing I know we're running into the forest.

The chattering things follow. A big wall of them whooshes through the forest, mirroring fiery wind that's blowing through Shrub City like a photo negative.

We nearly run into Kang, Arthur, and Esmerelda, who have noticed we aren't behind them anymore and are waiting for us at the bottom of a hill.

"Move," Seabrook says. Something is clogging his throat. The wave of chattering things is crashing through the trees behind us.

Esmerelda takes the lead, and we run through the thick trees, which thankfully don't claw at us like the monsters from the first day. Sometimes the chattering things are so close that they're almost on us.

Arthur trips.

A black thing lands on his back and scurries all over him with little lizard feet. Arthur's mouth looks like it's howling. He plucks the chattering thing off and flings it to the ground. He sprints past me, little red half-moons all over his arms and legs. He's bawling.

Then the fire disappears, and the chattering creatures fade into the distance. We're alone in the dark.

We stop to rest. I'm soaked with sweat, my chest is on fire, and I'm more scared than I've ever been. My pain and fear reservoir is gone. I can't conjure up . . . anything.

Soon, though, I see something flickering through the trees. It's the river. Esmerelda says we we're only a few hundred feet from its banks.

Arthur stands at the edge of the clearing, peering into the woods in the opposite direction. He isn't crying anymore. He scratches absently at the little wounds he has all over his arms and legs, but his mouth is pursed and his eyebrows hang low, and he stands there like you couldn't knock him down with a sledgehammer.

Seabrook isn't talking. He's collapsed on his stomach in the clearing, breath rattling in his chest.

"Are you okay, Doctor?" I ask.

"What's, like, the matter with him?" asks Esmerelda.

"He's been shot. In the back, I think."

Kang kneels next to the Doctor. "I'm all right," Seabrook mutters. Even in the darkness, I can see a big purple circle covering his right shoulder. The back of his green army shirt is soaked.

He props himself on an elbow. "Look," he says. His voice wavers. "There's nothing anybody can do about this until we get back to the boat. So let's get moving."

So we press on through the woods. I begin to hear the familiar gurgle of rushing water. It's weird how quickly you get used to something—I never thought I'd be so happy to smell that dead fish smell again.

Upriver and around a bend, a light glows. Voices shout orders. Flashlight beams sweep through the trees. I guess the Green Police believes the chattering things have made a meal of us, and now they're looking for the *Tamzene*.

We find her anchored where we left her, in the shoal hidden behind cedar branches. Everyone climbs aboard. Seabrook starts the engine without turning on the lights and pilots the boat back into river.

We're a mile away before Seabrook turns on the deck's floodlights. Most of the supplies are gone: the refrigerator is empty, and the boxes of equipment Kang keeps lashed to the deck are missing. Shrub People, I bet. They also bogarted a good bit of the hemp from the hold.

Seabrook stands behind the wheel and guns the engine until we're careening downriver at full speed. He's pale, and his face is shining with sweat. The blood drips from a small black hole above his right shoulder blade into a pool on the floor of the cabin.

A voice fizzes from the radio in the cabin, the one Seabrook says he uses to listen in on the Green Police: "*Opponents warned that poking new holes in the tundra would devastate this cathedral of nature. In Oklahoma, which has been a top-five oil producing state for more than eighty years, most people are puzzled by these apocalyptic predictions, as they live in harmony with more than one hundred thousand oil and gas wells.*"[6]

Kang touches Seabrook's other shoulder, but Seabrook shakes his head. "No, Kang," he snaps. "Not until we're clear of those boats."

Esmerelda's eyes won't stop moving. They dart from the old-fashioned gunwales to the mushroom-shaped smokestack, then to the hold, and finally the wake. She has green eyes, and her skin is freckled and deeply tanned. She looks even more beautiful in the barium-colored light, which makes her reddish locks and her eyes glow.

"All right, like, what the fuck is this place?" she whispers to me. "And, like, who the hell are you people, and what is this boat thing, and what are you doing out here?" She keeps asking questions, leaning closer to me, but I back off because my breath smells like day-old Salisbury steak.

Arthur collapses in a corner and falls asleep. The little red crescent moons all over his arms and legs are beginning to dry and get crusty.

I try to explain everything to this chick, but nothing comes out clearly. Finally, I say, "Look, the doctor will explain everything to you when we're safely away, okay?"

I leave her standing in the center of the deck and go lean on the side of the cabin next to Arthur, watching the woods rush past. I'm drifting off to sleep when I feel something pressing on my hip. Suddenly I remember the disc I pocketed, the one that had fallen out of Shwo-Rez's cigar box. I take it out and look at it.

What I see freaks me out more than any soldier in black or Shrub Person or chattering thing.

It's a circular patch—the kind Boy Scouts wear on their uniforms when they learn how to start fires and tie knots. The design is stitched in thick thread at the center of the circle: the profile of a snarling cat with long, fierce fangs. On the left side of the cat head is a large letter C; on the right curls an S. Circling it: *Duty to God, Country, and Species.*

I stare back at the woods and feel cold.

The same design is painted on the Bitchin' Poster that hangs over His Eminence's desk in his office.

his eminence

Want to know what I have to live up to?

Picture this: His Eminence, all of eighteen in the '70s, six-foot-two with good looks and publicspeak, already impressing the hell out of everybody and about to embark on a lightning political career when he makes his one big rebellious move—even more rebellious than lifting the car and driving west. He becomes an amateur boxer.

He did it for one summer between his senior year in high school and his freshman year in college, and it's where he first caught the eye of the Moms, who saw him in the stands and later went out with him for drinks. And he was good too—left with nose intact and ears uncauliflowered because he just whaled on the mofos he went up against. They never stood a chance.

His Eminence doesn't even *have* to give me the disappointment stares. It's obvious his four-foot-eleven offspring is far from the apple of his eye.

Not that I don't think I could handle myself in a fight, if it were to ever come down to that. I've played my share of vintage *Mortal Kombat*, people, and I can feel something animalistic in there; I know if I set it loose I'd just be a maniac.

But this, now . . . WTF does His Eminence have to do with the Green Police?

CHAPTER ELEVEN

the things in the box

They could tell the men didn't want to look at them. Even through the metal grate, the beings inside the box could tell the two men were terrified. They slumped in their shining gray chairs, hands clasped in steel bracelets behind them. The men looked at the ceiling of the white room, the fluorescent bulbs blotting out every shadow. They looked at the metal floor. They looked at their laps. They never looked at the box.

The things in the box had never seen men like these before. The men they usually saw wore green or gray uniforms with colored ribbons tied around their necks. These men were naked, filthy, and disheveled, one with white hair and the other with gray. They seemed less sinewy than other men, of softer flesh than the others they knew.

That's good, the things in the box thought.

The shiny black window on the wall blinked on. A face appeared, one the things had seen many times before in these situations, and were now indifferent to. If they had thought about it, they would have considered its immensity, its impossible roundness. But they didn't think about it.

It spoke in a language they'd heard many times before, one they lacked both the ability to understand and the desire to decipher. Its meaning was inconsequential; the soft men were important.

"*Mr. Schwartz. Mr. Crawley.*"

"Look. F—for the love of God, you don't need to do this," said the white-haired one.

"We want to cooperate. We have been cooperating," the gray one added.

"Jesus. Yes."

"*Well, you poor dears,*" said the large round face. "*There's no need to take on so. We're just going to have ourselves a little chat. I'm Maude Sweetwater.*"

"Oh my Christ."

"You've heard of me?"

"Oh fuck oh fuck oh fuck oh fuck . . ."

"Secretary Sweetwater, ma'am, we are completely willing to cooperate. We had no prior knowledge of any wrongdoing on the part of the representatives of Super Corp., and I am more than happy to turn over—" The white-haired man was sweating now. The things could smell it in their cage. It excited them.

"*Super Corp? Oh, your little federal indictment. Oh, Mr. Schwartz, we don't care a whit about that, dontchaknow.*"

"I don't. I . . . I'll sign anything, Ms. Sweetwater. It's what I do best. Gray-Aide. Chuck. Chuck'll tell you."

"*Well, I appreciate that, Mr. Schwartz, I really do. But all I care about is Doctor Marion Seabrook.*"

"Who?"

"She means the wraiths, Great Shwo-Rez—um, Bob. The wraiths."

"*A couple of men and two boys recently paid you gentlemen a visit. They were on a boat. I'd like to know what happened to that boat.*"

"The wraiths?" said the white-haired human.

"*The boat, gentlemen. Where is it?*"

"I don't . . . I don't . . ."

"*Ammospermophilus homoedo.*" That was particularly familiar to the things in the box.

"What?"

"*It's a breed of squirrel. Long name for a little squirrel, am I right? Ha ha. Well, this little squirrel used to be a very rare species found in the Midwestern United States and the Pacific Northwest. Thought to be entirely extinct by the dawn of the twentieth century—one of those poor, sweet, innocent victims of the Industrial Revolution. There wasn't a whole lot of human contact with the ammospermophilus ho- moedo, gentlemen, except for one relatively little-known incident that happened 'round about 1850. A wagon train—the Soup party, named for Mordeci Soup, the head of the party—was making its way across Kansas to Colorado when it had an encounter with this rare breed of squirrel.*

"*It wasn't until 1855 that the remains of the Soup party were dis- covered by another wagon train. Twenty-eight men, women, and chil- dren, their bones strewn among the wreckage of their wagons, mixed up with the clean, white bones of the horses, just baking in that hot Kansas sun—licked clean, mind you. A couple of skeletons of children were discovered a good ways away from the wreckage. Apparently some of them tried to run and were cut down.*

"*Well now, the pioneers that spotted them, they figured they were the victims of Indians. But there were no arrows or hoof marks—just lots of little tracks, from tiny animals that must have swarmed around that wagon train like piranhas.*

"*That's when the Stewart party—the wagon train that spotted the Soup party—became the first group of people to meet up with ammo- spermophilus homoedo and live to tell the tale. You see, ammospermo- philus homoedo is the man-eating squirrel.*

"*Now it just so happens that this rare breed of squirrel couldn't cope with the pollutants in the atmosphere from nearby cities and mostly died off. But, dontchaknow, life has a way of going on. In the early twentieth century, our predecessor organization happened to dis- cover a nucleus of these little man-eating squirrels and began a pro- gram to repopulate the species.*

"*We at Locksley Ponds have continued their work.*"

The soft men glanced for the first time at the beings swarming in the box.

The beings in the box chattered appreciatively.

"Jesus, Secretary Sweetwater. You don't have to do this."

"No, *I'm afraid I do. The Green Police have been tracking that boat for months. We almost had her on the Allwyn River, but there was a storm."*

"The Allwyn. That goes right past Oxnard Gulch Air Force Base."

"Shut the fuck up, Chuck."

"Yes it does, Mr. Crawley. Seems there was an incident there. The base was overrun by animals."

"I don't follow . . ."

"Bears, deer, and birds all broke through the gates at Oxnard Gulch, gentlemen. Destroyed four jets on takeoff—birds flying into the engines, dontchaknow. Bears took out ten men before we could carpet bomb the hills. And that boat, the Tamzene—*by then that illegal boat slipped through our clutches once again."*

"My God."

"So you see how important it is that we get that boat. How important it is—given the lives lost, the treasure lost, and knowing full well who that boat's allies are—that we capture that boat. So gentlemen. Where is it?"

"I don't . . . I don't . . ."

"I will ask one more time. And then you'll meet our furry little friends."

"Jesus Christ, Secretary Sweetwater, we don't know anything—"

The round face disappeared from the window on the wall as the hatch flung open, granting the beings access to the searing whiteness of the room. The men in the chairs made loud inconsequential noises.

The things in the box had been right.

The men were soft.

PART THREE

The Evil Lobster

Anything different—that's what they're gonna talk about—race, religion, ethnic and national background, jobs, income, education, social status, sexuality, anything they can do to keep us fighting with each other, so that they can keep going to the bank.
—George Carlin

Chapter Twelve

kang operates

At midmorning, Doctor Seabrook falls against the wheel and to the cabin floor with a moist splash.

Kang was expecting it. He drags him to the hold, where he has already laid bedding in a corner. Arthur and I each take a leg, and Kang grabs Seabrook's shoulders. We carry him down the steps like that, despite his groggy protests that he needs to keep piloting the boat. Kang anchors us on the lee side of a small island, under some enormous weeping willows.

Belowdecks, the doctor, lying on his stomach, closes his eyes and passes out. Kang cuts off Seabrook's army shirt, revealing an inch-wide crater that's splashed blood all over his back. It's nasty. Kang cleans the blood off with a rag soaked in water from a canteen, but more tarry ooze continues to froth from the hole. He orders Arthur to press down on the wound with a cloth and then goes up on deck.

Kang boils water in a tall pot on the grill. He places a pair of needle-nose pliers and a lobster pick into the boiling water. After a few minutes, he takes them out and goes back to Seabrook.

Watching Kang remove the bullet from Seabrook's back almost makes me hurl. I've seen lots of gunshot victims, of course; most heal up long before the movie ends. But seeing an actual wound and all that blood makes everything turn black around the edges of my vision. The skin looks more fragile and easily torn than I imagined it would—like candle wax. The blood is black and smells like metal.

Arthur is pale. When I sit down, though, he continues to mop the blood with a rag. Esmerelda wrinkles her nose and holds the pliers for Kang when he isn't using them.

i show my moves

Kang takes the boat another mile downstream and scans the banks for a hiding place. He finds one in another shoal behind trees that smell like the Moms's linen closet. After we anchor, Kang motions for us to stay on the boat. Then he climbs overboard, and we watch him disappear into the forest.

It isn't until I can no longer make out the silver and white feathers of his headdress that it occurs to me that he's gone off looking for a town, which sucks because I don't want to wait here—I want to tag along so we can start hitchhiking to California. The plan, as far as I'm concerned, can still be to hitch west, see the show, then tell His Eminence about this world-changing invention as a peace offering. Score one for Wimp Winthrop.

But I can't think about leaving Seabrook right now—we'll at least hang until the old man gets some help.

Silence envelops the deck after Kang disappears. The wind rushes through the trees, spreading that sweet closet smell over the dead fish odor. I feel shaky—and not just because I can't stop thinking about that patch I found, or because I saw a guy with a gaping hole in his back. I haven't eaten anything except a couple of Pop-Tarts and a seaweed citrus juice since before the Shrub People captured us.

"The concert is in six days, Arthur," I say. "Did you realize that?"

Arthur nods.

"I understand this time around they're opening up with tunes from the *Bruiser* album. 'Show Biz' is the first tune." I stand, walk to the center of the deck, and spread my legs wide. I grab a fake microphone, do a pirouette, and kneel, looking at Esmerelda for a reaction. This is my cool move, people—it's old school Axl Rose, from the heyday of badass front men. I'm a pro. I practice front man dance techniques in the mirror of my walk-in closet, and this move is one of the best in my repertoire—almost as killer as the one where I spin and do a flying scissor kick. Sometimes, though, when I do that move, I lose my balance and fall into a pile of laundry. The pirouette move is the safer bet. "Opening with 'Show Biz' is a shade on the obvious side, don't you think?"

Arthur nods and mouths the word *journeys*.

"Yeah, they opened with 'Journeys' in Berlin last year," I say. I whirl again and this time punctuate my landing with a karate kick. Something in my leg pops, and hot needles shoot up my hamstring. Grabbing my ass in pain would embarrass me in front of the chick, so I try to keep my face tight and kneel again.

"You guys are talking about the Red Grizzlies?" says Esmerelda. She's watching me dance with her arms crossed over her chest. I don't see any awe. In the night, she unfurled her tattered clothes and put them on normally. Now she wears ripped bell-bottom jeans and a tight AC/DC T-shirt.

"Yeah!" I say. "We're actually on our way to California to—"

"How can you guys, like, listen to that crap?"

Crap?!

"You . . ." I manage. "You don't like the Grizzlies?"

I look at Arthur, who seems to be taking this blasphemy pretty well for a true believer. In fact, Arthur is smiling. He sits up and turns toward Esmerelda.

"No," she says. She reclines on an elbow and looks up at the trees.

How could such a gorgeous thing be capable of so horrible a sin as bad-mouthing the Red Grizzlies?

"What's wrong with them?" I ask.

"You know," Esmerelda says, "maybe one of us should be, like, sitting down there with Doc Seabrook until Kang gets back."

My neck bristles. My head aches. "What's wrong with them?" I ask again, through clenched teeth.

"With what? The Grizzlies?" she says, smiling. "Oh, come on, stubby. Hello? How 'bout for starters that they're, like, not *real*?"

Arthur rolls over on his side, and a soft chirping sound comes from his mouth. The son of a bitch is laughing.

"Not real?" I might possibly be screaming. "Not real? The Greatest Band on Earth not *real?*"

"Unbunch your panties," Esmerelda says. "I don't mean to diss something that obviously you think is the shit."

"Well what do you mean, not *real?*"

She looks at me with half-lidded eyes. "Look, all I'm saying is that the Red Grizzlies are a corporate creation. Rim-Shot Records realized there was this post-grunge music revolution, like, a decade ago, and they, like, created a band out of session musicians and gave them a personality."

Arthur is totally *beaming* at her, and I will strangle that lame-o—right after I finish with her.

"That's bullshit!" I shout. Pigeons that were roosting in the laundry closet tree squawk and take flight. "That's such bullshit!" And I laugh! I am totally laughing at how stupid this chick is. I mean, come on. "They're the most influential rock band since Zeppelin!"

Esmerelda looks at Arthur and giggles. "Oh come on, guys! Like, wake up and smell the corporate propaganda! Indie rock is where it's at. Hit iTunes up for some tracks by the Porpoises or the Drier Sheets already. *That's* wicked badass."

I laugh again—a series of high-pitched bleats that would have embarrassed me ordinarily, but right now I'm too pissed to care about appearances. "The Drier Sheets! The . . . the Drier Sheets!" A thousand insults for her obviously inferior choice of music clog my head so that I can't get a single one out. "How could . . . The trouble with *that*, is . . . See . . ."

The hottie giggles and puts a hand over her mouth. I give her an ugly stare, then sit cross-legged on the deck, peering into the forest for Kang.

What a nut job. How can anybody hate the Greatest Band on Earth—especially somebody who looks like that? And what's up with Arthur? Earlier I swore I'd never pick on the kid, but right now, people, I want to hurl the most mentally-leveling insult in his general direction.

Arthur stands and rummages around in one of the boxes the Shrub People didn't take. He finds the pad and pen that Seabrook gave him earlier and sits next to Esmerelda. He scribbles something.

"*What's your story?*" she reads. "My story? Oh, well, I'm an orphan. My parents both bought it back in Nevada when I was a baby, and I've been kicked around from foster home to foster home ever since. My adopted parents in Lynnbrook were all right. That is to say they, like, treated me decent. But about a year and a half ago, my dad up and left. And my mom—well, she went a little haywire. She lost her job. We were damn close to living on the streets. Well, Mother was out doing the only thing she could do for cash at that point—hunting up aluminum cans for recycling—and she comes back and tells me we're going to live with these, like, Shrub People.

"Well, it wasn't as bad as it looked. I mean, like, at least there was food, which was more than we could say living in town. That Shwo-Rez asshole, he had lots of hunters that caught lots of fish and killed deer and stuff for everybody. And every so often, some of the more normal people would sneak off into town and pick up some, like, Twinkies and Ho Hos and pizza and stuff.

"But come on—we were living in cardboard boxes and pretending that Lynnbrook wasn't real. Mother had totally, like, flicked the last marble out the ring at that point. She was even thinking of marrying that dude Yellow-Hunter. That would have got us a lot more food—hunters' wives are well fed—but winter wasn't that far away, and she was getting too comfortable. I mean, hello? A cardboard box in the *snow*? So here I am."

Arthur scribbles something else on the pad.

"Well," she says, "once you guys drop me off in a town someplace, I guess I'll figure it out. I don't know. I mean, I could talk to social services or something and tell them what's up. But I don't know if I want to deal with yet another family of assholes, thank you very much. Now, what's *your* story . . . Arthur is it?"

Arthur, the little traitor, reddens and stares at his pad as if he's embarrassed to look the hot chick in the eye. He starts to scribble like crazy. He writes for minutes, and Esmerelda cranes her neck to see what he's writing. Finally, he finishes and hands the pad back to her.

She reads for a few minutes, puts her hand just above her chest, and exhales. "Oh my God. That, like, totally sucks! Your vocal chords! So you can only talk in a whisper? That is so totally harsh, bud."

Arthur, who is now the color of the flames of hell that consume all traitors, takes the pad back from her, writes something else, and hands it back.

"Oh, you're welcome," she says. "So if you whispered something in my ear, I could, like, hear your voice?"

Arthur nods.

Esmerelda smiles. "Well," she breathes, "come here. Whisper something, Arthur."

Trembling, Arthur brings himself up to his knees and leans close to her ear, pressing the bullhorn of his PA system against her side. He buries his face into her reddish-blond curls and his mouth moves. A pretty smile spreads across Esmerelda's face. She giggles.

"Well holy shit, if it doesn't look like rain, you two!" I yell, jumping to my feet.

Arthur and Esmerelda flinch and glance up at the sky.

"It'd be really rough to be stuck out on this boat for another night in the rain, don't ya think, Arthur?" I stand over them and smile until my cheeks hurt.

"Oh, wow! That would suck!" Esmerelda says, frowning at the thick clouds. She stands and stretches. "I guess I'll go check on the Doc, guys."

Arthur glares at me and mouths several words I can't make out.

I know, I know. Pathetic, right? But come on, people, Arthur was a few rungs down the social ladder from me, remember?

And I saw her first.

The radio says: "*I believe that global warming is a myth. And so, therefore, I have no conscience problems at all and I'm going to buy a Suburban next time.*"[7]

we eat (at last)

It's pissing rain when Kang returns. He has first aid supplies like gauze pads and bandages, a plastic first aid kit to keep them in, and a bottle of whiskey because the store didn't have any rubbing alcohol for Seabrook's wounds. He also carries a small cooler full of groceries—including two bags of shrimp.

Seabrook regains consciousness while Kang redresses his wound. Kang points out on a map where we've anchored.

"Take us south, Kang," Seabrook says. His voice sounds as though his lungs have filled with fluid. "Take us south, and we'll try to pick up the Tennessee River west. They'll be looking for us on the Ohio."

By nightfall we still haven't seen a sign of the Green Police boats, so Kang takes off again. It is raining steadily, and the wind is tossing tree limbs in the woods. To the south, bursts of lightning split the sky and remind me of the artillery fire in *Battling Leathernecks*. Kang has bought four clear plastic ponchos from the store.

We house some boiled shrimp and potatoes and drink seaweed citrus juice. Esmerelda says it's the best she's eaten since she moved down from Boston. We throw the shells and soda cans into the grocery bags and place them in the aft corner of the boat.

kang makes a shoe

Kang drives through the night, and we seem to pass the storm. When I wake the next morning the scenery has changed. The monster trees are gone—at least the big claw parts of them that stick up out of the ground. I guess we're still in what once was a forest, but the forest must have really pissed somebody off—stumps stretch out all the way out to where the sky meets the ground. The trees have been mown down. Pieces of them lay in piles of sawdust.

Pipes line the hills and shoot up through the valleys. They're old and rusty, and blackish guck pulses out of them, steady as a heartbeat. The black stuff trickles from the ends of some of the pipes into the river, which is also black with a rainbow tinge to it. It stinks, and dead things float in it. Not just fish—the bodies of furry things so coated with goo that you can't tell what they were bounce off the hull of the *Tamzene* as we slide through.

It's like there was a war or something.

"What happened?" I ask Kang, but he must not hear because he keeps driving downriver.

Eventually the forest comes back. Kang takes the boat behind some trees and drops anchor. He makes some signs at Arthur. Arthur makes some signs back, but Kang looks pissed and shakes his head.

Arthur sighs and writes on his pad: "*Kang says we're out of hemp. He says he'll hide the boat here for a few days while the doctor recovers. He can't go get more hemp himself because he can't get any of the dealers to understand him. He says we need to get off the boat now because it's too dangerous for us to stay. He doesn't know exactly where we are, but it's safer for us to run.*"

I'm pumped, people, because we'll be able to hitch our way out of the wilderness to the promised land to see the World's Greatest Show. I tell Arthur, and he toes the ground.

"Should we go?" Esmerelda asks. "I mean, what if things get worse with the doc? Couldn't you use the help?"

Kang shakes his head.

We hang out for the rest of the day, helping to clean up the decks and wash everything down. Kang disappears late in the afternoon. He shows up again at nightfall wearing a new headdress. This one has deer horns poking out from the front and feathers that go all the way down his back to his ankles. He painted his face blue and orange.

He's carrying a bundle of weeds and twigs. He places it onto the deck and looks at each of us with this face that's so solemn it scares the shit out of me. He makes a few signs to Arthur, whose face brightens. Arthur nods at him with this big grin.

"What's he doing?" I ask.

"*Kang is going to perform an ancient Milliconquit blessing on us,*" Arthur writes. "*He's going to communicate with his ancestors who will guide his hands as he crafts for us the shoes of the Milliconquit, which will protect us on the rest of our journey.*"

"Wicked," Esmerelda says.

Well, I'm not one to mess with ancient religious stuff, no matter how freaky it looks. Somebody like His Eminence would probably flat-out tell Kang he's a nut bar—"Conquering these people was necessary for national progress," he likes to tell me when we watch old John Wayne flicks on the plasma screen. Also, I highly doubt he would get away with this if Seabrook was up and around. But I'm superstitious, and always let people do whatever they want.

Kang kneels before the bundle of sticks, holds his arms out straight, and stares at the horizon. The river water makes light spiders on his face. He mouths a few words, bows, brings his arms in like a praying mantis, and tucks his head. Then he juts them out to the sides again, sucks them back in, and bows again. He makes these motions about seven or eight times, then jumps to his feet, skips around the pile of twigs and grass four times in a circle, and falls to his knees. He grabs handfuls of the sticks and holds them up to the sky. He freezes like that for almost a minute, still mouthing something.

Arthur watches all of this with big eyes. It certainly looks freaky.

Then Kang thrusts the two handfuls of twigs together and begins bending and twisting them. Ever see one of those guys on TV do origami, where they rip and fold little pieces of paper with these fast hands until they've got a horse or a rooster? It's like that. His hands zip all over the pile of twigs. He doesn't look at them. His eyes are clamped shut, his nose pointing downriver. His breath comes faster, and his hands move quicker and quicker on this mangled pile of twigs until all at once he holds something up to the sky and opens his palms flat.

The twigs fall through the cracks between his fingers and blow away in the breeze.

The Indian's shoulders slump, and he looks at his feet, his eyes shifting around at us. He shrugs.

Arthur pats his back.

"That's it?" I ask. "Where's the shoe?"

Esmerelda smiles. "It's okay. We'll be all right, Kang. Thanks."

Chapter Thirteen

beavers

For centuries the beavers paid the two-legged pigs little mind. The pigs lived in the factory nearby, and further off, on a farm. The factory gave off large plumes of smoke, which the beavers knew hurt the trees and the water and sometimes made it hard to breathe. But they ignored it. Two-legged pigs will be two-legged pigs.

Then, one of their large, rumbling vehicles arrived with markings on the side that read *Pawtucket Toothpick Company*. The two-legged pigs buzzed and sawed and hammered and took the trees away.

The beavers defended their homes as best they could, but the two-legged pigs had discovered more efficient ways get rid of the beavers. Some were poisoned; others were shot when they stood up to the two-legged pigs. Still more died when the factory installed large metallic snakes where the trees once were and flooded the river with something toxic.

A small band of surviving beavers gathered one night at the edges of the forest where their homes once stood. Many were too weak to go on. Some argued that it was fruitless to fight anymore, that they should try to find another spot on the river, forgoing the home of their forefathers.

But one charismatic young beaver said the survivors should spend their last breath seeking revenge. He beat his tail upon the shore. Some of the younger beavers joined in, until there was a rush of applause rising from the trees.

The farm, it was decided, was an easier place than the factory for a suicide mission. The young beavers said goodbye to the older ones, the ones who decided it was best to begin again further downriver.

The young ones pressed into the woods at dusk. They scrambled up hills, through fields of fallen trees, and over round, hard circles laden with rainwater—orbs upon which the two-legged pigs rolled their vehicles, then discarded.

But things changed when they reached the top of the hill overlooking the farm. A sweet-smelling smoke filled the air. At first it meant little to them—another fire from those beasts who love fire was of no consequence.

But then they felt strange. The world seemed to spin. They fell against trees and trembled with something like laughter. They felt happy.

That farm was okay, the beavers decided, suddenly aware of the beauty of the world around them. These two-legged pigs are our brothers.

growing high farm

We're back in the woods again—hopefully for the last time. I can't wait for the snaps and crunches under my feet to turn into the solid feel of pavement and to only be scared of the occasional desperate homeless person, and not those chattering things we saw at the Shrub People camp.

I ask Arthur what the little monsters were. He writes on his pad and shines a flashlight on it:

Hair
Tails
Claws
Sharp teeth.

"Fucked up," I say. "So do you think those guys were really the feds?"

"Feds don't do stuff like that," Esmerelda says.

"What do you know about it?"

"If they were feds, like you say, then they must have been after all that pot you guys had in the hold there. Kang and the doc are going to be in a world of shit if they don't get out of there. I say we go back and help them out."

"You heard Kang," I say. "He doesn't want us there. Says it's too dangerous."

"Yeah, well, like, don't you want to help?"

"What are *we* going to do, man? You go back if you want, but Arthur and me are going on with the pilgrimage. Just remember, though—you're extra baggage, and if five-oh catches up to them those creepy-crawly things might not be as kind to you as they were to Arthur."

I look up at the charcoal sky and I'm glad there aren't stars. Stars make you feel small. I'm little enough. Maybe that's why people like His Eminence bust their asses so hard to become chief muckety-mucks. Maybe they looked at the stars and felt small.

In my pocket, the badge presses against my thigh. I can't figure it out, people. His Eminence is an old-school guy, a Skull and Bones society type, a stock market player—what could he possibly have in common with that nut job Shwo-Rez from Ohio? Are they part of the same club?

I wonder if there are stars over the Compound back in Philly. I wonder if the Moms is out there, leaning on those little red marks on her forearms, staring up at the stars through the trees.

Maybe we should just hitch back home.

We keep walking, and after a while the forest thins. Soon we're walking through a field of knee-high plants—like ferns, but in rows. In the distance I can make out the outline of a big house with gables. Around it there's a glow.

We press on through the tall plants toward the glow.

Somewhere, someone is playing country music on a big sound system. It's mostly flute and guitar with an old-fashioned beat, but somehow it sounds weirdly familiar. *I'm going up the country, babe, don't you wanna go? I'm going to some place where I've never been before.* I hate redneck noise personally, but since I haven't heard anything except the mental iPod in days, it's beautiful.

And there's this campfire odor everywhere that smells cozy.

Somebody runs past us, and we all flinch. It's a kid, probably a little younger than me, but taller.

"Dude!" I yell.

The kid turns. He is freckled with short red hair. For a moment, he looks out of it, confused, but then he smiles. "Duuuuude," he yells back.

What's with this kid? "Hey, little dude," I say. "What's going on up there?" I point toward where the light is glowing. It's wavering. But then everything is doing that. It's weird.

"It's the Tuesday night party! Don't miss the grub," the kid yells. He takes off through the field toward the light and the music.

As the house gets bigger, more and more people run past us through the field—old people, young people, black, white, Hispanic. Most of them are laughing as they hustle by. A couple of them turn and urge us to follow, but then they double over and laugh like something's really funny. Every once in a while you see somebody shuffling along timidly—an old lady or a couple of young guys who clasp their hands in front of them and walk like they're afraid they might fall over. They peer at you out of the corners of their eyes like they're paranoid.

Arthur and Esmerelda are starting to act funny too as we get closer to the light. Before they both seemed sad about leaving the *Tamzene*. But now every time somebody runs past they laugh and laugh like it's the funniest thing they've ever seen.

Come to think of it, I'm feeling pretty damn strange myself. I'm dizzy, but it isn't a dizziness I've ever felt before. It's like somebody placed this really heavy octopus on top of my brain, and the tentacles are hanging over the sides. My mouth is dry as a mofo. The lights are beautiful in a way I can't describe, and I'm mad hungry. I feel like I could eat a whole freezer of steaks myself.

Soon we're standing on the lawn of the house. Dozens of people are there. The glow comes from these big floodlights they've placed on top of poles, along with Chinese lanterns. There's a wooden dance floor with a deejay who, when we arrive, is spinning that country music bullshit.

Everybody is having a great time. And I mean *everybody*. Usually at a party, there's screaming kids or a crabby old person mucking up the works, but everybody on the dance floor is grinding and shaking and flailing their arms. Surrounding the dance floor are these metal folding chairs, and in them there are some other people who are smiling and looking up at the lights.

I forget about California and the *Tamzene* and all of that and get caught up in it. We're laughing and dancing and running around throwing stuff at each other, playing tag and going crazy. Some of the other kids our age join in, and soon *everybody* is in on this game we created. We call it paper plate tag—you have to touch the person with a paper plate instead of just your hand. It's really funny.

And the food. Oh my God, people, I've never loved food as much as I do now. They laid it out on two long tables behind the folding chairs. It's a potluck with ham, mashed potatoes, watercress salad, and German chocolate cake. We slather it onto paper plates and practically make out with it. We take big gooey mouthfuls.

This one character jumps up onstage and takes the mic from the deejay. At first I think it's a girl because there's all this gray hair, and somebody calls her Abbie. But then I hear the voice and see the beard, and I know it's a guy.

"Avoid all needle drugs," he says into the microphone. "The only dope worth shooting is Richard Nixon!"

Everybody howls. The guy with the microphone collapses into paroxysms of laughter.

"Maybe I should get some new material," Abbie says when he recovers. "In any case, welcome to Growing High!"

Everybody cheers.

An old black man steps onstage. He wears these wicked cool bell-bottoms but has a tangled halo of ash-colored hair. He picks up the badass left-handed Fender Strat. I expect it to suck because he's old, but he makes wild sounds with that thing, like he took lessons from The Edge or something. He starts singing about some kind of *"Purpa Haze, all in my brain."*

Everything spins. At some point we're talking to the Abbie guy. I try to explain about the boat, but it's getting harder and harder to talk, and it all seems totally hilarious.

"It's cool, man," he says. "I want you to meet my friend Tim."

A *really* old man with skin like paper, wearing a white lab coat, steps up out of the crowd. He's holding a silver tray upon which are squares of what look like jello.

"Actually, it's Dr. Leary," the old man says. Sharp for an old guy.

"You're probably wondering why we're all here," he says. "Myself, Mr. Hoffman, Mr. Hendrix, Miss Joplin." And he rambles into this long-winded speech I only partially understand. It's weird—I guess he thinks I should know who he is and who all these others are. So I smile and pretend to be impressed.

Evidently they were part of a group who did math or something. A counter culture, he calls them. Well, back in the '70s some of them ran afoul of the government and had to fake their own deaths. They had to hide out for a few years until they started this farm, and they've been here ever since.

Now this fat old lady with wild silver hair and wearing a muumuu is on the stage singing in this really deep, gravelly voice: *"I'm gonna show you, baby, that a woman can be tough. I want you to come on, come on, come on, come on and take it!"* And I'm like, wow, who'd want to take that old lady?

"Old hippies don't die, young man," Tim says. "They just move to Ohio and grow weed."

"Wow," Esmerelda says. "You're, like, really old."

The three of us laugh. Old Tim seems to take it in stride.

"The military industrial complex believed Timothy Francis Leary departed this mortal coil in 1996," he says. "I am ninety-four years old. Do you know the secret?"

We stare at him.

"LSD," he says. "It allows you to think for yourself and question authority. Taken responsibly, it also gives the patient what has proven to be a longer life. That, of course, comes at a price. To me, each one of you resembles a large, anthropomorphic horned melon." He holds out the tray. "Jello?" he asks.

We shake our heads and return to the party.

The floodlights and the Chinese lanterns make it seem like we're all dancing inside this big pretty Christmas tree. Everybody is so nice—I don't see an angry face anywhere. You know how at parties, some people dance woodenly, like they don't really want to dance and they're just doing it because they feel like they have to? That's me, usually—actually, I'm usually not dancing at all. That doesn't happen here. Everybody is really feeling the music. Some people look a little better than others—some people just look like they're having seizures—but everybody is having a great time.

Esmerelda grabs me around the waist, and we rock back and forth to some ancient song with a kick-ass guitar. "*Waterfall, nothing can harm me at all, my worries seem so very small with my waterfall . . .*"

Esmerelda is a good head taller than me. My nose is at her throat. I'd also technically never slow danced with a girl before. Both of these things would ordinarily have been enough to make me have to pee, but for some reason, tonight, I don't know, I just feel confident. I don't care. I hold her close and let the light from the Chinese lanterns hug us.

"I was mean to you," she says dreamily.

"Yeah?" I say. I'm laughing. *Stop laughing*, I tell myself, but I can't.

"I shouldn't have, like, dissed your rock 'n' roll band, man," she says. She stoops and puts her head on my shoulder.

"It's okay," I say. "Everything's cool. Do you ever miss your mom?"

"Sometimes," she says, "I keep meaning to go back to see her, but I just don't have the time, you know?"

"Okay," I say. "But I thought you said she sorta *died*."

She tenses up. She lifts her head and shakes it. "I mean my, uh, adoptive mom," she says. Fingers rub her eyes. "Winthrop, what's up, man?"

"I'm sorry," I say. "I didn't mean to bring you down."

"No, I mean, what's up with this place? Who are these people?"

I look at the dancing figures around me. A black guy with dreads and a pair of shades is slow dancing with a little old lady. "What? Everybody's just having a good time . . ." I say.

Somebody coughs into the PA system. I turn and realize it's Arthur. He's smiling and holding onto a cup of something. "Hi everyone out there," he says, not using his bullhorn. He smiles wide, and this choked little chirp whistles over the speakers.

"I just want to, you know, thank everybody here for all this and stuff. I only wish my friend Kang could be here to see you all. You've treated me and my friends—*friends*, everybody. That's like a foreign word to me. Back home in Pennsylvania, I don't have any friends. I'm such a loser. I don't even go to a regular school—I get homeschooled. My parents are afraid to let me outside because of this problem I have, and even when I go out there all the other kids pick on me and stuff. I was surprised they let me go to the camp, but the old man said it was a special camp and that I was kind of expected to go and that I better not embarrass him. But that's when I met *that* guy." He points at me. "Winthrop, everybody. He's just, well, he totally rules. Don't let his height fool you. He took me under his wing and treated me like a real friend. And that beautiful girl there, Esmerelda, she did the same. And now I have friends in all of you!"

Everybody howls and claps.

"Okay, okay. I got a question for all of you. You see, during my homeschooling, my mom gave me this book, kind of like a—what do you call it—a reference book. It provides all this information about drugs. And I can kind of tell that maybe what's making all this stuff here at your farm so beautiful tonight, from what I read about the affects of that drug cannabis, that it kind of feels a lot like *that*, you know? Like maybe we're all really feeling what they call a big contact high? I think I can smell it, that campfire odor."

The crowd cheers again.

"Yeah? Well, I was, that is to say *we* were, my friends and me—

friends, everybody!—we were hoping that maybe we could buy some off you and stuff."

Everyone laughs.

Arthur continues, "It's not for us, you understand. But you see, a couple of our friends couldn't be here tonight, and they've got this boat, and it's really cool. It like runs on this stuff. Marijuana, I mean. Or something like it. And they're stuck because they ran out. So maybe if you guys could maybe share some of your supply, then maybe we could help them out so they could get going again and stuff? Maybe?"

Abbie leaps to the stage. "Come on, people! What do you say? Let's help the little brother out!"

Since it's a warm, windy night, we sleep on the grass. When I wake up the next morning I notice the hills. The farmhouse is in the center of miles and miles of these rolling hills, which are covered with row upon row of what looks like green ferns. They're everywhere on the horizon, all the way down to the top of the house and barn and the spaces in between them.

That, Abbie explains to us, represents about 20 percent of the US government's marijuana crop. It's illegal for farmers to grow it in most states, Abbie tells us, but the feds continue to grow their own for research.

"In exchange for autonomy and immunity, we give them a percentage," he says. He shakes his head. "The '80s ruined this country. Everybody traded free love for tech stocks. I could have kept talking and let the Man put a bullet in my skull one day, but it wasn't worth it. So they offered me a deal and I took it. Here, at least, we can be free."

He smiles at me, like that incoherent blather is supposed to be profound. I find myself nodding along like I know what he's talking about. The nice old guy who played the guitar—forget the last name, but he spelled Jimmy with one M and an I—makes more sense to me now.

"This whole place is built on shit," he says. Every Tuesday night, the farmers burn their surplus. That leads to the kick-ass party.

I put on publicspeak and spill about how the *Tamzene* is being chased by those Green Police government goons, and Abbie immediately offers us all the weed we want and then some.

We hustle back to the boat.

"Abbie Hoffman says we can have all the weed we want!" I tell Kang, who is down in the hold changing Seabrook's bandages.

Kang frowns at me. He turns to Arthur and moves his hands rapidly, but keeps his frown on my face.

Kang says you're not allowed back on this boat unless you get rid of the acid, Arthur writes on his pad. Now suddenly Arthur can't talk anymore. What's with that?

"No," I said. "Dr. Leary tried to get me to take that stuff, but I didn't want to start seeing horned melons."

Kang explains to us that marijuana and hemp aren't the same thing. They're both varieties of this plant called cannabis, and they're both illegal. They also both contain this chemical called THC, which reacts with the stuff in the hemp cooker to burn hot enough to run the boat. So it'll work just the same. In fact, marijuana burns a little hotter.

The Indian guides the boat up to the little harbor on the north side of the farm.

Well, Abbie Hoffman even trucks it over to the *Tamzene* for us, people, a big flatbed truckload of enough bricks of marijuana to keep all of Philadelphia stoned for a year. Beat that, Burton Trotsky.

Kang looks at Hoffman with an odd face.

Hoffman holds up two fingers. "Peace, man," he says.

Kang shakes his head and shoves off.

My head feels like a wad of chewing gum, and I'm worried about whether or not the stuff we inhaled will stunt my growth. Esmerelda tells me that's something called an old wives' tale. I hope she's right.

As for the Growing High farm, it seems sort of sad, you know? It's a nice place, probably the nicest place I've ever been to. Back home in Philly you're lucky if you get a "Fuck you" from somebody passing you in the street, but there, black, white, old, young—everybody

dances with everybody else. Still, it isn't love that makes you so cool
at the farm, but some chemical that sends your mind away for a while.
I wonder what the farmers would think of that place just a few miles
upriver from them where all the trees have been cut down and all the
animals are dying in the oil. They probably wouldn't care at all.

Down in the cabin the Doctor looks really sick. His wound bled a
lot during the night. Arthur, Esmerelda, and I don't talk about leaving
again.

CHAPTER FOURTEEN

the doctor

I take the first shift looking after the doctor, which means Arthur and Esmerelda get to be alone on deck.

The doctor is in a lot of pain. Every now and then he moans or grumbles about something. Even though we don't say it, we all know hospitals are out of the question because, if that is the five-oh following us, the Green Police would have Doctor Seabrook in about thirty seconds.

I've never sat with anybody this sick before. One of His Eminence's favorite flicks is *Bridge on the River Kwai*, which came out a million years ago. There's this one scene where an old British officer takes a bullet to the foot, then collapses and orders everybody to go on without him. His Eminence said he admired the bravery, so I guess that's how sick people ought to be treated. He didn't say anything when the rest of the soldiers picked him up and carried him along anyway.

Every now and then Seabrook comes to and says something, usually asks where we are on the river, and when I don't know he tells me to go get Kang. By the time we come back he's passed out again.

"Ohio," I say this one time when he comes to.

He sighs and smiles up at me. He's lying on his stomach, his cheek shoved into the bedding. "Thank you, Mr. Brubaker," he says.

"How you feeling, Doctor?" I ask. "Does it hurt?"

He rolls his eyes.

I want to ask him about his wife, the one who died, but I remember how he was the last time the subject came up. I try on publicspeak again.

"So, uh, where did you get your degree?"

"My what?"

"Your degree. Your doctorate. Where did you go to school?"

"Why suddenly the curiosity, Mr. Brubaker?"

"I don't know. I'm just curious, that's all."

"McMaster Divinity . . ."

"Wow. Is that a liberal arts college?" I ask.

"It's a seminary."

"I never . . . good school?"

"I thought so."

There's a long pause. He closes his eyes. I ask, "What's your PhD in?"

"I don't have one."

"I don't get it," I say. "When did you . . . what are you a doctor of?"

He opens his eyes again. "Who told you I was a doctor, Mr. Brubaker?"

Well, the public relations video he showed me had dubbed him Doctor Marion Seabrook. He isn't wearing a stethoscope and doesn't have a degree pasted to the wall of the cabin, but . . . hell, there's been doctors all over the place! "Well I—you did! You introduced yourself as Doctor Seabrook."

"Doctor Seabrook. That's my name."

"But . . ."

Seabrook looks at me with eyes that are so sad, I feel horrible for having asked the question. "My middle name is Marion. My surname is Seabrook. My mother gave me the first name Doctor."

"But . . . but you built this boat. You're an expert on . . . on . . . energy and stuff . . ."

"I did, indeed, build this boat, and I am, in fact, an expert on *energy and stuff*. I am a man of science."

Up until now, the had doctor looked just fine in a mortarboard and robes, but suddenly the wind of that comment blows him down to his skivvies.

Seabrook breaks the silence. "My mother thought the name would give me some dignity and self-respect," he says. "Odd, isn't it? She thought it would give me a leg up in life. She was sure of it."

I think it would be cool to be named Doctor. Automatic nickname: Doc. His Eminence and the Moms named me after a character in a movie, although not a character that helped my self-esteem any. They could have named me something cool like Dixon Steele or Josey Wales or something. But no, they had to name me after Winthrop Paroo, the dorky little kid with a lisp Ron Howard played in *The Music Man*.

"It didn't give you a leg up?"

"No," Seabrook murmurs. "If you ever choose to have children, Mr. Brubaker, do not foist unrealistic expectations on them. I'm living proof."

"Oh."

He smiles uneasily. "Don't get me wrong, her heart was in the right place." He frowns again. "Her heart was *always* in the right place."

"Well, why is it such a bad thing? I mean, I would think it would be nice being named Doctor. People would think . . ."

"People would think you were a doctor," he says. "Yes, how wonderful that is. Let me ask you this—you just found out that I'm not who I say I am. Has your opinion of me changed in any way?"

I'm still thrown as to how someone who hasn't studied for millennia could build a device like the *Tamzene*.

"You don't have to answer," Seabrook says. He sighs. "When I tell people my name, they're always impressed at first, but then they find out the truth."

"Well, why don't you change it?" As soon as I turn eighteen, I'm going to jump into my Porsche, drive straight to the Philadelphia courthouse, and file the necessary forms to change my name to the ultracool Razor, the one I decided on after winnowing down a typewritten list of kick-ass monikers, which included Saber, Rifle, and Bubonic Plague.

"But your wife was a doctor, right?"

He closes his eyes again and begins to breathe heavily.

the flood

The river swells because there's been a big rainstorm. We cruise past a town where it's gone up over its banks—you can barely see the roofs of some of the houses, the water has gotten so high. Tires, chunks of wood, boxes, and furniture float in the water. People zip around the streets in little motorboats.

Kang has been hiding the *Tamzene* as best he can when we travel by day. We try to hug the bank farthest from the town and keep under the trees, but a man in a bass boat spots us and pulls up close.

"Thought you might have been supplies," he says. Greasy brown hair is smeared all over his scalp, and a three-day beard peppers his cheeks. He looks more annoyed that we aren't who he's expecting than he does shocked by the weirdness of our boat. "This is the third storm like this we've had in the past six months. Each and every time the government always shows up about two days too late to be of any use. This one's about it for me and mine—insurance has gone through the roof. Only thing left to do is pick up and head out of here. Hopefully someplace where there ain't no water. Y'all best get someplace high and dry. They say that storm might turn back around this way."

We thank him and keep moving downriver. Water stretches all the way out through the woods in some places, reflecting the trees and carrying small sheds and old tires that Kang either changes course to avoid or lets bounce off the hull.

For most of the day the air hangs thicker than the water, bugs swarm us, and the sun burns up at us off the river. Then, late in the day, a gray glacier crawls across the sky, flashing like gunfire.

the snake

For days the water moccasin's hunting grounds had grown.

This was happening with increasing frequency during the warm days. His ancestors had smaller territories in which to hunt; they had been forced to live within the confines of the riverbed.

Thanks to the big, two-legged mammals and their big, belching machines, the skies, the winds, the heat, and the water had changed. Now, his home became pregnant and burst forth from its boundaries. He swam through the forest on the hunt, through the lair of those very two-legged mammals. Down their streets, which had filled with water. Past many of the tree trunks of their legs, some of which he could tell—he could get very close without any of them noticing—had become whitened and chafed by the pestilential floodwaters.

On this day, the water moccasin swam in the center of the river, searching for the big fish he knew still lived there.

He failed to perceive the *whoosh-whoosh* of the clean boat that hugged the old shoreline as it passed. But close behind the clean boat, he sensed three mammal-made crafts of the suicidal variety.

Now the moccasin paused. What was passing through the air and the water? He lacked the ability to perceive something so complex yet meaningless, an aberration to the instinct that had guided him for nearly ten years. He was a very old water moccasin, old enough to have known and experienced all manner of alterations in the water.

This was a warning. These three passing boats were not to be taken lightly. They were to be obstructed.

The water moccasin felt the air change. There was to be nothing natural about this storm.

the storm

It isn't really a storm until midnight. What Kang should do is find a safe spot to port and wait it out, but we can practically feel the Green Police boats bearing down on us. The storm strikes when Kang has taken the *Tamzene* into a narrow crevice between two rock walls, through which knifes deep, fast-moving water. Jagged rocks surround us, and there's no place to anchor. The water throws us around like a volleyball. Arthur and I—Esmerelda is belowdecks with Seabrook—fall all over the deck, and the river water slaps at us. A couple of times, gusts nearly take me overboard.

A swell pitches the boat to the side and she careens out of control. Bellowing, Kang spins the wheel, but it's too late. The *Tamzene* crashes against the wall. The side of the boat throws itself at me, and the world goes black.

When I come to, everything is yellow and red. A fissure has snaked down the side of the hemp cooker, and I can see the fire blazing inside. Smoke boils from it. Then a blast of water crests over the boat, and the fire winks out with a hiss.

The wind howls like Fang on the *Live From the Meadowlands* opening track "I Conquer All," but over it I hear the humming noise of the engine fizzle and die.

Kang tries the wheel, but it doesn't respond. Without the engine to give the craft thrust, we're a dead hunk of wood and metal drifting down a river between jagged rocks.

Arthur scrambles from one side of the boat to the other, tying down equipment that has become untied.

"What can we do?" I shout.

The boat skids along over rapids, crashing against rocks. Kang tries to stoke the fire in the hemp chamber, but it won't start.

After a while, the rain slackens and the river grows more shallow and slow. Kang is able to steer the boat over to a sandy bank at the water's edge and drop anchor.

We collapse on the deck. The clouds have thinned. The boat rocks in the current, sloshing water back and forth over the deck boards. I allow the exhaustion to swallow me and sleep without a single dream.

we stop for repairs

I'm awoken by bright sunlight and chirping birds, and for a minute I think I'm back at my grandmother's house. It was an old farmhouse with a nasty old barn where Grandma used to park her car. She and the Moms would talk about old times in the kitchen—His Eminence never went with us on these visits. But we hadn't been back to Grandma's house since before we moved into the Compound, which was a long time ago. Grandma's farm—one of those half memories that don't come to you unless you're not thinking about anything in particular.

A rushing sound buzzes in my eardrums—Kang working on the

hemp cooker. He wears a black mask with a visor, and directs the flame of a blowtorch at the crack in the cooker. Arthur and Esmerelda stand slightly behind him, watching.

I also watch for a couple of minutes from my supine position, with my chin pressed against my chest. My skin is seriously pruny, and my clothes are soaked. Esmerelda turns and smiles when she hears me groaning.

"Hey, Sleepy Dwarf!" she says. My hair seems to be sticking up in a million places, and is plastered to my head in others. Plus I smell worse than the river. I edge away from her.

"What time is it?" I ask.

"It's like nearly nine. You're a heavy sleeper," she says. She helps me up. "That was some badass storm, Winthrop. The doc, well, he was thrown around a bit, but he'll be okay. I think he might not have a fever anymore. He was down there talking and everything."

"That's good," I say.

"The boat," she continues, "is a little worse for the storm. But Kang here says it'll be, like, up and running again by midday, isn't that right, Kang?"

A loud thud comes from the front of the boat, and we all turn. It's Doctor Seabrook, who has climbed up from the hold. He shuffles forward through the trash and debris on the deck.

"My boat," he says, his voice faint and airy. "What happened to my boat?"

He looks like the baddies in *Zombie Cannibals*. Two bloodshot eyes stare out at the world. Hair and muttonchops are tangled in a wild tilting halo. Blood has soaked through the gauze Kang tied around his shoulder.

Kang puts up his visor and lowers his torch, cutting off the flame. Arthur's mouth gapes.

"Doc," Esmerelda whispers, "are you high? What are you doing out of bed?" It occurs to me that it's not actually a bed, but a steaming hard metal corner of the hold. The man should be in a bed in a hospital somewhere.

"Kang, what happened?" he says, louder this time. He closes his eyes and reaches for the gunwales, pressing his weight into the railing as tremors pulse through his body. Then he calms and opens his eyes again.

"The boat hit a rock in the storm, Doctor," I say. "It put a hole in that cooker thing. Kang's patching it."

Seabrook's eyes widen, and they looked wicked red. "You're *welding* it? Kang, it'll never hold!" He pushes himself off the rail, loses his balance, and falls on his backside.

Kang drops his torch and helps Doctor up.

"Those welds will never hold, Kang," Seabrook says. "We have to patch the cooker with steel, don't you see?" Kang grabs him around the waist and helps him back to the hold. "And where the hell are we?" Seabrook bellows. "Good God, man, don't you see we're *exposed?* The Green Police will be all over us in a minute . . ."

Kang guides Doctor back below and redresses his wound. He continues to grumble for a while, but soon falls fast asleep.

we go for cigarettes

Time inches along. I watch the clouds make faces at me. I count the plastic bottles on the shore around the boat and up in the trees. I trace the picture of the cougar face on the patch with my index finger. Kang keeps clanging away at the hemp cooker.

"I need a smoke," Esmerelda says finally. "Maybe there's a convenience store or something nearby. You guys game?"

Kang clangs around the hemp cooker and wipes the sweat from his brow with a bandana. He doesn't seem to be listening.

"What if those guys in black come back?" I say.

"Are you an old lady or a rock star, stubby?" she asks. "I'm talking like five minutes. I'm jonesing."

Without another word she scrambles over the side. Arthur watches her disappear into the trees. Kang, absorbed in engine parts, pays no attention.

"This is crazy, right?" I say.

Shrugging, Arthur leaps over the side.

I follow.

We weave our way between the trees. Esmerelda walks ahead of Arthur and me.

"What do you think of her, man?" I ask him.

Arthur shrugs and smiles at the bullhorn on his chest.

"Yeah, she's all right," I say. "Smokin' bod. My girl back in Philly is way hotter. Bigger jugs, you know?" I try to quickly piece together an imaginary girl that will impress. "She's studying to be an acrobat. Can do all kinds of contortionist moves. We've got a killer sex life."

Arthur beams at me.

Making up shit again, eh? Wimp Winthrop says. *Pathetic.*

"What about you, man? Getting any?"

He chuckles and shakes his head.

"Yeah, well wait'll we get to California. More ass than sits on a toilet seat goes to those Grizzlies shows. Just stick with me."

Arthur shrugs, still sticking his teeth out in that same stupid grin.

"So what are you going to tell your folks?"

The smile wavers for a second, then comes back full force. He holds his arms out to his sides and shrugs.

"Yeah, mine'll be wicked pissed," I say. "But they're learning not to fuck with me. Sooner or later, you gotta take off the Pampers, cut the cord, you know . . ."

Then Esmerelda whirls on Arthur and presses herself into him. She taps him on the arm. Leaning close, she whispers, "Tag." She's rekindling the game we started at the Growing High farm. Arthur, who I bet is hornier than the Primose School band, flushes pink and chases after her.

I try to keep up, but their legs are longer. You might not believe this, people, but I'm beginning to envy Arthur. I mean, the kid is lower on the pecking order than I am. At Primrose, he wouldn't have lasted five minutes—none of us would have had anything to do with him. But out here in the woods it's different. The same kid who was bawling like a nancy boy just a couple of days ago has scored us a bunch of ganja, regularly chats with a badass Indian dude, and is now running around the woods with a blond hottie who I'm starting to get the feeling might be more interested in him than me.

I lose sight of them in the trees, but follow the sound of Esmerelda giggling. The mental iPhone is restocked with Grizzlies tunes, so I click on some of the numbers from the *Journeys* album.

That's when I hear the noise. It starts like a little chuckle, and at first I think it's Esmerelda giggling. But she's stopped. Then there's a humming—the bumblebee buzz of a gasoline engine. It rises up under the sounds of the crickets chirping. I can make out something white through the trees and black figures weaving around. Why did we get off the boat? Why did we get off the boat?

I stumble toward the boat, hot tears smearing all the trees. I yell for Arthur and Esmerelda to follow. My shoulder smashes against a tree, and I fall to the ground. The buzzing noise is getting louder, and a new noise climbs up over top of it—the chattering noise I heard in the woods in Ohio.

It's the black things again.

Esmerelda's white legs and browning Keds seesaw past me. "*Run!*" she screams.

Propping myself on an elbow, I look back into the burst of tree limbs—just the empty forest with the light streaming between the boughs. My shoulders ache. The chattering noise grows.

Then, all at once, the woods are streaked with shadows. Animals are everywhere. Small ones, no bigger than my hand, zipping up through the trees, bounding across the grass, swarming at me.

They're squirrels. Gray squirrels with puffy tails, the same ones I see leaping through the little trees back on Broad Street. They pile on top of one another, and soon a big boiling cloud of squirrels tumbles toward me, closer and closer.

Then two hands grab my shoulders and pick me up, and I'm running blindly behind Arthur back to the boat.

The squirrels follow.

Soon we wade into the water, climb the ladder, and collapse onto the deck. Kang has started the engine, and when I land on the deck next to Arthur, I see why: three white boats have appeared around a bend in the river where we'd crashed into the rock wall. They're closing in.

I look at the shore. Nothing but bottles and wrappers and junk. The squirrels are gone.

The *Tamzene* crawls along, bug-like, barely churning the water. Kang's eyes have gone wild. He signs something at Arthur, fingertips darting like gnats.

Arthur writes on his pad: "*The cooker isn't sealed. We can't get up to speed.*"

frogs

Evening was their time to shine. When the sun fell from the sky, the male frogs came to the rocky shore to sing. They swelled with air until they might burst, filling like balloons and forcing the air from themselves with a thrum. If they sang well the female frogs would come. Day was a time for keeping submerged, climbing occasionally from the water to catch insects, but mostly waiting for nightfall, when mates were won.

Then came a single, jarring thought, an obliterating whiteness that cut through all desire and instinct. The frogs swam without realizing that they were shoulder to shoulder with other frogs and had collected into a great mass of frogs.

That they were swimming directly into the path of an electric motor.

we get lucky

The white boats get bigger and bigger as the hemp cooker sputters and shakes. Kang turns to face the oncoming boats. He pulls the bowie knife from its scabbard and holds it at his side.

When they're almost upon us, I hear a grinding noise—like when His Eminence's gardener runs over one of my lightsabers in the courtyard. Then there's a deep-throated blast from the center boat as a plume of white smoke lifts from the cabin. The boat shudders. It turns and strikes the boat next to it. The third boat slows to a stop.

Green and white blobs bubble up in the black river. They're floating frogs—millions of them, many dead and showing their white underbellies. Some are just pieces, severed legs or shredded torsos.

"Dude!" Esmerelda says. "They must have run over, like, a colony of these things."

She's right. Evidently the white boats plowed over the top of a giant army of frogs, and the Green Police engines evidently weren't designed to sail through amphibians.

Kang lowers his knife and watches the boats as they disappear in white smoke.

CHAPTER FIFTEEN

the birmingham kid

The engine hiccups and spurts smoke. We turn up a stream and then down another, and come to rest in a lagoon at the bottom of a steep hill. A pipe runs down the hill and pours oil into the water near the boat.

This stopped being fun a long time ago, but now I'm completely freaked. This whole thing is so not cool. Squirrels bite? What would have happened if a bunch of them took after me like that one did to Arthur?

Kang clangs around with the hemp cooker some more, and the big lightning-shaped crack looks bigger. I wish I could get him to just keep going and put some more water between us and the white boats. How long does it take to repair frog damage?

Seabrook shouts from the hold. He's holding two fistfuls of gauze and tape—the bandages have been ripped from his shoulder blade. The hole on his back oozes through rust-colored crust, and his skin is the color of an early model iPod and speckled with sweat. Occasionally an electric current trembles through him. His eyes are open but probably blind behind his gooey tears. He mumbles something, gibberish mostly, but I can make out the name Lydia.

I want my mom. I know that sounds totally lame, but it's the truth. I want my mom worse than anything. I'd go off and find a phone, but I'm afraid those baddies in black would come back.

Kang redresses the wound and covers Seabrook in blankets. Soon Seabrook's eyes close again. He stops talking and starts to breathe heavily again.

* * *

Kang finishes welding the cooker. We help him reload it and then mop the deck while he revs the engine to test it. Nobody talks.

We finally get ready to head out again when we hear a popping noise. Everybody freezes.

I scan the tops of the trees. For a while there's nothing but the wind brushing past. Then I hear footsteps and heavy breathing. Someone is running through the forest.

Another bang.

"It's a gunshot!" I cry. "Kang, let's get out of here!"

A man darts out of the forest. He stops at the edge of the river and waves at us as we pull back from shore.

"Help! Help! Don't go nowheres without me!" He raises his arms over his head and jumps up and down. The man is sporting an undershirt beneath overalls and a blond bowl cut that nearly falls into his eyes—a style that's *so* '90s.

"It's one of those guys!" I say. "Keep going, Kang!"

But Esmerelda furrows her brow. "It doesn't look like a cop, Winthrop," she says.

She's right. On his back is a bright green knapsack. Another gunshot pops in the woods, and something thuds against our hull.

"Help me!" the man shouts again.

"They're shooting at him, Kang!" Esmerelda says. "Let him get on board."

I think that's crazy. I mean, what are we doing? We need to get to a town. It's a miracle we made it this far. Seabrook stuck his neck out for someone, and look at him.

But I don't say anything.

Kang stops the boat. The man wades into the water, taking off his knapsack and holding it over his head like it's full of mint-condition X-Men action figures. He climbs aboard, and Kang speeds away.

Over the engine, the radio sputters snatches of conversations: "*My responsibility,*" someone says, "*is to follow the Scriptures which call upon us to occupy the land until Jesus returns.*"[8]

The man rests against the gunwales, gasping for breath and clutching his backpack to his stomach with big, meat-slab hands. He smiles and nods a hello. A big jaw bites his upper lip, and he smells worse than a gym locker at school—why does everyone smell so awful out here? I back away.

"Y'all done me a huge favor," he says. He has an honest to God Southern drawl. "That's what you done. Y'all done Charlie Lee a big ol' honkin' favor."

"Hi," Esmerelda says, stepping forward and holding out her hand. "My name's Esmerelda. And this here's Winthrop and Arthur, and that there driving the boat is Kang."

"Name's Charlie Lee Bowden, and I'm pleased to meet y'all," Charlie Lee says. He nods at each of us in turn. He wrinkles his nose at the sight of Kang. Then he leans toward Esmerelda and whispers, "'Scuse me for saying, little lady, but is that there an Injun you got driving this here boat?"

Esmerelda frowns. "His name is Kang, and he's a Native American."

Charlie Lee leans back against the gunwales and nods. "I don't mean no disrespect, ma'am. I just never met an honest to goodness Injun—er, Native American before."

I cover my nose and moved further away from the guy. "So," I say, "who was shooting at you back there?"

"Po-lice," Charlie Lee says. He sits up straight and looks at Esmerelda and me, sticking his thick jaw out at us. "See, they's after me for doing the Lord's work."

Esmerelda glances at me. We just left a camp full of religious wackos, and now we've picked up a Southern evangelist? It isn't that I don't believe, people. I'm sure there's a heaven and a hell and that one of those celestial video game remotes holds sway over my destiny, but it's all too far away, and talk of it bores me worse than the news on TV.

"Like, just what exactly is the Lord's work, Mr. Bowden?" Esmerelda asks with narrow eyes.

"Well," he says, "I'm afraid, little lady, y'all done gone and picked yourselves up one honey of a hitchhiker. I'm the Birmingham Kid."

"The . . . what?"

Charlie Lee's eyes fall, and his smile slips from his face. "Come on now. Y'all mean to say you ain't never heard of the Birmingham Kid?"

"No," Esmerelda says.

"Well, they call me that because I'm from Birmingham. Only I ain't from there exactly—I'm from the town of Crawdad, Alabama, which is about an hour's drive away. They done called me Birmingham because it was the closest big town, and I daresay it wouldn't be right calling me the Crawdad Kid on account of my bidness."

"What business is that?" Esmerelda asks.

"Well, ma'am, I go from place to place doing the Lord's work."

"So you said," Esmerelda chirps. "And just what does that mean? Like, why were those cops shooting at you?"

"Well, the po-lice, they don't always take too kindly to my crusade, although most of the God-fearing people do." He hugs his backpack more tightly. "I just done a bit of work there in the town of Fenton, Kentucky, when the police caught on and run me off. Usually I find a house or some folks who appreciate the Birmingham Kid where I can lay up, but I didn't find nothing of the sort this time. That's how I come upon y'all, and thank heavens I did. Y'all done Charlie Lee a big ol' honkin' favor."

Just then, the doctor groans from the hold and something strikes the metal floor below. All of us, including Charlie Lee, go belowdecks—except Arthur, who takes the wheel from Kang.

Seabrook has attempted to crawl back out of bed, but he's collapsed before reaching the stairs. He's lying on the metal floor. Kang takes his shoulders and I grip his feet, and we carry him back to his bed.

"That man been shot?" Charlie Lee says.

"Yeah," I say. "Two days ago. Shot in the shoulder."

"Well, now that's a darn shame. Y'all ain't planning on taking him to no doctor, now are you?"

Esmerelda narrows her eyes. "Why?"

"Well, doctors are agents of the devil," Charlie Lee says. "They're all about taking people away from life everlasting and getting in the way of God's will."

"What?"

"Doctors," Charlie Lee snaps. "Don't listen to them, y'all. Y'all trust in the Lord. He'll see your friend through."

is there a doctor in the house?

The sky is just beginning to turn pink when we see the town. Houses poke up above the trees, and cars speed past on blacktop roads. Docks lined with bobbing white boats jut out from shore. Church spires rise into the sky, and a water tower that looks like an upside-down scallion pokes up from behind the rooftops.

"Why, that must be the town of Crofton," Charlie Lee says.

I suck wind until my lungs are ready to burst. Just beyond the house, two golden arches hump—McDonald's burgers are on the wind.

Kang anchors upstream and out of sight, waiting for dark when we can sneak by unseen.

Esmerelda comes up from the hold.

"Kang," she says, "he looks really bad."

We all go back down again. Seabrook is lying very still. His breath is coming in short, rasping spasms.

"He needs a doctor," Esmerelda says.

We all stare at her. A hospital, of course, we decided we can't do. But I don't know if I've ever seen any living person look that color before.

Esmerelda is crying. "I'm afraid he'll die. Kang, we have to go over to that town and find a doctor."

Kang stares at her gravely.

"We can make something up," she says, tossing a hand at him as if he'd refused. "I mean, I know doctors are supposed to report stuff like gunshot victims. But we can make something up and leave before anybody has a clue."

Kang nods.

Esmerelda exhales. "Okay. It's settled. I'll go."

Kang stiffens. He shakes his head vehemently.

"What else are we going to do? Talking isn't, like, your strongest suit, man. Plus, if something goes wrong, none of us knows how to drive this boat."

She and Kang go back and forth. Arthur signs at her. He doesn't want her to go by herself. Charlie Lee and I watch them blathering on and on.

As for yourstruly, I want neither option. I want to get off this ride, but what's waiting for us if we do? If only we had one of those invisible cloaks that they have in that *Larry Spackler and the Killer Animals* movie.

An idea pops in my head.

"We go secret–agent style," I say.

stealth mission

"This is ridiculous," Esmerelda says. "Everybody is staring at us."

We're hiding in an alley next to a drugstore. We make our way through the town, hiding in doorways.

Despite what Esmerelda says, my disguises are awesome. I took the ponchos Kang got us, then borrowed some of his feathers and a few ribbons of Seabrook's extra gauze tape to fashion us each miniature headdresses. Also, using some of the red paint Kang has for the hemp cooker, I gave us each a crimson war face.

"The point is," I say to Esmerelda, "those guys in black are going to be looking for three kids, right? Not three Native Americans."

When we first arrived in town, Charlie Lee, who'd been heehawing at our costumes, said he was off to get himself something to eat. We watched him saunter away, his overalls and backpack cruising down the hard pavement and right angles of a city street. He disappeared into a restaurant called the Steak Shack. The name made my stomach rumble.

I was so starved, I might have considered going with him if I hadn't spotted the man in the black suit. We'd been hiding in the entryway of a bank building with the *Closed* sign flipped over.

It wasn't a Green Police uniform—just a black business suit. He had a crew cut and sunglasses, and looked like a member of His Eminence's security detail.

But he passed us. He saw us, gave us a look with a knitted brow, and seemed in no hurry to loose saber-toothed rodents on us.

"Look," Esmerelda says. She's taken off her headdress. "I'm going in there to see if I can get some kind of painkiller or something for the Doc, and maybe see if we can use a phone."

Arthur follows her. I wait outside to keep a lookout.

Crofton sure isn't much of a town. One stoplight at the corner of Main Street divvies up a couple of bars, churches, and a Shell station. A handful of houses with rusting aluminum siding line the crumbling sidewalk. Probably zero music scene. Cars zip past without stopping, and the drivers don't seem to look out the windows.

I spot a metal box marked AT&T in the alley across from the drugstore. I run across the street to get to it, nearly into the path of an oncoming car. I glance over my shoulder to see if Arthur and Esmerelda can see me. Through the drugstore window I see a few adults moving around, but no sign of red faces and ponchos.

There's a push-button keypad at the center of the metal box, which bends and mangles my reflection. Attached to it is this super old receiver thing. What do they do in the movies? *Zero for operator,* it says.

I press it.

"Directory assistance."

"I want to call the Brubaker residence in Philadelphia."

"You want to make a collect call?"

"What's a collect call?"

"Sir, that means the party you're dialing will be responsible for the charges."

"Sure. Let's do that." I give the number.

From the corner of my eye, I see the man in the black suit again. He emerges from an alley and stops on the shoulder. His mirrored shades flash in the late afternoon sun.

I drop the receiver and let it dangle, then turn to run. I'm walled in on all sides by brick, and for a brief few seconds I wish I had the arms of those monster trees to dart back into.

When I search for the man in black again, his back is to me. He's wandering off in the direction of the restaurant where Charlie Lee had gone for dinner. *He's just a guy, he's not a baddie*, I tell myself.

I exhale. Still no sign of Arthur and Esmerelda.

I pick up the receiver and put it to my ear.

It'll be okay. His Eminence will send a car. Once he hears about the *Tamzene* and how great it is, he'll pull some strings and maybe even bring those black-uniformed baddies up on charges.

"They told me this was going to help your career," I say to myself, rehearsing, as the line clicks and beeps, presumably darting across the country to connect me with the Compound.

I realize how hollow I sound.

As for that patch thing, I tell myself, *it's sure to be some kind of coincidence. That's all.*

That sounds hollow too.

I shake my head. I'll tell Esmerelda and Arthur that it must have been a fluke. His Eminence's people must have just spotted us on a spy satellite or something.

They can't ever know. I just want my mom.

The phone rings once.

From inside the Steak Shack, where I'd last seen Charlie Lee, I hear a shout: "God is great!"

The door swings open and people scatter out. Old ladies and old men rush past with panicked looks in their eyes, mouths hanging open. Some of the people wear white, grease-covered clothing. Some of them are screaming.

No sign of the man in the black suit.

"Brubaker residence. Your security clearance code, please," says the voice on the phone.

The last person out the door is Charlie Lee. He has a smile on his face, and his eyes are flashing like crazy. He raises his knapsack over his head and bellows, "God is great!"

Esmerelda and Arthur emerge from the drugstore and freeze.

I hang up the receiver.

Charlie Lee lowers his shoulders and runs directly at us. "Y'all better run," he says, laughing as he passes us. He hustles down the incline in the direction of the *Tamzene*.

We all stand there like a pack of goons for a second or two. Behind us the restaurant explodes in a massive ball of flames and wood splinters.

We run after Charlie Lee.

cuisine

Ablack curlicue of smoke twists over Crofton. The wheeze and sigh of its fire alarm is just beginning when we reach the *Tamzene*. In the dim light, I can barely make out Charlie Lee running ahead of us. I hear him whooping and shouting in celebration. Behind us the lights of Crofton are disappearing into small yellow squares.

Charlie Lee climbs aboard first, shouting, "Start her up, Kang ol' buddy! Give her some gas!"

"Don't do it! Don't let him on board!" Esmerelda yells, but it's too late—the engine hums to life just as she, Arthur, and I reach the hull. As we climb aboard, Kang speeds away.

Esmerelda pushes past Charlie Lee and into the cabin. She glares, wicked pissed, at the Birmingham Kid from behind Kang.

"Throw his ass overboard," she growls.

Kang frowns and glances at Arthur, who nods and signs something at Kang.

Charlie Lee leans against the edge of the boat, gasping for air. The run made his cheeks red, and spread across them is that same psycho smile he was wearing just before the Steak Shack went up in flames. He turns the smile on Esmerelda. "Aw, now don't take on so, Esmerelda. It was God's will."

Crofton disappears around the bend. Cloudbursts of trees pile in on us and this psycho that might blow us out of the water. A few more digits into the phone, a quick story, and all this would have been finished.

I manage to stammer, "What . . . what the hell . . ."

"You're a murderer," Esmerelda says in a small voice.

I can't take my eyes off that green backpack that holds God knows what. I want Esmerelda to shut up. I want to keep Charlie Lee calm until the guys in the white coats show up.

"Aw, hush now," Charlie Lee says. "There *weren't* no innocent people in that restaurant. They all run out the front before that bomb went off. You saw 'em."

Kang continues to steer but glances at Charlie Lee. His muscles flicker.

Charlie Lee looks back at Kang, and he pales. "Now, y'all could throw me overboard, but who's to say I won't go to the first phone I see and put in an anonymous call to the po-lice and tell 'em about this here boat?" His cheeks allow a rubbery grin. "Oh yes. I can tell something is up with this here boat y'all are driving. You been looking over your shoulders all day long, and you didn't pull into Crofton like regular folks. You anchored downstream. And you got a man with a gunshot wound in the hold that none of you seems too anxious to take to a hospital—sinful doctors or no sinful doctors. I dare say ol' Charlie Lee telling the police what I know about the *Tamzene* and where y'all are is something you definitely don't want. Which is what would happen, Mister Injun, not long after this here backside punches a hole in that there water."

Esmerelda cringes and mouths the words: *Native American.*

Charlie Lee grips his bag to his midsection, and that mad scary smile reforms. "Now, the way I see it, y'all got two options. One, you kill me." He gulps. "Not the prettiest of options by a long shot. Not only for ol' Charlie Lee, but for yourself, Mister Injun. Y'all will not only have to explain to these here youngins what a cold-blooded savage you are, but you'd have a body to dispose of to boot. Not to mention it ain't a Christian thing to do. Or option two, you keep on driving this here boat downriver—no longer than just a night and a day—and you drop ol' Charlie Lee at the first town you come to, and ol' Charlie Lee will take his belongings, and you'll never see hide nor hair of him again. So help me God."

He pushes himself off the side of the boat and kneels, placing his backpack on the deck in front of him. Then he raises his arms up from his sides and spreads them out like wings.

"Lord," Charlie Lee says, "Charlie Lee is putting his life in Your hands now. Save me from the murderous hands of this heathen so that I may do Your work. Your will be done."

Kang steps out from the cabin and stands in front of Charlie Lee. Muscles tight, he takes a step toward the Birmingham Kid, but then stops, sighs, and rolls his eyes. He motions for Charlie Lee to stand. Then, slumping his shoulders, he returns to the cabin and takes the wheel back from Arthur.

"Thank you, Mister Injun," Charlie Lee says. He stands, clutches his backpack to his chest again, and leans on the railing. "And God bless you. God bless y'all, for that matter."

Esmerelda goes white. She wedges herself into the corner of the cabin and shakes her head.

"I—I don't believe this," she mutters. "I mean, hello? We're, like, gonna let this guy stay here? He's got a bag full of explosives!"

Shut up shut up shut up. This chick is always trying to act all grown-up and sophisticated and no-bullshit. She's going to get us killed.

But Charlie Lee is still super smiley, like we're all joking. "Esmerelda, what makes you think I'm gonna hurt you?" he says. "Did I hurt anyone? Did you see anyone hurt back there?"

Esmerelda doesn't look at him. Instead she turns to Arthur, who nods and shoots Charlie Lee a frown. *Like he's going to do something!* Both of them are pissing me off. Bringing this nut job on board was *their* idea to begin with!

"Well, I put it to you, Winthorpe . . ."

I don't bother to correct him.

". . . didn't it look to you like everybody got out in time?"

I lean against the side of the boat and wish I was still back in Crofton, which is now a yellow glow over the tops of the trees. "I don't know, Charlie Lee."

"Well, I think they all got out in time," he says. "Anyway, it was the Lord's will."

"Would you stop saying that, please," Esmerelda says, continuing to glare at Arthur. I want to throttle her, people. "We're going to drive you to where you need to go, but would you mind . . . oh, *shit*, man . . ."

Charlie Lee continues to smile. "Maybe you ought to calm down."

"What's in the bag, man? How did you do it—plastic explosive or something? Is it safe?"

"It's plenty safe," Charlie Lee says. "Y'all don't fret about it. I know what I'm doing"

"I'm sure," Esmerelda says. She rolls her eyes and clicks her tongue. "Well, *why* did you do it, then?"

"I didn't do nothing," Charlie Lee says. "*God* did it."

Esmerelda shakes her head. "Oh for Christ's sakes. Fine. Why did God blow up that restaurant, Charlie Lee?"

"Oh. On account of that restaurant was serving lobster roll."

"I'm serious!"

"So am I." He shakes his head. "Those people should have known better—that is an abomination and a sin. That's why I'm not that concerned whether or not there were any stragglers, you see. It was the Lord's will."

"You, like, *bombed* . . . a restaurant . . . because it was serving . . . *lobster?*" Esmerelda says. "I'm sorry, do you have any idea how fucking wacko that is?"

He takes a deep breath. "All right, y'all," he says. "Ahem: *And all that have not fins and scales in the seas, and in the rivers, of all that move in the waters, and of any living thing which is in the waters, they shall be an abomination unto you: They shall be even an abomination unto you; ye shall not eat of their flesh, but ye shall have their carcasses in abomination. Whatsoever hath no fins nor scales in the waters, that shall be an abomination unto you.* Leviticus, chapter eleven, verses ten through twelve."

Nobody says anything.

"Shellfish," he says. "Bible says it's an abomination to eat shellfish.

Them people back there at that restaurant was serving lobster roll.
That there is an abomination—a downright sin—and God smote them
with my hand."

Esmerelda continues to stare at him with a wide-open jaw, and
says, "You're out of your fucking mind."

Charlie Lee bristles. "Oh I *am*, am I? It's in the Bible, ma'am, the
word of God! And people all over just flaunt it by serving that stuff up
like there's not a thing in the world wrong with it. It's an out-and-out
sin, don't you see? Lookee here." He leans toward Esmerelda, who
bounces back to the cabin. "That same book of the Bible, Leviticus.
Why, just nine chapters later it says, *If a man also lie with mankind, as
he lieth with a woman, both of them have committed an abomination.*
That's your homosexuals. Bible says that's a sin too.

"Few years ago, this wasn't no problem. But those dang fools there
in Washington and in some of the states allow the queers to get married. Can you believe that? I know some fellers—good, God-fearing
boys, who are taking care of that abomination.

"Now all over the blessed thing, the Bible, it rambles on and on
about the gift of life. Heck, one of the Ten Commandments says: *Thou
shalt not kill.*" He smiles again and raises a finger. "Now that there is
your aborters, your pro-choicers.

"Now your aborters, that's even bigger. We been going after them
for years. You probably heard of the one feller, that Eric Rudolph. He
was taking care of *that* sin, smiting those who offend the Lord, by
blowing up the clinics where they murder all those babies."

He steps toward the cabin and leans inside. Arthur, arms akimbo
like he's a badass or something, leaps in front of Esmerelda and tries
to mimic Kang's most threatening expression.

"Well, now, you explain to me—all of you—why your homosexuals and your pro-choicers are getting their punishment for their sins,
and your shellfish eaters are getting off scot-free?"

Charlie Lee puts his bag at his feet, crosses his arms, and lifts his
chin. "Well now they're not, y'all. Thanks to the Birmingham Kid. I
done smoted twelve shellfish-serving restaurants in Alabama, four in

Georgia, and that one there, the Steak Shack of Crofton, was my sixth in Kentucky."

"That's twenty," Esmerelda says.

"So it is."

Lobster Newburg is one of Jean-Paul the chef's specialties. The Paste Eaters and I often hung out at the Long John Silver's at the King of Prussia mall and munched on popcorn shrimp. Just the other night, when Kang had steamed shrimp, I felt more at home than I had in days. Had I only known then it was a sin, I would have stuck with the potatoes. Jesus, it's all so confusing. You get the same bullies at the Primrose School—in certain hallways it means a Paste Eater's ass if he gets caught wearing a black turtleneck. But in others, it's acceptable. I just bet you there's a different group out there that says you have to eat shellfish, or *that's* a sin and you'll get blown up. Religion—it's the biggest bully there is.

"I didn't know you couldn't do that," I say. "Eat shellfish, I mean. So much is sacrilegious that I just didn't realize."

"A lot of people don't realize, Winthorpe," Charlie Lee says. "That's why, before I set off any of my plastique, I yell out, *God is great!* That sends them all scrambling out the exit doors quick as jackrabbits. And, like I say, if any stragglers are there . . . well, that's God's will."

I try to act like I'm interested, but the guy is mad crazy, so I try to sit as far away from him as I can. It's best to humor people like that. What does fighting with them get you?

But Esmerelda and her new little toady Arthur clearly don't agree. "Hey, like, how did you *know* that place served lobster, Charlie Lee?" Esmerelda asks. "You didn't have a chance. You were only in there for a couple of minutes. And it was called the Steak Shack, not the Seafood Shack."

He unzips the front of his backpack and pulls out a piece of purple paper. "They got it right here on the to-go menu. See? Lobster roll." He holds it out for Esmerelda, who snatches it from him and goes back into the cabin.

For a little while it's quiet, and I'm hoping Esmerelda is going to keep her fat yap shut. I watch the woods fly by. So much has happened, and my brain is just not working anymore. Something in my pocket is digging into my thigh—it's the patch, the one with the snarling cat face on it. I hold it and run my finger along the stitching, staring into the woods and wondering if I'll be able to sleep at all with a God-freak bomber on board.

Then Charlie Lee leans horrorshow close. "Say," he says, "what's that you got there?"

I try to speak, but just then something sucks all the moisture out of my throat. "It's . . . uh . . . well, I just found . . ."

He puts out a hand. I black out for a second. Now he's standing there holding the patch in front of that broad, underbite face.

He frowns. "Why, you're . . ." his voice is all trembly. "You're one of 'em!"

I feel numb. His eyes skip all over me like a wandering spider.

"No," I manage to say.

"Yes, you are too, ain't you? You're one of 'em!"

Mind reeling, reservoir long since blown to smithereens, I grunt.

Charlie Lee raises both his arms, everything blurs, and my heart pounds in my ears.

But the guy hugs me. Toe-cheese floods my sinuses. Horror and disgust tangle inside me.

"Well, I'll be!" he says, laughing in my ear. "I certainly will be. I never expected you was one of them!" He lets go. "Are all the rest of 'em—Esmerelda, Arthur, and that Injun—part of it too?" Tears fill the man's eyes. "Y'all were having fun with me. Pretending you didn't know the Birmingham Kid. Well, it surely is a pleasure."

He hands the patch back to me. "Oh, you mean this patch," I say. "No, I'm not one of . . . whoever. I just found this patch, is all."

Charlie Lee blinks. Then, the smile slides off his face. "You what?"

"I found it. In the woods up in Ohio."

He stands and scratches his scalp. "You found it?" he says. "In the woods? You mean to say you ain't one of 'em?"

"No," I say. "Sorry."

He nods and smiles sadly. "It's all right, Winthorpe."

Leaning his backpack on the side of the boat, he sits next to me. His smell burns my eyes, and I duck my nose into the remnants of my turtleneck. My own scent isn't much better, but I find my own brand of unwashed funk, a Campbell's chicken noodle soup odor, more tolerable.

"First time I seen that patch was about four years ago. I was living at my home in Crawdad, and one day a traveling preacher come into town, and he had a patch just like that."

"A traveling preacher?" I ask. The patch didn't look religious. In fact, it looked much more badass than that—something a biker might have on his jacket.

Charlie Lee nods. "Yep. He was a good man. The Reverend Harlan H. Spikes. Head of Higher Purpose Ministries, which is one of them government-funded, faith-based organizations. The good Reverend is the one who's responsible for saving the Birmingham Kid, Winthorpe."

"How?"

"Well, he saved me from the hellfire of eternal damnation." He reddens and lowers his head. "Fact is, down in Crawdad, I used to work on a . . . a shrimp boat. That's right. Used to make my bones catching them abominations. The Reverend come into town one day and pulled us aside and told us how what we was doing flew in the face of the Divine Plan, and that we could be saved. So a bunch of us boys in Crawdad went to his prayer meeting, which he had in a big old tent in the fairgrounds. Told us how he'd given spiritual council to that there Eric Rudolph fella years ago, and how simple human beings can become vessels for God's wrath. Simple human beings like me and my friends. And how you can get your reward in the sweet by-and-by. Big plots of real estate in heaven. Reverend Spikes told me I could get myself a nice little corner lot on several acres and just sit, drink my weight in Pabst, and strum a harp all day long in the kingdom of heaven. Never had nothing but a double-wide and a bug zapper here on the old blue marble.

"A few of us went back to his prayer meeting and met with him private. And that's when I seen he had a patch like that sewed onto an old army jacket. I asked him what it was, and he told me it was a special club he belonged to a long time ago, and that they were good God-fearing people who could do what needed to be done. And he said if I was to ever run into somebody with a patch like that, I was to show them respect because they were wonderful men of God who certainly would be watching my good deeds.

"Well now, Reverend Spikes didn't really organize or nothing. Just got us to studying on what was wrong in the world today and how a body can be God's instrument and stop it all. Some of my other buddies went out to states that's been lettin' queers get married and blowing up the court houses. Another fella is trying to get going on the abortion clinics."

Esmerelda steps out of the cabin. Her face is still red, but now she's smiling, like she just made it to level five in *Heckenluber*. "Well, Mr. Birmingham Kid, it looks like you've made a big-ass mistake."

She holds out the purple take-out menu for the Steak Shack. Charlie Lee takes it from her. "What's that, pray tell?" he says, returning her smile.

"Did you happen to notice the asterisk next to the lobster roll on that menu?" Esmerelda asks.

Charlie Lee glanced at the paper.

"And what, braniac, do you think the asterisk stands for? Look at the bottom of the page."

I look over Charlie Lee's shoulder. Next to an asterisk at the bottom of the page is typed: *Made of imitation lobster product/flounder.*

The Birmingham Kid's face sags.

"That's right, asshole," Esmerelda says. "That wasn't shellfish they were serving at the Steak Shack. It was *imitation* shellfish, made of flounder."

"Dear God," Charlie Lee murmurs.

"And last time I checked," Esmerelda continues, her voice getting louder, "the Bible doesn't say a whole hell of a lot about eating flounder. Which would make what you did a *sin!*" She gasps, mocking him.

"What are you doing?" I snap. "Quit poking him!"

She ignores me, again, so I stand up in her face—her throat, actually. "*You're going to get us all killed!*" I hiss.

She looks down at me. She blinks. What I'm saying is confusing her, I can tell. For the briefest moment she's scared, but then all at once it goes away, and the hard look is back in her eye like she's a cop on some TV show.

Charlie Lee drops the menu. Then he starts to cry. His shoulders fall, his face reddens, his mouth contorts.

Esmerelda frowns at him and crosses her arms. "So now you're upset," she says. "Good." She spins around, barks, "Asshole," over her shoulder, and walks back into the cabin.

Kang steps out. His fists are at his sides, and he watches Charlie Lee, who just sits, shoulders shaking in loud, moist sobs. Kang inches nearer to him, and I brace myself for what looks like a badass fight. But instead Kang reaches for the knapsack. Even though he's overwrought, Charlie Lee hugs it to his stomach. Hugs it like it's his baby. Kang stands there for a minute, blanches, then turns and goes back into the cabin.

I exhale and slump against the gunwale. If everybody just leaves this guy alone, maybe his killer baggage won't go off, and we'll drop him off and never see him again.

The Birmingham Kid slips the knapsack back over his shoulders. He grabs me by the neck and pulls my face down to meet his. We're nose to nose. Tears blur his eyes.

"They all got out, didn't they, Winthorpe?" he says. "You think they all made it out of there okay, don't you?"

I try to stand, but he holds me down. "I don't know, Charlie Lee. It—it looked like it."

He lets me go, buries his head in his hands, and makes choking sounds. Then he shouts, "God!" a few times; each time I shake like a mofo and almost pee.

And then: "What have I done? Atone! I must atone! I must make this right!"

At midnight Kang anchors in a tree-lined lagoon and cuts the engine. He goes down to check on Seabrook, who has been sleeping most of the day. Kang gives Seabrook more of the Tylenol Esmerelda bought in Crofton and changes the dressing on his wound.

Charlie Lee makes a racket, moaning and talking about how he needs to atone for his sin, how he has offended God and now he needs to do something to make it right.

We pile into the cabin, giving him the deck to pace. Esmerelda drifts off with her head in Arthur's lap, which would have turned the kid into a blithering spaz a couple days ago, but now he just sits there and watches the Birmingham Kid rant.

"She needs to chill," I whisper.

He doesn't react.

"Seriously, man. Who knows what's in that bag? And he was fine before she opened her big fat yap."

Arthur mouths, *I know.*

"So what are we going to do? Wait until he gets tired out and then jump him?" I look at Kang, who sits there and stares at the guy without changing his expression.

We don't jump him. We watch this crazy guy wandering back and forth over the deck. Why have we even stopped? Maybe Kang is thinking he'll go to sleep, and then he can separate him from that bag of his. I don't know.

When I finally drift off, I have another one of those freaky dreams I've been having lately. I'm at a cotillion in a white ballroom with bleached hardwood floors, and the Moms and His Eminence are there.

I am a crab.

His Eminence has donned his tuxedo, and the Moms is in her best gown, a blue number with blazing sequins around the neckline. On the breast pocket of His Eminence's tux is sewn that patch I have in my pocket—the one with the snarling cat face on it. The Moms has a similar patch on the bust of her gown.

A Grizzlies' tune is playing in the background. My fave: "*When the lightning flashes and the thunder rolls, I will not yield. I will stand fast and resolute.*"

All around, people are dancing. High heels, wing tips, and loafers nearly crush me.

When he sees me scuttling across the floor beneath the dancers, His Eminence smiles and lets out a bellow. He runs across the room, pushing dancers out of the way. Finally, he stands over me. When I look up at him, the old man's smile fades to a sneer. He raises his foot and tries to squash me. I dart out of the way just in time. Then Charlie Lee, who's there next to His Eminence wearing a powder-blue tux with big ruffles, tries to step on me. Next, the Moms aims a red leather pump at my head. Soon the whole room of people has stopped dancing—they're all trying to step on me, tap-dancing around me, pouncing at me, and firing lobster pickers in my direction.

All the guests are wearing patches.

I manage to claw my way up onto the banquet table and make it across, swerving to miss silver plates of hors d'oeuvres and champagne glasses. The partygoers stab at me with forks.

When I reach the end of the table, a large rotisserie the 'rents sometimes use for roasting pigs is at the end. Turning on the spit, over and over, is the pink, naked body of Doctor Seabrook.

Then I wake up. Before going to camp I barely ever had dreams, let alone nightmares—but now, minus television, my brain is mush.

It's early morning, and the sky is gray. The lagoon where we anchored the night before is a still pond. Big trees are everywhere, filled with cackling birds that make a dome of sound over the boat.

The radio is hissing and droning away. "*As you can possibly see, I have an injury myself—not here at the hospital, but in combat with a cedar,*" someone says through the static. "*I eventually won. The cedar gave me a little scratch.*"[9]

Arthur and Esmerelda sleep in opposite corners of the cabin. I don't see Kang, but I've never seen him sleep and figure he might be down in the hold with Seabrook.

But where's Charlie Lee? Maybe he took off into those woods, I hope, to "go make things right." Good riddance.

I stretch and cross the deck. We're probably still in Kentucky.

We have to reach another town before long. Maybe I can try the pay phone thing again. But I don't know. The patches. His Eminence's Bitchin' Poster. Now Charlie Lee. Ever get the feeling you're not in on everything?

Something is scattered across the floor in front of the hemp cooker. Miniscule orange filaments spilling from a plastic grocery bag.

As I approach, I realized what it is. After we ate shrimp and boiled potatoes the other night, Kang had gathered the trash into a grocery bag and dropped it in the aft corner of the boat. Someone found the bag, untied it, and dropped the shrimp shells on the deck.

Shellfish are an abomination.

Something pasted to the side of the hemp cooker catches my eye. Someone has smeared a gray plastic lump, about the size and thickness of a brick, across the hemp cooker. Wires protrude from it.

I've seen the gray stuff in at least a hundred movies.

Then Charlie Lee shouts in the woods. His voice, high-pitched and giddy, makes my skin crawl and a flock of birds take flight from the trees overhead.

"God is great!" Charlie Lee's yells. "God is great!"

heroism

For all anybody knows, life really might be a video game. Once somebody's life meter completely depletes, who can say for sure that's the end? After all, few people, if any, have gone into the light and made the U-turn back to reality to explain what's there. Maybe everything goes black for a second, and when the lights come back on, there you are—back on level three with a few less points and weapons but very much alive, at full energy, and with a chance to go for that same obstacle that killed you once before. And maybe this time you're equipped with the know-how to get beyond that obstacle—be it the Kevlar mutant in *Heckenluber* or that zombie with the fireballs in Attack Zombies—and move on to level four, and then higher and higher in the same way until you master the game.

And maybe, using one of those future lives, I would dash for the gob of plastic explosive smeared across the side of the hemp cooker, pluck it off, and throw it into the middle of the lagoon before it explodes, turning the *Tamzene* and all of us into a pile of cinders.

Instead Kang does it.

A second after the Birmingham Kid barks his warnings from the forest, the Indian appears out of nowhere and in one quick motion peals the explosive off the metal casing, thrusts it over his shoulder like a javelin, and hurls it in a steep arc into the center of the lagoon.

"Dern it!" Charlie Lee shouts from somewhere in the woods. "Mr. Injun, you're a lucky son of a gun! I would've blown you to smithereens if this dern detonator worked the way it was supposed to."

Esmerelda and Arthur are up. She has her arms wrapped around

Arthur and is pressing herself—boobs and all—hard against Arthur's PA system.

"All right, don't anybody move, now." The Birmingham Kid jumps up from behind a line of bushes on the bank next to the side of the boat. In his left hand he has an old revolver—what they call in the movies a Colt .45—which he holds at his waist.

"I'm coming back over there, and we're going to try this again, y'all." His voice is tired and worn. He must have been up all night, formulating his plan to atone for his sin in blowing up the Steak Shack, when he'd noticed the bag of shrimp shells.

Carrying his knapsack over his shoulder, Charlie Lee wades into the waste-deep water and climbs aboard the *Tamzene*, pointing the gun at where we've gathered on the deck.

"So, like, where in the Bible does it say anything about waving pistols around at people, Charlie Lee?" Esmerelda growls at him.

Charlie Lee scratches his head with the gun barrel. "The Lord helps those who . . . you've got to help yourself for the Lord . . . Shoot, don't it say something like *Be Prepared*?"

"That's the Boy Scouts," I say.

Charlie Lee shrugs and points the gun at us. "Well, I ain't never had to shoot nobody yet. But don't you think I won't, missy, if y'all try and prevent me from doing the Lord's work. Come here, Winthorpe."

Somebody has pushed an ice cube up my spine. "*Me?*"

"Right," Charlie Lee says. He lifts the backpack from his shoulder and places it on the deck. "I need you to set the explosive for me. I can't do that and hold the gun at the same time. The rest of y'all stand right there."

Hold on to hope, baby . . . no . . . *When the lightning* . . . the songs are whirling faster than the mental iPhone can catch them. I switch to movies—Jason Bourne dodging bullets, Clint Eastwood's Man with No Name fashioning a bulletproof vest out of a piece of scrap metal in *A Fistful of Dollars*.

I kneel and unzip the bag.

"That's it," Charlie Lee says. "Grab a big ol' handful of the gray stuff."

I reach into the bag and wrap my hands around what feels like dry clay. In *Sniper Dude X*, the hero takes a bullet to the forehead and he's still cool enough to make out with the Lizard Girl in the end. I imagine myself heaving the explosive stuff overboard and knocking the pistol out of Charlie Lee's hand.

"Now slather it on the side of that engine there," Charlie Lee says.

Esmerelda looks scared. It would have turned her on big time if I'd had the scrotum to make a move. Next to her, Arthur frowns and shakes his head. Kang never takes his eyes off the Birmingham Kid.

"Come on, son," Charlie Lee says. I look at him over my shoulder and see the gun barrel, and it's like the Wi-Fi hiccupped and everything's frozen, and there's a *Buffering* status report that keeps showing up.

I press the lump against the side of the hemp cooker.

"Attaboy," Charlie Lee says. "Now go on over there with the others."

Still holding his gun on us, Charlie Lee reopens the bag and pulls out long metal pipe cleaners, which he jams into the gray lump. Then he reaches into his pocket and produces a TV remote control.

"All right, y'all," Charlie Lee says, smiling at us. "Here we go again. Now, y'all are going to stay put right there. I'm going back over to the bank where I was. When I holler *God is great*, y'all better hustle off this here boat, or . . . like I say . . . God's will."

He backs toward the gunwales.

"I don't believe this," Esmerelda says. "Charlie Lee, come on, don't you think this is a little crazy? I mean, we're not a restaurant—"

"Crazy?" his eyes flash. "Y'all are the crazy ones! Read your Bible! Y'all ate of the forbidden shellfish, and this here is your judgment day!"

As he moves toward the side, Charlie Lee doesn't notice that Doctor Seabrook has climbed up the retractable stairway from the hold and is now tiptoeing toward him.

Seabrook is still the color of chalk. His mad funny hair juts in wild directions, but his eyes are sharp and clear and trained on the Birmingham Kid. He's holding a fire extinguisher.

"And by my atonement, y'all are gonna atone too. Sorry about that Doctor fella, but someday you'll come to understand that was all a part of God's—*unh!*"

Seabrook punches the back of Charlie Lee's head with the fire extinguisher. The Birmingham Kid grunts and falls into the pile of shrimp shells. When the fire extinguisher makes contact, the shellfish bomber flinches, squeezing the trigger on his Colt .45.

What happens then is in slow motion, like one of the fight scenes in *The Matrix*. The gun snaps, and I hear a whizzing noise, feel the breath of something like a fat dragonfly zipping past, traveling at breakneck speed directly at the person standing next to me—Esmerelda.

But as soon as the gun pops, Arthur dives in front of Esmerelda. The bullet thuds against him, and he crumples in midair and lands on the deck, draped over his PA system.

"Oh, God," Esmerelda breathes.

Arthur lies there, not moving.

"Oh, God," Esmerelda whispers. "Arthur?"

Arthur's pointy shoulder blades make an X through his pit-stained T-shirt.

This one time I saw this video where a woman's husband lost his head in a car accident, and she was left holding the head. She carried it a full city block because she was catatonic. The person making the video asked her what she was thinking, and she said all shaky, "It wasn't real."

This is.

Awful real.

Mad real.

No movie soundtrack violins or cool CGI or somebody screaming *No!* dramatically—the cackling birds, the *flop flop* of water hitting the hull, and the body of the kid I killed because I brought him here.

Burton Trotsky, the other Paste Eaters, and I always talk about going down to South Philly to watch a real-time gunfight. Trotsky, of course, claims he's already seen his share and has even been in a few himself, and that when you're in one it's like major John Woo, with pirouettes and slow-mo.

Trotsky is full of shit, of course. I know it.

Real-time gunfights aren't like that.

Just when I'm sprouting real tears, Arthur stirs. No blood on his shirt. Instead there are pieces of broken metal and plastic all over him and a big crack where the bullet connected with the bullhorn on his PA system.

"Are you all right?" Seabrook asks. He drops the fire extinguisher and kneels beside Arthur.

Arthur winces and rubs his chest. He gives the Doctor a thumbs-up sign.

I must be crying or something, because Seabrook asks me, "Mr. Brubaker, are you all right?"

So I nod, because I am.

"Kick-*ass*, dude," Esmerelda says. She throws her arms around Arthur's shoulders and leans into him, squashing her boobs against his PA system. She presses her face against his.

"You . . . like . . . saved my life, man," she says. "I will . . . *never* . . . forget you as long as I live." She cocks her head and plants her lips squarely on Arthur's. They sit like that for a long time, long enough for Arthur to change three shades of red.

When the kiss is finished, Kang picks Arthur up by the shoulders and gives him a bear hug.

I feel smaller than I ever have. I try to apologize, but I'm too embarrassed.

Esmerelda peels her face off of Arthur's and looks at me. "Hey, stubby," she says, smiling. "What could you do, man? The guy, like, had a gun. *I'm* the one who should feel bad. I told Kang to pick the guy up in the first place."

Seabrook stoops and picks up Charlie Lee's remote control and pistol. Then he goes to the hemp cooker and removes the plastic explosive. He stares at the gray lump in his hands.

"Kang, this would have destroyed my ship," he mutters. Frowning, Kang puts Arthur down.

"No hitchhikers, Kang." Seabrook glares at the Indian. His voice is hoarse, but he's speaking more clearly than he has in days. "We had no choice with the children, but no more hitchhikers." He leans over the hemp cooker, inspecting the blobs of melted and re-cooled metal where the Indian welded the broken machine shut after it crashed into the rock wall during the storm. His frown deepens to a scowl.

"Kang was only trying to help the man out," Esmerelda says. "Somebody was shooting at him."

"We are not in the business of charity," Seabrook says. "There are Green Police agents all over these woods. Side adventures will only sink us. Kang knows this." The wound on his shoulder must have hurt him just then, because he winces and places his hand on it.

"Damn," Seabrook mumbles. "Kang, I told you we needed to buy reinforced steel and patch this fissure. These welds will never hold. Why is it that you refuse to regard my orders?"

Kang bristles.

Just then, Charlie Lee groans. He rubs the back of his scalp, rolls to his side, and forces himself up onto his elbow. He makes a face like he's tasting something sour. Then he sputters and spits something into the palm of his hand.

It's a shrimp shell. When he fell, he must have sucked it into his mouth.

His eyes widen and he howls, then stops when Seabrook stands over him with the pistol.

"Get out of here," Seabrook growls.

The Birmingham Kid's face sags. "Mister, you don't understand! I'm trying to do the Lord's work here and you're . . ."

"The Lord," Seabrook snaps. "The *Lord?*" Spit flies from his mouth and his eyes go buggy. Sentences fly from his mouth like bullets: "*Get out of here now. Do you hear? Nobody is buying what you're selling. We don't want it here, do you understand me?*" His face goes bright red. He jams the pistol into the Birmingham Kid's face.

Seabrook is going to shoot him. He's gone loopy.

Charlie Lee scrambles to his feet, dusts the shrimp shells off his overalls, and walks toward the side of the boat. He turns toward his knapsack to pick it up.

"Leave that," Seabrook growls.

"But it's my property, Mister."

"Leave it," Seabrook says.

Kang grabs the knapsack away from Charlie Lee, who hangs his head and climbs over the side. He throws us all a hate-filled stare as he disappears.

"All right, Kang. Take her out of here—and slowly. We don't want to blow the hemp cooker," Seabrook says.

The engine roars. Charlie Lee shouts from shore: "Y'all ain't heard the last of the Birmingham Kid! I will atone for my sins! And so will all of you!"

As we pull away, I see him jumping up and down at the edge of the bank, face flushed purple.

CHAPTER EIGHTEEN

lydia

Seabrook doesn't speak for a while. He takes us downriver for several hours until it becomes dark, then anchors at the edge of a small island. He grabs the bottle of whiskey Kang was using to clean his wound—it's still almost full—and goes belowdecks, and we don't see him for a while.

When he emerges again, it's late, and Esmerelda, Arthur, and I are all sleeping on the deck. He's walking funny. He falls against the door to the cabin and stumbles, then trips over my feet and faceplants on the deck.

I get up to help him, but he waves me off. He leans against the hemp cooker.

I tiptoe to him. One hand dangles against his hip. In the other he holds his key chain, the one shaped like a crucifix. Between his knees is the whiskey bottle, which has only a splash left. He is staring downriver with his mouth agape.

"You all right?" I ask him.

He straightens up and looks at me hard. "Of course," he says. "You should be sleeping, Mr. Brubaker." Not all of the syllables in *Mr. Brubaker* make it out, but I know what he means.

"Can't sleep," I say.

We sit there listening to the crickets, which sound like one of the space cars from *The Jetsons* whirring away.

"She's not mine, you know" he says finally.

"What?"

"The *Tamzene*. She's not mine. You probably think I invented her, just like you thought I was a doctor. My wife. She did."

"Lydia?"

"Yes. How did you know that?" He shook his head. "Did you know she was a scientist?"

"Kang said something."

Seabrook nodded. "Did he tell you about me?"

"Just that she was a scientist and that she had . . . you know . . ."

"I am—or I was, I mean—a minister. Rev. Doctor Seabrook—the Reverend Doctor they used to call me. First Presbyterian Church in Love Canal, New York."

"When was this?" I ask.

"It was . . . thirty years ago, Mr. Brubaker." He narrows his eyes. "Has it been that long?"

"But you're not anymore," I say.

"No," he murmurs. "Not anymore."

He looks at the inky water rushing past.

"It was a good job. No taxes. Not a big paycheck, but a nice little spread not far from the 99th Street School. Steady. She gave birth to our first child that first year there. We were happy. Even though Lydia didn't believe . . . well, we didn't see eye to eye, needless to say. She was a woman of science. Just like I'm a man of science now. Back then I was a big power-of-prayer guy. *Pray for one another, that you may be healed.* One of those saps—that if you lead a good life and pray hard enough, blah, blah, blah. But the point is, we all loved one another and we respected one another and really—you'll find this out one day— that's all that's important."

He takes a final pull on the whiskey bottle, tipping the bottom straight up in the air, then moves as if he plans to pitch it over the side. Thinking better of it, drops it clattering on the deck.

I try to imagine him as a dad, with one of those wicked black-and-white collar deals, a wife at his side, and a baby in his arms. It isn't easy, but then it isn't easy to picture His Eminence as a dad either.

"But the *Tamzene* is hers. I just thought you should know. We'll tell your dad. Okay? It's her boat. She made it." He grabs my shoulder so hard I'm sure there'll be a bruise. It's the closest thing to a tender gesture I've ever seen him make. It just hurts, that's all.

He half smiles and looks back downriver. "She wasn't one of the first to get sick. By that time, everybody knew what was what. People were dying. They were dumping toxic waste. Occidental Petroleum had been dumping there since the '40s. Lydia knew all about it. She'd grown up in Love Canal. I was from Indiana. She knew it wasn't safe."

He rubs his eyes. He hasn't shaved in days, and his muttonchops have dribbled fragments of hair across his chin. The skin is still all chalky.

"She wanted to move," he says. His voice is thick and rasping. "I told her that my flock was there and that we had to stay. Jeffrey was going to start kindergarten soon. The falls were right there—Niagara Falls, you know. One of the most beautiful places on earth. Everything just seemed sort of set. But she *knew*." He grimaces. His voice becomes very sharp. "She knew and she stood by me because even though she didn't believe . . .

"She knew about the cancer before she *knew*. Before the doctors knew, she knew. I told her she was crazy, that God wouldn't cut down someone like her. Someone who was out working in her office all day and night trying to come up with better ways of living life on this planet. And then she got sick, and I told her still, God wouldn't. That God was just testing her, and if she believed, she'd be okay. So she said she believed."

He looks at me, his eyes wide with fear. "Because of me, she gave up all her work and started coming with me to church, started praying and wearing her crucifix." He holds up his key chain. "And I knew God wouldn't take her away because we both had faith and we both prayed so hard, and even as she got sicker and sicker we prayed. In fact, the sicker she got, the harder we prayed, and the more we believed she was going to be okay." His voice has been getting louder, but a wet choke stifles it.

"Religion makes people do fucked up things, Mr. Brubaker," he mutters after a moment. "It wasn't until after she died that I realized she'd been praying for *me* the whole time. To make *me* feel better. It was all my fault. She'd wanted to move, and I wanted to stay put."

He sighs. His eyes have become moist and his breathing rattles. "That should have been enough. That should have been it, Mr. Brubaker." He taps the bald part of his head. "Any sane person would have moved out of there after his wife died. But I wasn't sane. I was a man of God, Mr. Brubaker. Men of God are not sane. So we stayed, Jeffrey and me, in our little house near the 99th Street School. We read from Job: *The Lord blessed the latter part of Job's life more than the first. He had fourteen thousand sheep, six thousand camels, a thousand yoke of oxen, and a thousand donkeys.* All that stuff, you know. It helped. He was going to start kindergarten in the fall. But they diagnosed him that summer and I had to keep him out."

He buries his face into the crook of his arm for a moment. But when he raises his head, I don't see tears. His face is tight and angry. "Of course I prayed even harder then. Prayed that God would make him better again. Prayed that God would take the cancer out of him and put it into me. And the sicker he got, the more we both believed. He died November 12th, 1980. And I didn't know until then that it was all bullshit."

We sit in silence. I wonder if the others are awake listening to this.

"The *Tamzene*, her design for the hemp burning system, the design of the boat, was all just notes then, an idea Lydia had been scribbling on napkins and the backs of old bank statements. I found it in the garage in a box of her old stuff. The first thing I found was a picture she'd drawn. A picture of this." He put his palm on the hemp cooker. "It took me years to piece it all together. For every equation I found written on the back of an old receipt, I found I had another book to read—high school chemistry books, then books on thermal dynamics and finite math, and then really obscure complicated stuff sometimes written in Arabic that I had to translate. Then the image began to take shape. The boat. Lydia's boat."

"You're a man of science now," I say with conviction.

Seabrook nods. "I resigned the day after Jeffrey died. Burnt all of my books, Bibles, robes, crosses, and all the other paraphernalia in a big bonfire in the front yard. Abandoned the house. Hitchhiked out of town. They probably don't know to this day what happened to me. I took a bus back to my parents' in Indiana. I've devoted myself this past thirty years to finishing Lydia's work. So I guess I am a man of science now. She was right and I was wrong, you see. God couldn't save her. There is no God. People say there's a God because it absolves them of making their own decisions. Because they don't believe in themselves, they have to believe in *something*. There's no basis for it. I was too stupid to realize this before it was too late. Remember that, Mr. Brubaker. The *Tamzene* is a testament to that."

He raps on the cooker and it echoes because it's empty. "When we get to California, with your dad's help, we'll prove she was right all along."

"But you still carry that crucifix."

He looks at it and frowns. "It was hers. I just . . ."

We sit silently for a while.

"So I guess that's why you were so wigged out about the Birmingham Kid, then," I say.

He's still looking at the crucifix. "No," he says.

"Well, then what was up back there?"

"I was losing my mind, Mr. Brubaker," he says. "I'm all right now." Again he looks at the river. "Thirty years," he breathes. "Thirty years and you still scratch at it like an amputee at a lost leg in the middle of the night. I was losing my mind because when I was in the hold there I actually did it again. I was at the end of my rope."

"Did what?"

"Prayed," he says hollowly.

PART FOUR

Megapixels

"America is addicted to wars of distraction."

—Barbara Ehrenreich

CHAPTER NINETEEN

murder of crows

The murder of crows wanted to attack the white boats.

Three white boats in a row were anchored at the edge the lake where the crows lived. Men whose uniforms matched the color of the crows' feathers climbed around the boats' decks.

The white boats had been killing the crows. They took liquid from the ground and ate it. It came back up again in poisonous burps that billowed into clouds over the cities. Many crows died. Many young crows died in childbirth.

Crows are great listeners. They hide in branches, silence their cawing, and become shadows. They gather secrets into their great wings and fly over the cities, ominous as smoke.

This murder of crows had heard the stories: upriver, elsewhere, animals had begun attacking men.

Crows had never been ones to take orders. But a thought had occurred to them. It came uniformly in a way thoughts seldom come to crows.

Don't attack, the thought seemed to say. *Listen.*

So the murder of crows became shadows in the trees over the white boats and listened to their secrets.

Soon some of the men in black cut through the trees. Another man, not in black, was with them. The men in black dragged the other man along.

They made their prisoner sit on the deck of one of the boats. A man in black stood over him, menacing him with a gun.

They stayed that way for a long time, not saying anything. Finally another man in black emerged onto the deck.

"What is it you call yourself again, Mr. Bowden?" the man who'd emerged said. He carried a stack of tree skins.

"I call myself Charlie Lee," Bowden said. "Folks give me my nickname. Folks who appreciate the things I do in the name of the Lord."

"And that is?"

"They call me the Birmingham Kid."

The man paged through his stack of tree skins. "Religious zealotry. Explosives expert. Hatred of shellfish. Interesting. What were you doing there, Mr. Bowden?"

"I was looking for somebody."

"Awful long way for you to come looking for a seafood restaurant." The sitting man twisted his head from side to side. "Nope."

"No need to lie, Mr. Bowden. You're among friends here."

"I take pride in what I do, boy. I was looking for a boat."

"What boat?"

"Funny lookin' thing. Sets up on wheels that can drive over dry land. Jimmy Carter is the figurehead. Run by a bald limey, an Injun, and three youngins."

"The *Tamzene*?"

"That's the one. Them that's on it is the most sinful pack of so-and-sos I ever did run across. And I must atone for my sins with the Steak Shack in Crofton, Kentucky. They're gonna be smote to pay for my sins."

"You were aboard the *Tamzene*?"

"O-o-oh. Y'all were looking for it too? I knew the police must've been after them. They had a man shot and weren't taking him to no doctor—and not because modern medicine is a sin, neither. Yessir, I been aboard the *Tamzene*. Been tracking her downriver. And when I catch her, I'm gonna blow her to smithereens in the name of Jesus Christ, our Lord."

"Do you know where they're headed?"

"They're headed in the direction this boat's going in," Bowden said. "I sure as shootin' talked to them. I thought they were a Christian lot because they took me on board, and one of the young ones looked like he might be a member of the Holy Warriors of Jesus Church since he was carrying the patch with the cat face on it."

The man in black made a motion the crows couldn't see. "This one?"

"That's the one."

"Says here you were a member of the Holy Warriors of Jesus Church. Church of the Reverend Harlan Spikes?"

"Harlan Spikes," Bowden said. "Wonderful God-fearing man. He's the one who taught me and the rest of them about how your body can be a vessel for God's will. Eric Rudolph was his star pupil. We all aspire to—"

"What happened aboard the *Tamzene*?"

"Why, they're nothing but sinners there. Bunch of shellfish eaters. I done tried to do the Lord's work, and they stopped me. Took my bombs. Thought they got the best of me. But the Lord will smite them yet. By my hands too."

"You say somebody aboard the *Tamzene* had one of these?"

"Yessir. A boy. Winthorpe. I thought that . . ."

Another man in black appeared on deck. He whispered something to the other man.

"Give us a minute, will you, Mr. Bowden?"

Both men disappeared into the cabin.

Minutes passed. The crows waited, silent as shadows.

Both men stepped outside the door and stood next to the cabin. One waved his hands rapidly.

". . . can't in good conscience," he said. "I'm mean, but Christ, the guy's a fucking psychopath."

"But high functioning, right?"

"You mean to say you agree with this horseshit?"

Neither man said anything for a long time.

"He's one of Harlan Spikes' boys. A guerilla fighter."

"He's a psycho."

"Orders are orders."

One man in black let out a long sigh. Both men stood in front of Bowden.

"Charlie Lee Bowden," he said, "our orders are to take you to the nearest town and procure for you the best small boat money can buy. We're going to outfit you with as much plastique as said boat can carry. Then you're going to find the *Tamzene*. And . . . I've got a personal message for you from Rev. Spikes."

Bowden blinks. "You do?"

"*Keep up the good work. The Lord will reserve for you a special seat at the supper of the lamb.*"

Bowden's face breaks into a smile. "Well, I'll be," he says. "I certainly will be."

noise

An explosion awakens me.

The sky is still grayish pink. The loud snap echoes and wigs out the birds. They swarm out of the trees.

The forest is a canopy over the boat. Through the branches I can make out a few houses on shore. Is it the Green Police or Charlie Lee shooting at us? When I search the deck I see Kang and Seabrook on their knees, peering over the gunwales.

A rattling noise follows the bang. The trees roar, and the sky is suddenly filled with birds.

A man appears next to one of the houses. He rattles the inside of a pot with a ladle, and each time it clanks, birds scatter.

"What's he doing?" I ask Seabrook.

The Reverend Doctor is pale, his eyes blazing red. He leans against the side and rubs his temples. "I don't know. Scaring the birds, it looks like."

"Why are there so many of them?"

He looks skyward, but keeps both palms planted on his temples. "They look like grackles," he says.

"Where are we now, Doctor?" I ask.

"Missouri," he says. "But I'm not exactly sure where. My GPS locator doesn't seem to be getting a signal here. I think it's safe to go ask the gentleman where we are, Mr. Brubaker."

Arthur and Esmerelda are sleeping in the aft end. The two of them have been whispering and giggling lately. I'm right back where I was at Primrose, people. Arthur's the one she likes. Why does Arthur get all the chances to be cool, saving her life and everything?

So I make it a solo mission. I wade through the shallow river, which comes up to about my waist. When I'm about halfway through, another firecracker goes off and I fall in, soaking myself.

"Hey, you all right there?" yells the man from the shore. He's an old-timer with gray hair. He lets the pot and ladle slip from his hands.

I sputter and drag myself through the water the rest of the way toward shore.

"Sorry," the man says. "I didn't see you." He looks up. Birds are zooming everywhere, and the trees are still cheering. They look like pepper flowing through milk.

"Damn birds," the man says. "They make a god-awful mess. I've never seen anything like it."

"Why are there so many?"

He shrugs. "I read something about it in the newspaper. Weather is haywire this year. Usually they fly further south this time of year, but it's so warm here. Seems to get warmer all the time. They roost in the trees and sh"—he glances at me—"poop all over everything. That's why I got my boy out front with the firecrackers. And I bang these pots and pans. Beats cleaning bird poop."

While he talks the birds settle down. He bends, picks up the pot and ladle, and starts banging away again.

"What's the nearest town?" I yell.

"What did you say?" he shouts back.

"The nearest town!"

He stops clanging. The birds are mad loud. He tells me that if I follow the river about twenty miles or so, I'll reach the town of Blysse.

"But don't . . ." Another firecracker goes off in the front yard, so I miss what he says. I thank him and go back to the boat.

* * *

Back home the Paste Eaters are the most dependable guys I know. They're constant: other than a handful of righteous bands, movies, and video games, everyone and everything is *weak, rank* or, as Burton Trotsky says, *Dickensian.* Pep rally bonfires? *Gay.* Good grades in school? *Lame.* Dating a hot cheerleader? *Please, dude.*

Above all, one Paste Eater would never betray another—certainly not over a girl. Not that there ever was a girl, but I always assumed . . .

Arthur is no Paste Eater. He and Esmerelda stay in the back corner of the boat as we start heading downriver again. They lean against the back of the boat, Arthur scratching things on his pad, and Esmerelda giggling. When I come near, they both clam up. It makes me sick.

Beneath the humming from the hemp cooker is a new noise: a clattering sound. The giant pistons jut back and forth as always, thrusting the boat along, but now they're sputtering and steam is rising from them.

Seabrook looks at the engine and clicks his tongue. He holds a thermometer against the cooker, reads it, and shakes his head.

"They won't hold," he mutters.

The CB radio buzzes softly: "*Human beings are the primary species on this planet. Animals and everything else are subspecies whose position is subordinate to that of humans.*"[10]

Even though it's spazzing, the hemp cooker still needs to be refilled. And who does that? Yourstruly, of course. I march up and down the steps all by myself while Arthur and the chick sit back there and canoodle. Seabrook and Kang aren't talking much either, so neither of them tell the lovebirds to give me a hand.

"Mute Betrayer" is the name of the first song I compose that morning, and at its center is this searing guitar solo that would literally make concert-goers' ears burst into flames. Then I write an acoustic ballad called "Shrub Girl Gone" that gives me the misties. The Vienna Boys Choir is just starting its accompaniment on the refrain when Arthur appears at the top of the retractable stairway, grinning like the cat from *Alice in Wonderland.*

"What's your deal?" I say, passing him and dumping a bag into the hemp cooker.

When I return to the staircase, he's still standing there, same stupid grin wiped all over his face. He holds out his pad for me to take: *Need a little help?!* A curved line under the punctuation makes a smiley face.

I shove the pad back at him and go down into the hold. I say, "What's the point? It's almost done now. Where were you five minutes ago?"

I grab another bag of hemp off the pile, and when I turn, Arthur is there. He's still smiling, but it's eroded a little around the edges, and his eyes look somewhat concerned. Again he holds the pad out for me.

I sigh and throw the bag to the ground. "I'm never going to get done if I have to stop to read shit all the time. *Rain Man* was less of a hassle than you."

I read: *I've been thinking. Maybe we could bring Esmerelda along with us to the Grizzlies show. She's pretty street-smart, and there's safety in numbers after all.*

The words swim on the page. Just the day before, I squirted tears of frigging happiness that he'd survived a gunshot. Now I'm all alone again.

"I've planned this in great detail, Arthur. And now just because you got yourself a bitch, you're going to fuck the whole thing up."

He frowns at me.

"Look, I don't need this, Arthur. She's not even a Grizzlies disciple, man. She dissed the Greatest Band on Earth, and if we're going to this thing together then I want us to be pure. It was supposed to be just you and me, but hey, if that ho is more important to you than us Grizz-heads, suit yourself."

I don't wait for him to react. I stoop, pick up the sack of hemp, and start up the stairs. My eyes water as I tear open the bag and dump it into the cooker.

It isn't like he's doing anything wrong, people. I know that. Arthur isn't a bad dude. I'm being a prick—because, well, the hottie wants him and not me. I've been working my ass off to get her to notice me.

Like all chicks, she has not yet developed a palate discerning enough for the taste of Winthrop. But that's not Arthur's fault.

I decide to find Arthur and talk with him—not to apologize exactly, but Arthur held out an olive branch, and I'll be big enough to take it.

But then I hear him giggling again and I change my mind. *Artherelda* is back in the corner again, all draped over one another. Arthur is flushed pinker than the Pink Power Ranger. I figure they're laughing at me, so now I'm really burning.

I sweep the deck. When I get up close, I shove a great big cloud of dust all over them.

Esmerelda stands, coughing. She dusts off her AC/DC T-shirt. Arthur glares at me.

"Sorry," I say. "Maybe if I didn't have to do all the work around here myself I might not make so many mistakes."

"Like, what the hell, stubby?" Esmerelda growls. "You've been stomping around here like a goon since this morning. What's bunching your thong?"

"Nothing's wrong at all, Esmerelda. It might be better form if you two got a room, is all."

Her mouth falls open and her eyes smolder. Then she smiles and clicks her tongue. She looks to be about thirty years old just now, and it makes me uneasy. I move away.

She follows me. "Winthrop, like, what's your problem, man?"

I keep sweeping. "I don't have problem. I just don't like the idea of you tagging along to the Grizzlies show when just a little while ago you were dissing them."

"Look, I'm not going to put down your precious Grizzlies anymore. I mean, hello? It's just a rock 'n' roll band."

"That's what I'm talking about. Just a rock 'n' roll band."

She snorts and puts her hand on my arm. "Okay, okay," she says. "Look, I just obviously don't take that stuff as seriously as you do. I'm not going to say anything bad about them anymore. All right?"

I look at the chewed-up fingernails grasping the turtleneck. "I don't think we should be going to California with someone who doesn't take the band seriously."

"Winthrop, why do you, like, hate me? What the fuck have I ever done to you, man? Are you jealous or something?"

"No!"

"Well then, why . . ."

"Forget it," I say. "At the next town, let's all just go our separate ways, okay, Arthur?" I want them to beg to come along.

Arthur frowns and shakes his head.

"Look, I don't need this," I say. "You guys don't follow me from here on in, all right?"

"You're a whiny little prick, aren't you?" Esmerelda growls.

You're not supposed to hit chicks. Movies tell you that women are supposed to be weaker, softer, and protected like babies or an endangered species—even the ones with big biceps who look like they could unwrap and eat a man like a Hershey's Kiss.

Video games contradict that, though. In *Heckenluber* the female ninjas like Jade kick some serious ass, and I can punch women in the head, only to have them pummel me with throwing stars.

And Esmerelda is a good head taller than me.

"Shut up," I mutter. I go back to sweeping the deck.

Esmerelda opens her mouth to say something else when Seabrook shouts from the cabin: "We're coming up on something, ladies and gentlemen. Looks like it could be that town, Blysse, Mr. Brubaker. Get Kang and tell him we're pulling in."

Around a bend in the small creek, I see wooden docks poking out from the shore. The trees part, and there are a handful of rowboats bobbing up and down in the current. A whitewashed marina hugs the rear of the docks. From its empty parking lot, a road climbs up a stone and dirt embankment and disappears over a hill. I can't see over the embankment to the rest of the town.

The Reverend Doctor guides the boat past the town and down river for about three miles. Then he anchors on the bottom side of a small island.

The engine hisses and makes popping sounds as Seabrook shuts it off. He darts from the cabin to the aft side, stands before the engine, and clasps and unclasps his hands. When it stops, finally, he exhales.

"You're not coming?" Seabrook smiles at Arthur and Esmerelda when he sees them huddled in their corner.

"No, Doc," Esmerelda avoids his gaze. "We figured we'd hang back and watch the boat."

Bastards.

The radio cackles: "*We're out to kill the fuckers. We're simply trying to eliminate them. Our goal is to destroy environmentalism once and for all.*"[11]

Kang, Seabrook, and I wade through the shallow river to the opposite bank and climb up the flat rocks and into the forest. We hike upriver through the woods until we come upon a single-lane dirt road that winds past the trees in the direction of the town.

By this time, the clouds have piled in and weigh heavily on us as we march down the road, stones crunching beneath our feet. The weeds on both sides are tall, and bees and crickets pulse within them. No one says a word.

The road turns back and forth. Eventually, over the crest of a hill, we come upon a fallen tree. It's an oak, gigantic and leafless, and it forms a waist-high barrier across the road.

Seabrook frowns as he approaches it. He studies the tree, placing his hand on its side. Then he marches into the woods and looks at the part of the tree that's still poking up from the ground.

"There's moss growing in that stump," he says. "This must have happened months ago."

"So?" I mumble. I don't care. I stare at my Timberlands and let the wind from the incoming storm cool the sweat on my scalp. Back at the boat, Arthur is getting some. *Little son of a bitch.*

"So this road isn't navigable, Mr. Brubaker. Why would someone just leave this here?"

Behind Seabrook, the forest floor is strewn with the corpses of fallen trees, snapped from their roots and left to rot.

"Evidently there was a storm of some sort," Seabrook says. "And yet no one has cleared the mess."

Rain begins to fall, and the sky rumbles. We march faster down the winding road. Bolts of lightning knife through the clouds, and then the storm really kicks into gear, lashing us with hard sheets of rain.

Finally, up a long stone driveway, the dormers of a farmhouse gape at us. A tin-roof barn stands next to it. We run up the driveway through the rain, sloshing through mud puddles. A screen porch wraps around the first floor of the farmhouse, and the door to it is unlocked. We go inside and stand dripping on the gray porch planks. Rain roars on the roof.

The porch is wide, with a pair of wicker chairs and a few wicker tables strewn about. Everything is gray, like a worn photograph, beneath a thin layer of dirt. Hanging from the eaves are potted plants held up by chains. The plants have long since died, and the brown curled leaves look like pubic hair. One pot has fallen and formed a mound of shards and black dirt.

"I suppose we should go introduce ourselves," Seabrook says when no one comes to the front door. It's made of wood and glass and looks in on a kitchen with a linoleum floor. White lace curtains bracket the view.

Kang raps on the door. Minutes tick past. No one answers.

"I guess nobody's home," I say.

Seabrook is still frowning. "Has it been abandoned?" Stepping in front of Kang, he tries the knob. It turns, and he pushes the door open.

"Hey," I say, "what if you're wrong and it's not abandoned, and old Farmer Brown comes back? We'd be able to explain ourselves a lot better if we're standing on the porch, not . . ."

That's when the smell hits me. It's worse than dumpsters behind the lunchroom at the Primrose School, a sharp smell I want out of my nose the minute it enters.

The Reverend Doctor's heavy eyebrows push hard on the tops of his eyes. "Stay here," he says.

Kang and Seabrook walk into the house and leave the door ajar. I move as far away as I can from the smell, stepping around to the op-posite end of the porch. The rain is turning the driveway into a brown river, and at its end, the winding road where we'd been marching is no longer visible. I watch the rain. I wonder if Esmerelda and Arthur have to go belowdecks to do their thing among the bags of hemp. How does it feel to be next to her, to touch her, to feel her breath on your face?

After a while Kang and Seabrook reemerge. Seabrook holds a handkerchief to his face. Kang's cheeks shine with tears.

"Abandoned." Seabrook says. "Long ago. They left the larder full and the refrigerator stocked, and then someone shut the power off. They must have left in a hurry. And I believe they may once have had a pet of some sort—the husk of something lying in their living room."

It doesn't take long for the rain to fade to a drizzle, but it isn't soon enough for me. When at last I can see the road again, I burst from the porch. The screen door slaps behind me. We make our way down the driveway and back to the road to town.

"I don't get it, Doctor," I say. "Why would they just abandon their house like that? With a full fridge and a cat or dog or whatever just left to die?"

"Who knows, Mr. Brubaker," Seabrook mutters.

A few hundred yards from the house, the road turns into a steep hill. On both its sides, thick yellow weeds blow back and forth. I breathe deeply through my nose, letting the musty wet concrete smell of the rain replace the rotten odor from the abandoned farmhouse. At the foot of this hill sits the town we passed on the creek.

Or what's left of it.

The town has three long streets bisected by several alleys. Here and there brick and concrete houses poke skyward, but their roofs have collapsed. It looks a bit like that movie *Stalingrad*, where what's left of a few walls make right corners where there might once have been buildings, and you can see the grid pattern of the streets.

Mostly, however, it's a pile of broken brick, glass, board, and rubble.

blysse

A baby cries. Nothing else in Blysse makes a sound, except the *drip-drip* of a busted pipe and the *snap-crackle-pop* of a bare wire. Heaps of rubble and broken glass lean over the streets.

It's total bullshit, people, that after so much time in the woods dicking around with the trees, the first town without pot fields or Shrub People or seafood restaurant bombers is a pile of garbage. I know what irony is. We studied it in English. I hope God is laughing his ass off.

Here and there, a house has been spared from whatever smoked this place—Bricker's Hardware Store and Home Cookin' Diner haven't been touched. But their windows are dark.

I look around for the bawling baby, which turns out to be a hunk of metal moving around on its hinges—a weather vane. It must have once been on top of a building; it's now lying on its side near a tall mound of stone, held to a slab of roof shingles by a black iron rod nearly as tall as me. The cast metal figure of a knight on horseback forms the working portion of the weather vane, his lance pointing in the direction of the wind. Written in raised type on the knight's cape are the words: *Town of Blysse, Mo., Est. 1855.*

Nothing moves. Rats and snakes and creepy-crawlies probably live in the big piles, but they aren't moving. Only the weather vane bawls.

"What the hell happened?" I say. My voice sounds loud.

"Had to be a tornado," Seabrook says. "You can see the winding path it took."

All I can see are piles of debris leaning—and in some cases spilling—

over the road. The foundations of buildings still stand, and inside are couches, desks, and broken TVs. Poles and bits of wire mark where there were once traffic signals and streetlights. Reams of paper curl and dance in the breeze.

"What happened to the people?" I ask. It's like that old-school *Star Trek* episode where Kirk and the gang beam down to the planet and find buildings and electricity and stuff, but all the people are gone. Only they're not gone—they're just moving so fast you can't see them.

"Most likely they've evacuated." Seabrook stops walking. A blue-and-white striped couch with a University of Missouri throw blanket still draped across it sits on the sidewalk in front of him, just sitting there like it was put there on purpose. Seabrook sits on it. "Odd that they'd abandon their town instead of rebuilding, right?"

"Maybe there's somebody left," I say. "Some of the houses are still standing."

"Well, there was that hardware store in the center of town," Seabrook says. "Maybe they know of a lumber store nearby or might be able to help us find steel plates for the cooker."

The bell to Bricker's Hardware's front door jingles. Sunlight pours through the front window and makes long shadows on two rows of dust-covered boxes of nails and power tools. As the door swings shut, dust kittens scurry across the tile floor.

"Hello?" Seabrook calls, but the empty store swallows his voice. On one side, one set of shelves has collapsed onto another, spilling hammers and wood saws. No one is here. If it was a Toys 'R' Us or an FAO Schwartz, people, I would have shopping-spreed the Xbox department.

On the opposite end of the store is a lone checkout counter. Pasted on it are canceled checks from deadbeats who have bounced them, beneath a sign that reads: *Do not—even under fear of death—accept a check from.* A University of Missouri mug stuffed with pens sits next to an electric cash register. Digital zeros glow on the money display.

"Well, power is coming from somewhere," Seabrook says.

An electric buzzer sits in front of the register. Seabrook tries it three times, leaning on the button. A metallic buzzing noise sounds from somewhere in the back of the store.

Seabrook shrugs. "Let's try the diner across the street."

The Home Cookin' Diner is a metallic trailer with parking spaces in front. Inside, all the booths are empty. The giant vapor lamps over the grill are off, and no one is behind the counter.

Seabrook sits on one of the stools. "This is the damnedest thing I've ever seen," he mutters. "When there's a tornado, there are usually people around picking up the pieces afterward, right?"

"Maybe everyone died?" I offer.

"Impossible. Even in the most violent storm, only a small percentage of the population actually dies, Mr. Brubaker."

Kang makes signs at Seabrook.

Seabrook nods. "Yes, I suppose we could look through the wreckage to see what we might be able to salvage to fix the hemp cooker."

The sun is beginning to warm Blysse, and steam rises from the puddles. Seabrook selects a big pile, and we dig through the dissolving fragments of shredded wood and insulation in search of steel.

I'm still freaking on Arthur and Esmerelda. In 9½ Weeks, Kim Bassinger's were pointy like lightsabers. I imagine Arthur having mad skills, doing all kinds of porno-sexy moves on Esmerelda with Seabrook's refrigerated produce and Salisbury steak packets. Sweat gathers above my lips, and I fling a brick behind me with as much force as I can muster.

"What do you want?"

A voice from Bricker's Hardware bounces off the heaps. It's loud as hell and scares the crap out of me.

A woman stands in the doorway. She has one of those big schoolteacher 'dos, a monster hairsprayed fro, but it's drooping to her shoulders, and long matted tangles poke out of it. She wears bulging jeans and a flannel shirt. Her arms are crossed and her eyes are bloodshot all to hell, like we've woken her up.

No one says a word.

"I said," she snaps, "what do you people want? I ain't got all day."

"I beg your pardon," Seabrook says. "We're looking for . . . ma'am, what happened here?"

The woman rolls her bloodshot eyes and kicks the ground. "Y'know what, mister. I ain't missin' my turn for this. Y'all keep jawing at me and are gonna cost me my turn. Why don't you just take whatever the hell you want to and then git?"

She spins around and marches into the store.

"Ma'am?" Seabrook offers again. He hurries after her into the store. Kang and I go after him.

The woman whisks past the cash register and heads through a door at the rear, closing it behind her. Seabrook tries the knob, but it's locked. He mutters something about the possibility of a rear entrance, so we walk out the front door and go around to the back.

The woman is walking down the center of the street, picking her way over the fallen buildings. When she looks over her shoulder at us, she looks pissed and hustles.

We follow. She weaves and trips her way up the street. Soon she reaches one of the few buildings that's been left intact: a large cinder block building with Roman columns. On a cast-iron sign above the door are the words *Blysse City Courthouse*. The woman scrambles up the steps and disappears into the long shadows created by the columns.

We stop at the foot of the steps.

"What's her deal?" I ask.

Seabrook turns. "Perhaps we'd best get back to the boat," he mutters, and starts back down the street. Kang follows.

"Hey, what's the matter?" I stand there and watch them going. Seabrook trips over a mound of debris, but picks himself up and scrambles on.

"The city courthouse is a government institution," he barks over his shoulder. "It's probably best not to . . ."

"You there. Stop."

Seabrook and Kang freeze.

The voice echoes from within the shadows of the columns. Two men emerge and walk down the steps. One is small and shaped like a bullet. The other is taller, clad in a flannel shirt, bib overalls, and a mesh John Deere baseball cap.

Both men hold hunting rifles.

Ever fantasize about what you'd do if somebody held a gun on you? Up until a few days ago, I always believed that if mugger or somebody threatened me with a piece, I'd poke out my chest and, at just the right moment, swing for the gun and run off. After all, how many baddies fire tons of shots at Sniper Dude X? And he's barely been grazed.

Now I know different. I've been held at gunpoint two times in the past few days, so I know: Michael Bay has it all wrong, people. Adrenaline doesn't make you pirouette and freeze in midair. All you do is stand there and hope you don't get killed.

"Okay," I manage. "Okay, man."

The gun barrels peer at me as the men draw closer. I don't want to make a move that might flip them out, so I pull my hands in. I start scratching the right front pocket of my shorts.

Both men speak to me through long beards and look at me with glazed red eyes. Have they been drinking? Smoking a J? They look like they haven't slept in weeks. The tall one spits a stream of tobacco juice at my feet. The stocky one points his gun at Kang and Seabrook.

"Get over here," he snaps in a high-pitched voice.

"Who are ya and what's your business here?" the tall one says. He is all bones. The flannel shirt he wears hangs from his shoulders and gathers around his midsection as if there's nothing there but air.

I keep rubbing my pocket. Beneath my fingers I feel the patch with the cat face. I stare at the tall man's red eyes. They're somewhere else. They're not alive.

"Our boat," Seabrook says loudly, not looking at the tall man, "was damaged during a storm. We're looking for scrap metal to make some repairs."

The man stares at Seabrook through his half-lidded eyes for what seems like minutes. There's no noise but the soft whimper of the weather vane's metal hinge.

"What boat?" he says. "Where is it?"

Seabrook frowns, and I can tell the tall man's eyes have thrown him off his game. "We slammed into some rocks and parked it about ten miles upstream from here. Perhaps you could let us know where we might find some scrap metal, and then we'll be on our way."

The man says nothing. His red eyes stare. They're a painting. His skin doesn't look like skin at all—plaster of Paris, or maybe bone.

Seabrook looks at the ground. So does Kang.

"Hurry it up, Roy," the stocky one says. He shifts his weight from side to side and winces. "We're going to miss our turn if you don't watch it."

"What are y'all doin' out on a boat near Blysse?" says the tall one.

Seabrook says nothing for a moment, and the tall one jabs him lightly with the gun. "You can answer," he says.

Seabrook looks him in the eye and freezes. "Fishing," he breathes.

For another long moment there's no noise. The weather vane whimpers in the dying breeze. A newspaper flutters past. The short man shuffles in place. The tall man continues to hold Seabrook in his stare.

"Ain't no more of you, are there?" the tall man asks. "It's just the three of you?"

Seabrook nods.

The man says nothing. He raises a calloused finger and buries it into his beard, scratching some part of his face. Then he clutches his rifle and presses it firmly against his shoulder.

"Good," he says, cocking the gun. "Then all there is to take care of is y'all."

Seabrook's jaw unhinges. He backs away. He loses his footing on a heap of stone and falls on his back. Kang's eyes flash, but he stands frozen.

The short one grabs me by what's left of my turtleneck, pressing the barrel of his gun into my chest. Movies suddenly dissolve. Even the Grizzlies seem hollow. *Hold on to hope, baby . . .* What hope? What do you hold on to when there is no hope?

The tall one clicks the lever on the rifle backward, cocking it.

"What's in your pocket, boy?" the short man screeches. "Out with it. What you got there?"

"It's nothing," I say. I dig into my pocket and pull out the snarling cat patch. I hold it up for the short man to see.

The short man releases his grip and stumbles backward. His red eyes blink.

"Why, you're . . ." he starts. "You're . . . Hey, Roy! Take a look!"

The tall one glances over his shoulder and instantly relaxes his rifle. A hollow black space appears beneath his beard as his mouth hangs open.

"It's you," he murmurs. "Well, why din't you say nothing? You come to fix it, didn't you?"

Both men lower their rifles. The short one grins. "Well, c'mon. Maybe you can fix her before my turn," he says.

They start up the steps and beckon us to follow.

CHAPTER TWENTY-ONE

the winds

The winds never knew the name of the towns through which they blew. They only knew that here in the flat part of the country, they could whip with ease through the canyons of brick and metal and stone the men built, carrying paper and hats and kites and voices away in their arms.

When the snow melted and the ice receded every year, the winds in this part of the world wreaked havoc, sometimes turning over and over on themselves until they became what they sometimes heard the snatches of voices they carried call *Fingers of God*.

Spring had passed. It was not the season for the Fingers of God. But when the thought came, they rose from lazy summer slumber and chased one another round and round until they formed a point.

The point plowed northwest through forest and fields until it sliced into the town. It uprooted houses, consumed buildings, livestock, trees, and gardens. It cut into stone and blacktop until it reached the place the thought had ordained.

It meant nothing to the wind—just another of the stone boxes men build. It had seen stronger and it had seen much weaker. But the thought had ordained this place, so the winds went round and round and round and round, faster and faster.

The stone box did not budge, so the Finger of God rolled onward until it died.

Amid the wreckage of the town, the stone box was one of few surviving structures.

And what was inside remained unharmed.

george romero

Seabrook was right about the tornado. Roy says it was a category F-5 bastard that started out in Alabama and burrowed its way northwest. It took a right around Memphis and tore into Missouri, hugging Pemiscott, Butler, Carter, and Oregon counties before it hit its first town: Blysse. It roared through at about two a.m., leveling nearly everything in its path, and withered and died almost immediately after exiting the city limits.

No one in Blysse died in the tornado, Roy says.

The first things we see when he leads us in through the front doors are large storage containers stacked to the ceiling of the lobby. They're piled between the receptionists' desks and copy machines and take up most of the first floor. Some are marked *Campbell's Tomato Soup*, others *Bounty Paper Towels* and *Ramen Noodles*.

"Come on," says Horace, the short one. He leads us up a flight of steps lined with boxes of toiletries and Deer Park water.

The staircase leads to a long hallway. At the end of it, a metal detector flanked by two folding tables arches over a mammoth wooden door. A brass sign hangs over the door, etched with the words: *Parish County Court of Common Pleas.*

"We got her set up in there, but then you knew that," Horace says. "Y'all wait here a spell while Roy and me let them know you're coming."

Horace and Roy go through the door and close it behind them.

When we're alone I show Seabrook and Kang the patch and tell them it was in Shwo-Rez's cigar box. Seabrook says Horace and Roy think we're there to fix something, that the patch must be a repairman's logo. I don't buy it, because why would His Eminence have it on his wall at home? And why would Charlie Lee have carried on about it? And why would it have been in Shwo-Rez's box? But Seabrook says we'd be nuts not to play along like we're the repairmen. Maybe we'll be able to fix whatever they need and make it out of here with our hides.

Just then the wooden door swings open, and a bespectacled man steps out. A rumpled suit billows down from his shoulders, and a long beard clings to his necktie. His eyes are as red as Horace's and Roy's. A smell follows him. It reminds me of the time in seventh grade when the starting linebacker on the varsity team at Primrose held me down and forced me to sniff his unwashed jock. I cover my nose.

A smile flares beneath the man's beard. "You'll be the repairmen, then," he says. "I'm Lawrence Peckwood, the mayor of Blysse. Glad y'all could make it. A lot of folks here will be glad to see you."

Mayor Peckwood frowns at me. "You're awful young, aren't you, son?"

"A prodigy," Seabrook says, clapping me on the shoulder. "The kid's the best in the business."

I try a His Eminence smile on for size.

"Well, no matter. Let me take you to it."

The mayor turns and swings the door open.

Inside, stained wooden benches stretch across the center of the room, parted by a narrow aisle. At the front, a mahogany desk towers over the room, and a smaller one, a witness stand, stands next to it. Latin phrases are etched into the wood trim just beneath the ceiling. Light streams into the room from windows behind the desks.

Everywhere—lying on the benches, milling in the aisles, seated atop the judge's bench, and sprawled on the tables—are people. Some sleep, splayed across the seats and floor like they fainted. Others sit cross-legged and slurp cold Campbell's tomato soup from the can or munch dry ramen noodles. Children sit looking at nothing in particular, their fuchsia-colored eyes motionless, as if they're waiting for something a long way off. All the men have beards. All the women looked disheveled, and those who wear makeup have acquired a crusty shell or a bright sheen.

All have the same red-rimmed eyes.

The blast of warmth from the room feels like someone turned on a heater. Sweat hangs rancid in the air, and the only noise, since everyone sits nearly motionless and no one speaks, is the loud buzzing of flies.

"We can fit about three hundred in here," Peckwood says, weaving between the prostrate forms. Glancing over his shoulder, he gives us a yellow-toothed smile. "The rest we got put up in the municipal offices and in the hallways in the back. Things are a lot better now that we got the store owners to agree to move their stock here. Since the storm the supply chain has been cut off, but y'all got through, so maybe that's changing."

We step over and around the people, who don't seem to notice we're there. I trip over a little girl, curled at the feet of a woman who is sitting on a bench near the front of the courtroom, staring into space. My head strikes the woman on the rib cage, and I nearly throw her to the floor. I struggle to push off of her, but in doing so pull myself up so that I'm sitting in her lap.

The woman hasn't moved. She continues to stare, jaw dangling, red eyes dazed. She doesn't look at me.

"Excuse me," I say.

The woman continues to stare.

"Holy shit!" I say to myself. "This is some horrifying stuff. This is major league George Romero."

Without changing her expression, the woman's mouth begins to move. She whispers: "George Romero. George A. Romero was the writer and director of *Night of the Living Dead*. Of his movie *Diary of the Dead*, Desson Thomson said, *We want to high-five Romero for finding new ways to off his lifeless marauders . . .*"

Even her tone is like a zombie. I push off of her and follow the mayor and my crewmates out of the room through a door opposite the entrance.

". . . so we allow our shop owners to hook up their service bells to the fire alarm system here, so they can attend to their stores when someone rings the bell," the mayor is saying. He steps over people either sleeping or deceased, thrown rudely into the dark hallway outside the courtroom. "We've got it going in shifts, you see. The best place for it was in the judge's chambers here, on account of the fact that it's soundproof and we can lower the blinds. Trouble is, we can only fit about twenty at a time in there. Blysse has about two thousand residents, which means we can grant them about twenty-four minutes apiece on a rotating basis. We've found it works best if we rotate on the half hour, shuffle folks into the courtroom as the main waiting area, then out and around from office to office as each shift ends. We'd love to do more, but hell, this is the biggest venue in Blysse that's dark enough."

We make our way down the hallway, rounding the sleeping forms that line the way to a door at the other end. The door is marked *Judge's Chambers*.

The mayor leans against the door and rubs his chin. "All right," he says. "I reckon only one of you will fit in there right now. I guess that'll be you . . . Winthrop was it?" He looks at his watch. "The next shift don't come on for another fifteen minutes, so when you're in there, hush. You'll be able to see what the problem is once you're in. Horace and Roy will come in there and round everybody up. If you have to shut her down, just try and keep it to five minutes when the next group comes in."

He smiles weakly. "I understand y'all had a run-in with them outside. Sorry about that. They do a good job making sure we don't have no others horning in and throwing a monkey wrench into the rotation. Twenty-four minutes apiece ain't hardly enough time for anybody. Horace and Roy were sheriff and deputy back in the days before y'all introduced the device."

He turns the knob on the door. "All right," he whispers. "Quietly, now."

sharpness

The door swings open, and I'm staring into a crowd of people. All their backs are to me, and they stand shoulder to shoulder. A blast of sound reverberates all around—a roar, like a million people clapping. I've never heard a sound like it, people, not even from the Red Grizzlies. It comes in through my ears and floods every part of my mind, makes a downward turn at my spinal column, and zips through every nerve ending until the tips of my fingers tingle.

In front of the people, something glows—a light that, even shaded by the forms in the room, sears my eyes. Mayor Peckwood and I push our way through the people toward the light.

"*Tiger Woods has eagled the ninth here at Augusta, ladies and gentleman,*" says a voice that seems to be inside my head. It washes through, knocking over old memories and filling in all the folds and wrinkles between my synapses.

"Golf today," the mayor whispers in my ear.

"Shhhhh!" hisses one of the people.

The sound weakens my knees. I stumble forward, knocking into people who bounce off of me like saplings. Finally I reach the other end of the people forest.

Before me is an enormous flat-screen TV that is more like a gaping window: it looks out across an expanse of grass lined with tall pine trees.

Everything is sharp. The blades of grass all have sharp edges, sharper even than real blades of grass I've seen between strips of sidewalk back home. I can see each and every one of them, even blades of grass that must be a mile off. Every pine needle on every tree is a tiny dagger. Each needle is slightly different from the other, something I have never noticed even after a week of floating through millions of them on the river.

Stranger still, everything seems to be lit with a glowing inner light. The sun blooming in the top left corner of the window breathes warmth through me. The soft wind outside seems to thunder through my ears like a freeway full of traffic. A crowd of people stands near the trees—giants! I can even make out the textures of polyester shirts and the soft leather of shoes.

The brightness and sound fills every corner of my brain. I feel myself floating through the window and hovering above this bright, better world. Then I'm forced downward to the grass.

Inexplicably, words appeared in front of me. White and yellow words: *Tiger Woods. 4 under par.* Next to them, someone has painted a great yellow eye, and beneath it the letters *CBS*.

Somewhere in the back of my mind, the last portion that hasn't been encumbered, thinks, *It's a TV. I'm looking at a TV.* And then that last untouched crevasse of my brain is filled with sound and light.

Suddenly the image shakes. It wiggles for less than a second, as though the victim of a power surge.

"See there!" someone whispers. The mayor, again. "That's the problem. That's what we need you to fix."

Then the screen goes dark, and the lights come on.

"All right." It's Roy's voice. "Twenty-four minutes. Move on to Conference Room B down the hall."

The crowd lets out a groan and shuffles out the door. The mayor and I are alone. Now that the sound and the light are gone, I ache. I feel hollow. Every part of me is empty. I ache like I'd carried an entire pallet of hemp up from the hold.

I look at the window, wanting more. It is about the size of a small billboard and an inch in width. The residents of Blysse hung the screen on the oak-paneled wall of some local judge's office. Sound comes from an oblong set of speakers that stand on the floor beneath the screen.

"What . . . what the hell is it?" I manage to say.

The mayor frowns. "The flicker, you mean? We were hoping you could tell us! Started about a month ago. Sam Cook, our local TV repairman, can't remember enough to even take a gander at the dern thing, so we remained hopeful one of y'all would come along. Been handling these mega high-def things long?"

"What?" I say.

"Mega high-def TVs. Ours is just a prototype, from my understanding. Has there been many changes in the past six months to these babies?" he asks hopefully.

I stare at a kid with the grungy hair and torn-up turtleneck and realize it's my reflection in the shiny black screen. The set feels hot and smooth under my hand, nearly as warm as the sun over Augusta. The reflection of my hand rises to meet me.

In the lower right hand corner, a red button says *On/Off.* I press it.

The world hums. Fire blazes. I watch the most beautiful Coke commercial ever. What sounds like a choir of angels sings the lyrics to "Always Coca-Cola."

When that's over, a commercial for the Red Grizzlies' new album flashes on the screen.

"*Hold on to hope, baby.*" Fang appears. I can see even the most minute blemish on his skin. Fang looks more real than he would probably seem in real life, and the music . . . the wall of sound . . . I nearly faint.

People file in all around, including a woman with a thick southern drawl in the back who keeps yelling, "I want to see my stories!" until they switch the channel to *Days of Our Lives*. Passion and sex flow from the screen in reds and violets, and before the first commercial break, I am convinced I am no longer a virgin.

I begin to forget. First I can no longer remember exactly what state we're in. The rivers begin to evaporate and the *Tamzene* flows upstream, and all the hemp goes back down into the hold. Seabrook and Kang disappear, and even Arthur and Esmerelda fade away, and soon it's just me and the hourglass from *Days of Our Lives*.

Twenty-four minutes tick by like thirty seconds, and then the screen goes black. I feel hollow. More people shuffle in.

"Springer!" someone yells. "Dad gum, y'all got to watch them soap operas last time. I want to watch Jerry!"

The TV comes on like an atomic bomb. For twenty-four minutes I feel white-hot rage. The screams of the guests, particularly a transsexual prostitute who has duped a dwarf lesbian into marrying her, are like souls screaming in hell. The angry crowd shouts back like a Greek chorus. And what they shout is more poetic than any Shakespeare play we ever had to read in school.

Twenty-four minutes later the TV goes black, and Roy says, "Move on to Conference Room B down the hall."

Somebody has ripped out my insides. Everything is dark. The hollowness hurts.

I fall.

Then someone is carrying me. Someone shirtless, painted with brown war paint.

It's Kang. People file into the room all around him.

A man is leaning against the wall, dozing. He opens his red eyes. *That's the mayor,* I remember. *Mayor . . . something.*

The mayor's eyes snap open. They're red and look ready to bleed down his face. "Well?" he says. "Can y'all fix it?"

"I think so," I hear Doctor Seabrook say. "Just a slight tweak needs to be made to the power coupling. We have to return to our boat to get the necessary parts."

"Y'all want an escort?" the mayor says.

"No, we'll be right back. Come on, Kang."

Kang and the Doctor carry me through the supine forms in the hallway and past the crowd of people sleeping in the courtroom. We walk out through the metal detector and down the steps lined with water and paper towels. We march through the lobby and out into the empty streets of Blysse.

The sun rides high overhead. It is warm, but not as warm as the sun from the TV.

Kang carries me out of town, stopping only once to pick up a weather vane. They're going to use it to patch the hemp cooker.

As we walk, Seabrook tells me a joke. It's a long joke, and it makes me feel tired. He says he heard it from Roy out in the hall while I was watching. Once there was this little town, and some big muckety-mucks from the city came and asked for permission to run some tests on this new product they'd developed. A new high-def TV. One of the men was wearing an army uniform with a patch on it just like the one I had in my pocket. The visitors said they wanted to set up a display in the courthouse. They set it up that very day, turned it on, and left. Little by little people from the town came in to check it out, and once they came they never left. Wives came in to get husbands and stayed; husbands came to get wives and stayed. People came in to complain that the police weren't doing their duty or that the trash company hadn't collected in months, and they stayed too. Children came in after their parents and stayed. Soon everybody moved into the courthouse. Nobody wanted to stop watching TV. Then the businesses ground to a halt. People stopped going to work, nobody went to church, kids stopped going to school, the mail stopped coming. A tornado hit the town one day and nobody came to help. Everybody knew about the storm. The picture of it ravaging their town on CNN was so gorgeous, they all stayed planted and just watched the whole thing on the television. The phones stopped ringing. No cars drove past on the streets. Electricity was coming from somewhere, but nobody questioned where from, because the people could still watch TV and that's all they cared about.

If they have electricity, somebody is providing it.

It's an experiment.

Seabrook talks until we get back to the *Tamzene* and set sail again, but I don't care.

Everything looks dull and gray and boring.

It all would look so much better on that huge flat screen, high-def TV.

CHAPTER TWENTY-TWO

dullness

Arthur and Esmerelda come up from the hold, adjusting their clothes. Arthur's mouth looks red. I'm not sure. I don't care. He writes something on his pad. I don't understand.

Seabrook and Kang build a bonfire in the woods downriver from Blysse. They lay the pieces of the weather vane on rocks stacked up within the fire until they glow. Then Kang hammers the weather vane flat. He bolts the metal to the hemp cooker over the places where it had cracked during the storm. Seabrook heats the bolts with the blowtorch.

I sit and wait.

The deck boards stretch in dull gray lines.

The others galonk around the maroon hemp cooker for a while, silhouetted in front of the pinkening sky—a faded, washed-out pink, like somebody bleached a salmon.

They talk. I can't make out much of anything.

Once in a while, they look at me with frowny faces.

I sit and wait.

The moon rises. On the TV in Blysse it will blaze.

I think about George Lucas. That will be something, even if it's the old cheesy '70s version of *Star Wars* without the CGI effects. Would laser beams and lightsabers actually hurt to watch? How would the Grizzlies sound if they played their show right between my brain lobes? Their San Fran concert will be on pay-per-view.

Arthur drapes a blanket over my shoulders. It warms me. I don't care. He lies down next to me on the deck. Then Seabrook lies down and so does Esmerelda, and Kang isn't here anymore.

I can't make my move right away. I wait until they're all breathing heavily. I wait until Arthur stops flipping around in his sleep.

Then I quietly get up and weave my way around the sleepers. I go over the side of the boat.

I slip into the waist-deep water and move as slowly as I can so I won't slosh any water around. When I reach the shore, I crawl up into the trees.

Kang, I think. Kang could still stop me. Where does Kang go in the night? He never sleeps on the boat. He is there one minute and then not there a minute later.

I start into the woods and hope I don't run into Kang. Then a voice makes me hide behind the trees.

I peer into the dark. After a few minutes I see a blue glow. It reminds me of something I've seen before, another blue glow in the woods. It moves back and forth.

Somebody is pacing in the woods, talking on a cell phone.

"I know," says the voice. It's a man. "I know, I know, I know. We've been through this."

I see what looks like long silver hair. It's Kang. Talking on a cell phone.

"We've been through it, Mom," he says. It's freaky. His voice is high and nasally.

"I don't know why I bother sometimes," he says. "Yeah, yeah. Every night. I call you every night, Mom. Because I love you. Don't you love me?" Hearing him speak and pace with a cell phone squeezed between his shoulder and his cheek is sort of like when you see the guy who plays Gollum in the *Lord of the Rings* movies: you can't picture anybody but the CGI beastie, but then there's this ugly little British guy making those noises. It's a rip-off, and even though you can't put your finger on what exactly is wrong with it, you feel betrayed just the same.

My badass Indian is a mama's boy.

"I'm not coming back, Mom," he says. "This is who I am now.

What do I always say? What do I always say? You are who you choose to be." He snaps the phone closed, and everything is dark again.

I stay hidden for a while until I hear him move off down the river, tripping over roots and muttering about it. Then I get up and head back upstream toward Blysse.

I have lots of questions. I mean, where in the world has he kept a cell phone all this time? How does he keep the battery charged? And who the hell is this guy? I don't know why it didn't seem weird to me before. Indians with war paint and headdresses just aren't around anymore. But there are psychos everywhere.

I brush off the questions. I'm focused on getting back to the TV in Blysse. Seabrook, Arthur, and Esmerelda don't need me. Arthur will find his way back home. Plus, with me out of the picture, he's got whats-her-name all to himself. And Seabrook's avoided the Green Police so far without me, after all. I'll tell His Eminence all about the *Tamzene* and how it really does work and is an honest-to-goodness good thing he ought to help with some government funding, and everything will be all right.

Truth be told, people, if I have to nuke the boat and the crew with it, at this moment, I'll press the button.

I stumble along. I trip and bloody my arms and knees. After a long time, I see a searing white light. It's Blysse.

It's the TV slicing through the darkness.

It bleeds through the trees ahead. I run toward it. I fall again and cut my legs and arms. I'm bleeding pretty badly, but I don't care because that light is getting closer and closer and brighter and brighter.

But when I get there I discover it isn't Blysse at all, but a set of floodlights attached to poles at a campsite. The camp is full of people dressed in black. When I run into the camp, they all stop and stare at me with surprised, sagging looks on their faces, metal army plates full of food in their hands, and the Green Police logos on their uniforms. Some of them wear the patches on their chests—the same patches I found in the woods that Charlie Lee and the people from Blysse recognized, the same patch that's in my pocket, and the same logo that's on the poster in the office of His Eminence.

Deep inside me a little voice says, *Stop*.

Everyone freezes. We stare at one another.

Whatever is speaking inside me has a movie projector—not a flat screen, not a mega high-def or anything like what's in Blysse, but an old chattering reel-to-reel job like they had decades ago.

The movie that plays is Arthur pushing the stool over to me so I don't embarrass myself for being short that one day on the *Tamzene*. There are images of Arthur and me laughing. There are some great shots of Arthur jumping in the way of that bullet just a couple of mornings ago. The movie is also Seabrook: cradling Arthur's ankle, clutching me by the arm on a night when he's hurting, punching Shwo-Rez in the back of the head.

As I realize I'm running back into the dark woods, the movie continues to play. I see Kang next, wrapping his arms around Arthur and me with that closed-lipped smile . . .

"*You there! Halt!*"

. . . standing, holding his knife at his side on the deck of the *Tamzene*, facing down the burning white yachts.

And I'm plunging into the woods, trees crisscrossing behind me. I can see silhouettes of the men on my heels, but I am pulling away from them now. The TV, Blysse, my parents, the Grizzlies—all of it be damned. For once I'm going to be the hero, people. Winthrop Brubaker is going to save the day. I realize now that I'm making it, I'm pulling away, they're tangled in the trees. I'm making it. I'm making it. I'm—

Sharp pain slices into the back of my neck. I fall forward into blackness.

PART FIVE

Survival of the Fittest

"What didn't go right?"

—President George W. Bush after Hurricane Katrina

Chapter Twenty-Three

jorge

They'd been given two big ones and a small one. The big ones were nothing new: men, sinewy and covered in hair. But the things in the box had never seen such a young, tender one as this before. A large metal mouth gaped from a box that joined the young one's chest.

It would be hard to chew.

The humans sat in the white room. The young one's handcuffs jangled against the chair. The two big ones sat, heads bowed, in expressions the things in the box had grown to know. Though they had learned little about the minds of men, they believed the expressions were ones of hopeless fear.

The shiny black eye opened, and a face appeared. Inconsequential noises commenced.

"*Doctor Marion Seabrook.*"

"Yes."

"*Your companions are Kang and . . . Arthur, is it? . . . I'm afraid we have no record of either of you . . . Your name, Mr. Kang? . . . Okay, we'll skip names. Where is the Tamzene? . . . Gentleman, I can promise you this will go much easier if you cooperate.*"

"What's a *Tamzene?*"

"*Hmmmph. Gentlemen, we found you in the woods downriver from the last known whereabouts of your invention, Doctor Seabrook. You were clearly searching for your escaped hostage, Winthrop Brubaker. It's only a matter of time before we locate your boat. Why don't you make it easier on yourself and tell me where the Tamzene is.*"

"I don't know what you're talking about. We were fishing."

"Look to your left, gentlemen."

For the first time the three humans glanced in the direction of the things in the box. The things in the box chattered. The young one opened his mouth in a silent howl.

"*Do you have any idea what the things in that box can do to you if I release even one? So a little cooperation please, gentlemen. Sharing is caring, right? . . . Mr. Kang, your full name . . . Your full name, Mr. Kang . . . Is it Jorge? Jorge Zuniga? I can see by your face that rings a bell. We have a winner! I have here an Arizona driver's license for a Jorge Miguel Zuniga of 225 Crestview Terrace, Flagstaff. Not the best picture. You had short hair and glasses. But I'll wager dollars to donuts this is you, Mr. Kang.*"

"Kang?"

"*Didn't tell you that, Doctor Seabrook, did he? You thought he was a Native American named Kang? He's a con artist. He's been telling that story for five years, Doctor Seabrook. Or should I say Rev. Seabrook, pastor of the Love Canal First Presbyterian Church, last seen in Niagara Falls, New York, 1980? . . . We know all about you, gentlemen, so it's useless to continue with this charade.*"

The dark one stared at the floor. The young one and the older one seemed to study him, mouths agape. Then the things in the box chattered, and the humans all flinched.

"*Doctor Seabrook, a scientist such as yourself must be familiar with amospermophilus homoedo . . .*"

movement

The trees along the river were one hundred years old. They'd been saplings when men first settled in the nearby towns. In their youths the river had been strong. Fish with speckled bellies plunged through the clear-running channels. Deer drank from the pools the river made in its shallow reaches.

In those days, the trees wished they'd been given the ability to move. When the water swept past their roots, it was so strong it threatened to drag them along. *If only*, the trees had thought in those days,

*we'd been gifted with the swiftness of mind and fleetness of branch to
climb further into the forest to protect ourselves.*

As the years passed, the rush of the water subsided. The river withered like a vine dying of thirst. The channels turned brown, and the fish
died. Again the trees wished they'd been gifted with musculatures and
joints and nervous systems to pull up their roots and march through
the forest to a land where the air wasn't so choked with poison, where
the streams flowed with clean, sweet water.

The night the order arrived, the trees were dying claws leaning
over a slackened dirt-colored sluice. *Now?* some of them thought. *After so much has happened? After all has been lost?*

But they obeyed. They strained within their branches. Strain was
something they'd previously been unable to know and feel, but now
here it was, something foreign yet not foreign, something ubiquitous
yet never before seen, willing their arms to move.

They wrapped themselves around the man-made thing, the boat
with the metal smokestack. Great cracking noises filled the forest as
their weaker limbs snapped free. They felt their bows dipping into the
river.

Soon, they'd hidden the boat from view.

As sheets of rain fell, the river began to swell.

innocents

It starts out innocently enough. We're sitting at the table in the front
salon on one of those nights—you can count them on your fingers—
when His Eminence is home. Nobody talks. Nothing strange here. I'm
staring at my plate full of roast duck and so is the Moms. His Eminence is spooning heap after heap into his face, surveying the room
with that searchlight expression, the kind that you hope won't land
on you if you suck your neck deeply enough between your shoulder
blades. The Moms and I are trying our best to avoid it, but eventually
it lands on me, and His Eminence asks how school was.

"Okay," I say, which is what I always say.

"Ready for camp?" he asks me.

"Sure," I say.

And everything is quiet once again.

"Let me ask you something," His Eminence says. "Is that fork bothering you?"

His question throws me because it's bizarre, so I give him three words instead of one: "I guess not."

So we eat a while longer. The Moms is staring at her plate, looking at neither me nor His Eminence. Nothing is out of the ordinary.

After a few minutes His Eminence slams his fork down on the table, and that's the first time I notice he has yellow eyes.

"You're a Brubaker," he says, "and it's a disgrace that any Brubaker would ever eat with a knife and fork. That's your mother's influence."

And then I realize that the His Eminence's face is false. He tears is off like it's a *Mission: Impossible* rubber mask, and underneath is the face of a cougar.

"We'll teach you proper table manners," the cat says to me, and then bends down and starts scarfing up food. He jumps up on the table and wolfs down the asparagus, roast duck, and potatoes au gratin.

The Moms is just sitting there with tears rolling down her face. She looks at me and screams, *"Run!"*

I wake up lying in a white room with long curtains that arch over a view of a sun-covered field of grass that stretches all the way to a row of trees. Beyond that, the river glimmers.

The bed is soft. The blue comforter is pillowy. A big black desk on the far wall sits next to a cushioned chair with a pair of khaki slacks and a white shirt folded on it. A blue vase crammed with flowers rests on the desk.

I stand and scoop up the clothes. They've been draped over a pair of polished wing tips, a leather belt, a pair of black socks, and a pair of boxer shorts. On top of them is a note written in cursive on a thick sheet of high-grade paper:

Master Brubaker, dial 7 for room service. We hope you have a pleasant stay with us. The Management. PS—Ms. Sweetwater

*has requested that you join her on the front range at your ear-
liest convenience.*

The letterhead at the top of the page says *Locksley Ponds.*

The plush carpet squeezes between my toes. Everything smells like
flowers. This is like one of the upscale five-star hotels we stayed at
when His Eminence needed me and the Moms on his campaign tours. I
wonder if all of it was a dream. The *Tamzene*, Seabrook, Kang, Arthur,
Esmerelda—they're like comic book characters, like a crazy B movie,
them and Shrub People and biting squirrels and that high-def TV.

Then I look in the mirror over the desk and almost lose my shit.

A skinny little beastie stares back, somebody with skin the color of
Hershey's syrup, greasy hair poking everywhere, a big scratch on his
grimy little arm, and other little bruises and scrapes everywhere. The
kid is only in his skivvies, and his chest, arms, and neck are pale where
his turtleneck—now nowhere to be seen—had once been. It takes me
two looks before I realize the whole *Tamzene* trip was the real deal.

I go to the bathroom, your typical five-star shitter with marble
floors and porcelain everything. I shower, watch the dirt streak off me,
and wonder where the hell I am. I remember the faces of the men in
the camp. The black uniforms. The lights on the poles. Then nothing.

The hot water licks me like a big tongue. The field and the trees
and the river outside the windows seem a million miles away. The stillness is strange. I can't feel the wind anymore. The river's fishy smell is
gone, and the potpourri flowers make me queasy. The walls feel like
they're getting closer. I want to get out.

The starchy clothes chafe me as I pull them on. I cross the bathroom in three steps and make it to the door out in five.

When I open the door, I'm face-to-face with a moose.

It freaks me out at first—seeing the antlers and the glassy, staring
eyes—but then I realize it has no body. It's one of those trophy heads
attached to a piece of wood mounted on the wall. A little brass plate
under the moose's chin reads *Cervus Elaphus Canadensis—The East-
ern Elk.*

A hallway stretches to my right and left. Brass electric candles attached to the wallpapered walls every few feet emit the only light in the hallway. Other animal heads are mounted between the candles. Their eyes twinkle at me.

I turn right and walk. After a while I see a woman in a dark pantsuit. She smiles at me. There are a few potted plants on the wall, but no place to hide.

"Hi, Winthrop," she says. "Enjoying your stay with us?"

"I guess," I say.

"The director decided to let you sleep. She's out on the range already. Go down the stairs and out the front door. Just keep walking straight and you'll see her."

She turns and points down the hallway.

I walk past her. She smiles the whole time—not like she's a freaky-deaky psycho killer, but like she's an employee working for tips or something. You see a lot of those smiles when you're a congressman's kid.

White rails line the spiral staircase, which snakes down to a tile foyer. More animal heads hang over the old-fashioned hat racks and benches in the entryway. By the time I reach it, I'm walking fast because I really want to get outside and everything is feeling really close. I open the door and quickly step outside.

I walk off the porch and out onto a brick driveway and look up at the big mansion where I've been. It's built of yellow stone, and the windows are black. I keep backing up to try to get a better look at it, but it just keeps stretching, and eventually I back into the field.

Tall grass rises and falls all the way down to a treeline way off in the distance. Beyond that is a river lined with a boardwalk. A handful of buildings huddle over the planks, and I see tables and chairs outside of a pair of restaurants—Le Gavroche and the Crab Shack.

I walk into the field.

After a while I crest a hill, and there's a woman sitting there in the grass next to a boulder. She looks as big as a house and wears a wide-brimmed straw hat beneath a light green sash. A pale green sundress hangs from her shoulders. Or maybe it's one of those muumuu things husky people wear.

"Winthrop!" she says when she sees me. A pair of horn-rimmed glasses—the kind I guess they wore in the '50s—pinch her large pink head. She struggles and sways back and forth four or five times and finally stands, heaving this grunt that makes her shake all over. It makes me feel bad for her, carrying all that extra weight.

"I'm Maude Sweetwater. I'm a friend and admirer of your father." Her voice is small and cute. She sticks out a big hand capped with dainty fingers. "I'm pleased as punch to meet you. We're happy to have you out here with us at Locksley, dontchaknow. Come. Sit."

She squats again, and the air she sucked in to stand bellows outward. I sit cross-legged on the ground next to her.

The little face at the center of her giant melon head is smiling. "We've phoned your father and told him that we found you and everything is all right. He's sent for you. He's been worried sick, dontchaknow."

Wimp Winthrop has locked my jaw. I am busted. Primrose will be a fond memory. Duseldorf Military School for Boys is something His Eminence waves around to scare me sometimes.

"Before you leave, Winthrop, I thought I'd take the opportunity to show you around Locksley Ponds. We couldn't have built old Locksley without your dad's help in Congress," she says.

"What's Locksley Ponds?"

"Why, look around you, dear boy. This beautiful estate. Two hundred and seventy-seven acres. It's a rather ingenious little revenue producer for us at the Green Police."

"*You're* the Green Police?"

She smiles again. "I'm the head bean, as it were. The CEO of our little organization." She pats my elbow. "I just want you to know that, on behalf of all of us here, we apologize for everything you've gone through. If we'd known *you* were on that boat, Winthrop, we wouldn't have . . . well, of course you know . . ."

"What's the Green Police?"

"We're what's known as a government corporation, son. Kind of works like the Post Office, dontchaknow. We make a profit like a regular business, but our board is a congressional oversight committee, and people like myself are appointed by people like your dad."

We watch the grass. There's no noise but the wind blowing through the tall blades.

"You're familiar with the passenger pigeon, aren't you, Winthrop?" Her head had turns toward the mansion so I can see only the rear of her hat.

"The passenger pigeon," she repeats. "Ectopistes migratorius. Once it was the most common bird on the planet. Their flocks were a mile wide and three hundred miles long. People say they blotted out the sun for days, huge black storm fronts full of birds, just moving across the sky."

She turns and smiles at me again.

"Then came the Industrial Revolution. Deforestation. Growth of cities across the countryside. Not to mention those birds were good eating, so people just walked out and shot 'em down, like picking apples off a tree. About 1850 or so, their populations started to dwindle. Public reports have it that the last of the passenger pigeons died off in a zoo in Cincinnati in 1914. Amazing, isn't it? How something once so plentiful over a period of sixty-four years of serious industrial growth could be completely wiped away." She sighs. "Ah, the innocents always suffer for the wheels of mankind."

In the distance, I hear thunder. I scan the skyline: nothing but blue and little white clouds as far as I can see.

"Of course, the passenger pigeon wasn't *really* extinct, Winthrop. In the 1930s it was discovered that a wildlife collector name Aloysius Sims from Wausau, Wisconsin, had three such birds in captivity. Male and female. And he was attempting to revive the species."

The rolling thunder in the distance seems louder now, and more sustained.

"Well, of course government scientists wanted to study the bird, so they secured Mr. Sims's collection. In 1942, a secret breeding project was launched to see if it was possible to repopulate the species under federal protection in remote areas."

Above the river, a black cloud appears at the edge of the trees. The cloud grows larger and larger, and what sounds like a freight train a mile off chugs toward us.

"Imagine—bringing back this species to where it once was! Of course, one has to be careful what one tells the public, dontchaknow. If one were to tell people about the passenger pigeon, the government would be expected to enter in whenever any species is about to meet its maker and interrupt the natural flow of things. So in 1975, our covert ops took charge of the passenger pigeon project."

The cloud balloons to a massive storm front the size of a city. It towers over us, blotting out the sun.

They're birds—gray birds with reddish bellies and purple eyes. Millions of them. The flapping of their wings creates a roar.

"Look at them, Winthrop! Passenger pigeons," Sweetwater says through her pink smile over the roar. "Do you believe that we actually once had to grab them from the jaws of extinction?"

Millions of them are flying over my head. I've never seen so many birds in one place, people. Maybe Seabrook has the Green Police all wrong. If they're able to bring back something like this bird that died off, they can't be all bad.

"They'll be worth millions in accounts for us," Sweetwater says. She reaches down into the weeds where she's kneeling and picks up a black AK-47 machine gun.

She raises it to the sky and fires off several rounds into the cloud of birds.

Gray lumps fall like rain. Sweetwater fires in sweeping arcs. With each arc, twenty birds fall from the sky and plop on the ground.

I wig.

"Aw, tenderhearted lad, aren't you," she says, laughing. "Well, why do you think we've raised them, Winthrop? This is what we do here at Locksley. We've saved thirty so-called extinct species on our ranch here. Lesser fruit bats, African cats, several varieties of mountain lion.

It's a rather ingenious revenue producer. For a $700,000 fee, our guests can come here to hunt them.

"We put the hunters up in suites here at Locksley," Sweetwater goes on, seeming to add figures in her head, "at $2,000 a night. Additional fees for taxidermy services and facilities in the basement where they can clean their kill, plus an additional $20,000 for each passenger pigeon and fruit bat killed. $50,000 for your larger mammals. And of course, for the restaurant in Locksley's dining room and our two riverfront eateries, we skim a few animals such as these to fill out the menu, where a plate costs more than your average sitting at the Big Boy, let me tell ya.

"The Senate—thanks to your dad—approved it ten years ago in the budget omnibus. Granted, it's not our charter business, but this is sideline revenue that we use to fund our programs. It brings in nearly $10 million a year, dear boy. I'm sure I don't need to tell you how popular the novelty is of hunting species previously thought to be extinct—especially among the fiscally elite."

Sweetwater raises a walkie-talkie to her lips. "Okay, Somes. Bring the choppers in and collect them. I'll let you know when we're ready for another release. Over."

"Ten-four," a voice crackles.

I stare at the gray lumps on the ground. One of the lumps is struggling in the grass. The black cloud overhead has mostly passed by, and the sun blazes down once again.

"I'm wondering if you can help me with something," she says. "Before your mom and dad get here."

I don't say anything. I mean, the gun is seriously badass, and ordinarily I'd be asking to take a turn myself, but for some reason this whole thing has made me feel like puking.

"You'll be happy to know we've taken your captors prisoner," she says.

"You're not going to hurt them, are you?" I ask. "Doctor Seabrook, he doesn't mean to hurt anybody, he invented this—"

"They aren't going to harm you anymore, you can rest easy about that," Sweetwater says, looking away from me. "Doctor Seabrook is a dangerous psychotic, and his associate, Jorge Zaniga . . ."

"Who?"

The pink smile returns. "Told you his name was Kang, did he? In my day we called that type of fellow a Pretendian—somebody who pretends to be Native American. He's a known con man—"

"No."

She ignores me. "—wanted in his home state of Arizona for fraud, dontchaknow. Your dad assured us that you'd cooperate with us, Winthrop. The trouble is, we're having a hard time finding that illegal boat. Can you help us?"

"The *Tamzene*? You mean you didn't find it? Where are my friends? Where's Esmerelda?"

She frowns. "Who?"

They must not have captured her. "No one," I say.

"Winthrop?" she continues to frown. "Who is Esmerelda?"

"She's just this girl." My heart is pounding in my ears. "She hitched a ride with us for a while. Actually, come to think of it, she must have gotten out back when we were in that town with the TV."

"Would you be able to describe her?" she asks.

"Sure," I say. "So you guys can't find the *Tamzene*?"

Sweetwater chuckles. "This is a slippery bunch you helped us capture here, Winthrop," she says. "They managed to hide this thing. Now, you were with them for days, young man, and I'm sure you've learned some of their MO. What do you say? Are you willing to help us out?"

"Look, I think somebody is making a mistake here. Doctor Seabrook isn't a bad dude, and this boat thing, I mean, I think it's a good thing and it really works."

She smiles and clucks her tongue. "Oh my," she says. And then the moving bird catches her eye.

"I understand how you feel, Winthrop. Happens sometimes when somebody spends too much time in captivity."

"No, you don't understand. Doctor Seabrook and Kang helped me, they didn't—"

"I believe it's called the Stockholm syndrome," she says, grunting to her feet again and raising her rifle. She smiles that pink smile. "Maybe it's time for somebody to watch a little television."

She stands over the wounded bird. A bullet has nicked its wing, rendering it flightless, and it tries to hop away from her. She clucks her tongue again.

"Poor thing. Suffer the innocents for the wheels of mankind."

She raises the gun, points the muzzle at the ground, and fires.

the river

It was as though the river had regained its youth. In its younger days, it had been mighty, wide, and deep. Age upon age of dry seasons had withered it, shrinking it to a mere trickle, a dry bed in some places.

Now, for a purpose it did not entirely understand, it was necessary for the old river to become young again. Sustained cloudbursts soaked the cracked bed, replenishing gullies, pouring down from mountainsides. Before long, the river stretched out to its original banks.

And it carried cargo. Swept along on its now vast waters was what to it was little more than a twig. But the river knew to take great care with this, an unmanned—but man-made—craft. A tall, odd-looking boat, with a strange metallic mushroom attached to it.

It carried the boat around its bends and eased it through its rapids, no matter how playful the river felt.

cougar scouts

The trees glow, as if lit from inside. Every leaf is so sharp it hurts my eyes. There are thousands of them, and they stretch all the way to the horizon, rising and falling over mountain peaks, each one bright as a fluorescent bulb. They throw themselves up to the electric blue sky, which is so phosphorescent that it sweeps through my mind, wiping everything clean. Soon, there's only the sky and the trees.

"*The Appalachian Mountains*," says a deep voice that rumbles in through my ears, down my spinal cord, and bleeds into every nerve ending. "*Untouched. Virginal. Beautiful.*"

The scene changes to a close-up of a tree. An eagle perches on a limb. I can make out each of the small fibers in its feathers. Its black eyes look into me just before it raises its wings and takes flight.

"*But unforgiving,*" the voice continues. "*Like the sirens of old, the verdant Appalachians have beguiled men, punished them, and lured them to their doom. Since the beginning of time, nature has stirred unnatural feelings within man. Nature has been his undoing, his weakness. It fills his mind with wonders, but offers no sanctuary. Nature is the enemy of mankind. Its attacks are seldom conventional, always merciless, always devastating.*

"*August, 79 AD. Pompeii, a thriving jewel in the Roman Empire's crown, was living in a golden age of civilization, until Mount Vesuvius erupted, encasing thousands in molten rock.*

"*1201 AD. 1.1 million people in Syria and Egypt die in the worst earthquake in recorded history.*

"*1587. One hundred British men, women, and children settle in Roanoke, Virginia. Three years later, they vanish.*

"*1887. Nine hundred thousand die when China's Yellow River bursts through its dams.*

"*Tsunamis. Droughts. Vicious, killer animals. Disease. Nature has many weapons in her arsenal, deadly and unstoppable. Nature is the enemy of civilization, and civilization is the enemy of nature.*"

Blinds slide up the windows, willed by unseen motions. We're in a darkened parlor somewhere within Locksley Ponds. The last rags of daylight are burning in the sky.

Time and place occur to me in short bursts.

"Please, turn the TV back on again," I say.

"No," says the blurry thing standing between me and the TV. "No, Winthrop. Too prolonged an exposure can result in acute addiction and mental incapacitation. Secretary Sweetwater said you're in need of mild reconditioning, but we want you lucid when your parents arrive. Which means we're going for a walk. Up now."

The blurry thing grabs me by the wrists and hoists me out of my chair. We go out into the blinding pink light and march. Soft grass purrs beneath my black wing tips. I throw a look back over my shoulder and see the big yellow mansion receding—and along with it, the TV.

The blurry thing is a man in a black uniform. Somewhere, underneath the big desire to go back and watch more TV, it occurs to me what he is.

"You are the Green Police," I say.

He smiles. "That's right."

We walk on, and everything is dull: the sun leaning on the river, the grass, the trees, the rifle slung across his back, the picture of the snarling cat on his chest.

The snarling cat picture seems important. I can't imagine why—sure, it would look nice on the TV, but other things would be more impressive on the high-def. Then I recognize it: the patch, the thing in His Eminence's office.

The man hums: *When the lightning flashes and the thunder rolls, I will not yield. I will stand fast and resolute.*

The man is humming the Grizzlies.

"Are you a fan of the Greatest Band on Earth?" I ask him.

"Excuse me?"

"That song. The Red Grizzlies."

"What song?"

"The one you're humming."

He laughs. "That's one of the songs the CO taught us in basic. Fancied himself a songwriter. It's an earworm, I'll give it that."

"The CO?"

"Brigadier General Harlan H. Spikes."

That name sounds familiar. Seems important. But I can't imagine it being that great on the TV, so I let it go.

"What about that patch?"

He taps the snarling cat face. "This?"

"Yeah."

"Oh, you'll get one of these one day," he says. "You get this when you get out of Cougar Scouts."

"What's that?"

"It's like the Boy Scouts, only better. Turn right here, we're going to go down to the Hero Garden."

We're at the top of a rise in the field, looking into a copse of trees. "How do you get in?"

"My scoutmaster picked me," he says, puffing out his chest. "That's how you know you belong. My dad didn't pull any strings." He gives me a worried look. "No offense."

I wave him off. "What is the Cougar Scouts?"

He frowns. "Well, it goes Cub Scouts, Boy Scouts, and then either Eagle Scouts or Cougar Scouts. Unless you bypass that. Like you did."

"What do you mean?" I say. "I'm not a Cougar Scout."

"Well, not yet," he says. "You skipped out on Godspeed Summer Camp, from what I hear."

I vaguely remember that name. The camp. The camp Arthur and I ran away from just days ago.

The guard shakes his head. "Should have hung around. Godspeed is what some of us call a kitten camp, for guys like you with dads who grease the wheels. But I hear it's fun. I hear on day five you actually club baby seals. Check this out, Winthrop. This is important."

I blink. We're standing inside the trees. Tall concrete columns surround a wide, flat patch of land completely covered in cement. Three rows of statues crisscross it. A path leads out of the trees to the docks, where I can see the Crab Shack and Le Gavroche.

Atop a pedestal in the center, etched onto a stone tablet, are the words: *Vir Apud Gens.*

"What is this place?" I ask.

"It's the Heroes of Civilization Sculpture Garden," the guy says. "The secretary had this installed personally."

We stroll among the rows of statues. One is a likeness of a man in an old-fashioned suit, staring intently at the horizon. Next to him is a big oil derrick, out of which trickles real oil that pools on top of a stone vase of what looks like dying flowers.

Luther B. Robertson, Inventor of the Oil Derrick, reads the gilt plaque below the statue.

"All these guys were Cougar Scouts," the guard says. "Anybody who is anybody. The secretary. The president. General Spikes. Your dad."

His Eminence? An image flashes of an old man in a Cub Scout uniform cradling a tumbler of scotch. But I'm still hollowed from the TV, so the thought falls in on itself until it's a tiny dot.

The other statues show likenesses of people I've never heard of before, with names like James Watt, Anne Gorsuch, and Ronald Reagan. One statue is of three smiling men standing aboard the deck of a ship. It's labeled: *Dedicated to William Murphy, Joe Hazelwood, Harry Claar, and the rest of the crew of the beloved* Valdez.

I hear a crackling noise, electronic buzzing, and a voice. "Carmison."

The man holds a black radio to his face. "Copy."

"We've got movement over in the south sector. Would you mind taking a look? Over."

"I've got the kid. Over."

"We just need you to look, Stu. Leave the kid in the garden for a minute."

The guard sighs. "Ten-four." He looks at me. "I need you to do me a favor, Winthrop."

"What?"

"I need you to sit tight here for just a second, okay? I have to go check something out. Just sit right here." He points to a stone bench across from the Valdez statue. "I'll be back in five minutes. Okay?"

"Then can I watch more TV?"

"Yeah. Then you can watch more TV."

I sit. On the TV, the Valdez guy statue would glow with an inner light. So would His Eminence in a scout uniform. How about that? Well, I guess it makes sense that if great people were part of this group, His Eminence would be too, right? And if I would have stuck around camp, then maybe I would have been part of it too. Somehow, though, that doesn't seem like a good thing.

"Stubby!" a voice hisses.

Esmerelda creeps out of the woods.

"Hi!" I say. "Hey, you've got to see this TV they've got here."

"I know all about the TV, Winthrop. I need you to listen."

"Okay. Why are you whispering?"

"Shhhh. Look. The've got the Doc, Kang, and Arthur locked up on the west side of the mansion."

"Did you know they think Kang isn't an Indian, but a Mexican?"

"*Keep your voice down!* Listen to me. I'm not who you think I am. I'm AICO."

"What's that? Did you know my dad was a Cougar Scout? And I'm going to be one too."

She grabs my face between her palms, and her green eyes look into mine. "They scrambled your brain, stubby. I need you to listen to me."

I move my jaw to kiss her, but she pushes me back. "Listen to me. I'm an AICO agent. Secretary Sweetwater is guilty of murder. I have proof. And we need to spring Kang, Arthur, and the Doc, or they're next. Do you understand me?" The words slip from her mouth like hailstones into a pond.

"Harlan Spikes . . . was a Cougar Scout. Isn't that the guy the Birmingham Kid talked about?"

She grimaces, a terrible twist of a smile. "I know all about Harlan Spikes. I need you to promise me something, stubby. Don't watch any more of that TV, okay? It's a mega high-def. It's an addictive TV, Winthrop. They use it to control people's minds. They introduce it when they need a docile populace. It's illegal. Don't watch it, Winthrop. Shut your eyes and think about something else."

"The Grizzlies?"

"If you have to . . . shit."

Esmerelda is gone. I hear her hiss into the leaves.

"Winthrop?" the guard says. He's standing next to me, gun slung over his shoulders.

"TV?" I ask.

The guard laughs. "A little more," he says. "But too much will rot your brain."

the war

"What people don't know, Winthrop," Sweetwater says, "in fact, what 98.2 percent of the population doesn't know, according to our most recent research, is that this nation is at war."

We're sitting in the room with the TV. She makes me take breaks every couple of hours. I hate these breaks. For most of the day, my head has been filled with this awesome history lesson—all about how settlers battled bears and crocodiles, how we dump drums of sludge in the ocean to kill sharks, how after Hurricane Katrina we carpet bombed the Galapagos Islands and killed twenty sea turtles.

"Sure they know," I say, "we're at war with . . ." but the name of the most recent one I occasionally catch glimpses of on Fox News escapes me. Something ending in –stan.

"Not that war, Winthrop," she says, her small face beams behind the horn-rims. "Wars like those are largely unimportant skirmishes, you'll find out. They're launched as distractions. We've been fighting the war I'm talking about for more than two hundred years. Now, this is something you'd learn after becoming a Cougar Scout, dontchaknow. But you're a legacy, and you have a right to know. I'm sure your father would approve my telling you.

"Did you ever notice how geese fly in perfect formation?" she says. But I'm only partly listening. I want to tell her that by the location of the sliver of moon just over the river, I can tell that it's getting close to nine p.m., and *Sniper Dude X* might literally blow my mind broadcasted on the giant TV just over her shoulder. I want to be there for the mushroom cloud.

"Geese fly in V shapes," she goes on, "because they were drilled to do it. Ants march in straight columns. Bee hives are geometrically perfect fortresses. Nature isn't just a wild collection of animals and plants and rocks that's there to be pretty for you. There's something intelligent behind it. Something organized. And it wants us all dead."

"Uh-huh."

Her delicate little hand grabs my arm.

"This is information the vast majority of the general public does not know, Winthrop. Only we select few. It's certainly something small-minded environmentalists like your psychotic friend Doctor Seabrook will never understand. Men of his ilk believe everybody should be driving hybrid cars, cuddling little fuzzy things, and making love to trees. Their kind doesn't understand the war. But a few enlightened souls—myself, your father—know the stakes."

"Can I watch some more TV?" I ask.

"We're at war, Winthrop," Sweetwater says, "with what romantics like Doctor Seabrook like to call the *forces of nature.*

"People like Seabrook don't get it," Sweetwater mutters, gazing out the window. "They think we should just ride around in horse-drawn carriages eating twigs and berries. Thank God our forefathers weren't fooled. They knew the beasts and the weather and the forests wanted to wipe them out. They knew nature is the enemy of man.

"The few members of the unenlightened public believe that when the government gives tax breaks to oil companies and undermines alternative energy concerns, they're protecting the interests of big business." Her pinkness flashes scarlet. "They don't know what's really happening. They can't see the forest for the trees. They don't know what oil is. Ever since the Industrial Revolution, we've known why it's such a valuable resource. It's more important than its ability to drive engines and make plastics. Hell, we have the ability to do that with sunlight now. These crazy spotted-owl porkers will never get it."

She flushes, embarrassed. "Excuse me," she says. "Oil is a weapon. It pollutes the air. It kills plants and animals. It's one of our most effective weapons, as a matter of fact, and it's my duty to keep wrongheaded people like Doctor Seabrook from trying to bring it down. Think about it. If it wasn't for fossil fuels polluting the atmosphere, plants and wildlife would flourish! They'd invade the cities and overpopulate the earth! We wouldn't stand a chance.

"We are a proud agency, Winthrop. We have a long and storied history of success. We have saved this country from the likes of Seabrook, time and time again, for more than two hundred years now. And one of these days this war is going to end.

"Nature wants the United States for itself. It wants the water, it wants the air, and it wants the land. When we try to take the land—which is our God-given right—it fights us. It sends its animals to attack us. It assaults us with storms, floods us, hits us with earthquakes, or tries to burn us up in forest fires. It's our destiny to control this country and all its resources, regardless of what we're up against."

"But, like, won't that kill the people too, if you destroy the water and air and stuff?" I ask.

"It's called mutually assured destruction, Winthrop," she says. "You might have witnessed the concept in microcosm during the Cold War with the Russkies. We can't weaken. Do you honestly believe that nature, if she really wanted to, couldn't wipe us all out with a monster volcano, a hurricane, or a great flood? Well, she wouldn't dare try because of our nuclear deterrent. The stalemate is what's keeping us alive for the moment. But that won't last forever.

"Now," Sweetwater says, "do you see why that boat can never make it to California? It would tip the balance. We have nature on the run, but tree huggers like Seabrook are giving her hope. Nature is warming up the atmosphere, threatening to melt the polar ice caps, hitting us with hurricanes. That boat is a danger, an unwitting capitulation from a peace-mongering pinko. Say Seabrook made it to California, and people actually listened to his nonsense. The trucking industry might just take a hit. That would cripple our air pollution arsenal. Trucks create a significant percentage of the air pollution in this country. We can't have that curtailed, Winthrop."

"Uh-huh." I want this conversation to end. "So why didn't you just set up a roadblock or drop a bomb or something?"

"We've tried. It's not that simple."

"Is this like a bin Laden thing?"

"I told you, we're fighting a war," Sweetwater said. "You were first spotted aboard the *Tamzene* on the Allwyn River in Pennsylvania. Remember?"

I barely do. Most of my being at the moment is concentrating on the power button to the bottom right of the TV.

"Do you recall what happened? Three of our boats almost overtook you."

"There was a big storm."

She looks at me over the horn-rims.

"I don't get it."

"In Pennsylvania, there was a storm. Another storm in Ohio. Bird attacks. Bear attacks. Suicidal frogs getting lodged in our engines. Whenever we're close, something happens. This *Tamzene* is clearly very important to our enemy, Winthrop. It recognizes the threat to our arsenal. That's why we've got to find it."

"Got ya," I say. "Now can I watch TV?"

She smiles. "In a moment, Winthrop. There's something I need your help with first, if you don't mind."

From nowhere, Sweetwater pulls a remote control and presses a button.

The room changes. On a secret conveyor belt, my recliner turns counterclockwise. The wall slides upward, clearing the way for a window into another room.

It is a room with whitewashed walls and a metal floor. Handcuffed to chairs in the room are Arthur, Seabrook, and Kang.

They look miserable. Their jaws are slack, and each of them has little crimson half-moons scattered up their arms and on their cheeks. Next to them—towering over them, actually—is a box made of black metal.

Tears sting my eyes. I want to go to them, but I feel so hollowed out and weak it's difficult to move.

"You know Arthur's dad is NSA, right?" I say.

"NSA?" she laughs. "We know all about your friend. The NSA are glorified postmen, Winthrop. He won't be missed. Now listen, we need your help. We're going to try one last time to find out from these Greenpeace wannabes where the heck they hid the *Tamzene*. I know it's painful, but if you catch them in a lie, speak up, all right?"

I stare into the other room, wishing against everything that I was somewhere else, that I'd never left camp, that Arthur and I could have just gone on and joined whatever stupid club His Eminence had me set for.

"Of course," Sweetwater adds. She seems to grow taller as she leans over my chair. "If you happen to know where the boat is yourself, why, you could tell me. Then we won't release what's in that box."

I look into the knowing slits she has for eyes.

"Do we understand each other?" she asks. She gives me one more look and leaves the room.

A moment later she's in the white room with two armed guards in black uniforms. She stands in front of Kang and chuckles.

"Gentlemen," she says to the guards, knifing Kang with her eyes. "This is a historic day. More than two hundred years ago, when this great war of ours was in its infancy, our forefathers realized that one way we could demoralize those pesky early environmentalists, the Native Americans, was to rob them of adequate footwear. So they systematically destroyed the Milliconquit tribe—which was what some scholars called the Shoe Salesman tribe."

Kang's face hardens. It grows tighter and tighter until tears bulge from his eyes.

"Took some doing too," Sweetwater continues. "But that was nothing a little smallpox couldn't fix. But I digress. Today we finish the job. Even though our friend Jorge here is only a faux Milliconquit."

Kang opens his mouth. "I," says the nasally voice I'd heard in the woods, "am a Milliconquit. My name is Kang."

"Well," Sweetwater laughs, "now you'll die like a Milliconquit."

"My name is Kang," he says again, this time his voice thundering. "I am a Milliconquit. Your people tried to kill the Milliconquit, but we survived. We hid ourselves among your people. We hid ourselves in the cities. We married you, and you bore our children."

Kang looks at Arthur. Tears are slipping down Kang's cheeks now. Arthur smiles. "I was born in Arizona. I lived in a little town in a little white house with a normal little white picket fence and lived a normal little life. And yes, I grew up as Jorge Zuniga, a normal little Latin American kid. I was nothing special. I took a normal little job as a normal computer programmer. But then I started researching who I was, and I learned that through my veins courses the blood of a great and powerful tribe, and I knew that I was Kang. I knew I was a Milliconquit. And I know there are others like me. And they're coming for you. I am Kang, the Milliconquit."

I hear what sounds like a bumblebee. It rumbles lazily somewhere outside. I glance behind me, out the tall windows that were hiding behind the blinds while I blindly watched TV. I look past the boats and the Crab Shack and the other building with the French name. Nothing but the moon glinting off the river and casting shadows through the trees.

"Yes, yes," Sweetwater says. "We know all about you, Mr. Zuniga." But she doesn't seem quite as sure of herself. She glances quickly at the officers behind her. "He went off his nut, dontchaknow. Had a nice job in Flagstaff—data entry. Then one day he shows up wearing no shirt and a big headdress full of feathers he probably bought at the Halloween shop. We are what we are, Mr. Zuniga. And I hate to break it to you, but you're no Indian shoe salesman."

"Oh, but I am," Kang says. "As my father was before me."

"A corpse," Sweetwater says. "That's what you're going to be." She goes to the metal container and places her hand on top of it. "Before we leave you alone with our furry little friends here, do you have any last requests?" she asked.

The buzzing noise grows louder. I crane my neck. I can see a faint light glowing around the bend in the river.

"No?" Sweetwater says. "Then I'm going to ask you one last time. If you fail to give me the location of the *Tamzene*, I will open the box. We'll carpet bomb the area. It's sloppy, we don't like to do things this way if we can avoid it, but it's been done bef—"

Her voice trails off. She looks through the window at something over my shoulder.

On the river, a boat emerges from a clump of trees. The craft is long and thin with a motor sputtering at its rear. The boat is heaped with boxes, and it slices into the moon-soaked shoal toward Locksley Ponds' docks.

The boat pulls behind the docks, and the driver cuts the engine. He's a heavyset man in bib overalls. A mop of blond hair glows silver in the moonlight.

It's the Birmingham Kid.

Sweetwater's face sags. She steps toward the glass. "Oh dear," she mumbles. "What's that asshole doing now?"

Charlie Lee turns toward his pile of boxes, opens one, and plunges his arm into it.

"Stop him," Sweetwater yells to the guards. One of them turns and jogs out the door.

Something catches Charlie Lee's eye—something by the dock. He stands and stares at it.

"God is great!" he yells. He stoops and pulls the chord on the engine. It sputters for a moment and then comes to life. Swerving, Charlie Lee aims his boat directly at the Crab Shack restaurant.

"No!" Sweetwater presses herself against the glass window.

Charlie Lee's boat slices through the water, aimed like a laser at the building. Just before he slams into the side of it, I see the Birmingham Kid raise his arms over his head and catch a glimpse of his howling face.

"God is great! God is . . ."

The Crab Shack explodes into an orange mushroom cloud. Next to it, the building with the French sign on it also bursts into flames. A giant arm of fire reaches up toward the heavens. A thunderclap echoes throughout Locksley Ponds.

In the white room, the lights flicker and die. Pale moonlight casts everything in a silver glow. The guards look rattled, glancing around uncomfortably.

Sweetwater peels herself from the window and turns. Her eyes are wild with fear.

"The animals," she says. "They're loose!"

the thought

I never much wondered where thoughts came from. They're just there.

They come from somewhere inside you. They're part of you. They don't have sizes or shapes or weight, really—they're just the electricity buzzing around in your head. I never bothered to ponder exactly where they come from beforehand, or if they arrive from someplace outside of you.

This thought, people, doesn't seem to come from the usual place. It comes from somewhere outside. I don't mean to say I've been possessed or some nut-job thing like that. But it's this concrete thing in my head. A voice.

"*Hi, Winthrop,*" it says.

I'm wondering where it came from, but I'm also kind of busy looking back and forth between the billowing orange fire outside the window and my friends handcuffed in the white room. So I don't say hi back.

"*She left her remote control behind,*" the voice says. It's this deep-throated, dumb-sounding voice. "*It's there on the window ledge.*"

I look, and sure enough, Sweetwater has left behind that gray rectangular remote she used to change the room into the mirrored wall.

"*The top center button in the remote unlocks the cage,*" the voice says amiably. "*Why don't you press it?*"

After that thought come others. These hangers-on are all mine, I can tell, and I know they come from my usual thought place because they're shapeless.

They divide. TV shows, Red Grizzly songs, the Moms' little pink pucker marks on the forearms, and the great TV are on one side. On the other, there's Arthur, Kang, Seabrook, Esmerelda, and the Shrub People.

You make a million choices every day. Most of them are rolls with loaded dice, or you hope you're playing the video game with the right key code so you can automatically get to the next level even if you lose all your lives.

You go in the third entrance at the front of the Primrose School every day because you always do.

You pick meat or veggies on your pizza because you were wired to do it, because it's what's expected of you.

You wear black turtlenecks and listen to the right music because it's what the guys around you want.

You run away from camp because deep down you think it's what your father wants.

I've never faced this before.

If I don't press the button, I know they'll probably fix whatever damage has been done to Locksley Ponds. I'll watch some more awesome TV, and in a couple of hours His Eminence and the Moms will show up and take me home.

If I press it, I don't know what will happen. What will the things in the box do? Will this kill my friends or set them free?

It's the biggest choice I've ever faced.

So I roll the dice.

I press the button.

just desserts

I am something of an expert on just desserts.

In *Star Wars*, for example, the evil Emperor got his in the end when a dying Darth Vader threw him down a bottomless pit. King Kong, of course, was beaned by biplanes on top of the Empire State Building before falling to his death. In this old movie called *Breakdown*, Kurt Russell killed the bad guy by squashing him with a tractor trailer he first dangled and aimed at him over the rail of a bridge.

Maude Sweetwater's end is up there with the very cream. When the hatch falls open, a squirrel scrambles out. It looks just an ordinary little squirrel, the same kind I see darting through the trees back home in Philadelphia. But Sweetwater shrieks at the sight of it, a wail like one of the co-eds in *Zombie Cannibals*.

Then thousands of squirrels surge out of the metal crate. They swarm all over her, more squirrels than I've ever seen. Thousands of puffy tails and needle-like claws and ears encircle her until she disappears within the cloud. First she screams. Then she makes animal noises like a bleating pig. Then the squirrels all fall in on her and dart away. All that's left is a clean white skeleton draped in a shredded green muumuu.

More squirrels engulf the guards, who fire randomly at them, even managing to pick off a few of the tiny creatures, which explode in red mist. Soon the guards, too, disappear, leaving nothing behind but bones, black uniforms, metal helmets, and machine guns. One guard shrieks in terror and runs for the door, but by the time his hand grasps the knob, it's a white cluster of bones.

But that's not the strangest part. The piranha squirrels haven't laid a tooth on the *Tamzene*'s crew. The feeding frenzy keeps its distance. And when it ends, the squirrels dart around the room, sniffing the air and waggling their tails as if foraging for nuts.

I go out the door I'd seen Sweetwater take. The hall outside is dark. I feel around for a doorknob, find one, and walk into a room.

Squirrels are everywhere, making wild chirps and clicking noises.

"Careful, Mr. Brubaker," Seabrook says.

"I don't think they're going to hurt us."

He nods. "Even so," he says. "Let's get out of here. Slowly."

Gingerly, each of them stands, dragging with them the chairs to which they are tied. They creep through the room, shuffling forward with the metal seats in tow, careful not to step on or bump into any squirrels. The squirrels chatter at us, some standing on their hind legs on tables and the backs of furniture.

"Try the pockets," Seabrook says. He nods toward the wet skeleton of one of the guards. I want to hurl. I feel ribs and hip bones—all moist with squirrel spit—and I find a wallet and a small set of keys.

I unlock all the cuffs. They've taken Arthur's PA system. It makes me wicked sad. So sad that I start crying.

"I'm sorry, man," I say.

He gets this big grin and hugs me.

"We've got to get out of here," Seabrook says.

We head toward the door, inching between the chattering squirrels. I try not to look. When I do, all of them stare back—thousands of them, each black eye a curved mirror that reflects the room. They stand everywhere, sniffing at the bones piled around the crate, on the backs of the chairs, atop the windowsill. These are silhouettes against the fire consuming the docks outside the window. Their chattering noises swell in the room.

I freeze. Why don't they attack? For a second I can't move. If make the slightest noise—even breathe the wrong way—it might mean something in squirrel-ese, and I'd be little more than an acorn at dinner time.

Outside in the dark hallway, voices gurgle from every direction, every now and then punctuated by a chorus of shouts. Bursts of machine-gun fire come from somewhere in the house. I feel my way down the hallway, bringing up the rear.

At the end of the hall, we pass through the doorway to the long corridor with the animal heads. The sconces along the wall have been doused, but orange light fans up the stairway from the windows in the lobby, and along with it the sounds of several voices screaming and the screeching of animals. The bursts of gunfire come in deafening blasts.

At the other end of the hall I see a shadowy figure. It crouches on all fours, and its tail coils and uncoils in the dim light. Its eyes glow with yellow fire.

It's a cougar.

"Everybody freeze," Seabrook says.

The cougar crouches on the carpet, holding us in its glowing gaze. Its tail flicks back and forth.

"Guess that power outage opened some cages," I say.

"What the hell is this place, Winthrop?" Seabrook yells.

We stare at one another—the cougar and the four of us—for what seems like hours. And then Esmerelda bounds up the stairs.

It must be Esmerelda, but she looks like one of the chicks from *Hot Force.* She's gripping this big-ass assault gun that's nearly as big as she is. Her frizzy blond hair has been slicked back, and her green eyes glow beneath the black stuff she's painted her face with. The cougar snarls at her and raises a paw. I hear myself scream.

Esmerelda never flinches.

"Easy!" she yells, like she's talking to a yapping Pekingese.

"Ms. Chicklis!" Seabrook says.

"Where's Sweetwater?" she growls.

"Squirrels got her," I say. "Oh yeah, guys, Esmerelda's, like, some kind of secret agent."

"Later," she says, and glances down stairs. "Let's go, guys." She notices we're all staring at the mammoth cat at her side. "Oh," she says. "She won't hurt you. I don't know why, but she won't. None of them will. Let's move."

We follow Esmerelda in single file toward the steps while the cougar watches, its eyes burning. I wait for it to pounce on us. *How would its claws feel, how would it roar on the high-def? Would fangs knifing through my flesh hurt worse in a billion megapixels?* I shake my head and focus on the stairs. The cougar never moves.

The lobby is chaos. Orange light from the fire at the docks streams in through the cavernous front windows. Green Police officers dart back and forth while an enormous flock of birds swoops everywhere, diving at them and slashing them with their talons and beaks. They are pigeons with slate-gray backs, scarlet eyes, and gray bellies.

In the great room, three grizzly bears hold four guards at bay. They stand on their hind legs and roar. The guards cower behind a sofa. One bear, riddled with bullet holes, lies dead next to the fireplace.

I count the splayed bodies of four guards in the opposite room. They aren't moving. Blood from beneath their helmets soaks through the carpet. Some of the gray birds are perched on them, pecking away.

From rooms elsewhere in the house, screams and loud volleys of machine-gun fire reverberate.

Outside the windows, other weird animals attack the guards. Several of them dart away from some sort of beast I can't identify, a gray hulking thing with floppy ears that rushes at them.

Guards run to and fro. If they see us, they don't seem to care.

"The munitions," one mutters as he passes. "If the animals get into the armory, God help us all."

Seabrook leads us through the entrance hall toward the front door. A guard darts in front of us, howling as a snarling brown cat of some sort runs after him. Others bat their arms helplessly at the flocks of birds that dive-bomb them, slicing their cheeks and hands.

None of the animals pay us the slightest attention. It's like we're ghosts.

When we reach the door, someone shouts, "Hey! Stop them! Don't let them get away!"

"You there! Halt!"

A machine gun goes off. I feel the hot air of the bullets whiz past my ankles. Esmerelda breaks into a run. We follow. We make it as far as the porch when everyone stops and stares at what hours before was the field where Maude Sweetwater gunned down the passenger pigeons.

A wall of woolly brown forms thunder past like traffic on a busy freeway, raising clouds of dust that shimmer in the moonlight. The rumbling noise blots out all the other sounds. They are thousands of buffalo, and their stampede is blocking our path to the river's edge.

At first I can't believe there are so many, and then I remember what Sweetwater told me about repopulating species. In history class, we learned that before Europeans moved to America, buffalo herds were as large as three hundred thousand animals. Some say even bigger.

"Don't move!" someone yells over the stampede.

Over my shoulder, I see a guard. His uniform is ripped, and blood trickles from a slash on his cheek. He points a machine gun at us.

"All of you, lie on the ground and put your hands on your heads!" he yells.

Esmerelda whirls. She hoists her beast-sized gun and points it at him.

I turn and face the dark forms of the buffalo charging past. Everything has been hollowed by the TV, so I have nothing—no games, no movies, no Grizzlies—to rescue me from my thoughts.

The dust from the stampeding herd billows over me and sticks to the sweat on my cheeks.

Then the guard lets out a cry. A cougar—possibly the same cougar that was crouching by the stairs—is wrapped around his supine body. He hammers on the big cat's shoulder blade with his fists. The cougar roars, baring its teeth.

And then there's an explosion.

At first it's a deep-throated boom, so loud my head can't contain the noise. Then everything goes silent. The noise sweeps through me and lifts me off the ground, suspending me in midair for a moment before casting me down hard. It also lifts the guard and the cougar, hurtling them into the air in a tangle of fur, black leather, arms, legs, and claws. When they land, guard and cougar bounce, and the gun clatters to the ground.

Everything goes white. Then the whiteness becomes orange, and I see orange light pouring from the holes that used to be the mansion's windows.

Heat scorches me.

I hear a loud ringing. Gradually I make out the tinkling noise of broken glass and the crackling of fire. Inside the mansion nothing moves except fire licking at the walls.

"We've got to get out of here!" a guard yells.

"This whole place could go up!" someone else yells back.

I sit up, ears still going off like cell phones. As I stand, shards of broken glass slip from me. The explosion didn't take out the buffalo stampede. If anything, the animals seem more frantic.

"Head for the river!" Seabrook yells.

"How?" I ask.

He's lying next to me, Arthur thrown on top of him. Next to him, Esmerelda and Kang looked dazed. Esmerelda's gun is nowhere in sight.

Seabrook looks at the herd, then back at the mansion, where jagged spikes of flame bloom through the windows.

He looks me in the face. I can't hear him just then, but I can read his lips.

We have no choice.

Stepping off the porch, he makes his way to the edge of the herd. Then he walks right into the middle of it.

The stream of buffalo swerves to miss him.

He takes another step. Then another. Then he stops and turns back toward the mansion.

Seabrook stands at the center of an ocean of brown beasts. I can't help thinking of that movie His Eminence always watches at Easter, the one with the guy from the National Rifle Association wearing a fake beard, parting an ocean so the Israelites can flee. It's the same here: the buffalo flow around the Reverend Doctor like he's sending them a personal signal. When one of the buffalo comes too close, he cringes, but the animal veers off just in time. Seabrook beckons for the rest of us to follow.

Each of us wades into the stampede. It feels like walking onto the freeway; all around are truck-sized animals charging past. The heat from their bodies feels nearly as hot as the explosion. They swerve to miss us, some coming within inches.

I know I must be recovering from my TV addiction because I wonder if the buffalo will cave in on the Green Police officers, like the water in His Eminence's favorite movie—that is, if any of them are crazy enough to chase us.

They're not.

Eventually we reach the other side. The cool air blowing off the river sooths my scorched skin, and I swallow deep mouthfuls into my lungs.

The docks are on fire, and several guards are attempting to hose them down. We run right past them. They either don't see us or are too confused to care.

Seabrook scrambles into the woods. But when we don't follow, he turns to look at us.

"Where are we going to go?" I ask.

"We'll hike downriver, I suppose. There has to be a town or something somewhere. But standing here isn't a—"

"Follow me," Esmerelda says, plunging off in an another direction. "Seriously. You guys are, like, never going to believe this."

A few hundred yards upriver from the burning mansion, hidden behind the low-hanging branches of some giant elm trees, the *Tamzene* bumps against the current.

Seabrook smiles. He frowns. He starts to cry, sputters, and wades into the river. Finally, laughing, he tries to hug the hull of the boat.

"How?" he manages. "When they caught us in Missouri, they put us in a truck, blindfolded us, and drove for hours."

"Beats the hell out of me," Esmerelda mutters.

By now Kang has already climbed aboard. He goes to the cabin, and the boat hums to life. Soon we're all aboard and moving out into the river.

I'm forgetting something important about Esmerelda. I rummage through memories.

"AICO," I say.

"Later," Esmerelda says.

"What is it?"

"Agency for Internal Covert Operations. Kind of, like, an internal police organization."

The *Tamzene* picks up steam. We barely make it past the blazing docks and the Green Police boats when another explosion rifles through Locksley Ponds, throwing mammoth chunks of sandstone into an orange sky. A great red claw of fire springs from the mansion's foundations.

Silhouetted against the flash are thousands of buffalo, birds, monkeys, and lions moving around the mansion. As Kang pilots the boat downriver and the burning remains of Locksley Ponds shrink in the *Tamzene*'s wake, the forest and animals disappear into the dark.

A voice blares over the static on the radio: "*Our goal is to destroy, to eradicate the environmental movement. We want to be able to exploit the environment for private gain, absolutely.*"[12]

Chapter Twenty-Four

secret agent girl

The *Tamzene* takes to the big water of the Missouri, rounds the bend onto the Mississippi, and plows north.

The Mississippi isn't as big as I imagined. In school they spend a lot of time talking about how important it is, but it looks like a brown trough with a shallow trickle running through it. Most of the river has dried at the edges, so Seabrook has to keep to the center.

At first, when I narc on Esmerelda for being a government stooge, I figure Seabrook is going to chuck her off the boat. And I'm not so sure that wouldn't be a bad move. I know enough now to realize I don't understand exactly what His Eminence is, but I'm guessing I'm in more trouble than getting carted off to military school now. If Esmerelda is five-oh, she's dangerous—I don't care how hot she is.

But then the news on the radio changes everything.

It isn't the radio Seabrook uses to listen in on the Green Police, the one that sputters all that noise. It's the little one he turned on the night he learned I was a senator's kid.

We have only been out a day when through the rush of static we hear about the fire at the secret government resort in Missouri: *"Federal sources say the resort had been under investigation when a fire destroyed it. A release from the Justice Department, unprecedented in its lack of specificity, said to expect 'major arrests within days.'"*

Esmerelda squeals. "They got it!" she shouts. "It went through!"

She picks up the radio and holds it to her ear, but that's all there is about the mansion. She fiddles with the knob, running through bursts of songs and ads and fuzz, but there's nothing more. Then she holds the radio over her head like it's a Grammy and dances, twerking her hips. She grabs Arthur and plants a big kiss on him.

"I have to, like, get to a TV," she says. "Kang! Seabrook! I have to get to a TV."

Seabrook looks confused. "It's too dangerous to stop right now."

"You don't understand," she says. "If what I think just happened really happened, there's nobody following you."

Kang takes the boat under some trees. Seabrook, Esmerelda, and I march through a thin copse and reach a ribbon of blacktop parted by a double yellow line.

After a moment or two, the roar of an engine comes up behind us. Seabrook and I scamper into the forest, but Esmerelda stands her ground.

"Don't be silly," she shouts back at us. "Get back here."

It's a pickup truck. The driver seems to consider how mad filthy we are. He tells us to sit in the bed of the truck.

Moments later we're bouncing along through the woods, past little houses. *If you and Arthur could have gotten this ride days ago, none of this would have happened,* Wimp Winthrop says.

Esmerelda peers over the side at the trees flying past. All we can get out of her is that just before the mansion exploded, she'd broken in and managed to find the evidence she needed. "I used their computer— their own fucking computer—to copy files to my HQ and a contact I know in Justice. The damn file was still uploading when the power went out." She closes her eyes and lets the wind rush through her hair. "But they got it," she says. "We did it."

"Got what?" Seabrook asks.

"Evidence," Esmerelda says.

The truck drops us at a Walmart, which I have naturally heard of but never set foot in. As we wander through the weird fluorescent lights, past school supplies and heads of lettuce, women in pajama bottoms pushing shopping carts either stare at us or pick up their children and hug them.

We stop at a bank of flat-screen TVs with price tags attached to them. All of them are showing baseball highlights.

"Give me a remote," Esmerelda barks at a man behind the counter.

She flips to CNN. ". . . *a very large and clandestine organization, paid for by misappropriated funds,*" the anchor is saying. "*The group's leader, we've been informed, was a woman named Maude Sweetwater, believed to have perished in the blaze at this government resort. Again, we're covering a major breaking story here and we'll continue to provide details as they come in. What we know now is that the Justice Department arrested forty-seven federal agents this morning . . .* '

Esmerelda whoops.

"*And, this just in, a warrant has been issued for Pennsylvania Republican Senator Mortimer Brubaker.*"

My stomach jumps from a high dive platform. It's falling . . .

". . . *the high-powered Republican lawmaker has barricaded himself within his home in the Philadelphia suburbs . . .*"

. . . falling . . .

". . . *charges include misappropriation of funds, conspiracy, malfeasance and, shocking as it sounds, murder . . .*"

. . . and I slump to my knees.

"Jesus," Esmerelda says, eyeing me. "That's, like, your dad."

I manage to grunt. My head is pounding beneath the weird fluorescent lights and glowing TVs. Boarding school? I'll be lucky if boarding school is all I get. I'll be grounded until I'm in my thirties.

"*Senator Brubaker has issued the following statement: 'I categorically deny any culpability and wrongdoing. I will cooperate fully with the investigation, which will prove beyond a shadow of a doubt that the charges levied against me are the lies and desperate machinations of a socialist administration bent on destroying the last vestiges of freedom in this land.' We now take you to Suzanne, who is outside the Brubaker compound . . .*"

The screen flashes. I see a quick burst of the outside of the Compound's brick wall, and suddenly the image goes dark. Another image appears.

It's the Red Grizzlies. A live concert. "*Hold on to hope baby . . .*"

"What is this shit?" Esmerelda says. Then she shakes her head. "It's APE."

"What?" I ask. She turns the channel to another news show. "Hey, I was watching that!"

It's Fox News now. A roundtable of men and women in suits are discussing the administration's inability to look tough in front of the visiting Argentinean ambassador.

"APE is the Agency for Public Education," Esmerelda says. "They're in charge of promoting religious and interracial violence and subliminal indoctrination. They'll only allow news like what happened to be broadcast for a short amount of time."

"*. . . and we are aware of the situation going on at Senator Brubaker's home in Philadelphia. And we're monitoring the—forgive me for editorializing—patently ridiculous charges that have been brought against him. Fortunately, we as a news organization will give no credence to vicious lies and rumors propagated by charlatans . . .*"

"Let's get out of here," Esmerelda mutters.

But I don't want to go. I just sit cross-legged as Esmerelda keeps flipping channels between brief flashes of news. Seabrook and Esmerelda both sit down on either side of me.

Empty is the only word I can think of to describe how I feel, people. Not empty like when I just watched the mega high-def TV.

Just empty.

CHAPTER TWENTY-FIVE

big finish

Well, I guess that sums it up.

I bet you're expecting a big finish after all that action. We blew up the baddies' place, I found out my dad is, like, Darth Vader, and there's some weird force everywhere. Here's an ending—we have this big celebration, and I look off in the distance and see some ghosts and Muppets grinning at me encouragingly.

Does that work for you?

Well, get this: life is not a movie.

Maybe you should stop watching so much TV and get outside for a change, people.

I'd like to say that we got to California. That Kang found his lost tribe, and Seabrook was elected president of the whole world. That Arthur started talking again. That Esmerelda let me get to second base with her. That I scored all kinds of hot chicks at the Grizzlies' concert.

None of that has happened. I am still floating down the river on this crazy-ass boat looking for the Pacific Ocean.

A couple of days ago, Arthur came the closest to one of those endings where the good guy rides off into the sunset with the big-boobed blonde on his lap.

On the radio that evening, we heard this: "*The Justice Department appears poised to drop all charges against Senator Mortimer Brubaker, citing a lack of evidence.*"

I hadn't yet decided what I was going to do. I just figured His Eminence was off to jail. But when that happened, I figured I'd find the Moms and we'd come up with some kind of plan. Collecting food stamps, maybe? Moving to a trailer somewhere?

Esmerelda slumped her shoulders, shaking her head. "What do you expect?" she said. "You can't fight the Society of Man."

"The what?"

Esmerelda arched her eyebrows. "You never heard of it? The whole thing goes way back to, like, colonial times. When the settlers first came to this country, they faced a lot of hardships—you know, animal attacks, Indian attacks, horrible storms, droughts, rough winters. The people sort of thought of nature as the Beast, you know?"

"Of course," Seabrook said. "You'll find it all throughout the literature. 'Young Goodman Brown,' for example. Or *Moby Dick*."

"Well, way back then, a group of these Puritans from Massachusetts got together and formed a sort of secret club. They called it the Society of Man. Basically, the club believes that nature, the trees and the animals and everything, are a kind of organized force. Like, an army. The legions of the Devil. And it's man's duty to destroy it. To be the master of the beasts of the field . . . there's some sort of Bible verse that goes with that or something."

Seabrook closed his eyes. He fumbled in his pocket for the crucifix key chain, but came up with nothing. They must have taken it when he was captured.

"Genesis, chapter one, verse twenty-six," he said. "*And God said, Let us make man in our image, after our likeness: and let them have dominion over the fish of the sea, and over the fowl of the air, and over the cattle, and over all the earth, and over every creeping thing that creepeth upon the earth.*"

"Right," Esmerelda said.

"The early colonists were horrified by nature. It stands to reason," Seabrook says.

"Well, this society grew and prospered throughout the seventeenth, eighteenth, and nineteenth centuries. Most of the members of the first continental congress were members."

"And?"

"Supposedly the Society of Man still exists. That's the theory, anyway. They're the ones really running the show. The Cougar Scouts, the Green Police, APE—the heads of all those agencies are card-carrying members of the Society of Man. So they say."

On the radio they were interviewing someone who only described himself as a government official. His voice was modulated.

"*What happened was not solely the result of a federal investigation,*" the voice said. "*An important arm of our government is in disarray because of the actions of a handful of nefarious persons. And my message to them is, beware. There will be retribution. You can run, but you can't hide. That goes for you . . . and your families.*"

That chilled me, and I didn't even have to worry. My family, after all, are among the ones responsible.

But it wigged out Arthur something chronic. In the wee hours that night, I found him staring into the forest.

"What's up?" I asked.

He was startled, but he shrugged and looked back out at the trees.

"I've been wondering," I said. "What happens now, man?"

He shrugged.

Going back to the Compound now scares the hell out of me. But I'm just a kid. Arthur's just a kid. What choice do we have but to go home?

Arthur seemed to read all of this. He wrote on his pad, *I'm not going back.*

"Okay," I said. "Say we hang with these guys until San Francisco? There's going to be cops and army guys and crazy shit all over the place. And if we survive, they'll just take us back anyway."

Arthur drew a line under his previous sentence.

"But we're just kids, Arthur," I said.

Shrugging, he walked away.

The next day, Kang and Arthur huddled with Seabrook in the cabin. I watched them talking through the glass. Seabrook shook his head. When I walked into the cabin they all stopped talking.

"What?" I asked.

Nobody answered.

Arthur and Kang went below to the hold.

So, it was Seabrook who broke the news. Arthur and Kang were both going home to warn their families. Arthur's dad works for the NSA, but Esmerelda said that, compared to the Green Police or the Society of Man types, that wouldn't mean much. They probably had no idea what Godspeed Summer Camp was really all about.

"Oh," I said. Hot tears flowed down my cheeks, to my great embarrassment. "Doc, Arthur's going to get back there, they're going to put another one of those PA system thingies on him, and he's going to be right back where he was."

Seabrook sighed and looked at me over his shoulder. "I'm altering the route. I'm hoping to hit the Pacific Ocean by way of Canada now. Kang and Arthur are going to try to catch up to us, once they get word to their parents. Then they're going off to Montana to look for more of their lost tribe."

"*Their* lost tribe?"

Seabrook nodded solemnly. "Kang has adopted Arthur as a Milliconquit."

This whole thing was completely unfair. Arthur was *my* friend. I helped the kid along when he was too afraid to do anything for himself. Now he was going to ditch me. Arthur wouldn't survive five seconds in the wild without me.

"He'll never make it, Doctor," I said.

"Oh, yes he will," Seabrook said. "He has you to thank for that, Mr. . . . Winthrop. He's not the same kid."

Just then, Arthur and Kang came up from the hold. Arthur had stripped off his shirt, ripped it, and tied it around his head like somebody out of an '80s metal group. Wedged into the back of his shirt was a lone silver-and-white feather that looked as though it had been plucked from Kang's headdress.

Arthur crossed the deck toward me. A week under the hot sun and wind had baked his skin to bronze, flecked with great patches of freckles. How did I miss this? Without the PA system, Arthur didn't look like such a goon any more. He looked badass. His head didn't flop anymore; he held it straight and walked tall, like a man.

"So," I said. "I guess you think you're hot shit now or something, is that it?"

He hugged me. At first I wanted to tell him off. He'd still be paddling driftwood down a creek in Pennsylvania with a pack of choir boys if it wasn't for Winthrop Brubaker. No chicks. No status. No friends at all.

But a shaky feeling crested over me, and then I was the one who couldn't talk

"I'm so sorry," I managed. "I'm so sorry I dragged you out here, man. I didn't . . ."

Arthur pushed himself back and held me by the shoulders. He seemed so much taller, and his eyes were clear. He looked me right in the face, and get this, people: I understood him. I couldn't make him out more clearly if he had a hundred PA systems.

Don't be sorry, he seemed to say. *You are my friend.*

I couldn't talk. My chest ached.

"Don't leave me," I whispered.

You'll be fine, Arthur's eyes said.

At last, I realized the kid really was going to be okay. *I* did that, people. What did I tell you? A kick-ass friend! I picked him, brought him right along, and look at him now.

He went to Esmerelda. Her Xbox-colored eyes looked moist. It occurred to me that he's a few years younger than this chick, and I'll bet he's made it to second base at least. Arthur is a legend.

"It's okay," she said.

They embraced. She whispered something. I think it was, "You're a great kid. You saved my life. Go save your family."

He kissed her. No tongue, as far as I could tell, but it definitely lasted longer than a peck.

He turned to me with eyebrows raised.

"Go," I said. "And be careful." Then to Kang: "Remember that scene in *A Man Called Horse*, where they hang Richard Harris up with the antlers through the nips to prove he's a man, and there's these really bad '70s special effects, but it looks like it hurts like a bitch anyway? Don't be doing that to my boy here just because he's a white dude."

Kang picked me up and squeezed me to his chest. Then he and Arthur scrambled over the side of the *Tamzene* and disappeared into the woods. The last things I saw were two silver wisps in the trees.

After they were gone, I turned to Seabrook and saw him standing there with his eyes squeezed shut.

"What was that?" I asked when he opened them.

He patted me on the shoulder.

He didn't need to say. He was praying.

We've seen a lot of shit in these woods, people, that aren't just cells and chemicals and periodic tables. Church stuff and science stuff aren't mutually exclusive.

The way I see it, Seabrook might have lost his crucifix in those woods, but he found something else.

He's the Reverend Doctor Seabrook, after all.

So not such a bad ending for Arthur, right? It's been a couple days now, and we haven't heard a peep. But if anybody is capable of making it through the wilderness to their families, it's Arthur and Kang.

As for me, Seabrook, and Esmerelda, we're still going. At the moment we're anchored somewhere in the boring flat states, where Seabrook says the *Tamzene* will have to jump up on its wheels and tick off a few miles because the water route doesn't extend through the continental divide. Before that, we'll go through something called the Ogallala Aquifer, which he says is this big strip of water under the states that grow all our corn. Seabrook says it's drying up so fast that in one place he believes we'll actually be able to travel by underground cave.

Sounds made-up to me.

Esmerelda is just settling in to sleep. Seabrook is dozing in the cabin. I'm watching the stars through the trees. The sky seems so much clearer out here.

The CB radio buzzes and coughs. "*The president's plan would in-*

deed cause a surge in electricity bills—costs stand to go up $17 billion
every year. But it would also shut down plants and potentially put an
average of 224,000 more people out of work every year."[13]

Seabrook asks me every so often what I mean to do. I honestly
don't know. Going back to the compound seems crazy now. But like I
said before, for four more years I'm just a kid.

Something whacks the side of the hull. My neck hair stands on
end.

I hear a scrambling on the side of the boat. I'm petrified, unable to
utter a word. I glance at Esmerelda. Her eyes are still closed, and her
head is resting on her arm. I can see Seabrook's feet propped against a
bench in the cabin.

Then, over the gunwales crawls the last guy I'd ever expect to see,
but the guy I want to see more than any other.

"Fang!" I say.

It's him! The Great Poet. The Writer of the Songs. The spokesman
of his generation.

He's wearing his trademark red bear costume, the one with the
black machetes for claws attached to the gloves. The suit of red hair
bulges everywhere and rises into a hood with pointy bear ears. On
his face, Fang wears thick crimson eye makeup and has a drooping
mustache.

He's standing on the deck now, BC Rich guitar slung across his back.

"Hi, Winthrop," he says.

He knows my name. Fang knows my name!

I say something like, "Hi."

"Where were you for the big show, man?" he says.

"I tried to get there, but . . ."

Underneath the mustache, I see teeth. "Stuff happened, because
that's what stuff does, huh? Am I right?"

"Yeah."

"It's cool, man. Cool boat you got here."

"Thanks."

Just standing here. Passing time. With Fang. This is something I've done in about a thousand dreams and a million fantasies, which is what I half figure this is.

"So listen," Fang says. "You never got to see the show, and I feel bad about it. But we're putting on this special, intimate performance at a club near here. And I want you to be the guest of honor."

Esmerelda stirs. She sits up and gapes at Fang.

He ignores her. "Your mom and dad set it up, man," he says. "They're worried sick."

"Jesus," Esmerelda says. "Doc!"

Fang points one of the black blades at Esmerelda. She jumps to her feet. "Easy, little lady," he growls. "My friend Winthrop and I are going to take a ride in my raft there"—he points over the side—"and if you just keep chilling, you won't get hurt."

"It's Fang, Esmerelda!" I hear myself say. At the moment my mind is hovering over the boat, watching this whole conversation.

"Winthrop, that's Harlan Spikes," Esmerelda says.

I stare at him. It's Fang, all right. The same rakish tilt to the bear ears, the wry wink and smile he trademarked earlier this year. I mean, right now he's waving his claws at Esmerelda, but I have no doubt I'm talking to the man himself.

"Who?" I say.

"Harlan Spikes. He's a brigadier general in the Green Police. My office sent me a dossier on him back in Ohio."

"Shut your hole, you little bitch," Fang snarls.

"No, he isn't," I say. "He's Fang."

But to tell you the truth, people, now I'm not so sure. Fang would never call a blond hottie like Esmerelda a little bitch. If he was angry, he'd put the pain down into his pain and fear reservoir and say, *Hey, baby, it's all good.*

"They're one and the same," Esmerelda says.

The songs have slowly been coming back to me ever since the mega high-def hollowed me out. *Hold on to hope, baby. When the lightning flashes and the thunder rolls, I will not yield. I will stand fast and resolute.*

"Don't listen to her," Fang says. "We're going to let you into the band, man. All you have to do is climb down off of this boat, get into my raft with me, and we'll get out of here."

I take a step toward him. Ordinarily I'd be leaping at the chance, but Esmerelda pipes up again from behind the hemp cooker. "It's APE, Winthrop."

I bristle. The muses of the modern era. The gods of the new rock. The great hope of rock 'n' roll, the soundtrack to the revolution . . .

"Nuh-unh," I manage.

Fang lunges at Esmerelda, who darts out of the way. He doesn't chase her. He seems to want to stay in my field of vision. He turns back to me.

"Come on, Winthrop. It's a free concert. Just for you. We're going to let you play guitar."

This definitely is a dream. I take another step toward Fang. He looks older somehow in person. There are crow's-feet spidering through his red makeup.

"Do you really think the Green Police are the only thing going on here?" Esmerelda says. "The Green Police are just a little fish in a big pond, man. This is the guy who trained the Birmingham Kid to blow up things in the name of religious purity."

"That's crazy," I say.

"She's lying," Fang says. "She just hates the band."

"They send subliminal messages to the general public," Esmerelda says.

"But . . ." I search for something scathing to say to her. I can't find anything. I slump my shoulders. "But their music . . . it . . . always kind of . . . spoke to me."

"It's designed to. Think about it. *When the lightning flashes and the thunder rolls, I will not yield. I will stand fast and resolute.* As in, stand still. Do nothing. Take whatever they dish out."

Fang snorts so hard his mustache flops. "Who are you going to believe, Winthrop: your own ears, or some crazy chick with awful taste in music?"

Fang has a point. "What are they trying to distract me from?"

"Think about it, stubby!"

So I think about it. That little projector plays again in my head. Images flash of monster trees and dead fish and furry things floating in rainbow-tinged water, fallen-in buildings and water moccasins and birds laying eggs that will never hatch. And pipes, pipes everywhere— running down hillsides, shooting up walls, turning on linked fittings at right angles, and burrowing deep into the earth, all trickling, oozing, and pouring black sludge.

Staying away means . . . God, I don't know what it means. Monster trees and crazy homeless people and big neon oranges and crazy squirrels and buffalo and struggling just to find a decent shower.

But going back means living like I did with the TV in Blysse. Spoon-fed, clothed and, yes, entertained.

But none of it real.

It's not fair. It's another choice. Fourteen is too young to make it.

I just wanted to go see a rock concert.

But I make my choice.

And then Seabrook tackles Fang from behind.

They scuffle. Seabrook's ring of hair flares wildly, and his bald pate and face go crimson. For a rock and roller, Fang fights like a badass. I guess that's the Green Police training.

But Seabrook has the element of surprise on his side, and soon puts the guy in the bear suit into a bear hug. Sputtering and hollering at both Seabrook and me, my idol is dragged to the edge of the boat and tossed—ears over big red feet—overboard.

When he lands I hear not a burst of water, but a pop.

Looking over the gunwales, I see that his claws have punctured a small blue raft, the raft I guess he meant to take me away in. Now it's little more than a sheet of rubber he's tangled himself in as he turns over and over and sputters curse words at us.

From here, even in the dim light, I can tell there is black print on the side of the raft.

Greeen Police.

"You can't just leave me here, Seabrook!" he yells. "I'm miles from the nearest town."

"You're a bear," Seabrook yells back. "Bears are great in the woods, last I heard."

He puts his arm over my shoulder. "Ladies and gentlemen," he says, "I don't think we've chosen a suitable spot to make camp. Shall we make our way westward?"

"Sure," I say, laughing.

"Then, by all means, take her out, Mr. Brubaker."

"Me?" I've never driven this thing before. I've never driven *anything* before.

"Of course," Seabrook says. "A first mate must be skilled at piloting the vessel, after all."

"I'm your first mate?"

Esmerelda clears her throat. "Uh, just so you know," she says with mock coldness, "I don't take orders, stubby."

By the time I reach the cabin, I can tell Fang has freed himself from the rubber flap that was once his raft. I hear his claws brush against the hull.

"Winthrop!" I hear him yell.

But by then I've pressed the ignition button. Smoke lifts from the hemp cooker, the pistons push back and forth, and the wheel vibrates under my palms. I turn her, and we're in the center of the river.

Seabrook and Esmerelda scan over the rail for rocks as I pilot the boat down the dark river.

Maybe it wasn't such a hard choice, after all.

Big choices always seem unfair, I guess. Especially when you're just a kid. You figure the really hard stuff will come later, when you grow up, start your band, and the chickies arrive. But that's never how it works. Whether I'm with the Moms and His Eminence or out here in the wilderness, anything can happen.

After all, nobody ever chooses anything.

Not really.

Chapter Twenty-Six

---

the trees

The object, the floating thing all the plants and animals in the forest believed was so important, floated away. The trees watched it go.

Before that, it dropped a red bear.

The red bear was not a bear at all, but a man dressed as a bear. He climbed from the river and clambered into the trees, making whimpering noises and shivering.

The trees wanted to kill the man in the red bear suit.

They didn't know why, exactly. It was another thought that circulated through the webwork of root systems, old oak to Methuselah pine.

Intruder among us.

But the trees knew that they had less of a chance of killing the man in the bear costume than others. A new creature that lived among them would do the deed. It was a squirrel that had sharp teeth and lived on flesh instead of seeds. Many squirrels such as these had come west recently, sweeping into the woods and mating with the local squirrels so that now their numbers had grown.

The squirrels tracked the man who had left the boat. The man could see their eyes shining in the darkness. The trees could tell because he shivered and looked all around at the chattering noises and made whimpering sounds.

The floating thing reached the middle of the river and made its way west. The trees wished it well, but they knew the floating thing had been less important than the thought had made it seem.

There had been so many others before it.

There had been a car years ago that ran without gasoline. Men had destroyed it. Its maker had been murdered.

There was an airplane that flew using only water that turned to steam. A man had shot the woman who had invented the steam airplane and dumped her into the river. Her body decomposed, turned to nutrients that became a bed of river grass. That, too, had died when men drove past on their dirty boats.

So many others. Balloons and boats and cars and homes that did less to hurt the trees and the things of the forest. All failures, death at the end of each attempt.

But the trees knew. The floating thing was of little consequence. There would be more after its time had passed.

It was as it would always continue to be.

Men were born. Through the course of their lives, they killed animals, murdered plants, blackened their soil, poisoned their air, and befouled their water. And then they died.

So the trees did not mourn when the squirrels swarmed around the man and ate him as he shrieked in his bear costume.

The trees sang.

They sang the only way trees can sing: silently but for the wind through their branches.

What did the trees sing? A human song, oddly. One they had heard in recent weeks, one that spoke to them because it spoke to the treedom of trees.

When the lightning flashes and the thunder rolls, I will not yield. I will stand fast and resolute.

Voices

1. From the Kansas Homeland Security Department website. Following the terrorist attacks of Sept. 11, 2001, US citizens were advised to prepare for potential terrorist attacks by keeping a full tank of gas at all times. http://www.kansashomelandsecurity.org/high.html
2. Jerry Falwell, from his March 4, 2006, "Listen America" column on *WorldNetDaily*. http://www.worldnetdaily.com/news/article. asp?ARTICLE_ID=49101
3. President George W. Bush, Sept. 23, 2002, Trenton, New Jersey.
4. Interior Department Assistant Secretary Craig Manson, appointed by President Bush to a position overseeing the Endangered Species Act, as quoted in the *Los Angeles Times*, Nov. 12, 2003.
5 Sen. James Inhofe, R-Okla, April 2011, on fracking, as quoted in *Popular Mechanics*. http://www.popularmechanics.com/science/energy/coal-oil-gas/top-10-myths-about-natural-gas-drilling-6386593#slide-4
6. Frank Keating, Governor of Oklahoma, on the ANWR oil exploration, as quoted on ANWR.org, a grassroots, nonprofit organization founded to expedite congressional and presidential approval of oil exploration and production within the Coastal Plain of the Arctic National Wildlife Refuge.
7. Jerry Falwell in a soundbyte on CNN, Nov. 20, 2002. For a transcript, see http://transcripts.cnn.com/TRANSCRIPTS/0211/20/ip.00.html
8. Former Interior Secretary James Watt in a *Washington Post* article from May 24, 1981, as quoted on http://www.reference.com/browse/wiki/James_G._Watt.

9. George W. Bush, Jan. 1, 2006, at the Amputee Care Center of Brooke Army Medical Center, San Antonio, Texas.

10. Rush Limbaugh, *The Way Things Ought To Be* (New York: Pocket Books), p.104–6.

11. Ron Arnold, executive vice president of the Center for the Defense of Free Enterprise and the founder of the Wise Use movement, as quoted in *The War Against the Greens,* by David Helvarg (San Francisco: Sierra Club Books), 1994, p.7. The Center is a nonprofit industry activist group. Among its members are former government officials and GOP congressional leaders. Wise Use is an industry-funded anti-environmentalist movement started in the late 1980s.

12. Ron Arnold, as quoted in the *Toronto Star* in 1991. Found on wikipedia.org at http://en.wikipedia.org/wiki/Ron_Arnold.

13. House Speaker John Boehner on Obama Administration efforts to lower carbon emissions at power plants, June 2, 2014. Read more at: http://www.speaker.gov/video/promise-made-promise-kept-electricity-rates-skyrocket#sthash.QUfpvntN.Se7mUjhx.dpuf

Acknowledgments

More people than I can thank have played at least a small role in the production of this book. I've been blessed with great friends, family, coworkers, and editors, all of whom were there at least to inspire or offer a kind word. But at the risk of insulting any of them, I'll name a few.

Aside from the aforementioned Kaylie Jones and Anne and Lance Landauer: Dr. Bonnie Culver, J. Michael Lennon, and the rest of the peerless Wilkes University crew who gave me a chance to learn and improve my craft; Marlon James and Dan MacArthur, two talented writer friends whose advice is to be found all through this volume; Justin Kassab, who looked at two messy drafts and had the stroke of genius to combine them; P. Casey Telesk, who gave great marketing ideas and art; Michelle Glass, who read the manuscript and provided encouragement, and her husband, Christopher Glass, my best friend, who was there for many of the inane road trips that inspired the book; John Opilo, who told me about mountain lions, and his wonderful, beautiful, and talented daughter, Emily Opilo, who understood, put up with my incessant tinkering, reading out loud (including this acknowledgment page, right now), and still talks of this ridiculous book with pride; Johnny Temple and all the great people at Kaylie Jones Books and Akashic Books; Dan Sheehan, a great writer, colleague, and friend who read the book and advised; Sean Snell, my best friend when I was twelve, with whom I became separated from a religious downriver canoe camp in Pennsylvania, spent twenty-five hours in the woods in the rain with nothing to eat, and no hemp-powered boat arrived to save us; and author Christopher Moore, whom I've never met but, when I was at my lowest, provided a simple response to an e-mail that gave me what I needed to keep going.